The Courier

To Jill & Eddie
with love from your
brother-in-law, Barry
aka
James R. Vance
September 2009

James R. Vance

RealTime Publishing
Limerick, Ireland

The Courier
James R. Vance

The Courier
James R. Vance

First Printing

This is work of fiction. Any similarity to persons alive or dead is purely coincidental.

ISBN: 978-1-906806-96-5
Published by: RealTime Publishing
Limerick, Ireland

The Courier
James R. Vance

Dedication

To the memory of my parents, Mona and James.

The Courier
James R. Vance

With acknowledgements to:

The staff of British Waterways Marinas based at Tequila Wharf,
Limehouse, London for their advice and information packs.

My daughter, Stephanie, for her constant London-based support
and research. Her sister, Jay, for her encouragement and belief
towards my goal of publishing my first novel.

The staff at Doggarts, Blackfriars, London for their indulgence
during my research at the venue.

George Enock for his detailed research at Paddington Station.

Cherie Rohn, author in her own right, who gave me sound advice.

The staff of Leicester General Hospital Coronary Care Unit,
Glenfields Catheter Suite and their Cardiac Rehabilitation
Services.

Richie O'Brien, RealTime Publishing, for his faith in me.

The Courier
James R. Vance

Preface

During the early years of the new millennium, immigration and terrorism had become the British government's two major issues in relation to national security. Though totally separate in substance, they were related by the controls implemented and exercised on the nation's borders by Her Majesty's Revenue & Customs.

It was freely admitted by the government that no precise figure could be attributed to the number of illegal immigrants in the country at that time; if that were the case, it could also be argued that it was not possible to assess the number of dormant or active terrorist cells at large in the United Kingdom. Publicly it was even stated by Scotland Yard that a terrorist atrocity, more devastating than 9/11 or the London tube bombings was 'waiting to happen'.

Integrated international intelligence and security forces were operating at the highest levels, but maybe the intensity and the methodology were too sophisticated and consequently they were missing the obvious.........

Part One   Brickwalls

(*PERCEPTIONS of WEEK ONE*)

Chapter 1

FRIDAY AFTERNOON: It was just another Friday, another autumn day in late October. The black spun off two cushions and dropped neatly into the corner pocket. Unfortunately the white cue ball followed suit.

Detective Inspector Massey grinned. "That's another pint you owe me!"

Detective Sergeant Turner leaned on his cue. "Double or quits?"

"It's like taking candy," said Massey. "Set 'em up then."

Turner shook his head in disbelief. As he stooped to place a coin in the table's mechanism, Massey's mobile phone churned out Chuck Berry's 'My Ding A Ling', announcing an incoming call.

"You really should change that ring tone," said Turner.

Massey walked towards one of the windows of the Ring public house and looked across from The Cut towards Blackfriars Bridge whilst he listened to the call. Turner hovered over the pool table with his coin until his boss had finished.

"It's your lucky day," said Massey, slipping the mobile into the breast pocket of his leather jacket. "The game will have to wait until next time. The Beamer used in the drug deal at London Bridge has been found up near Camden Lock. Uniform are keeping an eye on it until we get there."

Turner gulped the last dregs of his beer before following Massey towards their unmarked police car parked on Blackfriars Road. Forty minutes later they were handing the abandoned B.M.W. over to forensics, when Massey's mobile rang once again.

The Courier
James R. Vance

This time their task was to investigate a bizarre briefcase mix-up at a main-line railway station.

*****

The station approach was deserted apart from the burly frame of Sergeant Dawkins as he patrolled the concourse leading to the platforms. Fluckley Green was an unmanned railway station, a legacy of the numerous cost-cutting measures introduced at the turn of the century. Recently, a steady rise in petty vandalism had warranted a British Transport Police presence at specific times as a deterrent.

The initial duties of this role had made a pleasant change for him. Chasing illegal immigrants who had crossed over or under the channel could be quite wearisome. Besides, the paperwork resulting from the arrest of miscreants plying their criminal activity in the vicinity of the various stations and trackside was an unwelcome chore.

A trip through the pleasant Kent countryside, especially during the milder months of the year, was an added bonus. Dawkins was an 'old-school' type of police officer who had served his time in the force and was now content to see out his days with the Transport Division until his fast-approaching retirement. This unusual role suited his geniality and patient demeanour. After all, had he not seen it all during his long career? However, after several spells of waiting for the local comprehensive school to disgorge its daily quota of teenagers and monitoring their behaviour on railway property, the novelty was beginning to wear somewhat thin.

He glanced at his watch. Three thirty three. "Any moment, now", he muttered and a crescendo of youthful clamour confirmed his thoughts. The first group of youngsters appeared on the horizon. They approached the station, shouting and screaming at each other as if in celebration of the forthcoming half-term break.

He made his presence noticeable by standing at the main entrance to the 'up' platform. This was where the majority of young commuters congregated to catch the three fifty 'stopper' which eventually terminated at Waterloo station in the capital.

The Courier
James R. Vance

Some pupils knew him by now and exchanged pleasantries. Others seemed wary and a certain few still tried to test the limits of his authority with their obnoxious attitude and behaviour. Whilst travelling with them to the end of the line, he patrolled the corridors of the train, trying constantly to keep them seated and away from the doors. He could never understand why they (especially the girls) had to stand in groups between compartments or near dangerous doors. They blocked corridors and obstructed other passengers when there were plenty of seats available.

They've too much excess energy after an easy day at school. In my day, blah, blah, blah......!

Most of them shouldered small rucksacks or sports bags. Some even flaunted designer bags like Burberry or, occasionally, Louis Vuitton. The more studious types carried briefcases and large art folders. Irrespective of the type of hand luggage for their schoolwork and other daily needs, each was in itself a potential weapon in the sporadic battles which took place en route.

Patience and good communication skills were the sergeant's main strengths in controlling the excessive exuberances of this display of youthful vitality. A good old clip round the ear would sort this lot out, he often thought, but in this politically correct society it would have cost him his career.

Following the several trips which he had made in this alternative role, he had become aware of a young student who appeared to be a loner. He was always seated by a window with a briefcase on his lap. He was never in conversation nor involved with the other pupils. Maybe he was new or too studious to be engaged in the small-talk and repartee of his school mates. He was certainly smart and well-groomed, appearing quite mature for his age, which Dawkins put at about sixteen or seventeen.

He was probably more noticeable as he was one of only a handful of students who completed the whole trip to the capital. The sergeant's job became more relaxed as the atmosphere turned less boisterous with the decreasing numbers which alighted at each station along the track. Consequently, the ones who remained on board became more memorable with each trip.

The Courier
James R. Vance

Normally Dawkins took the next train back to Fluckley Green to retrieve his car and drive home to Ashford after completing his shift. Today, however, he was hungry and on arrival at the terminus he decided to wander over to the main concourse for a snack at one of the fast food bars to satisfy his appetite.

The loner preceded him from the platform and headed towards the stationery shop. He stood outside by a news stand and a row of seating, where he stayed as though he was waiting for someone. The area was extremely busy as rush hour commuters swarmed in different directions. The spot where the loner was standing was a melee of people rushing to buy copies of the Evening Standard and snacks from the shop to sustain them on their journeys home.

Opposite this hive of activity stood the burger bar where Dawkins purchased a Cajun chicken baguette and a beaker of tea. He seated himself at a table on the terrace outside, sat back in his chair and surveyed the busy scene before him. As he tucked into his snack and took a sip of his tea he became aware of a slight disturbance by the news stand.

At first glance it appeared to focus on the end where the loner was standing. He replaced the half-eaten sandwich back in its wrapper and turned towards the distraction. Rising from his chair, he walked across to the minor commotion where the youth seemed to be the centre of attention. The group of people who had gathered around the student parted at the sight of a uniformed officer as he approached the anxious looking youngster.

"What seems to be the problem?" inquired Dawkins, fixing his gaze on the student.

"It's my briefcase," he replied, glancing and pointing towards his feet. "Someone's stolen it."

The policeman followed the youth's outstretched finger to see a black briefcase at his feet. "So, what's that then?" he demanded.

The Courier
James R. Vance

"It's not mine," replied the youngster. "It's the same, but mine has my initials in gold letters beneath the handle and this one hasn't. Someone must have picked it up by mistake."

At that point two armed patrol officers approached, attracted by the disturbance. The sergeant outlined the problem and they walked away to resume their surveillance duties.

"Okay," said Dawkins, putting his hand on the student's shoulder, whilst bending down to pick up the substituted briefcase. "Come over here with me and tell me exactly what took place."

He led the way towards his table and the unfinished snack. "Sit there." He pointed to a vacant chair by the table.

"I'm meeting my mother," interjected the youngster, "over there by the shop."

"Well, keep an eye open for her whilst you explain what happened," said Dawkins, hoping for an opportunity to take a mouthful of chicken. "Now first of all, what's your name?"

"Scott," he replied, "Scott Morgan."

"Okay, Scott, take your time. I'll just make a few notes." Dawkins took a small pad from his tunic pocket and started writing.

"I was just standing there, waiting for my mum and just, well, just watching people and reading the headlines on the newspapers in the racks. My briefcase was on the floor, pushed up against one of the seats nearby. I suppose I wasn't really concentrating on anything in particular. For some reason I looked down and it was still there, but it wasn't up against the chair anymore and when I looked again, more closely this time, I realised that it was different. You see, the gold letters had disappeared."

Scott stopped and pointed to the space under the handle of the briefcase, which Dawkins had since placed on the table. "That's when I started asking everyone, and the man selling newspapers, if anyone had picked up my briefcase by mistake. But nobody came forward with it. They just started shouting and asking each other around where I was stood, and then you appeared." His voice trailed off a little. "That's it really."

The Courier
James R. Vance

Dawkins detected slight dismay in his tone and a look that begged the question why it had happened in the presence of a policeman. He put on a more officious air.

"And you're quite certain that you didn't notice anyone stood close by you who may have taken yours by mistake?"

"No. No, I suppose that I was too busy reading the newspapers when it happened. I don't know." He buried his head in his hands. "It's all my fault. Mother will kill me."

"I hope not," quipped Dawkins, now trying to lighten the conversation to console the youth. "I don't want a murder as well."

He drummed the end of his pen on the table and continued. "Tell me, Scott, is there anything in your case with your name and address on it, your phone number maybe, or any kind of I.D. which may help the other person to contact you? I'm assuming that it wasn't locked."

"No, nothing really. Only school books. The school's name is on some of them, though, and no, it wasn't locked."

"Well, they may even return to the news stand, if they realise their mistake soon enough. And if not, they could still trace you through the school. Talking of school, I know you have to wear a regulation school tie, but I noticed that, until last week, you wore a black tie. Any particular reason?"

The sergeant attempted to adopt a less formal approach, affording himself the chance of a sly munch of the baguette. The youngster fingered his striped school tie nervously.

"My father died recently with a heart attack and I've been wearing it since the funeral until this week, out of a sort of respect, I think. I'm not really sure. I just thought it the right thing to do. That's why I'm here. I used to live with my dad. They're divorced, you see. We lived near the school, so I've only been making this trip for three weeks, 'cos I'm with my mum now and she wants me to stay on there until I've finished my exams. She lives in Docklands but works close by the station and picks me up here each day."

The Courier
James R. Vance

"I'm sorry," said Dawkins quietly. "It must be difficult adjusting to new routines." He began to understand why the youngster sat alone on the train. He drew the briefcase towards him. "Anyway, let's see if there's any I.D. in here which might help to trace the owner of this one, provided it's not locked."

He swung the case around to lift the lid away from himself to see if it could be opened. At first the case appeared to be locked but as he forced down on the lid, the clasps sprang open with loud clicks and the lid popped slightly upwards. The sergeant opened it to about a forty five degree angle.

"Bloody hell," he cursed under his breath, but loud enough for Scott to hear. He quickly closed it again and rested both hands firmly on the lid.

"What's up?" asked Scott.

The owner of this little lot will definitely be in touch, thought Dawkins, "Er, nothing to worry about," he said, leaning over the case possessively.

"Why, what's in..?" Scott broke off suddenly and stood up pointing towards the shop. "There's my mother!" he exclaimed.

"You'd better fetch her over," said Dawkins, relieved by the interruption.

Scott rose and went across the concourse towards the news stand to greet his mother affectionately. After a few words, he led her to where the sergeant was seated, still looking at the briefcase which he had drawn closer to himself.

"This is my mother," interrupted Scott.

Dawkins rose and held out his hand. "Pleased to meet you, Mrs...," he glanced down at his notepad, "...Mrs Morgan. Please take a seat and join us."

He guessed that she was about late thirties, early forties. She was elegantly dressed in a navy blue suit matched by a pale blue silk blouse. Her blond hair was meticulously styled, cut quite short with a diagonal fringe, which gently favoured the left side of her forehead. Very nice, thought the officer.

The Courier
James R. Vance

"Scott says that someone has taken his briefcase in error and left their own briefcase in its place," she remarked, placing her navy blue handbag on the table before her.

"Would you like some tea?" asked Dawkins, conscious of his unfinished snack.

"No, thank you, officer," replied Scott's mother. "We really must get home. I have company this evening."

She leaned forwards more intently. "What can you do to retrieve my son's property? Will we have to attend a police station and make a statement?"

"Maybe, ma'am, but it can wait until tomorrow," replied Dawkins. "For now I'd just be grateful to record the details of your address and telephone number. I already have a brief statement from Scott which will suffice in the meantime, thank you."

He proceeded to note down the details which he had requested, thanked them and bade both farewell, stating that they would be contacted sometime tomorrow.

As mother and son walked away, Scott turned to the police officer. "By the way, sergeant, what was in the briefcase?"

"Oh, just lots of paper," replied Dawkins.

Scott smiled. "Are you staying to see if the other person returns for their briefcase?" he asked.

"I'll hang on for a little while yet," said Dawkins, more concerned about his snack than resolving the briefcase mix-up.

Scott gripped his mother's arm and they both disappeared amongst the commuters thronging the concourse.

Dawkins finally got the chance to munch the remains of the baguette. His mug of tea was now rather lukewarm. After a few mouthfuls, he picked up his phone and contacted headquarters to report the situation. He was told to stay put and await the arrival of the local C.I.D. He took another bite and settled back in his chair, placing the briefcase firmly between his legs under the table. His eyes wandered across towards the shop, at the same time observing the numerous commuters passing to and fro across the concourse.

His attention was drawn to a youngster standing adjacent to another news stand at the far side of the shop. At first he thought it was Scott as he was similarly attired, wearing a dark jacket and striped tie, but the resemblance finished there. Scott's demeanour was calm and confident, despite his loss. This student looked ill at ease, quite edgy in fact.

Dawkins finished the baguette and thought about buying a fresh mug of tea. He looked across at the news stand. The youngster was still there looking just as agitated.

The sergeant glanced at his watch. Don't suppose it'll be a rapid response, he thought, trying to assess whether he had time to purchase further sustenance before C.I.D. arrived. Gripping the briefcase tightly, he headed towards the snack counter.

The Courier
James R. Vance

Chapter 2

FRIDAY EVENING: The detectives stopped by the snack bar. Massey looked across the concourse.

What the hell am I doing here? This is a job for the local plod. They must think that I'm a soft touch coming down from the north. Bloody cockneys!

He spun round to face the uniformed British Transport Officer. Sergeant Dawkins looked up, alerted by the shadows of two men dressed casually in jeans, sweatshirts and trainers who approached his table.

"Sergeant Dawkins?" inquired the taller man, who was also wearing a black leather jacket.

Dawkins nodded and invited them to sit down. "You took your time," he said, spluttering crumbs across the table as he munched his second chicken baguette.

"D.I. Massey and D.S. Turner," said the inspector brushing away the crumbs. "We had a slight problem on Park Lane," he added curtly, still smarting from his surprise encounter with a suspect from a previous murder case.

"That stretch is always snarled up during rush hour," said Dawkins.

"I don't think he was referring to the traffic," added Turner, the hint of a smile on his face.

"What's with this briefcase business, then?" said the inspector, ignoring the banter.

Dawkins pushed the mug of cold tea to one side and glanced across towards the shop. The other youngster had disappeared. Before opening the briefcase to furtively display its contents, he related the sequence of events which he had witnessed and Scott's explanation of what had taken place.

The Courier
James R. Vance

The detective inspector considered the situation for several seconds. "C'mon, let's go and find Sammy."

He stood and moved away from the table. D.S. Turner joined him.

"Who's Sammy?" inquired Dawkins.

"You must know Sammy if you work this station," replied Massey, automatically assuming that Dawkins was a regular at Waterloo. "He's based over there with your lot on security. I believe that he's shit hot with the closed circuit camera tapes. Let's see what he's picked up. Maybe we can get a positive on the phantom case swapper."

The two detectives strode across the concourse with Dawkins in pursuit, tightly clutching the briefcase and the remnants of his sandwich. They headed for some offices above the station entrance adjacent to the stairs for the underground. Sammy was about to leave, but offered to help out before he finished his shift.

On entering the room where the monitors were housed, Dawkins was amazed at its size. "It's like a bloody tardis," he exclaimed.

"Big Brother is watching you," said Sammy with dramatic effect. "We've got everywhere covered here, inside and out. Now, what you looking for...and what sort of time frame?"

"The news-stand and shop opposite the burger bar," replied Massey.

"Time?" asked Sammy.

Massey turned to Dawkins. "What approximate time are we looking at?"

Dawkins, in true methodical fashion, pulled out his notebook. "Well the commotion kicked off at 17.50, so anytime between 17.30 and 17.50, I suppose."

Sammy soon found the appropriate tape and ran it over the specified time period, part play and part fast-forward. The three policemen crowded round him peering intently at the screen.

The Courier
James R. Vance

Just under the first five minutes of tape into the run, Dawkins shouted, "Stop it, stop it there. See it's a woman! Can you run it back a bit?"

Sammy rewound the tape and ran it again at slow speed and they all watched a young lady approach the stand, place her briefcase by Scott's case, purchase a newspaper at the stall and calmly pick up Scott's briefcase and walk away.

"Sod's law, guv," remarked Turner. "Back view only, no sight of her face."

Massey turned to Sammy. "Where's she heading for in that direction?"

"Either the booking hall, the toilets or outside," replied the security man, yawning and checking his watch.

"Can we pick her up on any of those?"

"Let's have a look-see shall we," said Sammy, already anticipating the request by moving to a different bank of screens. He ran another tape.

They all watched as the young lady appeared on the security video of the terminal's main entrance. She got into a taxi and disappeared from view.

"Still no front view," added Turner, glumly.

"No, but run it back again, Sammy. Give me a close up of the back of that taxi. Make a note of its reg. and licence number, sergeant," asked Massey peering intently at the image before him.

"Can we go back to the news stand afterwards?" asked Dawkins, "I'd like to get a closer look at the other schoolboy. It'll be sometime after 18.00 hours I imagine."

"What other schoolboy?" asked Massey.

Dawkins explained about the boy similarly dressed near the other news stand at the far side of the shop. Turner proceeded to take down the taxi details. They returned to the previous monitor, where they watched the eventual arrival of another youth in school uniform. He entered the shop, came out with some magazine in his hand and stood by the far news stand with a black briefcase by his feet.

The Courier
James R. Vance

Dawkins started sketching in his notepad. He turned to Sammy. "Would I be a pain if I asked you to run it back to when the girl arrived?"

"Yes," replied Sammy curtly, aware of the time. He rewound the tape as requested.

Dawkins studied the screen, looked down at his notebook and announced, "It's not the same school."

"What's not the same school?" asked Massey.

"I reckon the mark was the second student and the girl mistakenly chose Scott," continued Dawkins. "At first I thought the other youth attended the same school as Scott, but look at their ties. The stripes are both diagonal but in different directions; they're both blue and gold but the other lad's tie also has a green stripe. In addition, though both are wearing what appears to be dark suits, the other lad's jacket is a blazer...with a badge!"

"Go back to that, Sammy," asked Massey, "let's get a close up of this badge."

"Am I getting overtime for this?" moaned the security man.

"We'll mention you in dispatches," joked Turner.

"You're nothing but trouble, you two," ribbed Sammy. "There you go, and there's the blazer. Close up of the badge, you said?" He zoomed in and they all leaned forwards towards the screen.

"It's just a shield with gold and blue quadrants," remarked Turner.

"There's writing below it," said Sammy, zooming closer still.

"Looks like 'semper ad bellum'. Latin, I reckon," spelled out Massey. "Anyone know any Latin?"

"I think it means 'always at war'," said Turner.

"Sounds like a school for bloody mercenaries," interjected Dawkins. "Anyway, whatever it is, I reckon we need to find it."

The room fell silent. They seemed transfixed by what they had witnessed on the screen. Sammy interrupted their individual thoughts.

The Courier
James R. Vance

"I hope you don't mind me butting in to this scintillating detective work, but I think you're missing something."

They all turned towards the security man. Their combined expressions asked the obvious question.

"His briefcase was also changed," stated Sammy waving his arm towards the monitor.

"Play it again, Sam," quipped Turner.

*****

"Someone's stitchin` us up...sumfin`s gone bloody pear-shaped. Yer were given this case of shite?"

The young boy nodded in agreement and opened his mouth to speak, but his father cut him short again, turning brusquely to face the sallow youth.

"Don't like it, don't like it one bit. And I'm stuck with this bloody worthless crap." He pointed at the black briefcase on the table before him. He scratched the back of his close cropped head and turned to face a younger well-built man.

"Danny, take the case down the cellar and stick it in the `ole for the time bein`. I might need it later as evidence."

He was referring to his concealed hole in the wall. It was set behind a removable false block of stone, which secreted all vestiges of what lay behind it. Even the trusted Danny was not party to the contents of various boxes and packages lying within the depths of the hole.

"I'll phone Mickey and Vince before any more shit `its the fan."

Danny picked up the briefcase and left the room. Frank Cannon looked at his Gucci watch before turning to his son, Luke. "Are yer bloody sure yer saw no-one swappin` the cases?"

"I've told you, dad, it was dead busy. I waited ages but I fought there was no show. I didn't see the swap. I was too busy eyeballin` that copper."

"Copper? What bloody copper?" Frank exploded. "Yer never mentioned a copper before!" He leaned over towards the boy, both hands stretched out on the table. Bluish veins pumped up from the stretched skin on both his fists and his forehead, such was his stress. Staring directly into his son's face, he snarled. "And where was this bloody copper?"

His son reacted by stepping back from the table and, though somewhat nervous inside, displayed an assured air of bravado by crossing his arms. His role in his father's illegal affairs had endowed him with a certain amount of swagger, almost to the point of arrogance. He had quickly learned to stand his ground when confronted by authority or any behaviour which posed a threat.

"Sittin' over by the burger bar talkin' to some guys," he calmly replied.

"And?" snapped Cannon.

"Nuffin'. They were just talkin'," added his son. "I 'ung around a bit, but fought I'd better move on 'cos it seemed no-one 'ad showed.....with the fuzz bein' around and that."

"If 'e was busy chattin' to some other blokes, what was the problem?"

"Well, nuffin' really, but I fink he kept lookin' at me."

"Bloody 'ell!" yelled Cannon, more veins protruding from his forehead. "We started with nuffin'. Now we've got yer under police surveillance! Anyfin' else you fink I should know?"

"No, no...that's it. 'E just looked over a couple of times."

"And who were the other two blokes wiv 'im?"

"'Ow the 'ell should I know. They just looked like regular guys. Maybe they were lost or sumfin'."

"I don't fuckin' believe this," muttered Cannon as he paced the room throwing his hands in the air in exasperation. "Go and get lost yerself while I fink this frew."

He dismissed the boy with a wave of his hand and reached for his mobile phone. He dialled and continued to pace up and down, spitting obscenities while waiting for a connection. Luke always considered an early exit from the room to be a favourite course of action when his father was in this kind of mood.

"Mickey? ...Frank 'ere. Call Vince. Set up a meetin' a.s.a.p......no, not 'ere, back room at the W.C, nine firty tonight. What? ....No, just a complete fuck up. See yer there."

22

The Courier
James R. Vance

Cannon slipped the phone into his pocket and kicked out at a chair. "Bollocks!"

Danny reappeared from downstairs. "More trouble, boss?"

"Pour me a scotch. Someone's fuckin` me about. When... and I do mean when I find out ooh it is, they're dead meat."

*****

"Never send a woman to do a man's job."

"I've never been before. I did exactly as you told me."

"So how come I've lashed out a fortune for a case full of schoolbooks? Are these priceless first editions? No, I'll tell you what they are. They're educational fodder, probably full of lies and out of date ideology."

"Don't get your knickers in a twist. Obviously they've tricked you."

"Two years, two years has been spent perfecting this. Everyone's on the make, big time. Why would one of them suddenly pull a fast one? There's no sense to that. No, my girl, you've screwed up."

"He was there, dressed like you said, in the right place, at the right time. I'm sorry, but it's not my fault. It's obviously not as perfect as you thought."

A silence ensued as Isaac Joseph slumped into a leather armchair. Rebecca, his niece, stood by the window looking out at the shadows cast by the streetlamps in the square outside. The pale glow cast an eerie gloom in the twilight of a damp autumn day. A car swept by, blowing dead brown and golden leaves upwards. They floated in the air as though trying to re-attach themselves to the bare branches from which they had fallen.

She gazed at the airborne foliage. *My life all over, reaching out to my previous roots. And look at me now, running fruitless errands for a crooked uncle. So he's lost some money. Well, he can afford it. Serves him right for cheating my father out of the business and driving him to an early grave. Why, oh why do I continue to work for him?*

23

The Courier
James R. Vance

She turned to face the old man, staring defiantly at him from the window. "If your usual errand boy hadn't crashed the car, I wouldn't have had to go."

"You should be sorry for your cousin. He was lucky to escape with just a few cuts and bruises," he replied. "Anyway, where is the lazy so-and-so? I hope he's not gone back to Barnes. I told him to stay here until he's properly recovered."

His son had his own house between Barnes and Mortlake on the river Thames with a terraced garden leading down to the water's edge. This ideal location with its own mooring and top of the range cruiser was an indulgence which occupied most of David's leisure time.

"If he'd taken me to dinner as promised, he would have done the run as usual and you wouldn't be in this mess, so don't blame me. He's your son. Have a go at him. Don't take it out on me. I followed your instructions. It was obviously the wrong boy. So find out who he is and ask for your case back. It's as simple as that."

Rebecca had lost her mother through cancer before she had reached her teens and her father had brought her up until his death twelve months ago. He had been Isaac's partner but over the course of several years, her uncle had assumed total control and eventually ruined him financially. The stroke, which finally led to his premature death, was due in no small part to the stress caused by Isaac's devious business deals.

Whether through guilt or a sense of family duty, her uncle had taken Rebecca into his care and since leaving college she had recently started to work for him in one of his retail shops. It was an uneasy relationship as the nineteen year old privately blamed Isaac for the death of her father, but at the same time was reluctantly grateful for a roof over her head. She was biding her time and held no concerns if this latest escapade brought her uncle down. She had a close relationship with her cousin, David, but his untimely car crash the previous day had resulted in her involvement in the briefcase mix-up.

The Courier
James R. Vance

"Maybe you're right," conceded Isaac. He crossed to his desk and once again opened the briefcase. "Mind you, all there is to go on is the name of the school."

"Well, that's a start," added Rebecca, moving away from the window towards her uncle. "Surely there must be the student's name on at least one of the books or files in there."

"Nothing, I've already looked. Here, you have a sift through them." He pushed the open case towards her.

Rebecca took everything out and scrutinised each item closely. She found no name or any other kind of identification on the books or the paperwork, not even a signature. Giving up, she started to replace the various documents and struggled to push some files into one of the compartments of the lid. She removed the files and slid her hand down to find the cause of the obstruction. A plastic ruler was jammed across the divider and with a gentle tug she drew it out.

"Bingo!" she cried, waving it at her uncle. "See what I've found." In the centre of the plastic measure between the twelve and eighteen centimetre marks was a self-adhesive white label. Printed on the label in bold, black uppercase lettering was the name: **SCOTT MORGAN**.

*****

Sammy's replacement, Wayne, arrived at the security office, munching a cheeseburger. He was briefly made aware of the situation and joined the others round one of the monitors. They watched a figure in a hooded anorak and dark glasses approach Frank Cannon's son and exchange briefcases whilst the youth was reading his magazine. The 'anorak' disappeared and could not be found on any of the tapes which covered the other areas of the station.

Eventually, Sammy fast-forwarded the original tape to the point where Luke made a move. The youth rolled up his magazine, stuffed it in his pocket, glanced at his watch, picked up the substituted briefcase, looked around the station concourse and made off towards the stairs leading to the London Underground.

The Courier
James R. Vance

D.S. Turner broke the silence. "Two drops at the same place, both with schoolkids," he uttered. "What do you reckon is going on?"

"Something's not right," replied D.I.Massey. "In my mind it doesn't stack up. If the first drop involving the girl was a case of mistaken identity with the innocent school-kid, as Dawkins suggested, why would the real target be hit by someone else? Assuming that the other youth was the target and the girl had chosen him, why would briefcases be switched a second time?"

"You've not a lot to go on, apart from a young lad who's lost his briefcase, three unknown suspects and a briefcase full of money," said Dawkins.

"Plus an eyeball on the taxi that picked up the girl," added Turner.

"Okay, maybe that's enough," said Massey. He turned to Dawkins. "Sergeant, can you make some inquiries on your train-watch duties about the other school uniform? Maybe the kids from Scott whatsisname's school can shed some light...."

The uniformed policeman interrupted him. "The only problem is that they're on half term holiday for a week and I'm assigned to other duties, probably back to the ports chasing illegals again."

"Well do what you can and come back with any info, however slight," replied Massey. He addressed Turner. "Relieve Sammy of the tapes and follow up the taxi. See if you can find out where he took the girl. I'm going to have another chat to our schoolboy. He could be at risk if it's assumed that he still has the briefcase with the money and they trace him through his school. Thanks for all your help, Sammy, I'd buy you a beer but I need to get this lot under lock and key." He nodded towards the briefcase.

"No problem, sir. I'm sure Wayne and I could keep an eye on it for you!" Sammy winked and nudged Wayne, still devouring his burger.

"Sure," acknowledged Massey, picking up the case, "but I think forensics should take a look at it before it becomes awash with ketchup and burger relish."

26

They all walked out of the office, leaving Wayne licking the remains of the snack from his lips.

*****

The Windsor Castle was a small terraced public house situated in a narrow mews-style street, tucked away between Little Venice and Maida Vale. Frank Cannon tended to socialise at home, unless he was indulging in a night out in club-land in the West End. Business meetings with associates, however, were mostly conducted in a private back room of the W.C. The pub had changed little since its Watney Mann and Truman Brewers days apart from the fact that now it was leased from a private company.

The current licensee was an elegant lady of considerable trade experience. She stood no nonsense and maintained a high standard throughout. Her inflated prices were commensurate with the genre of clientele which she targeted. The exterior reflected this quality image with its polished brass lanterns and all-year round floral displays.

Inside the pub, the customer seating area was fairly limited. The majority of regulars tended to congregate around the bar itself which was bedecked with appropriately placed vases of cut flowers and silver-plated tureens filled with fresh ice. There was no music and the only concession towards any type of slot machine was a cigarette cabinet discreetly positioned in the corridor leading to the toilets.

Another passageway led to a small rear courtyard. Furnished with wrought iron tables and chairs, it was rarely used apart from hot summer days. Situated not far from Lords cricket ground, it was a popular venue for post-match analysis amongst local patrons of Marylbone Cricket Club afficionados. Along this corridor behind a door marked private was a small meeting room.

When Frank Cannon, accompanied by Danny and his son Luke entered this room, Mickey and Vince were already seated along one side of the oval mahogany table in the centre of the room. Luke (whose nickname was 'Loose' for obvious reasons) sat down next to Danny facing the two men who had responded to

Frank's earlier phone call. His father walked across to a hatch on the wall and opened two small wood-panelled doors, revealing access to the back of the bar.

"Evenin` Caffy darlin`. Can we `ave a tub of ice, five of your finest cut-glass tumblers, a bottle of Scotch and an orange juice for the boy, luv."

He turned back into the room and seated himself at the head of the table, simultaneously throwing the now infamous black briefcase in front of him with such force that it slid along the polished tabletop. It came to rest in front of his son, Luke.

"Well, `e's lived up to `is bloody name today. Go on, Loose, fire `em a broadside and open the case," barked Cannon.

"Frank, the `atch is open," whispered Mickey.

"Good point. Close the `atch, Danny, don't want to be a laffin` stock," replied Frank, sarcastically. Danny rose from his chair.

"No, don't bovva," continued Frank. "Sit yerself down...no, better still, bring the drinks across."

Frank took centre stage, obviously enjoying the opportunity to humiliate his son, despite the harmful consequences of the blunder. "Loose, show `em yer treasure trove."

Luke opened the briefcase to reveal its contents. Frank leaned back in his chair with his arms folded across his chest. The two men opposite Luke leaned over and stared at a case full of toilet tissue shreds.

Danny returned from the hatch and put the drinks on the table. "Here, you may need this." He started pouring the whisky.

"It's a load of bog roll," shouted Mickey.

"At least you can `ave a good shit," joked Vince.

"It'll be the most expensive crap ever," retorted Frank.

"They're all cut up into diamond shapes," remarked Vince, spreading toilet tissue all over the table.

"Obviously some dipstick with a sense of `umour," added Mickey, drily. "I reckon we've been infiltrated."

"Or stitched up," suggested Danny.

"Did you recognise `im?" asked Mickey, addressing Luke.

The Courier
James R. Vance

"Recognise `im? `E didn't even see the switch," interrupted his father, answering for the lad. "`E was too busy watchin` a copper."

"The pigs were there?" exclaimed Vince.

"No, only one, sat outside the burger bar," explained Luke. "`E kept lookin` at me."

"Anyway," went on Frank, ignoring his son's remark, "we've got a problem. After more than two years of unqualified success, sumfin`s gone tits-up. We never know ooh the client is, so we can only contact The Fixer and report in. Iver of you two got any drops sorted?"

"I've nuffin` lined up," replied Vince.

"And I've nuffin` for two weeks, `cos, don't forget, the lads are on `oliday for a week, you know, `alf term or somefin`, same as the normal schools," added Mickey.

"Well we can't sit on this for two bloody weeks. I'll `ave to make the call," moaned Frank. "Besides I'm well out of pocket with this poxy lot. Someone's gonna pay for this ... with blood!"

He pointed at the briefcase, whereupon Luke discretely swept up the toilet tissue from the table, stuffed it back into the case and carefully closed the lid.

"It could be just a bloody stupid mistake, but I'm not takin` any fuckin` chances. There's too much at stake for all of us. Mickey, can yer contact the other lads and warn `em. It might be an idea to suspend operations. At least, if yer right about the`olidays, we `ave two weeks before there are any more runs. If it can't be sorted by then, we're all in the shit."

He rose up. "`Elp yourself to more Scotch, I need a pee." He walked from the room and left them all staring at the black briefcase.

29

Chapter 3

SATURDAY MORNING: Massey decided to find Scott
Morgan's address early in case shopping was on the agenda for
mother and son. He had considered a courtesy telephone call to
make a firm appointment, but thought the element of surprise
without time to prepare what to say might elicit more facts from
the youth.

The house in Docklands was fairly new with a small garden
at the front, modest in appearance but quite pricey in the current
market. An ornate terracotta pot on each side of the entrance
contained miniature Buddleia trees still profusing their purple-blue
blossom. He waited a few minutes after ringing the doorbell,
wondering if his tactic was a mistake. He rang once more, waited
and turned to walk away, cursing his assumptions. He had taken
only a few steps when he heard the click of a mortise lock and the
opening of the Morgan household's front door.

Scott's mother stood in the doorway, blinking in the early
morning sunlight. She wore a flowing beige satin robe and not
much else from the detective's perspective.

"Good morning. You rang?" she enquired.

"Sorry to bother you so early, ma'am, but are you Mrs.
Morgan, Scott's mother?" asked D.I. Massey as he fished out his
warrant card.

She merely nodded in the affirmative.

"I wonder if I could have a word with him about the
incident which took place at the station yesterday?" he continued.

"He told the officer everything he knew shortly
afterwards," she replied, still commanding the doorway.

"I'm aware of that, ma'am, but there are one or two issues I
need to clarify, if you don't mind."

30

The Courier
James R. Vance

"You'd better come in, then," she said, stepping back from the doorway. "You may have to wait a while, though. You see, my son's still asleep. We had a rather late night. Sit yourself down in there and I'll let him know that you're here."

She motioned the detective into a tastefully furnished lounge and disappeared into the hallway.

Massey chose to seat himself on a cream leather sofa with his back to the bright sunlit window. He hoped to manoeuvre Scott into sitting facing him with the light full on his face. He glanced around. Most of the furniture appeared fairly new in a style which suggested Ikea was a favourite shopping haunt.

"Ah, there you are." Mrs Morgan glided into the room. "Would you like some tea or coffee whilst you are waiting?"

"That would be fine. Coffee please, white without." The detective rose and sat down again in one motion.

The young man's mother swept across the room and seemed to evaporate into the predominantly cream décor of an open plan kitchen area. "Have you found the owner of the briefcase?" she inquired, as she busied herself with the coffee.

"No, not yet," replied Massey. "There was no identification to go on." *How much simpler life would be, if that were the case. Maybe forensics would come up trumps.*

"Oh, never mind. Scott says there were only some old schoolbooks in his case and maybe they'll be able to contact him through the school."

"Yes, that's what I came to discuss, really," continued Massey. "You see, there were some items of value in the other briefcase and I think it would be unwise to allow any unsupervised contact. They may believe that Scott deliberately switched cases in order to steal the contents."

He was attempting to be cautious, choosing his words so as not to alarm her, but at the same time to protect her son.

"Oh, Scott would never do such a thing. He's so honest. I mean, for instance, he handed over the briefcase to your policeman friend."

The Courier
James R. Vance

"Be that as it may, ma'am, but you never know what goes through people's minds when under stress," he argued persuasively to make her aware that the mix-up with the cases was not as simple as it first appeared.

"I'm sure that when they realise how public-spirited my son has been, they will probably want to reward him for his honesty," she replied, appearing with a tray containing a pot of coffee, a cream jug and two willow pattern china coffee mugs.

"There you are," she said, placing the tray on a low glass-topped table between the sofa and two matching leather armchairs. She settled into one of the vacant chairs. "Help yourself, now."

The inspector leaned forward and poured some hot coffee into one of the mugs, adding a little cream and gently stirring the mixture. He was aware that he had still not convinced Mrs. Morgan of the seriousness of the situation, but to set alarm bells ringing at this stage of the investigation could be a little premature.

"It's the honesty of the other party that is questionable," said Massey. "You see, we have reason to believe that there may have been some criminal activity involved and we need to ensure that every effort is made to publicly exonerate Scott of any complicity in the matter."

"And how do you propose to manage that?" asked the young man's mother, suddenly unsure whether to be concerned for or proud of her son.

"Sergeant Dawkins…that was the uniformed officer to whom you spoke at the station…has informed us that there is now a half-term holiday at the school. This gives us a period of time to give maximum publicity to the incident, highlighting Scott's public-spirited action, as you described it."

"Do you mean that Scott would be in the newspapers or on television?" asked Mrs. Morgan, her face now betraying a mixture of concern and pride.

At that moment Scott appeared in the doorway, wearing navy blue jogging pants and a t-shirt promoting The Darkness.

"Good morning," he yawned, greeting the inspector with a quizzical nod. Standing by the window, he became partially silhouetted against the bright sunlight outside. He turned towards his mother. "What's that about television?"

"Good morning. Scott, I presume?" Massey stood up and faced the young man. "I'm Detective Inspector Massey. If you'd be kind enough to sit down, I'd like to explain to you what I propose concerning the handling of yesterday's incident at the station."

"Now, dear," interjected Scott's mother, "would you like some coffee or would you prefer some cold juice from the 'fridge?"

"Juice please," replied her son, sitting on the sofa alongside the Inspector.

Massey proceeded to repeat the main points of his earlier conversation with the boy's mother, all the time evaluating Scott's reactions. The young man appeared quite cool and unperturbed until the inspector explained the plan to publicise his public-spirited handling of the situation, in particular his handing over of the misplaced briefcase to the police.

"Please, you don't understand," pleaded Scott. "I don't want my name in the papers."

"I'm sorry," interjected Massey, "maybe I've misled you. There would be no identification of who you are. We would just issue a statement of what had taken place and refer to you as a public-spirited individual who had acted honestly and with the utmost integrity. That way, there would be no chance of the owners of the briefcase linking it to you in person and simultaneously it would be a way of informing them that it was now in police hands."

Mrs Morgan re-appeared with the fruit juice. "There you are, dear." She handed the glass to Scott and sank once again into the armchair opposite. "I think that's very sensible. I just hope that they return your briefcase to the school," she added.

"I doubt it," said Massey, "and quite honestly, I hope the publicity will deter them from approaching the school at all. Contact with this possible type of individual should be avoided. It is advisable to let the police handle everything."

The Courier
James R. Vance

The inspector reached across the table and replaced his coffee mug. "You have probably realised that we are extremely anxious to trace the owner of the other briefcase." He turned to Scott. "Have you any recollection, any at all, of the person who could have switched the cases?"

"None at all," replied Scott. "He must have done it, whilst I was looking at the newspapers."

"You said he. What makes you think it was a man?" asked Massey.

Scott shrugged his shoulders. "I just assumed it would be a man," he replied

"Any particular reason?" asked the detective.

"It's a sort of, well you know, a sort of man's type of briefcase," suggested the young man, hesitantly.

"Did you notice any women particularly close to you at the kiosk?" Massey continued to probe.

"Not really. I was trying not to look…" Scott broke off abruptly.

"Not to look at what?" demanded Massey.

"Well, what I meant was…I was not…I mean I was looking for my mother," stammered the youth, tightening his grip on his glass of juice.

"Mrs. Morgan," Massey turned towards Scott's mother, "any chance of another coffee, please?"

"Certainly, Inspector. More juice, Scott?" His mother rose and, in one movement, picked up the coffee pot and glided off into the open plan kitchen.

Massey turned back and leaned into the young man's face. "Look, sonny," he snarled quietly, "we're possibly dealing with villains here, men of violence. If you're holding something back, which I believe you are, now is the time to open your mouth and maybe save your skin and my time. We can do it quietly now or we can go down to the station and do it the hard way. What's it to be?"

"Would you like some biscuits with it, Inspector?" trilled a voice from the kitchen

34

The Courier
James R. Vance

"Fine," said Massey, hearing the voice but not really listening to what she had said.

"What was in the briefcase, then?" asked Scott, trying to take advantage of the interruption.

"More money than you could imagine," replied the detective. "Why do you ask?"

Scott smiled. "The sergeant said it was full of paper. I should have guessed. I don't suppose it makes much difference, anyway," continued the young man. "I'm already a target."

"I suggest that you fill me in now and stop prevaricating."

Scott rose from the sofa and sat in the armchair vacated by his mother. He now faced the policeman. He leaned towards the inspector, clasping together his moist hands and nervously twitched his thumbs. "I was approached by a man," he said quietly.

"When, yesterday?" asked Massey.

"No, about a week ago. I was there, waiting for my mother. He asked me if I'd like to earn some money. At first I thought he was propositioning me for a trip to the gents toilet, you know, but then he explained that someone would come along and switch my briefcase on the following Friday, that is to say, yesterday. All I would have to do would be to take the replacement briefcase into the gents, where he would be waiting. I would lose my own briefcase, but he said that I would be well compensated. He explained that I would be handed an envelope which would contain £500 on delivery of the briefcase."

"Not a bad return for him," interjected the inspector. "Go on."

"At first I thought he was some crackpot, but he opened his jacket to reveal wads of £50 notes stuffed in his inside pocket. My first reaction was to tell him to get lost, but then I thought, what the heck, it could be a bit of fun. Even if I didn't get the £500, all I would lose would be my briefcase and some old schoolbooks. That's why my usual bits were missing from my case yesterday."

Deep down it was more than 'a bit of fun'. Scott had been strangely excited by the proposition. Being asked to participate in something mysterious, possibly illegal, had stimulated his imagination. He had looked around at all the commuters on the station concourse and felt special to be involved in some covert and maybe criminal activity. The innate fantasies of his youthful years had lured him from reality into a magical world of intrigue. It was a spur of the moment decision, which would result in more than just 'a bit of fun'.

"And he didn't reveal or hint what the substitute briefcase might contain?" asked Massey.

"No, he told me not to ask. He said it was better for me not to know, but assured me that it wasn't drugs or a bomb. I don't know why, but I believed him. I did ask why he couldn't take delivery himself and be involved in the switch. He just said it had to be a schoolboy, but gave no reason. He showed me where to stand and told me the specific time, but said that on no account should I be aware of the switch taking place."

"Can you describe him?"

"Probably about twenty five to thirty years old, quite good looking, slightly shorter than me, I suppose. He had light brown hair in a neat ponytail and a kind of thin Craig David type of moustache. He wore a suit. Oh and dark glasses, not sunglasses, but with a sort of smoked lens. He looked quite smart, really. You would have thought he was just a normal businessman by his appearance. He certainly didn't strike me as a criminal. He was quite pleasant towards me.

I got the impression that it was some kind of prank, you know, on a mate at work or something, quite an expensive one, considering the offer of £500, but I suppose that's peanuts for some of these high-flyers in the city."

"Forgive my ignorance but what's a Craig David moustache?"

"You know, a sort of faint line, a bit Mexican looking but not as droopy."

"Really…..Did he give you his name?"

"No, and I never asked."

"Would you recognise him, if you saw him again," inquired Massey, "say in a line-up?"

"Probably," replied Scott. "Why, do you think you know who he is?"

"Not a clue," admitted Massey.

Mrs. Morgan breezed back into the room. "Sorry I've been so long, but I suddenly realised I had a hair appointment and, anyway, I've managed to re-arrange it for this afternoon." She placed a huge plateful of biscuits and a fresh pot of coffee on the small table. "Now, help yourself, Inspector. Have you boys been having a nice chat?" she asked, looking at each of them in turn.

"Your son has entertained me exceptionally well, ma'am," replied Massey. He leaned across to pour out more coffee and selected a chocolate digestive from the array of biscuits.

He turned to face Scott, pleased that the light was now on the young man's face. His gut feeling led him to believe the explanation which he had just received, convinced also by the young man's eyes, expressions and his overall body language.

"If I accept your story," he added, "it begs the question what went wrong? Why create the commotion which attracted Sergeant Dawkins' attention?"

"Quite simple," replied Scott. "I bottled it with the policeman being there. I guessed he would react if I made a fuss. He would end up with the briefcase as lost property so then I'd be off the hook."

"Far from it," countered Massey. "Someone has received a load of old schoolbooks in exchange for a briefcase full of money. The booty expected by your partner in crime has ended up in police custody. There are some very unhappy people around who were probably pretty nasty in the first place."

He rose from the sofa and walked to the window, munching his digestive. "At least we have a week's grace."

"How do you mean, a week?" asked Scott.

"Well, from what you have told me, it's almost certain that nobody knows who you are. According to Sergeant Dawkins, you won't be back on that station concourse to be recognised until school starts again following your half-term break. So, we have a week to trace these people. In the meantime, if you think of anything else, which may help us, here's my card. I can be reached on that mobile number twenty four seven, okay?" Massey handed his card to Scott.

Scott, in turn, handed it to his mother.

"You should keep it, dear," she said handing the card back to him. "You've lost me."

"Maybe you both should have one," added Massey, taking another card from his pocket.

"Have I missed something?" interjected Mrs. Morgan.

"Not really," replied Massey. "We've very little to go on." He looked across the paved walkway outside. Apart from the girl, he reflected to himself.

*****

"Hurry up, David. The M25 will soon be chock-a-block with traffic. It's Saturday, you know, shopping day, and I don't fancy spending most of it sat in a jam on either the North Circular or the motorway."

Rebecca leaned over the balustrade and looked impatiently upstairs. David had arrived back at his father's house late on Friday night following the accident on Thursday.

Isaac appeared in the entrance hall. "I'm glad you're going with him. Apart from the trauma of the accident, you know how headstrong he can be. Take the B.M.W. It'll be more comfortable for both of you. I'll still have the Audi if I need to go out today. Keep an eye on him for me, please."

David had been determined to uncover the whereabouts of the schoolboy as soon as Rebecca had found his name on the ruler. He had even wanted to drive to Kent the previous evening, but had been dissuaded from setting off by his father and then by his cousin. They had argued that nothing could be gained and that he needed more time to recover from the mishap in his car.

"I doubt you will find anyone who might help you at the school on a weekend," continued Isaac.

"David thinks there may be cleaners or a caretaker there," replied his niece, "so he's determined to go. He blames himself for the mix-up entirely and he's too stressed out to hang on until next Monday. I think this may be his way of exonerating me from blame, by tracing the boy and hopefully recovering the briefcase."

Her cousin bounded down the stairs. "Right, ready. Here, you drive. I've already pranged one this week. Better not scratch dad's as well," he joked, tossing a set of keys to Rebecca.

Twenty minutes later they were speeding along the M25 motorway towards the Queen Elizabeth II bridge which spanned the river Thames estuary at the Dartford crossing. David spread a map over his knees in the passenger seat.

"Follow the signs for the M20 and the Channel Tunnel after the toll bridge," he advised his cousin. "I'll give you directions to the school from the motorway."

"David, what if there is nobody at the school? The trip could be a complete waste of our time."

"Don't worry. I'll find out where this lad lives whether there's anyone there or not."

Rebecca sighed. "I give up. If you intend to break in, there could be alarms. They are bound to have some kind of security system, especially these days."

"I'll find a way. Besides, I'm not stealing anything. I only want an address."

Neither spoke after that until Rebecca asked him for money at the toll. The remainder of the journey was also undertaken in silence. Rebecca felt uneasy by his mood. He was so intense. He finally spoke in order to direct her from the motorway system towards Fluckley. They stopped at a newsagents to buy some canned drinks and to ask directions to the school.

Just past the railway station, they spotted the sign and came across an open gateway with a stone arch above it. A gravel drive led to an imposing ivy-clad stone building which towered over a wide rectangular courtyard. The centre-piece was a waterless ornamental stone fountain. Two wings spread from each end of the main building itself, extending into a vast playing field area on one side and additional more modern purpose-built buildings on the other side.

The Courier
James R. Vance

Rebecca stopped the car opposite this entrance giving them a full view of the school complex. David smiled for the first time since they had left home.

"It must be our lucky day. It looks like open house."

Several vans and a few cars were parked near the main entrance in the courtyard. A posse of men in overalls were busy on ladders and scaffolding, painting the exterior woodwork of the building.

"Wait here," said David. "No, on second thoughts, I'll wait here whilst you go over there and work your charm on those workmen. Find out what's going on, how long they're here for, if there's a caretaker on site, you know, make it up as you go."

"Thanks, David….and then what?" Rebecca was not impressed.

"Come back and give me the s.p."

Rebecca shrugged her shoulders and sighed. "Why me, David?" She looked across at him. Why is he treating me like this she wondered?

Expecting no reply to her spoken question, she opened the car door and walked up the driveway, crunching the gravel beneath her knee-length leather boots. Some of the workmen spotted her and a few wolf-whistles echoed around the large courtyard.

David opened a can of fizzy orange and leaned back in his seat, confident that he was about to make some progress by taking this trip today. He took a couple of sips, placed the can on the dashboard and watched as Rebecca engaged one of the workmen in conversation.

A few minutes later, she was striding confidently back down the driveway, watched by several pairs of hungry male eyes. She opened the driving door and leaned in through the gap, one arm on the roof, the other across the top of the open door.

"Well?" asked David eagerly.

"They're here all week, it's half-term and the school is closed."

"Brilliant!" enthused her cousin.

The Courier
James R. Vance

"Apparently there are two lots of contractors here, one lot doing the exterior and the other lot painting the classrooms inside. And I thought there was no money in education," she added.

"Never mind that. Two companies, one inside and one outside, you say?" He closed his eyes for about thirty seconds. "What about a caretaker?"

"He was here first thing this morning to open up and returns at five to lock up again."

David nodded, stroked the back of his head and quickly turned to face her. "Jump in, we're going shopping," he exclaimed excitedly.

"Shopping? Where to? What for?" asked Rebecca, totally bemused by his sudden enthusiasm.

"Wait and see. First turn the car around and head back towards Ashford. By the way, what colour paint are they using?"

After two stops to ask directions, they found a D.I.Y. store near Ashford town centre where David purchased some cotton painters overalls, a couple of paint brushes, a screwdriver set, a chisel and a tub of cream emulsion. On the way back to the school, David ordered her to pull into a lay-by where he donned the work clothes. At his request she splashed him sparingly with splodges of the paint.

Back at the school they reconnoitred the boundaries of the grounds to find a suitable drop-off point. This would enable him to slip unnoticed into the confines of the main buildings and it would make an ideal rendezvous for his return. Carrying his can of paint, he crept into the grounds near a sports pavilion and made his way across a deserted quadrangle to an open doorway.

Once inside the building nobody challenged him and he found complete freedom to check out the staff and administration rooms, which he found on the ground floor. He tried a door marked SECRETARY, but it was firmly locked. Sod's law that's the one, he thought.

Further along the same corridor another door bore the sign ADMINISTRATION. He turned the knob and surprisingly the door opened revealing a large room containing several desks with

computers and a row of grey filing cabinets. He closed the door
behind him, placing his tub of paint on the parquet floor against the
door in case he was disturbed. He moved along the filing system.

Some drawers were marked with various school year
levels. What would be Scott's year, he wondered? He decided to
check one out to see what it contained. Taking the chisel from an
overall pocket, he prised open a drawer to expose a tight jam of
files with pupils' names. He slid one out to discover that it
contained copies of reports and academic records, but no personal
details. He cursed inwardly and moved on to break into the next
cabinet.

Outside in the comparative safety of the car, Rebecca slid
back her driving seat and adopted the recline position. She
switched on the C.D. player and closed her eyes. Within minutes
she had dozed off. Twenty minutes had passed when she was
startled by the opening of the passenger door. She looked across to
see a decorator stood by the open door. As she flicked the button to
raise her seat upright again, the man stooped to peer in.

David's grinning face appeared below the door-frame.
"Success!" he cried, still smiling. "Start her up. Let's go, we're out
of here!"

Rebecca turned the key in the ignition and powered the
BMW down the lane towards the main road by the railway station.
"I take it that you got what you came for?" she asked through a
huge yawn. "Where to now? Back home?"

"No, head for Ashford again, he lives not far away," replied
her cousin, poring over the map again.

On entering the next village, they stopped a man walking
his dog, to find the exact location of the address, which David had
extracted from Scott Morgan's file. Finally they pulled up outside
the house, which was a brick-built detached Victorian residence
with original sash windows. It was set back from the road behind a
neatly trimmed privet hedge and a mature but tidy front garden,
though the lawn was in need of a mow. There was a large gate to
the right affording access to a tarmac drive and a modern brick

garage. A small gate to the left opened onto a paved pathway leading to the front door.

Rebecca turned to face her cousin. "Now what?" she asked.

"Go over to the house and see if he's at home."

"Why me again?"

"Come on Becky. Just say you're a college friend. You're young enough to get away with that."

"And then what? I want a date with him or something? Or should I just ask if I can have my briefcase back, please?"

"I don't know. Say you need some help on a project or something."

"And what if he answers the door?"

"Just get him over here to the car. You'll think of something."

Rebecca sighed, but resigned herself to being used as the foil for David's quest. She walked to the gate, lifted the wrought iron latch and strolled tentatively up the path to the front door. Taking a deep breath, she rang the bell, waited a few moments, rang again and finally rattled the door with the brass letter box flap. There was still no movement within the house. She opened the flap and peered through. The hallway was littered with an assortment of envelopes, circulars and free newspapers.

"Nobody there, darling`."

She was startled by a man's voice behind her. The path was deserted, but to her right stood the source of the voice standing in next door's garden by a lawnmower. He was wiping his hands on an oily cloth and had obviously been tinkering with the machine.

"I must `ave bin on me knees when you rolled up," continued the man, stepping towards the low beech hedge which separated the two front gardens.

"I beg your pardon?" uttered Rebecca.

"It's been cantankerous ever since I bought it, but it usually gets goin` after I've fiddled with it."

"Sorry?" said Rebecca, quizzically, wondering what on earth he was chattering about.

"The mower," replied the man, pointing at the machine.

"Oh, I see." The picture in her mind of the man on his knees now started to make sense. "You said there's nobody at home?"

"They've gone, darlin', `e's dead, the lad's gone off to the smoke and it's up for sale."

"Dead?" queried Rebecca still confused.

"Yes, the old man died a few weeks ago, nice old guy, not that old really. Sad it was, `eart attack they reckon, so the young lad's gone to live with `is mum in London, somewhere."

"You mean Scott?" probed Rebecca.

"Yes that's `im. You a mate, are you?"

"Just an old friend. I was in the area, thought I'd look him up. I'd no idea...."

"Pity that. Nice lad, very clever they reckon, always askin` me questions, `e was. Never catch `im out, mind you, too clever by far, that one. Reckon `e'll do well in life. Good lookin` lad too. Close friend are you?"

Rebecca could see where this was leading and quickly asked, "You wouldn't have his new address, would you?"

"Sorry, darling`. One minute `e was `ere, next `e was gone. Didn't even say goodbye, but there again, `e was probably upset, `is dad dyin` and the funeral and all that."

"Well thanks, all the same," said Rebecca, retreating down the path. She stopped and turned towards the neighbour again. "You don't know which estate agent's handling the sale, do you?"

"No boards up yet, darlin`," replied the man waving his arm towards the empty lawn in front of the house. "I'm sure it won't be long though."

"Never mind. Thank you again for your help."

She closed the gate behind her and crossed to a smug looking David, who was sprawled across the reclining passenger seat. The neighbour dropped to his knees again and disappeared from view.

"No joy, then?" asked David, as she strapped herself into the seat belt. She related the conversation, which she had held with the lawnmower man.

44

"Let's head home, then," said David, apparently resigned to the fact that they had failed to locate the schoolboy.

Rebecca said nothing. She heard a muffled bang as she drove gently off in the direction of the motorway again. She glanced in her rear-view mirror and spotted a wisp of grey smoke rising above the neighbour's hedge. *He's finally started the mower or blown it up.*

She glanced at David and was mystified that he had accepted the dead-end to their mission so coolly. He had been so fired up since the previous day in his resolve to find the schoolboy. Confronted now with failure to do so, she expected him to be angry or irritable at the very least.

As she turned on to the slip-road to join the M20 motorway, she looked across at him once more. He was still reclining in his seat with his eyes closed and his hands clasped across his lap. She detected a faint smile in his facial expression. There was something strange about his manner since they had left the school. The youth had not been located, but still he appeared not to mind.

*****

D.I. Massey was still sitting in his car near the Morgan house deciding the next course of action, when his mobile rang. It was Turner with news about the girl. His inquiries had revealed that the taxi driver had dropped her on Maida Vale at the corner of Greville Place, close to Kilburn High Road, but no address was given. As the cabbie had made a u-turn towards Kilburn, he had seen her cross Greville Place and turn into a road on the left. He had also given a moderate description of the girl.

"Where are you now?" asked Massey.

"Just turning into Praed Street at Paddington," replied Turner, "heading for Maida Vale."

"Okay. Well, have a snoop around where she was dropped and see if there are any residents who may know her. It's a bloody shame that we couldn't get a good visual off that security video."

The Courier
James R. Vance

"I've pulled off a still of her. I know it's only a rear view, but someone may recognise her striking blonde hair. It's worth a chance, eh?"

"Good man, best of luck."

"By the way, any joy with the young lad?"

"Not a lot to go on, but there's a new slant to his story and I think we need a rethink. Meet me in the Clifton off Abbey Road at noon and I'll fetch you up to speed."

Massey set his mobile down on the passenger seat and reclined his own seat. Scott's story had given a different perspective to the situation. What had appeared as a badly executed switch was now further complicated by some pre-arranged scam.

His original intention of publicising the fact that Scott had handed the briefcase in to the police was no longer appropriate. Whoever had contacted the young man on the previous Friday was not going to be too pleased with his actions. Scott now needed protection but Massey needed to entice one or more of the players out into the open.

Against his better judgement, an idea was already forming in his head. He raised his seat back to a good driving position, clicked on his seat belt, turned the key in the ignition and set off towards Holborn where he joined the queue of traffic heading for the West End, totally unaware of the activity in Kent.

Chapter 4

SATURDAY AFTERNOON: It had started to cloud over and a chill wind was gusting as Massey parked his car on a meter near Clifton Hill. Turning his coat collar up for warmth, he dashed across to the public house, which was partly hidden by the trees which lined this fashionable backwater of St. Johns Wood. The surrounding houses were mostly large detached, some recently converted into apartments. One glance at the cars which were parked in 'residents only' parking spaces was enough to depict an area where only the wealthy could afford to live.

The pub itself was an impressive building, covered on the exterior by trailing wisteria and fronted by a small intimate patio which housed a few wooden bench sets, rising up from a sea of fallen autumn leaves. There were no umbrellas with their gaudy adverts. The only colour was provided by some planters on the patio and several hanging baskets containing the remnants of the summer's floral display. A sign boldly displayed the name, THE CLIFTON.

Massey slipped in through a side entrance, which led into the main vestibule and the bar. Turner was already into his first pint of Adnams Broadside, seated in the spacious lounge by a roaring log fire. There were a few customers in the back bar, but only an elderly couple in the main lounge. They had obviously ordered lunch as condiments and cutlery were laid before them on the polished copper-topped table.

Massey ordered a half of Shepherd Neame and joined his colleague near the ornately tiled Victorian fireplace. "Weather's taken a turn for the worse," commented the senior of the two.

"Why do you think I'm sat here," replied Turner, taking another sip of his beer. "What's the state of play, then?"

The Courier
James R. Vance

Massey related Scott's revised version of what had taken place at the railway station. He emphasised the desire to retain the youth's anonymity for his protection on the one hand, but outlined the need to flush out the mystery man who had made contact with Scott. It could involve publicising Scott's actions through the media, thereby causing a security nightmare for the police and major problems for the officers involved.

"Here's what I have in mind," explained Massey. "I reckon we have two options. First one, we could go to the media and announce Scott's public spirited actions, giving press and TV coverage with interviews and fairly substantial clues as to where he lives. The media will soon root that out anyhow. That would mean re-locating Scott and his mum to a safe house and lying in wait for the guy who approached Scott to attempt the retrieval of his cash or to exact some kind of retribution. Could be a long shot, that one."

The inspector took a sip of his beer. "Second option is that we say nothing and shut out the media completely. As Scott's on half term for the next week, even if they try to trace him through his schoolbooks, he will be relatively safe because he won't be commuting and keeping to his routine timetable. That will also give us time during that period to follow up any leads, for example, the girl. When he returns to school, we could keep him under tight surveillance, assuming the D.C.I. can spare the manpower, and use him as bait to drag our guy out into the open."

"With either option aren't we endangering the lad's safety?" asked Turner.

"That's why I tend to favour the second option. It's most likely that at this moment in time our man at the station and probably the girl who made the switch think he has the briefcase containing the money, but they won't be able to trace him until he's back at school. So we need to keep our involvement under wraps, no publicity, no press leaks, nothing."

"But what happens when he returns to school and we still haven't traced this mystery guy?"

"That's the only downside, Scott's security, whilst attending school if we haven't made that breakthrough before term starts again. Unfortunately, at the moment we don't know who or what we're dealing with. We just have to take a chance. What d'you think?"

"What if he saw Scott hand the briefcase to Dawkins?" asked Turner.

"Well, if that's the case, he'll know that we have the loot and Scott's probably in the clear. It means we're back to square one and maybe have to concentrate on the only lead which we have currently, namely the girl and this mystery school that Dawkins is investigating."

"Sorry to sound negative, but what if this guy at the station does seek some kind of revenge against Scott whatever option we choose?"

"That's why we need surveillance when he goes back to school and, if he does, well fine. We nab our man and maybe find out what's going on."

"So Scott's bait, whatever the scenario?" suggested Turner.

"If you were the guy who had made the deal with him, you'd either want your money if you thought he'd nicked it, or you'd want to sort him out if you thought he'd double crossed you by running to the cops. Either way, Scott's a target."

"Do you reckon the girl's an accomplice?"

"Why hand over all that money when it's already in your possession? No, it looks as if the girl's also been stitched up and Scott's cocked it all up by crying wolf."

Turner slurped the rest of his beer. "Want another?"

"Just a half. I'm hungry. Fancy a sandwich or something?"

"Good idea. What's on offer?"

"Not a clue. Just order something at the bar whilst you're getting the beers."

Turner tutted. *Great! When will I ever learn? Fell for that one again. Ah, well, thank goodness for expenses!*

The pub started to fill with lunch-time diners, so they moved down the steps and had their food served at a table in the conservatory area. It was quieter and away from the majority of the clientele.

"So, what progress with the girl?" asked Massey, munching his cheese and pickle mini baguette.

"The taxi driver's description didn't add much to what we'd already seen on the video. He reckoned she had a normal southern accent and was probably late teens, early twenties. After she left his cab, he radioed in and decided to nip home for a bite to eat, as he lives just near Kilburn Park tube station. He made a u-turn towards the High Road and that's when he saw her walking into a road off Greville Place."

Turner took a bite of his sandwich before continuing with his report. "Now here's the interesting bit. There are security cameras all the way down that road, you know, neighbourhood watch stuff. If they're working, we should get a good pic of her and maybe which house she went into." Turner smiled smugly and took another huge bite from his sandwich.

"So who owns the cameras?"

"The Met' believe it or not. I got that info off one of the lampposts," muttered Turner, spraying crumbs across the table.

"You're disgusting," joked Massey. "Made any contact yet?"

"I'll try the local nick this afternoon to see if they know where the feed goes to. I would imagine that there's some central unit which is responsible for the whole St. Johns Wood area."

"Any joy with residents in that area?"

"Hardly a busy street. Tried one passer-by who didn't even live round there. It seems to be a cut through for pedestrians from Abbey Road via Greville Place to the Kilburn High Road. Tried several houses, but nobody at home apart from one and she wasn't forthcoming. I gained the impression that, despite the presence of a neighbourhood watch scheme, it wasn't a very neighbourly environment, but I suppose that's city life and indicative of the times in which we live."

Massey nodded in agreement. "Doesn't make our job easy. Maybe we'll get some answers from the cameras. Thank goodness for technology. Talking of cameras, I'm still mystified about the second switched briefcase. What could have been in that one and was it related to the first swap?"

"And more to the point, where did it come from?" added Turner.

"It obviously contained something of value if it was to have been exchanged for the one containing all that cash, but......in the hands of a schoolboy? And you're right, where did he get it from?"

"More importantly still, where was it going to?"

"Fair point. If the switch had gone to plan, the girl would have brought the contents back here to St. Johns Wood, unless it was destined for Kilburn. What could be the connection with Kilburn?"

"The multicultural environment of Kilburn High Road?"

"And what's in Kilburn High Road besides traders?"

"Pubs? Irish pubs? No, all that's history now, surely?"

"Worth checking out. Call in Kilburn Park nick on your way home. Take the girl's photo and check if there are any records of suspect criminal activity connected with your neighbourhood watch road. Other than that, let's call it a day. I can't see that we can achieve much more. I'm going back to Blackfriars to have a word with forensics about the briefcase and then I'm off home. Keep your mobile on, just in case. If nothing crops up, I'll see you Monday morning. Have a good one."

Massey stood and drew up his collar again ready to confront the inclement weather. He glanced down at his watch. *Actually I might go down the Valley this afternoon to watch Charlton stuff the Geordies.*

He left the conservatory. Turner stuffed the remains of his sandwich into his mouth and washed it down with another gulp of beer. He looked at the empty glass for a moment and returned to the bar.

"Fill it up again, guv."

*****

The Courier
James R. Vance

"This had better be a life or death situation, especially on a Saturday. I trust you're using a public call box?"

"We've bin done over. Lost a complete assignment."

"I think you mean consignment. And what's with this 'done over' remark?"

Frank Cannon proceeded to relate how his son's briefcase had been switched for a case full of worthless paper instead of the expected payment for the contents of Luke's case.

"Give me the time and place and I'll track the scheduled contact. I can't do more than that. You'll be updated when I have the facts."

Cannon passed on the necessary information and started to elaborate on the facts, when he realised that the conversation with The Fixer was over. He glanced down at the handset, muttered some obscenity and replaced it on its cradle.

"Fanks, Caffy. Shove one more scotch in there, darlin`. Make it a large one." He moved along the bar away from the counter-top telephone in the corner and settled on a stool. He glanced around the bar. "Bit quiet in `ere today innit?"

"Always is when the kids are not at school. I think they must drag their parents off on retail therapy or something. Your Luke not with you today?"

"Don't talk to me about that dipstick," moaned Frank.

"What's he been up to now, poor lad? You're always on his back."

"He's got a lot to learn, yet."

"I thought he was doing well, `specially since he started that new school. Where'd you say it was.... somewhere abroad?"

Cannon ignored the question, finished his drink and walked out of the warmth and relaxing atmosphere of the Windsor Castle into a blustery October afternoon.

*****

"Took five different sets of prints from the briefcase, some inside, some outside. Ran them through the computer; all negative, none on the system. Notes were mostly used fifties, untraceable."

The Courier
James R. Vance

Massey's forensic colleague stood back with his hands on his hips. "Not much to go on, I'm afraid, apart from this maybe." He placed a sealed plastic bag containing a small coin on the table in front of the detective.

"Found it jammed between the lining of the base and the side of the briefcase after I'd removed all the cash."

"What is it?" asked Massey as he bent down to pick it up.

"It's a fifty cent euro coin, Irish to be exact."

"Interesting. Are euros dated?"

"2002, this one."

"And definitely Irish?"

"Yes, each country in the union has its own characteristic, in this case the Celtic harp, but it could have turned up in any E.U. country where the euro is currency."

"So it could just as easily have come from the continent?"

"Quite easily."

The detective twirled the small plastic bag between his fingers. "If only you could speak," he sighed. Replacing it on the table near the briefcase, he turned to Anderson, the forensic scientist. "Is that it, then?"

"I'm afraid so. Sorry I can't be more helpful."

"They're just pieces of the puzzle, Tony. Label everything, log them and store them. I'm sure we'll need them as evidence eventually, I hope."

"What crime has been committed?"

Massey smiled. "Your guess is as good as mine."

The inspector turned away and simultaneously turned his thoughts to football. He was becoming disillusioned with the whole affair. Each time he felt a sense of progress, there appeared to be a brick wall in front of him. He was beginning to question why he was bothering with the case at all. Anderson's question had highlighted the obvious.

On the surface no crime had been committed, only a hint of something illegal. Even the theft of Scott's briefcase was overwhelmingly compensated by its replacement. There was something going on and it was this enigma which intrigued him.

The Courier
James R. Vance

He was still uncertain whether he was abusing his authority to involve Scott, but he was trying to anticipate the next move by entering the mind of the person who had lost control of the money. His thoughts were interrupted as he passed the front desk.

"Telephone call has just come through for you, sir. A sergeant Dawkins," shouted the officer, leaning through the hatch. "You can take it here, if you like."

Massey turned away from the main doors, entered the front office and picked up the telephone. "Afternoon, sergeant. Any joy?" he asked, hopefully.

Dawkins explained that he had visited the school at lunchtime, but it was closed for the holiday and was in the process of being re-painted by a posse of decorators. There was no-one of any authority from the school, so he had left his number for the caretaker to contact him later when he came to lock up.

"What about the other school uniform?" inquired the detective.

"Nothing," replied the sergeant. "I made some general inquiries in the area, but drew a blank each time. Nobody even acknowledged that there was a similar uniform. I even spoke with a teacher in the local supermarket who was quite bemused by my suggestion. It's definitely not a school round here."

Another brick wall, thought Massey and continued speaking. "We're assuming that the other youth came from the same train. He could have appeared from anywhere, even from the capital itself, I suppose."

"Can I make a suggestion, sir," asked Dawkins, without waiting for an answer. "Why not review some more of those security tapes at the station to see if we can spot the lad arriving and maybe pinpoint which direction he came from?"

"Not a bad idea, sergeant. I'll contact Sammy and ask him to do a little digging on our behalf. Besides, how else do these security guys occupy their time?"

"Munching cheeseburgers?" offered Dawkins.

They both laughed and Massey gave him his mobile number in case the school caretaker had anything to offer. He suddenly felt reassured by his conversation with the sergeant that some progress might be forthcoming. The man seemed a little ponderous in his manner, but gave the detective the impression that he was disciplined and extremely thorough in everything he carried out. Before leaving the police station, he phoned and left a message for Sammy and eventually set out to drive down to the Valley for the football match.

As Massey squeezed himself through the turnstiles into Charlton Athletic's football ground, Turner strolled into St. John's Wood police station and Mrs Morgan breezed out of the hairdressers in Canary Wharf, proudly displaying her latest coiffure. A visit to the salon always gave her a lift mentally and today was no exception. She decided to spend the remainder of the day shopping, as Scott would normally spend Saturday afternoon glued to the sports channels on television, especially as the weather today had turned quite dull and chilly. With great ease she convinced herself that she was due some new underwear and, with that in mind, she headed for the selection of shops around Canada Place Mall.

*****

"You're out of luck, I'm afraid," said the young police constable. "They were only installed last week and the system's not up and running yet. Some technical glitch, apparently. It's bloody amazin`, innit? We can send pictures back from Mars and half the other planets in the solar system, yet we can't get one from just round the soddin` corner."

"I suppose it's been done on the cheap as usual," replied Turner, "but why install security cameras just in that particular road?"

"Oh, it's a trial run. I expect they chose that one, `cos there's been quite a few break-ins over the past six to twelve months along that stretch."

"Any special reason?" inquired Turner.

The Courier
James R. Vance

"Dunno, really. Maybe 'cos it's the closest posh part to Kilburn. I'm not sure. It beats me. Anyway, what's your interest in it?"

"I'm looking for a girl." Turner pulled out the still from the security video at the station. "Trouble is, I've only got a rear view. That's why I thought your cameras might have a better photo of her, as she was dropped there by a taxi yesterday." He handed the picture to the young constable.

"Can't even tell her age from this."

"No, but the taxi driver gave us a description. He reckoned she was late teens to early twenties, about five eight, pretty face, long blond hair, smartly dressed and carrying a briefcase. Ring a bell?"

"From what you've just said, she can ring my bell anytime," joked the constable. "Nah, sorry. You could try house to house."

"Been down that route. Hardly a friendly lot. Never mind, I'll leave you the pic and here's my card. If you could ask around, I'd be grateful.If you come up with any possibles, give me a ring. Oh, by the way, where's Kilburn nick?"

"Closed down. Nearest one's Queens Park. Mind you, doubt if they'll be much help. The area you're looking at is covered by our lot."

Turner stood up, thanked the young man for his time and walked out of St. John's Wood police station into the cool breeze of an overcast autumn afternoon. Having heard nothing from Massey since they parted company, he decided to cross the river and head towards Blackfriars. Instead of calling in at police headquarters, he opted for a couple of pints and a game of pool at The Ring before calling it a day.

Chapter 5

SATURDAY EVENING: Massey left the stadium just before the end of the match, missing Shearer's last minute goal to send the Geordies home in raptures. Partly due to a rather boring game with no goals (until his departure) and partly due to his pre-occupation with this current mystery case, he decided to head home to Streatham, take a shower, change into something casual and eat out at one of the many bar restaurants along Streatham High Road.

This had become common practice for him at weekends. During the week, if he made it home early enough, he would make do with a takeaway or a freezer-to-microwave ready meal. His justifications for this unhealthy lifestyle were the irregular hours of the job and the fact that he lived alone.

Although he was approaching forty, he was happy with the occasional relationship, but had no inclination to settle down again, following a marriage of eight years which had resulted in divorce and little else. Most of his close colleagues reckoned he was now married to the job and, in many ways, he had once again become a 'man's man'.

His first floor flat was situated in a quiet, unpretentious backwater, close to Streatham Hill station and within walking distance of the main shops, restaurants and café bars. He parked his car in a 'residents only' parking space and picked up his mail from the hallway before climbing the stairs to his two-bedroom flat. One look at the envelopes told him they were all bills and casting them to one side, he decided to make himself a coffee before heading for the shower. He carried the instant coffee into the lounge, sprawled across the settee and flicked on the television with the remote. Within a couple of minutes he was sleeping.

The Courier
James R. Vance

He was awakened by the shrill tune from his mobile in the pocket of his jacket. It was draped over an easy chair by the window. Stretching himself back into the land of the living, he staggered across the room, glancing at his watch…six fifty. The ten minute snooze had seemed like an eternity.

"Hello, Massey here," he said to the 'number unknown'.

He was surprised to hear the voice of Mrs Morgan, seemingly extremely stressed to have returned home to find Scott missing. On the verge of suggesting that she should not worry too unduly, she hit him with a bombshell.

"There was a note taped to the television in the lounge. He's been kidnapped!"

Massey told her not to touch anything, he would be straight over. He telephoned Turner to get the Scene of Crime team over there as quickly as possible and at the same time arranged to meet his colleague at the house in Docklands. He donned his jacket and left the flat, suddenly refreshed despite having to forego his shower. *Maybe the brick wall is beginning to crumble.*

Several minutes later he was hurtling down Brixton Hill Road with blue lights flashing from the front grill. He decided to head for Tower Bridge rather than risk being held up at the Blackwall Tunnel. Once across the river, he swung right past St. Katherine's Dock and headed towards Limehouse.

Traffic was particularly heavy in both directions and, using his new in-depth knowledge of this part of the City, he turned down towards the river onto Narrow Street, passing Victoria Wharf before reaching Limehouse Causeway. He passed by the Docklands Light Railway and skirted around Westferry Circus. Within minutes he was racing down Westferry Road and pulling up outside the Morgans' house in Burrells Wharf.

*****

Meanwhile, in London NW8, Isaac Joseph was answering his mobile.

The Courier
James R. Vance

"I believe there was an incident twenty four hours ago which you should have reported to me," said the voice on the line. It was The Fixer.

Isaac described what had happened at the railway station involving Rebecca . "I was going to contact you later. I'm just waiting for my son and my niece to return. They've gone to track down the mistaken schoolboy and to recover the missing briefcase. I'm sure they'll be back soon," he lied. David and Rebecca had returned empty handed shortly after lunchtime.

"Good. I'll be in touch later." The line went dead.

Rebecca entered the room. "Was that David?" she inquired.

"No," murmured Isaac, deep in thought. "Anyway, where is he?"

"Not a clue," snapped his niece, still angry with her cousin for ignoring her all the way back from Kent. "He took off in the car, leaving me at the shop. He's up to something, but won't confide in me, so how should I know where he is?"

Isaac stood up and wrung his hands. "I'm not happy with waiting a whole week for the kids to go back to school. There's too much at stake. We should be out there finding that boy."

Her uncle wandered aimlessly around the lounge, appearing very agitated and nervous. "What if we can't find him? It doesn't bear thinking about."

"Don't worry. We know who he is. I'll put together a list of estate agents in the Ashford area. One of them is bound to be handling the sale of his previous house and that will give us his new address." She didn't really care, but felt slightly responsible by her faux pas at the station. "Anyway, I fancy a drink. Care to join me?"

Isaac nodded and slumped into an armchair, wondering what the outcome would be. A few minutes later the following text message went out from The Fixer to numerous mobile phones, including Isaac's: 'All transactions cancelled forthwith until further notice. NO EXCEPTIONS'.

*****

The Courier
James R. Vance

Massey was standing in the garden talking to a uniformed police sergeant when Turner drew up outside. "You took your time," remarked Massey. "Managed to tear yourself away from the Clifton?"

"I was in The Ring, actually and winning at pool for once!" replied his colleague.

"You should have said. I could have picked you up en route."

Turner nodded towards the activity of the forensic team as they busied themselves inside the house. "Any joy yet?"

"There's a couple of uniform doing house to house for witnesses, this lot's dusting inside and there's a WPC with Mrs Morgan. But come and look at this. Tell me what you think." He led the way back inside the house to the corner of the lounge where the television stood.

Taped to the screen was a sheet of A4 paper on which was typed the following message:

IF YOU WANT TO SEE SCOT ALIVE AGAIN, THE POLICE MUST RETURN THE MONEY. STAY BY THE PHONE YOU'LL BE CONTACTED

"It was typed on Scott's computer upstairs in his room," said Massey, "and the pc's been left on showing that original message on the screen. Why? And why go to the trouble of changing the font from its default to that weird style of type? Also, according to Mrs. Morgan, they've misspelt Scott's name. I can't get my head round all this. At times I think we're dealing with highly skilled pros, especially with the amount of money involved and then, at other times, it's like chasing a gang of kids having a laugh at us."

"I tend to agree. How can they make such a complete balls-up at the station and yet trace Scott so quickly?"

"You're right. I've been so pre-occupied with this, that it hadn't crossed my mind. How the hell did they find him? I suppose we have to follow up what we've got, which isn't much. At last we now have a case to investigate even if it is abduction. Can you organise a phone-tap and surveillance equipment here asap?"

"Sure, no problem. Oh, by the way, some possible good news. My man at St. John's Wood has been in touch. We may have an ID on the girl."

"At last, a break," said Massey with some relief. "But you only said possible."

"Yes, a uniformed PC thinks he may have spoken to her a month or two ago during a house to house following a break-in and a GBH in the area. He's tracking back through the witness statements to find an address."

"Let's keep our fingers crossed on that one." Massey's mobile rang. It was Dawkins.

He wandered out into the garden again to get a better reception and to lose some of the noise from inside the house. Despite the cold air, he suddenly warmed inside as he listened to what the sergeant had to say.

"Well, that answers an earlier question," remarked the inspector as he re-joined Turner inside the house. "That was Dawkins. Apparently he's had a call from the caretaker at Scott's school. There's been a break-in earlier today in one of the offices where pupils' records are kept. No witnesses, but there were some decorators working outside who reported being spoken to by some young blonde female. They assumed that she was a local girl out for a stroll who just wanted to pass the time of day. You'd better chase up your man with his house to house records. They have to be one and the same."

"I think we're dealing with pros who occasionally like to take the piss," remarked Turner.

"If that's the case, we had better take this seriously," added Massey, indicating the message taped to the television screen.

The remainder of the weekend passed off without further incident. At the Morgan house D.S. Turner co-ordinated a rota of two on, two off to monitor the telephone surveillance operation, each pair consisting of a PC and a WPC. However, no call was received from Scott's possible kidnapper and nothing was forthcoming from St. John's Wood police station.

Sergeant Dawkins had failed to discover the whereabouts of the other school and Massey was unable to add to that part of the investigation, as Sammy had not come back to him with any information from the security tapes. Forensics worked over the weekend on all the evidence (mostly an assortment of fingerprints) from Westferry Road.

The only additional data they could give to Massey was the fact that the font on Scott's computer had been changed from Times New Roman (his default font format) to Comic Sans. There had been no sign of a struggle, no forced entry. The only evidence of Scott's abduction was the note taped to the television and the message on the computer.

Slumped once again across the settee in his Streatham flat, Massey was becoming extremely frustrated. He had spent almost two days investigating a crime without any real concrete evidence that a crime had been committed and if there was a crime, what the hell was it, he kept asking himself. He could sense the brick wall rising up again. Maybe he was focusing on the wrong boy. If the money had been earmarked for the other youth, there must have been something of great value in his briefcase.

What did he receive in return? Was it a legitimate exchange or was it part of the obvious scam that took place with Scott's briefcase? Turner had a point. If it was meant for the girl, she would be pretty upset to receive schoolbooks instead of something valuable. So what could have been in the other briefcase? Drugs? Diamonds? Gold? Top secret documents? Counterfeit notes? The possibilities were endless.

Why make the exchange there, in a public place and why cloak and dagger? It had to be something illegal, profitable and extremely valuable. And then there was the euro coin which forensics had found beneath the bundles of banknotes. Maybe the contents were coming in from abroad, maybe it was duty avoidance, but where did the schoolboys fit in?

The Courier
James R. Vance

    He determined that first thing Monday morning he would tap into Sergeant Dawkins' knowledge of Revenue and Customs. Yes, he had spent time tracking illegal immigrants, so he would have some experience of that agency. Massey suddenly realised that he'd not taken that shower, nor had he eaten. He kicked off his shoes, poured another scotch and thought, sod it.

Chapter 6

MONDAY: Giulio Fabrizzi was an Eastender, born in England of Italian parents. With his dark wavy hair, almond eyes and Mediterranean complexion he looked every inch a native of Puglia in the 'heel' of Italy, from where his family originated, that is, until he opened his mouth and spoke in his locally acquired dialect.

His grandparents had arrived in England shortly after World War II and set up a small catering business importing cheeses and pasta from suppliers at home. This venture had expanded over a period of time into a lucrative family wholesale import enterprise in a unit adjacent to London Docklands.

In time the business passed to Giulio's father and before the death of his grandfather, the young Giulio spent many happy hours with the old man, watching the cargo-laden ships steaming up the river Thames. Here the two generations of the Fabrizzi family would sit for hours and the youngster would listen, enraptured by his grandfather's stories of the trading ships, which sailed the world to bring their precious cargoes to the nearby dockside.

Sadly all that had now changed to be replaced by modern dwellings and upmarket waterside apartments. The area which was once thronged by merchants and traders had become a haven for well-off city types and stockbroker traders.

The love of the river and the fascination for the various vessels which steamed and sailed into the Port of London remained with Giulio throughout his childhood, his adolescence and on into adulthood. At the age of twenty one he eventually saved sufficient money to buy his own 20 ft Searay cruiser, which he named Giuseppe after his late grandfather.

The Courier
James R. Vance

Brought up in the Docklands area, he was ideally placed to have also purchased his first property in St. Katherine's dock with its own mooring. His income from the family business supported a comfortable lifestyle, where he could indulge in his favourite pastime of messing around with boats. Having recently acquired a young friend to share his passion, they would spend most evenings and weekends tinkering with the cruiser and trialling the results on the history-steeped stretch of river between Tower Bridge and London Bridge.

Further upstream lay Blackfriars Bridge with its own little piece of history. Thomas Doggett was an 18th century Irish actor and comedian, who became very interested in the Watermen of the river Thames, boatmen who could be compared to the modern day cabbies of the city of London. To commemorate the accession of George 1st to the throne, he inaugurated and funded a race between the oarsmen of the numerous boats, which plied their trade along the embankments of the river. To the six rowers of the winning boat (Watermen in the first year of their Freedom) he gave to each an annual prize of a Waterman's coat adorned with a silver badge on the sleeve.

The first race took place in 1715 and continues to this day, albeit in a different format, and covers the distance between London Bridge and Chelsea. At the southern end of Blackfriars Bridge, adjacent to the river, stands a public house, which carries the name of this historic race, Doggetts Coat and Badge. This renowned tavern and the Giuseppe were about to play a dramatic part in the partial destruction of Massey's brick wall.

*****

The lack of food and the abundance of whisky ensured a sound night's sleep for D. I. Massey, so much so, that it took several cups of coffee to recover sufficiently for the day ahead. He reached the office at Blackfriars shortly before nine o'clock. Turner breezed in with a couple of machine-produced coffees in plastic beakers.

"You must have read my mind."

The Courier
James R. Vance

"Bad night, then?"

"Crap weekend, really. Bloody Shearer started it!" moaned Massey, reflecting on the football match. "Then all that stuff with Scott. I can't make any sense of it. I assume we've heard nothing. What's your take on it all?"

Turner slurped his coffee and sat on a well-worn wooden chair across the desk from his superior. "At first, I thought drugs. Then I figured money laundering. Then illegal immigrant payments. Then prostitution. Then porn. Then I thought, maybe it's all something legal. Then I had another beer and thought bollocks. I haven't a damn clue!"

Massey smiled, partly in amusement, partly in agreement. "Nothing follows the norm. Two drops at once, which appear to have gone pear-shaped, the involvement of school-kids, a botched preconceived scam, mysterious suspects who disappear without trace and a possible kidnap with a ransom demand only for the money they lost…the whole business linked to some sort of criminal activity without an apparent crime, until Scott's disappearance. All we can do is wait."

Turner emptied his beaker and tossed it into the waste bin. "I'll give Dawkins a bell to see if he's come up with anything."

"You could ask him to use his contacts in Revenue and Customs to see if they've any angle on this or if there's any unusual activity which currently they might be clocking. I know it sounds like clutching at straws, but you never know. Tell him to come back to us on our mobiles. I fancy a trip to St. Johns Wood again. What d'you reckon?"

"Well, she's keeps cropping up every time. Searching for some young blonde female quite appeals to me on a dank October morning," quipped Turner.

They telephoned ahead to St. Johns Wood police station for an electoral list on the Greville Road area and at eleven fifteen they were knocking on the first door. By twelve forty five they were cold, wet and hungry with nothing to show for their endeavours.

"C'mon, let's eat. I'm bloody famished," grumbled Massey.

The Courier
James R. Vance

"The Clifton again?"

"Why not? It's just down the road. We can walk it."

"By the way, I think it's your turn at the bar," remarked Turner.

The pub was fairly quiet, probably as much due to the weather as to it being a Monday. Massey ordered some hot beef sandwiches with horseradish and they retired to the empty conservatory area with two halves of Shepherd Neame.

"It's sod's law. When you want paperwork it's always bloody missing," commented Massey. "If your mate at the local nick was more competent at keeping records, we could have probably found the young blonde by now."

"You mean like the one who's just walked in," replied Turner.

The inspector looked up to see a young couple walk down the steps to sit by the log fire. She wore a black, full-length leather coat, which flared open to reveal a short, beige woollen skirt and black, knee-length leather boots. Her companion, slightly older looking, wore a stylish, navy pin-stripe suit, white shirt and powder blue silk tie. He carried their drinks and placed them on the table by the fireplace.

"She's a bit tasty and worth a bob or two, I'd say," said Turner.

"Out of your league. Bet it's boss and secretary."

"Or kidnapper and accomplice," suggested the detective sergeant.

"They hardly look in need of money."

"No, but they look as though they could afford to fill a briefcase."

"Look at their expressions. Do they appear distressed enough to have lost a briefcase full of money, hard enough to have kidnapped a young schoolboy under threat of death?"

"First impressions can be very deceptive."

"Tell me about it," said Massey, reflecting on previous experiences, but not yet aware of how true Turner's comment would become during this current investigation.

The Courier
James R. Vance

Their sandwiches arrived at that moment and the light-hearted conversation drifted towards football, the fortunes of the Arsenal and the continuing success of the Premiership leaders. Eventually they decided to resume their door-to-door slog and left the young couple chatting animatedly by the blazing fire.

"Do you want me to stay on and follow the blonde?" asked Turner.

"Not likely with your track record," remarked Massey, "but, if she opens one of those doors later, I'll let you arrest her. C'mon, let's crack on and try to trace the real one."

It was about four o'clock when Isaac Joseph turned the black Audi TT into his driveway. He hardly noticed the two men walking towards his gates, such was his preoccupation with his own current situation. He parked up, climbed out of the driver's seat, secured the door with the central locking key and crunched across the gravel towards the house. He eventually became aware of the strangers' presence when the noise from the gravel increased as their footsteps drew closer. He turned to face them.

"Mr Joseph?" inquired the detective inspector.

"Who wants to know?" asked the old man, continuing to walk towards the safety of his front door.

"I'm Detective Inspector Massey and this is Detective Sergeant Turner," replied Massey, flashing his warrant card.

Isaac stopped abruptly and tried to compose himself before turning to face them again. "And what can I do for you?" he asked quietly.

"Just routine, sir. We're checking our records with regard to the commencement of the video surveillance system in this area. We have you down as the householder here. Anyone else live with you?"

"What does it say on your sheet, officer?" Isaac nodded towards the electoral roll, which Turner was flicking through on a clipboard.

Isaac knew that neither his son nor his niece had been registered for the community charge and he wondered whether the authorities had finally caught up.

The Courier
James R. Vance

"What should it say, sir?" asked Turner.

"Just me, if you've got your facts right."

"Quite so," smiled Turner.

"Whilst we're here, sir," continued Massey, "can you recollect seeing a young blonde lady who may live in the area?"

"Don't see anybody," snapped Isaac, turning to find the key for his front door lock. "I'm too busy to socialise with neighbours. Now, if you've finished, I've work to do." He opened the door and slammed it behind him. Once inside, he wiped the sweat from his brow and ran towards the telephone.

"Charming," remarked Turner. "I told you it was a most un-neighbourly neighbourhood."

"Miserable sod," added Massey. "Let's call it a day. I'll get some uniform bods to finish off tomorrow."

They walked back down the driveway, watched closely by Isaac Joseph as he contacted Rebecca to ensure that she returned home after dark.

The two detectives headed back to Blackfriars via Marylebone, Mayfair and St. James's, where the traffic started to become heavier as rush hour approached. They crossed into Lambeth via Westminster Bridge, continuing on into Southwark. The Inspector dropped Turner off to retrieve his own car at the rear of the police station and parked up himself, before calling in to pick up any messages. There were none.

Maybe no news is good news, he thought and, having decided to finish early for the day, left for his flat in Streatham.

Chapter 7

TUESDAY: The morning passed in much the same way. Massey contacted Mrs. Morgan to reassure her that they were exploring every lead and that it was only a matter of time before Scott was safely back at home. He knew that it sounded rather trite and was an often used delaying tactic, but how else could he offer any peace of mind to the young man's mother? In reality however, he was extremely concerned and desperate for any slight lead which they might follow. Even a telephone call from the kidnapper would have been a relief.

He also had a word with the police liaison officer at the Morgan house and she reported that Scott's mother was keeping unusually calm considering that her son had now been missing for three days. Perhaps it was because he had been living with his father and she was not yet used to having him around her all the time. On the other hand, it could have been some kind of delayed reaction. Massey asked her to keep a close eye on her and to keep him posted.

Sammy and Dawkins seemed to have disappeared off the face of the earth, as neither had returned his calls despite having left several messages. Obviously they had nothing to report, which frustrated him even more. Lunchtime came and went without incident, but Turner could see that the lack of any kind of progress was getting to his superior.

"How are the guys doing out at St. John's Wood? Any feedback yet?" asked Turner.

"Not a bloody word. The girl's disappeared. Scott's disappeared. Every bastard's disappeared. Even bloody Dawkins and Sammy have apparently been abducted by aliens. Bollocks to it all. I'm off for a beer. Fancy one?"

The Courier
James R. Vance

They left the office and made for the Ring public house on the corner of The Cut, their regular nearby haunt. They spent the next hour playing pool and consuming several pints of London Pride. At three o'clock they were back in the office, feeling less stressed than when they left, but still without having made any headway.

Massey returned to his desk and, for the umpteenth time opened the file on the case, trying to draw inspiration from its limited contents. His thoughts were interrupted by the ringing of his mobile as it vibrated across his desk.

"Hello, Detective Inspec…" he started to introduce himself.

"You Detective Massey?" The voice was muffled, but staccato and direct. "We want our money, you want Scott Morgan."

Massey's heart skipped. He stood up waving his free arm, frantically trying to attract Turner's attention and simultaneously pointing at his mobile. It suddenly clicked with the detective sergeant and he raced across the office.

"Listen," continued the voice, "you will place all the money in a thick industrial weight, black bin liner. You will tie the loose plastic end into one tight knot. You will place that inside another similar black liner and tie the surplus into two tight knots. At precisely six fourteen tonight you will stand alone with this bag of money outside Doggetts Coat and Badge at Blackfriars Bridge with your mobile phone fully charged and switched on. You will enlist no back-up. Any deviation from these instructions and Scott Morgan will die immediately."

The line went dead.

Massey looked down at his phone, then across at Turner. "I think we're dealing with pros after all," he commented in a tone of resigned realisation. He passed his mobile to a W.P.C. who had joined them. "Debbie, see if you can get a trace on that last call, but get the phone back here asap."

Turner sat down by the desk. "Well?" he inquired.

Massey related the details of the one-way conversation.

"At least, it's just around the corner," said Turner.

The Courier
James R. Vance

"Rush hour time," mused Massey. "All those people about. It could be any one of them. And he wants my phone charged up. It sounds like I'm going to be receiving several instructions to move around. But how did he know my mobile number and why bin liners?"

"Disguised as refuse?" offered Turner. "Maybe it's going to end up on a rubbish dump. You'll have to keep an eye on it, especially in black bags. It goes dark about half six," he added with a smile. "Rush hour, dusk, busy open public place. Some thought's been put into this. Need to organise surveillance. What do you reckon, both ends of the bridge?"

"Absolutely." Massey glanced at his watch. "Three hours, not a lot of time. I'll also need wiring up. Do we go with the money, or fake it? What do you think? Can we take a risk with Scott's life?"

He was thinking aloud, expressing his concerns with rhetorical questions and oblivious to any comments from his sergeant. "And when and where does the exchange take place even if they keep their word?" He finally looked across at Turner, knowing full well that they had no answer to his last question.

"Why Doggetts?" added Turner, "And, as you said, how did they get your mobile number?"

"Obviously from Scott. I gave him my card," replied Massey, having given that point some thought. "Anyway let's get moving. I want to cover every possibility, every loophole on this one." He stood up, hands on hips. "At last the brick wall's starting to crumble. By the way, what's the weather like out there?"

"Lashing down," said Turner. "Maybe that's the reason for the bin liners."

"Why bin liners?" echoed Massey as he walked away.

The telephone rang on Massey's desk. Turner answered it. It was Sammy from the security office at the railway station.

"Your boss wanted me to check the tapes on that second youth to find out how he entered the station."

"Well?" asked Turner, waiting for his report.

"Is he there, then?"

The Courier
James R. Vance

"He's just left the office. What've you got?"

"Guess where he came from," challenged Sammy, smugly.

"An alien spacecraft!" replied Turner, not really in the mood for Sammy's guessing game.

"Try a train," chuckled Sammy.

"Well, would you believe it? He arrived at the railway station in a train!" retorted Turner sarcastically. "Was it on time?"

"I reckon so, 'cos it was the next train after the one which the other lad came off. And guess what?"

"I can't wait. Go on, amaze me."

"There were several of them."

"Well, it is a bloody station and it was rush hour. Trains come and go all the time, don't they?"

"No, you stupid bastard. Several more lads, all wearing the same uniform, you know, the blazer with the badge."

Turner went silent for a moment. "Sammy, hold the line. Don't go away. Let me see if the inspector's still around."

He dropped the handset on the desk and shot out of the office. Taking the stairs two at a time, he spotted Massey at the front desk.

"There's a phone call for you," he shouted rather breathlessly.

"Just finding out if we've got any bin liners. Who is it?"

"Sammy. I think you ought to speak with him."

"Can't you deal with it?"

"I think you should speak with him," repeated Turner, emphasising the point by nodding his head knowingly.

"See what you can do," said Massey to the uniformed constable behind the desk. "I'll pick them up later and don't forget, two of them, heavy duty."

The two detectives raced back up the staircase and Massey picked up the unattended handset.

"Hi, Sammy, what's the score?"

The security man related an abbreviated and less humorous version of his conversation with Turner, whilst the inspector listened intently.

The Courier
James R. Vance

"Where do you reckon they caught the train?" asked Massey.

"Don't know, but I thought I might get hold of that railway police guy...Dawson...and ask him to do some ferreting."

"You mean Dawkins. He's already on the case, but not come up with anything so far."

"Would it help if I sent you some mug shots of them all?"

"You mean you've got full frontals?"

"On most of them, yes. Some better than others, 'cos some are a bit obscured, but I can pick out the best shots of them as they came off the platform."

"Brilliant. Can you send a copy of the video tape also?"

"No problem. Glad to be of service."

"That's another one I owe you. Send copies to Dawkins also. You'll probably find him through the railway police at Folkestone or Dover. And while I think about it, are you on duty next Monday morning, when the kids go back to school?"

"Don't know offhand, need to check the rota."

"Try and work it that you are and see if you can spot any of them, other than our friend at the kiosk. We need to find out where the school is. If we crack it before then, I'll let you know. Keep it low key, be discreet and thanks."

Massey replaced the handset and looked at Turner. "Things are hotting up at last. Let's concentrate on tonight's escapade now."

*****

Massey stood under an umbrella outside Doggetts Coat and Badge. He checked his watch. Six o'clock. Across the Thames, the chimes of Big Ben verified the precision of his timepiece. He radioed down to Turner who was standing outside the terrace bar of the public house overlooking the river.

"Phone me on your mobile and ask one of your young ladies to monitor our conversation with your radio. I just want to check you can listen in to both ends of the mobile chitchat."

74

The Courier
James R. Vance

The detective sergeant was accompanied by two plainclothes police women to assist in the operation and also to provide him with some innocent looking cover. The fact that they were stood outside the pub, drinking fruit juices on a dull, drizzling October evening, was beside the point. Early doors customers were scarce in the cold, damp atmosphere. Most commuters were hurrying home before the weather deteriorated further.

"What would you like me to say when I phone you?"

"The first thing that springs to mind or any useless chat. In other words, just be your normal self."

Across from Doggetts two policemen were masquerading as telephone engineers working on a cabling installation outside an office block. Over the bridge a surveillance unit staked out the area from an unmarked van, parked up on the Embankment. In the office block adjacent to the pub was a team of several police officers to coordinate the operation. In addition to communication systems, some of them manned camcorders and binoculars with night-sights, trained on the bridge and its immediate area.

Despite the back-up surrounding him, Massey still felt rather isolated and vulnerable. The radio surveillance checked out, confirmed not only by Turner's colleagues, but also by all the other strategically placed support teams.

"Hope you've got a tight grip on your bin liner," quipped Turner.

"Don't worry, it stays with me until Scott's handed over," replied Massey.

He checked his mobile phone again, that it was fully charged with a good signal. He glanced at his watch. Six thirteen.

Commuters were crossing Blackfriars Bridge in huge numbers, both on foot and in a slowly moving crawl of rush hour traffic. Dusk was falling rapidly and the light from the street lamps cast an eerie glow in the fine curtain of mist and rain above the river.

Another glance at the watch. Almost six fifteen. Still no contact. In the distance Big Ben chimed the quarter hour. Massey focussed on all the people hurrying and scurrying past him, homeward bound.

He suddenly jumped, startled by the ring of his mobile. He released the umbrella to answer the call.

"Inspector?" inquired the muffled voice.

Massey confirmed it was he and simultaneously tightened his grip on the bin liner. He stepped backwards towards the shelter of the pub wall to avoid the passing pedestrians and the incessant drizzle.

"Keep your mobile open. I need to check that you don't speak. Walk across the bridge keeping to the Doggetts side until you reach the third small recess jutting out over the river. Stop there and say 'I'm here'. Do not speak or ask questions. Go now."

Massey started walking towards the embankment side of the river, where St. Paul's Cathedral danced in the halo of its floodlights on the far side. It was quite difficult to negotiate the other pedestrians as most of the commuters were heading towards him. He glanced to his left and managed to spot Turner and his colleagues standing on the pub terrace huddled under a rain-soaked table umbrella.

"Are you carrying the money?" asked the voice via his mobile.

"Yes," replied Massey, "in bin liners as requested."

Massey now realised that he couldn't be seen or was the voice just checking that the mobile was still switched on? He passed the first two recesses and stopped at the third one. Climbing onto the raised part, he looked about him. Raising his mobile to his mouth, he said, "I'm here."

"Step into the recess, walk to the parapet of the bridge and look over," ordered the voice. "What do you see?"

Massey was already in the recess. He can't see me, thought the inspector, so where the hell is he?

He leaned over and surveyed the river. Below him, bobbing about on the black and gold shimmering water was a boat, a cruiser. He could just about hear the throbbing of its engine above the noise of the traffic and the downpour splashing the stonework of the bridge. Someone wearing a close-fitting, hooded waterproof jacket was looking up at him. A length of rope dangling from the stern of the boat into the water was attached to a small inflatable dinghy. Another person was in the dinghy, similarly attired.

"Scott's in the RIB tied up. He's quite safe provided you play ball. Drop the bin liner to me in the cruiser and I'll set him free."

"What if I miss?" asked Massey, playing for time and hoping that one of the back-up teams had clocked the situation and had the initiative to call up the river police from Waterloo Bridge.

"Just drop the bag. If you miss, the lad goes in as well."

Massey decided to play safe for Scott's sake. He reckoned that between the river police and the mobile back-up on each side of the Thames, there was no way out for the man in the cruiser. He dangled the bag over the parapet, sighting it over the open cockpit of the boat below. He let go. The bag thudded into the boat rocking it adding to the existing motion caused by the swell of the river.

The man drew a knife and slashed through the bin liners to check the contents. Satisfied with what he found, he cut the rope, setting the rubber inflatable free. Suddenly the cruiser roared into life and disappeared under Blackfriars Bridge. The inflatable drifted away into the shadows.

"Go, go, he's heading east," screamed Massey into his radio and started dodging through the pedestrians and the traffic on the bridge in an attempt to catch sight of the drifting dinghy on the other side. Turner was contacting the river police as he raced through Doggetts, pursued by his two female colleagues. There was no response.

He reached his vehicle in time to hear the observers above him radio that they had lost visual contact with the cruiser as it became obscured by the high-rise offices. The weather was also against them and the slight curve in the river made it even more difficult.

Turner tried the Port of London Authority and managed to marshal some assistance from Greenwich. Within minutes he and the two young policewomen were in his car speeding eastwards

along Southwark Street towards London Bridge, missing out a
complete stretch of the river, in the hope of gaining some distance
on the boat.

Meanwhile, having negotiated the traffic, Massey had
crossed to the other side of Blackfriars Bridge in a final attempt to
eyeball the drifting dinghy. It had now passed beneath the arches
of the road bridge and was slowly floating towards the pillars of
the railway bridge, which crossed the river from Blackfriars
station.

The unmarked van had already raced into Upper Thames
Street in pursuit of the cruiser, even though it had completely
disappeared from view. The inspector was now screaming for
back-up, partly to assist in rescuing Scott from the dinghy, but also
to provide him with wheels to track the fugitive.

The team in the office block by Doggetts had finally
summoned the river police from Waterloo Bridge, who were
approaching the dinghy below the railway bridge. Massey radioed
them to ignore the inflatable and pursue the cruiser in an attempt to
locate it further downstream. More police sirens and blue flashing
lights signalled the arrival of further support brought in by the co-
ordination team.

Gradually the evening commuters became aware of the
frenzied activity in proximity to the bridge with the result that the
rush hour escape from the city slowly ground to a halt, causing
further congestion for the police. Spectators thronged the bridge on
both sides, trying to find evidence to support the various theories,
which were rapidly spreading amongst them. London had become
so used to activity like this that it was quickly rumoured to be yet
another terrorist threat.

Turner swung a left past Southwark Cathedral and skidded
to a halt on London Bridge. Several vessels were gently making
their way in both directions along the river, but there was no sign
of the cruiser, or indeed of any speeding boat. He returned to the
car, made a swift u-turn with lights still flashing and, following the
river eastwards, turned into Tooley Street. Just past the London
Dungeon, he took a sharp left into the newly developed quayside

walkways and leaving the vehicle in a service road, the three of them raced through Hays Galleria.

They spread out to reconnoitre the stretch of river where H.M.S. Belfast lay at anchor below Tower Bridge. The area was busy with office workers, business people and tourists, either passing through or visiting the various café bars and restaurants in the mall. On the river itself there seemed to be little activity and the descending darkness made it difficult to see anything clearly.

It was no surprise, therefore, that none of the three police officers took particular notice of the individual with the rucksack. He appeared from the gloomy direction of the river, walked past Café Rouge and crossed the street to London Bridge tube station.

Massey ran down Hopton Street towards Falcon Point Piazza and, passing the Tate Modern, finally caught up with several officers who were busy fixing a holding line to the drifting dinghy. By this time it had washed up onto an exposed shale strewn bank of the river below the Founders Arms on Thames Path. Breathless and exasperated, he was even more frustrated by what confronted him.

"Bastard," was all he could utter, followed by, "Clever bastard." Then there was a short silence as he looked skywards, as though demanding some form of divine intervention.

"What shall we do with it, sir?" asked one of the officers.

The inspector felt like telling him to stick it, but it was evidence and possibly important evidence at that.

"Get it off the river before we lose it." He looked along the exposed bank. "Carry it up the steps onto Queens Walk and try not to handle it too much. Can someone call forensics and stay with it until they arrive? We'll need a van to take it away. Can someone sort that as well?"

He walked back up the steps and crossed to Falcon Point, where he contacted Turner. "Where are you?"

"About halfway between London Bridge and Tower Bridge, but there's nothing here. Spoken to Port of London lads. They've a couple of boats on the way and I've just asked the police launch to work with them to check the whole area from Southwark to Wapping. I'm going to carry on to Greenwich. Could do with someone covering the other side as far as, maybe, the Isle of Dogs. What d'you reckon?"

"Fine. Sort what you can. Contact that lot next to Doggetts, have them send more search teams. Mind you, I doubt we shall find him. We've been shafted and out-manoeuvred on this one. I'm seeing those brick walls again."

"What's with these bloody brick walls of yours?"

"Oh, don't mind me. It's pure frustration."

"Well, at least we've got Scott back, haven't we?"

"It looked like Scott from the bridge and probably looked like Scott from the riverside, but there was no Scott in the dinghy. We merely found a dummy dressed to look like Scott."

"You're bloody joking!"

"Like I said, shafted."

"Oh, shit! How much of the money was fake?"

"All of it. I thought the darkness would cover it and to some degree it seems to have worked. He checked it out in the boat before taking off, so he must have been satisfied."

"Not good news for Scott, though, when our fugitive finds out he's been mugged."

"Maybe, maybe not. When he discovers the stitch-up, he'll be mad, but he'll still want his loot and we can bargain with the fact that he cheated us with the dummy."

"Do you think I should still go to Greenwich?"

"Might be worth a look. Don't waste too much time. I'm going to see if forensics come up with any leads from the dinghy. Meet me back at the nick later, but phone if you or the waterboys find anything."

Massey hitched a lift back to the police station in one of the patrol cars and left a message at the front desk to be contacted as soon as the forensic team returned with the dinghy. He retired to his office and telephoned the liaison officer at Mrs. Morgan's house to relate the events, which had just taken place. Scott's mother had not been made aware of the planned exchange, so it was sensible not to involve her until there was some definite news on her son.

Until Turner returned he spent the next hour in contact with the patrol boats on the river Thames and at nine o'clock a decision was made to call off the search until daylight the following day. Ten minutes later, Anderson called to say they were ready to examine the dinghy. The two detectives went down to forensics to watch the detailed examination of the inflatable craft and its inflatable passenger.

The outcome was of little value to the investigation. The rubber inflatable boat was of the type sold in most chandleries and outdoor pursuit centres. It had no significant manufacturer's markings which might have denoted where it had been purchased.

The dummy was a cheap sex shop or joke shop style of blow-up doll, again which would have been difficult to trace. It appeared to be dressed in jeans, sweater, hooded anorak and a knitted wool hat, all of which could have belonged to Scott or any other youth of that build. Massey asked for the clothing to be bagged and tagged for Turner to check with Mrs. Morgan on the following day.

There was nothing else in the boat apart from two pieces of narrow timber planking, which had been nailed together in an 'L-shape'. The dummy had been attached to this to hold it in an upright sitting position. The only observation made by Anderson about the wooden structure related to the wood itself.

"Considering that the frame was merely to hold the dummy upright, whoever constructed it used some pretty expensive timber."

"The point being?" asked Massey.

"Well, one would have thought any cheap old wood could have served the purpose, but this is marine ply, not cheap by any means. Maybe it was the only timber available at the time."

"Meaning?"

"It's feasible that it was hastily put together at the last minute. Perhaps it was an afterthought, possibly because the dummy kept falling over in the dinghy."

The Courier
James R. Vance

"So the origin of this chunk of wood could lead us to the home of the speedboat?"

"Just an assumption. Problem is that marine ply like this could be found in thousands of boatyards and the like from the Thames estuary to Oxford and beyond. Possibly, it could have been lying in someone's boathouse, maybe belonging to a keen D.I.Y boat enthusiast."

"Thanks a bunch. Anything else?"

"You might work on the assumption that the cruiser and maybe even the inflatable were both stolen. Who would pull a stunt like this using their own craft and if they did, they'd have to have somewhere fairly close at hand to get the cruiser quickly under cover, and moreover, to get them both in a handy place beforehand without drawing too much attention."

"Thank you, Sherlock," said Massey, smiling. "You may not be far off the mark."

"I'd concentrate on the area from Wapping to the Isle of Dogs, St. Katherine's Dock, you know, Docklands area. There are a lot of new marina berths in that locality."

"Docklands," repeated Turner, thoughtfully. "That's interesting."

"In the meantime, I'll dust everything for prints, but I don't hold out much hope. Everything's covered with an oily film from the river. The timber may provide some clues…we'll see. Bring the clothing back when it's been identified but keep it bagged and I'll test it for D.N.A."

The two detectives left together, dismayed but not without hope.

Chapter 8

WEDNESDAY: Rebecca was in the kitchen making coffee and buttering some toast before she left for the shop, when her uncle steamed into the room.

"What happened to David again last night?" demanded Isaac, grumpily. "He's not in his room and his bed hasn't been slept in."

"I'm not my cousin's keeper. Anyway, he's probably gone back to Barnes," retorted his niece.

"What's he doing about the missing briefcase? I thought you and he were supposed to be recovering it from that lad."

"He tells me nothing. I tried various estate agents yesterday and none of them have the boy's previous house for sale, so I've done my bit. If David's got some other plan in mind, well, he doesn't confide in me."

Rebecca poured herself some coffee. "Want some?" she asked, filling another mug without waiting for a reply. "Anyway, why are you so twitchy all of a sudden? I thought you were content to let David sort it all."

"There's questions being asked and I can't provide any answers, apart from the fact that a great deal of cash has gone walkabouts."

"I'm sure your son has it all under control," she replied with a hint of sarcasm in her voice. "So who's asking questions?"

"Look, an operation of this magnitude has to be organised to perfection. Slip-ups like the one you made throw a spanner in the works, so it has to be investigated to prevent it happening again."

"I told you before, it was not my mistake. The perfection, as you put it, was not that perfect." Rebecca picked up a bread knife. Pointing the weapon at Isaac, she glared at him defiantly.

The Courier
James R. Vance

"And who is this so-called investigator?" She leaned back, cut two more slices of bread and popped them in the toaster.

"He's just the head of the organisation," replied Isaac, waving his hand dismissively.

"Do I know him?" asked his niece.

"No, nor do I. Nobody knows him."

"You mean this, this dodgy business in which you're involved, is run by someone whom nobody knows and he has the balls to question any minor mistakes?"

"Losing a briefcase full of money is not a minor mistake, young lady, and anyway someone has to oversee what goes on."

"Don't you patronise me." Rebecca banged the kitchen table and the toast shot out of the toaster. "I can't believe that you're running some illicit business for someone whom you don't actually know. How did you get conned into that? And besides, I thought it was your money. What's it got to do with him?"

"It's not that simple," explained her uncle. "There's a lot of people involved. We all work for ourselves, but someone is needed to co-ordinate everything. It's far too complex to explain. You wouldn't understand."

"Try me," snapped Rebecca, irritated by his manner and rapidly spreading butter on Isaac's toast.

"Not now, my dear. Some other time, maybe."

"Well, as far as I'm concerned, the whole thing stinks. Go and play your nasty little games, but don't ever, ever ask me to help out again." Snatching his toast from the plate, she stormed out of the room. Not only was she annoyed with her uncle, but deep down she was troubled by her cousin's attitude and his reluctance to confide in her.

Isaac Joseph sighed, shook his head in despair and watched her stride out of the driveway. He sipped his coffee and waited for the inevitable phone call, for which he still had no answers.

*****

The Courier
James R. Vance

D.S. Turner had gone straight to Westferry Road to see Scott's mother in order to check out the clothes which had been removed from the dummy in the dinghy.

D.I. Massey had driven to Blackfriars police station with a view to meeting up with his sergeant later in the morning. On arrival, he snatched a coffee from the machine, but was waylaid by one of the admin staff before he could reach his office.

"Excuse me, sir, but this e-mail you sent out about logging all boat thefts in the Thames area during the last week," she asked. "Does it include today?"

Massey walked on towards his office. "You mean stolen today or reported today?" asked the inspector, taking a sip of his coffee before placing it on his desk.

"Reported first thing this morning, sir, to the river police. They faxed it through. The owner noticed it was missing about eight o'clock and his description pretty well matches the one you gave out."

"When was it actually stolen and from where?"

"He's not sure. He thinks, maybe some time yesterday. It was definitely there yesterday morning, but apparently he was away all day and didn't arrive home until late last night."

"And where did it disappear from?"

"Oh, yes. Sorry. St. Katherine's Dock."

"Thanks, Sarah. Can you contact D.S. Turner and give him the details? He's over in that direction at this moment. Ask him to check it out and see what else he can dig up. Oh, and make a copy of the fax for me too. I assume we have this guy's name and address?"

"Oh yes, sir." She giggled. "I hope the sergeant's good at languages."

"Why's that?"

"Well, he sounds Italian. His name's Giulio Fabrizzi."

"With a name like that, he's probably a cockney!"

They both laughed and Sarah turned to leave, but stopped in the doorway of Massey's office. "Oh, I nearly forgot. Can you phone a Sergeant Dawson at Ashford nick?"

The Courier
James R. Vance

"Dawkins," muttered the inspector. "Yes okay. Did he say why?"

"Only that it was urgent."

She left and headed for the photocopier. Massey put through the call to Ashford and surprisingly got hold of Dawkins instantly.

"I believe you wanted me urgently. Some good news, I hope?"

"Possibly," replied Dawkins. "I hope you don't mind, but I've been doing a bit of snooping around at this end, you know, being here on the ground as it were."

"That's what good police work is all about, sergeant," commented the inspector, wondering what was coming next.

"Well, 'cos I was back in the office yesterday, I was going through the scene of crime reports, the ones on the break-in at the school on Saturday. Apparently, the only file that was opened in the pupils' records was Scott Morgan's. It was left out on a desk and nearby was one of those post-it pads, blank, but with an imprint of what had been written on the top sheet. They checked it out and it had Scott's address written on it."

"Not surprising," added Massey.

"No, but what is surprising was the fact that both his old address and his new one were written on the missing sheet, despite the fact that his previous address was struck through in the school's records and the new one written in its place."

"Meaning what?" asked the detective.

"Well, I found it strange that they would make a note of his old address when it was obvious that he had moved house. Anyway, I decided to check out his old address as it isn't far from where I live. It was all locked up as expected. I had a look around the place, but it was pretty deserted and, when I looked through the letterbox, there was a load of junk mail, letters and newspapers in the hallway. I was about to leave when the next door neighbour appeared on the scene from his greenhouse. He was quite chatty and in the course of our conversation told me about a visitor to the house last Saturday. Guess who!"

"Off the top of my head, the intruder from the school, but I bet you're going to tell me otherwise."

"A young lady with long blonde hair, same description as the one chatting to the decorators at the school earlier in the day."

"Most probably the same as the one on the security video at the station and in the taxi to Maida Vale. We need to find this young lady pretty sharpish. That reminds me, did Sammy send you those pics of the schoolboys?"

"Yes, but I didn't recognise any of them. I'll keep my eyes open next week, when they're back."

"Good man. Well, thanks for following that up," began Massey. "Maybe in the meantime you could keep a discreet eye on the house. Any luck with Revenue and Customs?"

"Nothing that ties in with this little lot."

"Ok, give me a call if anything comes up at your end."

Massey leaned back in his chair more confused than ever. He decided to meet up with Turner and drive to St. John's Wood again. The constant appearance of the young girl was beginning to annoy him. After the previous night's fiasco on the river, he was beginning to doubt his own judgement and expertise. The brick wall was rising up before him again. The admin girl brought him a copy of the fax from the river police.

"Excuse me, sir. I hope you don't mind me saying so, but you don't look very well. To put it bluntly, you look like shit."

"Too many late nights," he replied with a smile, "and thanks for your concern."

"You want to look after yourself. No job's worth sacrificing your health for."

"Quite right. Thanks." Too much booze and too little food, he reflected. It was fortunate that there was no mirror in his office to support the secretary's remarks or he would have realised the reason for her concern. During the past few days, the pressure and frustration of this particular case had taken its toll on him. His face had become tight and drawn, the skin taken on a greyish pallor and dark bags were appearing beneath his eyes. He promised himself some leave when it was all over. When what was over?

The Courier
James R. Vance

He phoned Turner to see what progress he was making. "Where are you now?" asked the inspector.

"Just left Mrs. M.'s on my way to see a certain Mr. Fabbysomething."

"Any joy with Scott's mum?"

"Oh, yes. Definitely the lad's clothing."

"Well, keep them bagged and take them back to forensics later. Let's hope they can provide something positive for once. How did she react?"

"Quite calm, actually. I don't think she realises how serious the situation could become."

"Let's hope that she won't have to." Massey went on to relate his discussion with Dawkins and his concern about the girl, especially that, having accepted her to be an important link in the affair, she had not been traced.

"I'll meet up with you outside the City Quay apartments at St. Katherine's dock. I've got the details. After we've spoken to the 'Iti' we'll head up to St. John's Wood again. Someone must know her or at least have seen her. Let's face it, she was a bit of a head turner."

He was about to leave when Debbie, the uniformed P.C. stopped him. "River police have just confirmed that they have recovered a motor cruiser, abandoned overnight at London Bridge City Pier. Description matches. They want to know what to do with it."

"Tell them on no account to touch or remove it. I'm heading to see the possible owner. He'll need to identify it. Oh, and ask Anderson in forensics to get his team down there in double quick time. I'll meet him at the pier."

Twenty five minutes later, Massey parked his car alongside the cottages on the marina in St. Katherine's Dock. Turner was already there and walked towards him. A gusty wind was blowing from the east, rippling the ropes and pulleys against the masts of the yachts and sailing dinghies berthed there, creating a cacophony of jangling sounds.

The Courier
James R. Vance

"Have you spoken with him yet?" asked Massey, closing his driving door.

"No, thought I'd wait for you."

"I don't speak Italian, either."

They both laughed and as they walked across the terracotta paving towards the apartment blocks, Massey told him about the boat found on the river. At the main entrance an intercom was activated by pressing the button alongside Fabrizzi's apartment number. They announced themselves and the door was unlocked with a low-pitched buzz. On reaching the first floor they found the Italian's flat and rang the bell.

"Thank you for coming over so quickly," he said, inviting the detectives into a minimalist interior in an art nouveau style.

"We may have some good news for you," interjected Massey, relieved that the Italian spoke perfect English, albeit with a slight east London accent. "A cruiser's been found near London Bridge. If you could accompany us, hopefully you will be able to identify it and on the way tell us more about its disappearance."

Giulio looked relieved, grabbed a leather jacket and followed the two detectives downstairs to the parked cars. Leaving Massey's vehicle on the quayside, Turner took the wheel and they sped off towards Tower Bridge.

Within a few minutes they were heading down Thomas Street to navigate the one-way system which would bring them to London Bridge and the City Pier by the Hays Galleria.

En route, Giulio described his boat and gave them as much detail as he could about its mooring, his last sighting and the discovery of its theft.

"I understand that the marina is enclosed by a lock gate," commented Massey.

"Yes, but it opens at eight in the morning and closes at six at the moment," replied the young man.

"I'm clueless with boats," added Turner, "but surely you must have an ignition key or something similar to start the engine."

"Absolutely," said the Anglo-Italian.

"So, how could it have been stolen?" asked Massey

The Courier
James R. Vance

"I suppose there are ways round the wiring system the same as hot-wiring cars," offered Giulio, "unless you have a key."

"Do you have a spare key?" asked the sergeant.

"Only one."

"And where's that?"

"My friend, who helps me with work on the boat. He has it."

"And have you checked with him, if he still has the key? Maybe he lost it." suggested Massey.

"No, I haven't seen Scott since the weekend," replied Giulio.

The detectives turned and looked at each other. "Scott?" they asked, in unison.

*****

Isaac Joseph snipped the last dead flowers from his rose bush, slipped the secateurs into their plastic holster and carried the cardboard box containing the debris from the garden to the wheelie-bin. He emptied the contents into the plastic liner and walked over to the garden shed to replace the pruning cutters in the neat little rack containing some of his gardening tools.

Still holding the box, he headed for the house across the immaculately mown lawn. He opened the conservatory door in time to hear the telephone ringing. He shuddered momentarily, not from the cool, late afternoon air, but from the dread of the potential caller. He entered the hallway and picked up the handset. It was the voice of The Fixer. Another chill ran down his spine.

"I take it from your silence that you have not recovered your money."

"Er no, not yet, there's some trouble locating the youth who took the briefcase," stammered Isaac.

"Allow me to clarify your position," continued the voice. "Your cash conveniently disappeared at the same time as the merchandise, which was intended for you, vanished without a trace. I find that a remarkable coincidence, but unfortunately, I do not believe in long shots. I'm more of a dead cert man, if you

90

follow my drift. Only three parties were privy to that exchange, the delivery boy acting for the seller, me, and the purchaser, you.

Now, my integrity is not in question, nor is the honesty of our friend, who is distraught at having lost his goods in exchange for a briefcase full of paper. Of the three parties involved in this clandestine transaction, there remains only one who can be a winner, one who, by knowing the system, can walk away with a case full of cash and a case full of goodies, not to mention my percentage."

"But I know nothing of the other briefcase. We've just lost…"

"Oh, yes. You have lost. You have two days to rectify this debacle. Noon on Friday or you will pay the price."

Isaac heard the click as the phone went dead. He wiped his brow, not for the first time that afternoon, and slumped into the nearest chair.

He re-lived the events of the past week in his mind. First, there had been David's accident, then Rebecca's mistake with the schoolboy, their unsuccessful trip to Kent, David's strange behaviour followed by his disappearance and finally the two policemen who had confronted him on his doorstep. Was that also a coincidence or had they discovered something? The Fixer was correct in believing that something was untoward.

It had been a week of unforeseen events and it had all started with David's mysterious accident. What was he up to? Did he know what was going on? Was he involved? How much did Rebecca know? Two days to find some answers. He picked up the handset again and dialled the shop. His niece answered the call.

"I must contact David. Do you know where he is?"

"His mobile's still switched off and there's no reply from his house," replied Rebecca. "I haven't a clue as to his whereabouts."

"It's urgent," protested Isaac. "We desperately need to talk. When will you be home?"

"The usual time." She detected a faint tremor in his voice. Though only communicating by phone, she sensed that Isaac was greatly disturbed. "What's happened?"

"Wait until you're home, but if you can find a way to contact David, it's vital, so very vital..." His voice trailed off and, despite their tenuous relationship, Rebecca felt deep concern for her uncle.

*****

Turner stopped the car in a narrow street alongside the Horniman at Hays as close as possible to London Bridge City Pier and he and Massey turned to face their passenger.

"This friend of yours, Scott. Where does he live?" asked the inspector.

"Not sure," replied Giulio. "I've only known him a few weeks. We just got chatting one day. He was watching me doing some repair work on the engine and he offered some advice. He seemed to know what he was talking about and it started from there."

"Yet you entrusted him with a set of keys?" added Turner.

"Well, yes. He helped me out quite a bit and sometimes, with me working and him being still at college, he came down to work on it when I wasn't around. In return he had a few trips on the river with me. He's an okay guy, dead intelligent for his age and good company. He's a good mate."

"But you don't know his address?"

"Somewhere in Docklands, I think he said."

"What about his surname?"

"He did tell me. Sorry, can't remember. I'm not good with names."

"When did you last see him?"

"I told you, weekend, Saturday, I think. Yes, it was Saturday afternoon. He didn't stay long. Said he had to do some shopping. Do you think Scott took the boat?"

The Courier
James R. Vance

Massey stepped out of the vehicle. "If you would be so kind to accompany us to the pier, maybe we could first ascertain that it is your boat which has been recovered."

The two detectives and the young man walked towards the river, the area of which was dominated at that point by the huge superstructure of H.M.S. Belfast. They headed towards a group of individuals standing beyond the blue and white police tape which had cordoned off most of Queens Walk from the Horniman to Cottons Centre. Anderson and his team were already at work on the cruiser which had been securely tethered to the pier itself. They continued across a short jetty to reach the forensic team.

"Well?" asked the inspector, turning to Giulio.

"It's not my boat."

Massey looked out across the Thames and saw the brick wall again. They continued walking briskly along the pier, pursued by Giulio. As they reached the forensic team inspecting the cruiser, he confirmed his initial reaction to the stolen craft.

Massey muttered a disappointed 'thank you' to the young man and stepped down to speak briefly with Anderson. He was standing in the well of the boat in his white protective suit, contrasting starkly with the grey murkiness of the river.

The forensic team leader looked up. "Is this the one, d'you think?"

"More than likely. Difficult to be absolutely sure, but it appears to look like the one below the bridge. Found anything yet?"

"A few prints and the trailing rope fibres. If we can match them to the trailing dinghy rope, I'd put my pension on it."

Massey smiled. "The way things have been going so far with this bloody case, I wouldn't put my loose change on it."

"Oh, ye of little faith," joked Anderson. "Is he the owner?" he nodded in Giulio's direction.

"Until a couple of minutes ago, but strangely enough, there is a connection. That's what's pissing me off. Every time I find a strong lead, something crops up to contradict it. It's a bloody nightmare. Anyway, just make sure they do a thorough job on this. Any clues as to the owner?"

"No license, no paperwork, nothing. The name's been sanded off the hull and even the craft number has been obliterated from the coaming around the hatch. It's been almost wiped clean, I'd say. However, it might be possible to reveal the craft number if it was originally etched into the woodwork. That would give us a trace through the Port of London Authority."

"How come it wasn't found last night?"

"It was secured to that metal ladder over there," replied Anderson, pointing further up the quayside towards the end where they had left the car.

The detectives turned and looked at a galvanised ladder bolted to the river wall, which rose steeply from the water towards the railings which ran along Queens Walk.

"I assume it wasn't spotted in the confusion as it would have been well obscured by the Belfast," added Anderson, "and of course it was dark."

Turner edged away wondering how he and his colleagues had missed it. He said nothing to the inspector.

"Bloody river police," muttered Massey. "Catch you later, then."

He caught up with Turner and they drove Giulio back to St. Katherine's dock where they took a written detailed statement from him about the theft of his cruiser and asked him to call them if he received any contact from his friend, Scott.

They cancelled the visit to St. John's Wood, preferring to return to Blackfriars to update and re-assess the situation. The inspector had one wall of his office covered with two wipe boards and a cork board. All three were littered with a disjointed collection of lists, names, fuzzy video stills and maps of various parts of London joined together by lines and arrows.

"Let's start from scratch again," he suggested, starting to clear some of the items from the wall. "We've spent almost one week chasing shadows up our own backsides and still nothing to show. What the fuck are we investigating?"

The Courier
James R. Vance

He was erasing the lines and the writing from the wipe-boards with increasing vigour as he spoke. Turner bent to pick up some of the photos which were flying off the boards as Massey's frustration scattered everything in its path.

"How about kidnap, extortion and theft for starters and then there's possibly money laundering, drugs, smuggling, racketeering and leading D.I. Massey on a wild goose chase," said the detective sergeant.

"We're missing something," retorted the inspector, ignoring his colleague's witticism.

"Do you want me to list them again? Kidnapping, theft, er, should I go on?"

Massey turned and held his hand up towards his sergeant. "You know what I mean. There's got to be some link, something that connects all this and all these events together." He waved his hand expansively towards the half-empty boards.

Turner held up the blurred video still of the girl getting into the taxi. "I still reckon she's the key."

"You're probably right, but who the hell is she?" Massey now stood with his hands stuffed deep in his trouser pockets. He looked through the window into the murkiness of a London skyline about to be eclipsed by the impending darkness. Without turning, he said, "You know the old adage 'two heads are better than one', well in this case, even two are insufficient. It's time to involve the whole team. Bring them in first thing in the morning. I'm off home."

The inspector glanced at the remnants of the boards, which were strewn across his desk. "I'll leave you to decide what's useful in that lot. Bring along anything relevant and set up the meeting for nine in the incident room. See you."

Without another word, he left the office.

*****

Rebecca checked and activated the alarm system, locked the shop door and pulled down the reinforced metal shutters. She bent forwards to lock them in place and completed her routine by double checking the windows. Satisfied that everything was secure she decided to hail a black cab to speed her homeward journey.

Her concern for her uncle had stayed with her all day. Within a minute she was seated in the back of one of the familiar London hackney carriages heading for St. Johns Wood. Normally she would walk down to Chancery Lane and take a tube to Oxford Circus where she would pick up the Bakerloo line for Kilburn Park, but today she had a feeling and it was not good.

The taxi was part way up Grays Inn Road when her mobile rang. Dreading the worst, she looked at the illuminated screen. She was somewhat relieved to see that it was David.

"Hi, it's me, I thought...."

Rebecca cut him short. "Where the hell have you been?" She screamed, so loudly that the cab driver jumped in his seat despite the barrier of the closed glass window divider. "Your father's almost demented and I have to keep fielding his constant questions about you. What in hell's name are you up to?"

"Look, just keep him sweet for one more day. I've been chasing up the lost money."

"And have you recovered it?" demanded Rebecca, becoming more irritated with every lurch of the taxi as it twisted and turned through the back streets towards Euston Road.

"Er, well not exactly," offered David, "but don't worry, I'll have definite news tomorrow, so I'll call you then."

"Keep your mobile switched on, you bastard."

The line went dead. Rebecca called his number. No contact. David had switched off his mobile. Rebecca leaned forward and banged on the window.

"Do you always drive like a maniac?" she ranted at the driver. She was still fuming as the taxi cut through Regents Park and skirted Lord's cricket ground, the home of the M.C.C. It turned right into Grove End Road and snaked onto Abbey Road towards the turning for Greville Place.

As it sped past the parade of local shops with the driver seemingly intent on disgorging his passenger as quickly as possible, she tapped on the intervening window. "You can drop me at the bottom of the road, just before Maida Vale."

The driver eventually stopped as she had commanded and Rebecca stepped out of the taxi. She paid the cabbie and walked briskly back up Greville Place, partly annoyed with David, partly concerned about Isaac. Her uncle met her at the front door of the house, appearing extremely agitated.

"What on earth has happened?" she enquired, as she ushered him inside.

Isaac put his hands to his head. "I don't know what to do," he wailed.

"Well, you can start by pouring me a drink," continued his niece. "That taxi driver was a maniac and as for bloody David, he's just a shit."

"David!" exclaimed Isaac. "You've spoken to David?"

"Oh, yes, I've spoken to David, for about ten seconds. And no, before you ask, I don't know where he is or what he's up to."

*****

For a mid-week Wednesday evening, the Windsor Castle was extremely busy. Frank Cannon had to shoulder his way to the bar.

"Jesus, Caffy, is it free beer night?" he shouted to the landlady.

"Evenin', Frank. Be with you in a minute," she replied as she filled two pints simultaneously.

"Is the room available tonight? I've not booked it." He nodded towards the corridor.

"Just help yourself. The door's not locked," she replied.

Cannon nudged his way through the crowd, beckoning his son to follow. They entered the room and Frank glanced towards the serving hatch. "Ask 'er to serve up the usual when she's right," he instructed.

At that moment the door opened again, admitting Mickey and Vince with two youths.

The Courier
James R. Vance

"Bloody murder out there," cried Mickey. "What the fuck's goin' on?"

"Probably some posh git 'avin' a party," suggested Vince.

"No matter," retorted Frank. "Come in and shut that bloody door. Can't 'ear yourself fink wiv 'alf of Sloane Square out there. Loose's getting the usual for us. What'll the lads 'ave?"

The taller of the two boys sat down near Cannon. "I'll 'ave a pint of lager, Frank."

"You bloody won't," countered his father, Mickey, as he swiped him gently across his shaved head. "Get them both a coke apiece, Loose." He sat down opposite Frank. "No Danny tonight?"

"Nah, told 'im to take a night off. I fink 'e's gone down the Bridge to watch some European game."

"Yeah, they're playing that Italian team tonight...Milan," added the other youth, Vince's son.

"Which one?" asked Luke, carrying the drinks to the table.

"The one from Milan, you dipstick," replied Vince's son.

"There's two Milans, smartarse, Inter Milan and A.C. Milan," pointed out Luke sneering across the table.

"'Ow the fuck should I know. They're bofe Italian, so who cares?" he snapped back.

"Alright, alright," shouted Cannon. "We're not 'ere for a fuckin' geography lesson." The room went quiet.

"What's the meeting for, then, Frank?" asked Vince, trying to show some interest in front of his son.

"We need to find out what's goin' on. I suppose you all got the message that everyfin''s suspended at the moment." They all nodded in unison. "Well I can't 'ang about for bloody ever, so I fink we ought to do some diggin'."

"'Ave they buried them?" enquired Vince, totally serious.

"Buried them? Buried who? What yer fuckin' goin' on about?" demanded Frank.

"The diamonds," replied Vince.

"'Ow the fuck should I know!" ranted Cannon, losing his patience. "When I said diggin', I meant investigatin'. You know, doin` a bit of research of our own. Question is...where do we start?"

"It's got to be somebody in the syndicate," offered Mickey.

"My foughts entirely," agreed Frank. "If muggin`s `ere `ad lost the briefcase fru a genuine mistake, we'd `ave `ad a proper briefcase in our possession wiv, you know, proper briefcase fings inside it."

"Like a cheese and pickle sandwich," joked Vince.

Frank glowered at him and continued. "A case full of bog roll cut into diamond shapes was planted by somebody in the know."

"Too fuckin` true," added Mickey. "So what d'you suggest?"

"Well, I asked you to bring the lads, `cos somebody knows sumfin` and if they're back at the Manor next week, they've gotta get their bloody ears to the ground and pick up any loose talk amongst the other lads. I'm going to get onto The Fixer again and see if there's anyfin` going down `ere that we can get involved wiv."

The meeting began to degenerate into general banter among the men while the youths amused themselves flicking beer-mats off the table. The busy bar soon began to empty as the partygoers made their way to some poor soul's house to finish off their celebrations. Cannon and his associates stayed until the bottle of whisky was empty and, after several attempts to dial a correct number, ordered a taxi to take them home.

Chapter 9

THURSDAY: Guilio reached out and switched off his alarm, turned over and snuggled back underneath the warm duvet. He thought about a lie-in, but decided against another day away from work after spending a wasted day helping the police with their enquiries. He made for the bathroom, thanking the inventor of central heating, as the pale rays of an October sun struggled to announce the arrival of dawn.

Ten minutes later he was rushing partly dressed around the kitchen, toast in one hand, a steaming mug of coffee in the other. He wandered across to the picture window overlooking the marina and the toast stopped in mid-flight towards his open mouth.

Through the early morning haze and milky sunlight he thought he saw his cruiser. Placing the coffee on a nearby table, he edged closer to the misty window and peered again, intently focusing on his berth below. Cramming the half-eaten toast into his mouth, he turned and grabbed his sweater, slipped into some trainers and raced downstairs.

Looking absolutely magnificent the Seaway cruiser swayed gently with the slight swell from the river. He swore later that the craft was laughing, as though she had been on a furtive liaison and a successful one at that! He ran up and down the quay, hardly believing his eyes. He started laughing, spreading his arms in a wild gesture indicative of his Italian ancestry that could only mean welcome home darling!

Several early commuters stopped and turned to watch his strange behaviour. In better weather, maybe he would have attracted an audience by his antics. Most spectators shook their heads, smiled and continued their journeys to work. Giulio scrambled aboard, fumbling for his keys, but he had left them in the apartment.

Everything looked in perfect order. He wanted to hug her, having been convinced that he would never see the boat again. Delighted, he skipped along the quay to finish his breakfast and dress for work. Suddenly he thought of Detective Inspector Massey. He'll be pleased! Reaching for his mobile phone he dialled the inspector's number. No reply, only an answering service. He left a high-spirited message.

*****

Massey picked up Giulio's message as he walked from his car into Blackfriar's police station just after 8.30 in the morning.

"Bollocks," he said out loud, attracting the attention of the desk sergeant, who seemed glad that he was not working on his team today.

Turner had organised the incident room and some members of the team were already sat around, mostly drinking coffee and making small-talk. Massey relayed the latest news to his sergeant.

"Well, that's one problem solved," commented Turner

"Just the bloody opposite," retorted his boss. "Where's the bloody boat been? Who nicked the bastard and then took it back again? And why for God's sake?"

"Maybe he got pissed on his night out and just misplaced it."

"You can't misplace a bloody boat, can you? No, it's too much of a coincidence. The night of the drop, Scott's possible involvement and Docklands again. Either he knows something that we don't or someone's taking the piss again."

Massey walked across to the boards where Turner had pinned all the current information relative to the case. He waved his hand at the storyboard. "Not one iota of this crap makes any sense whatsoever."

The other officers in the room stopped their conversations and looked at Massey in bewilderment. "Bloody hell," whispered one of them, "and the briefing's not started yet."

The Courier
James R. Vance

Turner, concerned for his boss's agitated state of mind, stepped towards the inspector. "Let's get a coffee before we start. How about if I brief the team on the story so far and you chip in with the detail or anything relevant that I may have missed?"

Massey nodded in agreement, fearing the brick wall syndrome might kick in and ruin the briefing. The door swung open at that moment and a uniformed officer beckoned him towards her.

"Can you contact a Sergeant Dawkins urgently? I've written his number down." She handed Massey a yellow post-it note. "Oh, and someone else has phoned in about a missing boat and the description matches."

"Matches what?" asked Massey.

"The boat which the forensic team are fiddling with," she replied as she left the briefing room.

His face breaking into a smile, the inspector waved the piece of paper at Turner. "I don't bloody believe it! Dawkins has phoned and we've got a lead on our boat. Start the briefing and I'll see what he wants."

*****

The little yellow Renault, inscribed with the words La Poste in navy blue on its door, slithered to a halt in the pouring rain. The postman grabbed a bundle of mail and was about to run through the downpour to the metal letter-box embedded in the stone wall, when he spotted one of the large wrought iron gates starting to swing open. Monsieur Faudet appeared clutching an umbrella.

"Mauvais temps, n'est-ce pas?" he shouted as he approached the vehicle.

The postman wound down his window and handed the bundle of mail to Faudet's outstretched hand. "Faudet, ça va?" he shouted through the sheeting rain.

"Eh, bien. Comme ci, comme ça," he replied hurriedly.

The Courier
James R. Vance

They exchanged a few minor pleasantries before the postman drove off to his next port of call and M. Faudet returned to the shelter of Le Manoir at the end of the driveway.

Madame Blanchard, the cook, heard him as he entered the main hall. She shouted from the kitchen doorway. "There's some hot fish soup here. Come and get it now, it'll warm you up."

Faudet placed the letters on an oak settle by the front door of the large rectangular entrance hall and dutifully wandered down the corridor towards the kitchen. The whole building had a hollow ring to it, particularly in the areas where there was no carpeting over the tiled floors, but this was normal during the holiday period.

The cleaners and housekeeping staff were not due back until the following weekend to prepare for the arrival of the boarders. The cook and Faudet, the caretaker, were the only staff still on duty, apart from Marcel, the gardener who turned up each day unofficially.

He was only employed part-time and was not expected to work during holiday periods, but took great pride in the gardens and especially the vegetable plot and felt a need to be on hand to nurture them on a regular basis. He would arrive each morning in his forty year old Citroen Dyane, park it between the barn and the woodshed and head for the greenhouses. Here he would sit, fill his pipe with fresh Samson tobacco and puff away in deep contemplation for ten minutes or so, before starting his morning routines.

It was rumoured that he had once been the owner of Le Manoir several years previously and had stayed on as gardener for the new owners, but he never talked about it and it was the French custom not to pry into personal affairs.

Mme. Blanchard enjoyed inviting the caretaker into her kitchen as she always considered it to be her personal domain, thereby affording her complete control over all who entered, despite the fact that Faudet held seniority in the staff hierarchy. He pulled out a chair and sat at the scrubbed pine table in the centre of the large room, where the aroma of fish soup mingled with the smoky essence of smouldering oak and chestnut logs from the

Godin wood-burning stove. Faudet was grateful for the opportunity to sit and relax in the damp warmth of the kitchen. A draught caught his legs beneath the table as the rear door was thrust open.

Marcel shuffled in, shaking the excess rainwater from his battered felt hat.

"I can smell fish," he remarked, thrusting his nose towards the ceiling.

"Sit yourself down," snapped the cook, "and don't make a mess on my spotless floor with your muddy boots. I hope you wiped them clean."

The octogenarian nodded and, glancing down at his feet to double check the state of his dark green Hunters, he removed his wet oilskin and hung it on a peg behind the door. He wore a heavy knitted woollen cardigan over a old beige jumper which had seen better days. Beneath the sweater, a green check flannel shirt was buttoned to the neck. Rubbing his hands to warm them, he crossed to the table and took a seat opposite Faudet, helping himself to a chunk of brioche from the basket between them.

The caretaker and he were old friends of forty years despite the age gap between them. When Thiery Faudet was interviewed for the position of caretaker at Le Manoir, Marcel Dubois recommended him to the owners. He was aware of the younger man's expertise and had vouched for his integrity based on their long term association.

"This soup reminds me of Dunquerke," said Marcel, winking mischievously at Thiery.

"When were you last in Dunquerke?" snapped Mme. Blanchard defensively.

"June, nineteen forty," said Marcel, grinning. "We were retreating from the Boche!"

"So what's that got to do with my soup?"

"The closer that we came towards the docks, the stronger the stink of fish," said the gardener.

"But I thought that you were captured by the Germans?" added Thiery, tucking into the steaming potage.

The Courier
James R. Vance

"That's true," replied Marcel. "I was taken prisoner at Bergues and eventually thrown onto a transport to Germany. Fortunately, three of us managed to escape near Charleroi and made our way into Switzerland."

"I still don't know what all this has to do with my soup" demanded the cook, becoming irritated by the old man's war stories, which she had already endured on several previous occasions.

"It was the smell of fish," insisted Marcel. "It stuck in my nostrils right through the war!"

"But you told me that you ended up with the Maquis somewhere near Limoges. That's nowhere near the sea," retorted Mme. Blanchard, joining them at the table.

"How did you find your way there?" asked Thiery, happy to prolong the old man's reminiscences, though he too had absorbed various versions of Marcel's faded memories of his exploits.

"Well, after Pétain capitulated to the Nazis and moved the government to Vichy, I headed for unoccupied France as it was less populated by the Wehrmacht. I experienced two years with the Resistance, sabotaging their military movements and installations."

He chuckled. "They searched everywhere for us, but with limited success. They couldn't cope with the mountainous forest region. Did I tell you about the time when six of us hid in the tunnels under the ruins of the castle at La Perrière?"

"Yes, many times," groaned his companions in unison.

"Eat your soup before it gets cold," said the cook.

"Isn't that where you met some young girl?" asked Thiery.

Marcel broke off a chunk of bread from the crusty baguette which lay amongst a carpet of crumbs on the table.

"Actually, I met her in the Monts de Blond." He slurped a spoonful of soup. "She kept me warm for several days in those damn tunnels. Merde, it was cold down there!" The old man winked at the caretaker.

"We don't need to know about all that," said Mme. Blanchard, crossly.

Marcel took another mouthful of soup. He leaned across towards Thiery. "You know, I could still smell the stink of that fish even in those tunnels!"

"Don't be ridiculous!" rapped the cook.

"I swear," said Marcel. He pressed his nose towards the bowl of soup. "It was just like this...ah, the memories!" He leaned back, whilst breaking off another large piece of bread.

"You do talk some nonsense," said the cook. "How could you possibly smell fish in an underground tunnel?"

"It was the girl," replied Marcel. "She worked in a fishmonger's!"

The two men rocked with laughter, whereupon Mme. Blanchard grabbed her empty soup bowl and stormed across to the deep enamel sink. "You're both as daft as each other," she cried. "Besides, I thought that you had lots of work to finish."

Marcel ignored her and continued his tale. "She was a lovely girl, despite the fishy smell! I often wondered what became of her." He stared across the room as though he were lost in the mists of time.

"She was captured, wasn't she?" asked Thiery, interrupting his reverie.

"S.S. Das Reich division picked her up near Bellac and interrogated her at Limoges prison. We scattered when we heard the news...just in case." He shook his head, saddened by the image in his mind. "She must have kept stum, because they took her off to Paris, probably to be tortured."

"Doubtless sent east to a concentration camp, if she survived the Gestapo," added Thiery.

"Without doubt," sighed Marcel. "I had to move on. In the spring of forty four I ended up in Gibraltar."

"Why there?" asked Mme. Blanchard, re-joining them at the table. She placed an earthenware jug containing red wine and three glasses before them.

"It was the only chance to link up with the Allies to carry on the fight."

"That must have been some journey," said Thiery.

The Courier
James R. Vance

"Crossing the Basque region was not too difficult. Spain was the problem, you didn't know who to trust. There were fascists everywhere. Eventually, I made it and was taken to England where I joined de Gaulle's Free French Army. At the end of August, under General Leclerc, we fought our way through from the north to liberate Paris."

"You told me that you were injured near Argentan," said Thiery.

"That's true. I entered Paris via the Porte d'Orléans in a blood-wagon, but what a celebration in front of the Hotel de Ville!"

The cook raised her glass. "Vive la Liberté!"

"Et l'Egalité!" said the caretaker.

"La Fraternité!" added the gardner.

They finished the jug before returning to their respective duties.

*****

"Good morning, sergeant. I believe you've got some info," said Massey enthusiastically. His mood had suddenly stepped up a gear.

Dawkins seemed just as excited on the other end of the telephone line. "I think I've found your mystery school."

"Well done," exclaimed Massey. "Central London, I bet."

"A bit further out, I'm afraid. In fact a lot further out. Try across the channel."

"Which channel?"

"The bloody English Channel. France to be exact."

"France!" cried the inspector. "What's an English school doing in bloody France?"

"Apparently, according to my Revenue and Customs contacts, it's been up and running for several years. It's a sort of boarding school with some staying for a term and some commuting weekly. They reckon it's a bit nobby, you know, exclusive like. The lads, boys only you see, come and go on the cross-channel ferry quite regular like. Customs just wave them through."

The Courier
James R. Vance

"I bet they do," interjected Massey, "and I bet the youngsters take full advantage."

"The lads at Dover said they used to check them at first, but they don't bother now, 'cos it was just school stuff and dirty washing they were bringing back."

"Bet my pension there's more than soiled underpants being brought in now."

"Do you want them checked out?"

"Good God, no way," cried Massey. "Speak with your mate soon as poss. If there's stuff coming into the country that way, we need to set up tracking ops at both ends. Bloody hell, who'd have thought it….kids! Make sure the word goes out that none of them gets stopped. You could check out the school, though. You know, background, who owns it, is it French or English, who works there, et cetera. And I could do with a map of its location."

"I'll fax the details through to you. And customs will be sorted today," replied Dawkins. "Any luck with the girl yet?"

"Zilch. Mind you, we may have a lead on the boat used in the drop on Tuesday night. That's my next line of enquiry. Still no news on Scott, either. Any luck with the Ashford house?"

"No, it still appears to be vacant. The old chap next door keeps twittering on about people being in there but, from what I've seen, there's no evidence of that. Mind you, this morning our nosey neighbour phoned in 'cos he reckons he saw Scott leaving the house."

"But that's impossible."

"I thought the same. Perhaps it was a paper boy or some lad delivering leaflets, but he was adamant that it was Scott."

"Did he speak to him?"

"No. He said he called out to him, but the young man continued to walk away. He didn't actually see him leave the house, but said that he first spotted him walking down the path towards the front gate."

"And where was our busybody at the time?"

"Watching from an upstairs window apparently, which he opened in order to shout to him."

The Courier
James R. Vance

"What do you reckon?"

"Not totally convinced, but he seemed pretty damn sure. I think he's a bit away with the fairies, if you get my drift."

"Well, thanks again for all your work. The news about the school's the best break we've had since this thing kicked off. Keep in touch." Massey replaced the handset and returned to the incident room, where Turner was covering the missing boat situation with the rest of the team.

"Any news on the latest boat?" he asked the inspector.

"Need to go down to forensics and also chase up the potential owner. I'm keeping my fingers crossed it's not another Italian job."

The team smiled, having just listened to Turner's account of Fabrizzi's wandering cruiser.

Massey turned to the group. "Anyone here speak French?"

The members of his team looked at each other, wondering what that had to do with the inquiry. A solitary hand went up.

"I'm not fluent, but I can get by if the frogs speak slowly and one at a time."

"Well, that's a damned sight better than me," said the inspector. "Got an up to date passport?"

"Yes, sir," replied the young detective constable.

"What's your name?"

The D.C. hesitated slightly, looking around the room rather nervously. Some of his close associates chuckled.

"French, sir. John French," said the detective.

In an instant the whole team burst into laughter with lots of unsavoury repartee. Controlling his own mirth to a faint smile, Massey used his outspread hands to calm them down.

"Very appropriate," he commented. "You'd better get off and pack your toothbrush. You and I are off to the land of snails and frogs legs tonight. You'll need to be ready to leave here, say about four o'clock this afternoon. I'll fill you in en route, as they say."

The Courier
James R. Vance

The rest of the team jeered sarcastically. Turner looked quizzically at his boss, waiting for an explanation. What was the boss up to?

Massey recognised his concern. "Don't worry, I'll explain in detail later. I want you to concentrate on the missing pieces of the puzzle over here. We need someone to interview the new guy who's lost his boat, some guys to unearth that wretched girl, forensics to check out the Italian's boat and oh, yes, you'd better also contact Fabrizzi to tell him to keep off his boat 'till we've examined it. Plus, it might be a good idea if you could go and interview him again. Take Mullen with you. He'll be good for a soft-hard approach. See what you can get out of him. I'm sure he knows more than he's letting on."

Massey's whole demeanour was in overdrive, as a more lucid image was beginning to take shape in his mind. A new strategy based on new ideas was evolving as he spoke.

He continued. "Get someone to contact Sammy and ask for copies of those school-kids' pics and also the videotapes. He'll know what's needed. See if they can get any matches on the database. And most important of all try and locate Scott Morgan. The clock's ticking on that one. Get Dawkins to thoroughly check out his old house at Ashford. Tell him to break in if necessary, and I didn't say that, of course.

Also it might be a good idea for someone to touch base with Scott's mother, just to keep her sweet. Can you sort all that with them, while I arrange this impromptu trip abroad? Don't worry, we'll talk later and prioritise everything. Okay?"

Turner nodded, rather mystified. Massey was about to leave the briefing room, but hesitated and turned once more to face the assembled team.

"I've just had a thought. I could also make use of a female officer," he declared. Everyone turned to look at each other. Turner leaned across looking rather startled.

"Again, with some knowledge of the lingo. Maybe I should briefly explain. I've just received information that suggests there's a French connection related to this case. A rather devious approach using a husband and wife team as a front may be useful. Is there anyone who fancies some undercover work in France?" Massey smiled and spread his arms.

"Can I be your son, sir?" interjected a male voice from the back of the room. This was greeted by a round of applause, some jeers and lots of laughter. Two W.D.C.'s waved their hands in response to the inspector's request.

Massey addressed the younger of the two. "Well, thanks for your enthusiasm and commitment but, with respect Kelly, I think you would pass off better as my daughter."

Massey smiled and turned towards the other volunteer. "What about you, Amanda, do you reckon you could pull it off?" He suddenly realized his poor choice of words as the room once more exploded into jeers and laughter.

W.P.C. Croft blushed, "I prefer 'Mandy', sir and yes, we could play the roles, no problem."

"Well, that's settled then. Mandy it is. Hope your passport's in date. Can you be packed and ready to go from here at four?"

D.C. French stood up. "Where does that leave me, sir?"

"Just start calling Amanda mummy," yelled another voice from the group amid more jeers and cheers.

"Well, I still need an interpreter and another set of eyes and ears wouldn't go amiss. I'm sure we could invent a role for you. We'll make up a cover story for all of us during the journey. In the meantime, I've lots to organize rather quickly. I'm leaving D.S. Turner in charge as there's a shed-load of work for you all on this side of the channel and hopefully by the weekend we should have made some real headway. Thanks for your time."

Addressing Turner, he said, "When you've finished here pop into my office and bring Croft and French with you." He patted his sergeant on the shoulder as he left, signalling that at last the investigation was moving in the right direction.

Despite the amount of work involved, he was satisfied that the team was about to make a huge leap forwards. In his own mind the brick walls were about to come crashing down. Massey was quite buoyant for a change. The recent grey pallor had melted from his face to be replaced by a revitalised glow. A stranger may have attributed such a dramatic change to some cosmetic influence.

*****

Isaac Joseph heard the car crunching up his driveway. He tentatively moved from the kitchen at the rear of the house into the main hallway. The car drew to a halt and the engine stopped. He heard a loud click as the door was opened.

Stepping gently into his study he could see the outline of the vehicle through the partially open Sanderson blinds shading a side window. He breathed a heavy sigh of relief as he saw David heading for the main entrance. As his son entered the house carrying a black briefcase, he returned to the hallway.

"Oh, David, I'm so, so glad to see you," he cried. Glancing at the case, he added, "You have the money?"

David smiled and hugged his father. "Don't worry so much. Everything is going to be fine." He entered the lounge and sprawled in an armchair. "Where's Becky?"

"She's at the shop as usual. She's worried about you."

"I told her yesterday that it would be okay. She's too intense. She should chill a little."

"Chill a little, cool it, whatever young people say these days. It's just difficult to relax when you disappear into thin air."

"Barnes is hardly thin air. I had things to do and needed my space. Anyway it was only a few days."

"Why could you not phone? You have all these fancy mobiles with the latest technology. You could have even sent me a picture to let me know you were safe."

"And what do I send it to? You don't have a mobile which receives pictures."

"Well, one of those telex things."

"You mean a text message."

"Text, telex, whatever. You know what I mean."

"I phoned Becky. Didn't she say?"

The Courier
James R. Vance

"But that was only yesterday. You've been missing since the weekend and with my car!"

"I told you. I had things to do. Besides, I wanted to wait until I had some positive news. You can have your car back now. The repairs on mine are completed, so I'll be going home in my own car later. Oh, and by the way, if anyone asks, I've been here with you and Becky since I crashed the car last Thursday. Now calm down and let's have a glass of wine together."

"How can I calm down when I am accused of stealing our own money plus the delivery and maybe threatened with my life?" Isaac related the content and menacing tone of the phone call which he had received from The Fixer.

"It was our bloody money for goodness sake. Why should we hand it over without receiving anything in exchange?"

"He thinks we also have the other briefcase."

"And how does he work that one out?"

"I don't know, but he wants it all sorted out before tomorrow."

"He's bluffing," retorted David. "How do we know that the courier's not double crossed us?"

His father spread his hands dismissively. "He'll be calling tomorrow. Are you going to argue the toss?"

"Too bloody true. From what you have said about his phone call, he doesn't have a clue, so why should we shoulder the blame?"

Isaac sighed and shrugged his shoulders. He considered that his son was up to something, but what? He walked back towards the doorway, stopped and turned to face him. "I'll fetch you that wine. You'd better lock the briefcase in the safe."

As his father left the room David looked down at the case beneath his feet and smiled. If he only knew.

*****

D.S. Turner entered Massey's office followed by D.C. French and D.C. Croft. The inspector motioned them to close the door and take a seat around the desk. Massey related the details of the phone call which Dawkins had made and showed them a fax with a map of the school's location which had arrived in the meantime.

"Thankfully the trip's been sanctioned by the powers above. We leave Folkestone at 7.20 pm via Eurotunnel. Sarah's booked us rooms in the Holiday Inn at Coquelles which I believe is only a few minutes from the terminal on the other side. I thought it would be preferable to have a car as we need the flexibility to travel to Ardres about twenty kilometers from Calais and other possible locations.

It seems likely that this school could be the source for the stuff which these schoolkids are possibly bringing in. If we can contrive a situation where we can snoop around by gaining entry, the visit could be rewarding. You never know what one of us may spot and I thought that posing as a family looking to enrol our fictitious son in the school could give us a fairly convincing cover story."

"Fictitious son?" asked Croft, laughing. "You mean that we'll be posing as mum and dad?"

"I'm afraid so," replied Massey. "I can't think of a more logical reason to visit the school. We could play it by the book as police officers, but, if it is bogus, we lose our initiative."

"So what will be the details of our cover story, sir?"

"We'll discuss that en route. We all need to be on the same wavelength."

French leaned earnestly across the desk "Is it a legit school with a few dodgy lads or are we assuming that the whole outfit has been set up as a front?"

"At this point, I don't know. I've asked Dawkins to dig up some background details." He turned to his sergeant. "If any useful info arrives after I've left, you'd best email it. I'll take the laptop. There's a fax facility at the hotel, but it may be unwise to use it. You never know who may have access."

"Are you going to liaise with the French police?" queried Turner.

"Let's see what we uncover first," replied Massey. "If this proves to be the link we've been waiting for, I'm sure there's going to be increased activity, certainly covert initially, on both sides of the channel, probably involving customs and other agencies."

"If we're just operating undercover on this trip, what's the dress code, sir?" asked Croft.

"Well, certainly not like police officers. I suggest smart casual with, maybe something more formal for the school visit, you know something sensible. Think about the scenario."

"And what will be my role for the scenario?" asked French.

"We'll think of something on the way unless you have any ideas."

"Uncle or maybe Godfather to this fictitious son?" he suggested.

"I prefer uncle," replied Croft. "You don't look like a godfather. Now, Al Pacino, he was something else."

Croft smiled, French blushed and Turner sniggered. Massey continued.

"Okay. That's settled, then. Let's go for Uncle John. Can you both make it back for about four p.m.?"

The two D.C.'s nodded in agreement and Massey bade them farewell until later in the day. The inspector left early to go home to Streatham for a change of clothes and an overnight bag. The activity produced by the new developments had reduced his stress level. He was perceptively more relaxed. Though he was looking forward to some meaningful detective work across the channel, he was still a little concerned, however, at the lack of progress at home.

There were still lots of unanswered questions hindered by conflicting evidence. He hoped that, now the whole team was involved, there may be a breakthrough, however slight or insignificant it may be. From past experience he knew that one small piece of evidence invariably led to another and so on like a falling set of dominoes.

The Courier
James R. Vance

Having arrived at his flat, he showered, donned a pair of fairly new Calvin Klein jeans and chunky roll-neck sweater. He packed a small canvas bag with his toiletries and a change of clothes, which included a shirt and tie to wear with his leather jacket for the more formal visit to the school. Within the hour he was heading back towards Blackfriars.

Turner, in the meantime, had dispatched the other members of the team to cover the areas of investigation highlighted by Massey at the meeting. He was chatting to French and Croft when the inspector arrived.

"All packed and ready for the off, then?" asked Massey breezily.

Both detective constables nodded in the affirmative and Turner outlined the various processes which he had already set in motion. He had assigned two detectives to meet the guy whose boat had been stolen. That visit had been arranged for later when the owner would be home from work. He and Mullen had postponed the repeat visit to Fabrizzi until after Massey's departure and the rest of the team were already following up on the inspector's other suggestions.

"Well, everything seems to be in good hands," beamed Massey. "May I suggest that we all make a move before the rush hour delays us?"

He once more addressed Turner. "Sarah's got our itinerary and hotel details and remember, I'll have my laptop and mobile with me, so keep me posted, progress or no progress."

As fate would have it, more bricks were to tumble out of Massey's brick wall before he had even reached terra firma on the far side of the English Channel.

*****

Turner was pulling up outside the City Quay apartments at St. Katherine's Dock with D.S. Mullen when his mobile rang. Expecting it to be Massey, he glanced at his watch. Six thirty p.m. He would probably be at Folkestone by now, he thought. However,

116

the call came from P.C. Wilson, one of the uniform police who had been sent to see the man whose boat had been stolen.

"Any joy?" asked Turner.

"Well, I've shown him the photo and he seems certain that it's his cruiser," answered the constable.

"When can he get down to the City Pier to identify it?"

"I've arranged to meet him there at eight thirty tomorrow morning."

"Fine. If it's a positive I.D. escort him up to the nick and get a full statement from him. When did he notice it was missing?"

"He reckons this morning. Apparently, he's been staying at his father's house for the past week 'cos he crashed his car and only got it back from the garage today."

"Have you checked that out?"

"Yes, he showed me the repair bill for some replacement bodywork. It was dated from last week and receipted as paid with today's date. He said he called at the house to pick up some stuff, heard the boathouse door banging in the wind and walked down the garden to investigate. That's when he found the lock on the riverside doors smashed in and the boat missing. He reported it to the river police and they got in touch with us, knowing the situation, et cetera."

"Where's his house situated?"

"Alongside the river at Barnes."

"Sounds nice. Have you had a look at the damaged doors?"

"Yes, and I've arranged for forensics to come over and check out the scene of crime."

"I take it then that he doesn't know when it was stolen?"

"No. As I said, he's been away all week."

"So you said, at his father's. Where was that?"

"He didn't say and sorry, I didn't ask. When he showed me the repair bill, it all seemed to stack up."

"Okay, not to worry. It sounds pretty genuine. Mind you, it may be worth checking out the garage to confirm what he has said. Where was it, local?"

"Er, not sure. I don't think so. Hang on, I'll ask P.C. Lomas, 'cos he checked out the details."

The line went momentarily quiet, while the two uniformed police conferred.

"Looks like another dead end," commented Turner to his passenger, "unless forensics turn up something."

After a brief discussion with his partner, Wilson came back on the line. "The garage was Michael Bates & Sons, Alexandra Road, Swiss Cottage."

A long way from Barnes, reflected Turner, and in the area of St Johns Wood. He asked D.S. Mullen to get out the A to Z and locate it precisely. And there it was, just off Loudoun Road between Finchley Road and Abbey Road.

"Now is that a coincidence or not a coincidence?" asked Turner rhetorically. He spoke into the mobile once more. "What was the boat owner's name again, constable?"

"Joseph, David Joseph."

Turner went quiet for a few seconds. "I know that name," he said gently. "Where've I come across it before?" He tapped the dashboard with his spare hand. "Joseph, Joseph. Come on," he demanded of himself. "It's recent. It's come up before."

He sighed, shook his head and spoke to Wilson again. "Where are you now?"

"Still in Barnes."

"Get over to the garage and find out if he left his father's address with them while the car..."

"It's almost seven, sir," interrupted the constable. "It's more than likely to be closed by now."

"Point taken. Meet the guy at City Pier tomorrow as arranged and I'll check out the garage first thing in the morning. Delay him as long as possible. Take him back to Blackfriars to make a statement and keep him there until you hear from me."

"What if it's not his boat?"

"From what you've said, it seems highly likely to be his boat." Turner paused slightly. "Bloody hell, got it!" he exclaimed suddenly, deafening Wilson down the phone and making Mullen jump in his seat beside him. "The grumpy old man!"

*****

Massey and the two D.C.'s made good time to the Channel Tunnel terminal and consequently caught an earlier shuttle. They spent the thirty minute journey discussing a suitable game plan to gain entry to the school, thereby creating an opportunity for some clandestine snooping whilst they were inside the premises. D.C. French thought it may be a good idea to reconnoitre the whole area around the school first and perhaps make some general enquiries at the local Mairie prior to the actual visit.

D.C. Croft suggested a 'courtesy' visit to the Ardres gendarmerie, but Massey reminded them that he didn't want to arouse any specific attention towards the school too prematurely in case some loose talk gave prior warning of a potential investigation. If it was considered that some surveillance was required at that end, of course it would have to be co-ordinated with their French counterparts.

The train pulled out of the tunnel at Coquelles and Massey switched his mobile back on. It bleeped with a text message, informing him that he was now linked to the local S.F.R. network. As the elongated string of carriages smoothly swung left in a wide arc towards the French terminal, his mobile bleeped again. This time it was a text message from Turner asking him to call urgently.

The train was crawling to a halt and the information monitors were displaying the procedures for driving off the decks onto the adjacent platforms. He decided to make the call from the hotel as it was only a few minutes away and he did not expect too much of a delay passing through any customs control.

They all checked in at the hotel reception and arranged to reconvene half an hour later to find a nearby restaurant. Massey slung his hold-all and laptop onto the bed, checked out the en-suite facility, used the loo, had a quick freshen-up and sat near the window to phone D.S. Turner in response to the earlier text message. He got through immediately.

The Courier
James R. Vance

Excitedly, Turner related the discussion with the two D.C.'s about their investigation at Barnes, finishing with the same question which he himself had answered earlier.

"Remember the grumpy old man we met on the house to house visits?" he asked Massey. Without waiting for an answer, he continued.

"Well, since I sent the text message, I've asked Debbie to check the database and guess what, the old man, Isaac Joseph has a record. He was done about six years ago for receiving stolen goods and got six months suspended. He was a partner with his brother in a jewellery business in Wood Green. His brother was not involved but about a year ago the brother died.

The business is now located in Hatton Gardens, so, in no time at all, trade seems to have boomed and the son, David, who reported the stolen boat for reasons, I might add, which are totally beyond me, seems to be running the show. It's rather bizarre that a boat possibly involved with Scott and the ransom demand could be owned by the son of a guy, with form, in the jewellery business. In addition, he lives in the vicinity of the mysterious blonde. What do you reckon?"

"Interesting but nothing conclusive as yet," replied Massey, "so we need to keep our options open. Without any hard evidence we're not in a position to arrest anyone, nor have we any charge we can lay against them. I would keep it low key, stick some surveillance on the son's house at Barnes and the old man's place at St. Johns Wood.

If there is a connection, it'll be the girl. If she comes into the frame, we'll know that we're onto the right individuals. Let the son think that we're on his side, aiming to track down the thief who nicked his boat, if it is his boat. I tend to agree with you, why did he report it?"

"Maybe he thinks it will throw us off the scent but, having said that, there was nothing to suggest that he was a suspect in the first place, so why attract us? There's got to be a reason, but what?"

120

The Courier
James R. Vance

"Well, at this point, we don't know, but at least it's moving in the right direction. Bear in mind also, that if there's a connection over here, the last thing we want to do is set alarm bells ringing on either side of the channel. How does the saying go, 'softly, softly, catchee monkey'?

Let's see what evidence we can dig up in the meantime. Also there's the pressing concern about Scott's whereabouts and of course his safety. Unless something over here contradicts our assumptions, I still believe the girl's the key. Call me if there's any further development. If not, I'll be in touch when I get back. By the way, how did you get on with Mister Fabrizzi?"

"No joy there I'm afraid. We tried a little bullying but we both reckon he's on the level."

Massey ended the call and looked through the window towards the familiar clock tower rising above the skyline of Calais. In his mind he visualized the innumerable tumbling brick walls of the port during W.W.II as the allies forced the Nazis back towards Germany. How quickly would his walls come tumbling down and for how long would they stay down?

The symbolism reminded him of those bizarre toy figures on a spring base, when the base was pressed inwards, the figure collapsed and immediately shot upright again when the pressure was released, crumbling only to rise up again with similar alacrity.

He felt a slight pain in his chest and, putting it down to indigestion, turned his thoughts to food. He welcomed the luxury of an evening meal in the convivial atmosphere of a restaurant. It felt a long way from Streatham.

*****

A fine drizzle descended forcing the young detective constable to intermittently flick on the wipers to clear the screen. Despite the air conditioning a mist was also forming on the inside of the window making visibility difficult.

"How much longer, sarge?" enquired the junior officer.

"All night if we have to," snapped Turner, already resigned to an uncomfortable stakeout. There were still lights shining in the downstairs window of Isaac Joseph's house. Two of the team had already been diverted to Barnes to carry out surveillance on David Joseph's riverside residence. Turner had elected himself to take first watch in St. Johns Wood, principally to convince himself of the existence of the girl at this address.

Having seen no-one enter or leave during the past two hours, he was now wishing that he had delegated the surveillance to other team members. He glanced down at his watch. Almost eight thirty, three and a half hours until the relief arrived.

"Is there anything to eat, sarge? I'm starving," uttered his colleague, aware that the detective sergeant knew full well that he had been summoned at short notice with no time to organize any refreshments.

"There are several takeaways on Kilburn High Road if you fancy a stroll. Get me a coffee and a kebab," replied Turner, virtually ordering his companion to make the trip.

"Got any dosh?" asked the young detective. "I'm skint. Didn't know we were eatin` out."

Turner smiled, thinking that they learn quickly these days. He dug a ten pound note from his pocket. "Here, and don't forget the change."

The D.C. made a dash towards Kilburn Priory, pulling up his coat collar as he made off into the lamp-lit dankness of an autumn night. Across the road an upstairs light flicked on. Turner strained his eyes to catch sight of anyone passing a window. Another light appeared in what seemed to be a bedroom. Seconds later a light went out in a room downstairs.

It took a few moments for the detective to realize the significance of what he had just witnessed. He sat bolt upright in the passenger seat and involuntarily wiped the haze from the windscreen, as if in disbelief. His suspicions had finally been confirmed. Reaching into his jacket pocket he withdrew his mobile and made a call to Massey.

*****

The Courier
James R. Vance

The receptionist had recommended either a trip into the town centre of Calais where there was a choice of restaurants, a drive across the motorway into the Cité Europe where bars and restaurants were 'en masse' in one specific area or a stroll down the road to a Buffalo Grill. Despite the various options, all three elected to take a taxi to the gourmet paradise across the A16 principally on the premise that there was a preponderance of bars including a typical London pub and an Irish bar.

A taxi eventually arrived about fifteen minutes later than ordered and by nine o'clock local time they were passing through the revolving doors between MacDonald's and The John Bull Pub into the vibrant eating-out area of the Cité Europe.

Though the main shopping mall was now closed, shoppers, cinema goers, visitors and tourists of different nationalities thronged the open concourse of the mall. The three detectives were immediately drawn towards the British pub which advertised many well known beers from across the channel. It was decided to have a quick one in there, a meal at the pizza restaurant opposite and finish the night off in the Irish bar around the corner. They sat at a table on a raised area where a waiter came over to take their order.

Massey felt relaxed for the first time in weeks. He was aware that the strain and stresses of the job were always a threat to his general health but recently the pressures had been building and he welcomed this opportunity to wind down. Their drinks arrived and he proposed a toast to a successful outcome from their visit to France.

D.C. Croft joked that D.C. French was superfluous to requirements as everyone appeared to speak English. In fact, as they looked about them, they could have been on the far side of the channel surrounded as they were by adverts, signs and products in their native language.

"What's the game plan tomorrow, sir?" she asked.

"I think it may be a good idea to get rid of the 'sir' bit first, as we're not here in our official capacity," suggested Massey.

"So what do we call you?"

"Probably best if we can keep to first names for the duration of the trip."

"And what might that be, sir?"

"You can call me Ray," whispered Massey as though apologizing for the name.

"Ray? Ah, Raymond. As in Raymond Massey?" asked Croft.

The inspector nodded in agreement.

"Who?" interjected French.

"Raymond Massey, the film star," retorted Croft.

The inspector realized that an explanation was due. "My mother was apparently a fan of Doctor Kildare and naturally with the surname 'Massey' she christened me Raymond Gillespie Massey after the actor and the character in the series and unfortunately I've had to live with it ever since." He took a mouthful of beer as if to wash away his words. "Anyway how does someone of your age recollect Raymond Massey? He was a star of the thirties, forties and fifties."

"I watched East of Eden when I was younger, a second generation James Dean fan and Raymond Massey played his father in the film. I've always been a film buff."

The conversation drifted towards favourite films, who starred in what film, personal video and DVD collections and the time quickly passed in a relaxed and convivial atmosphere. The ambience was interrupted by the ringing of Massey's mobile. It was Turner from his car in Greville Road.

END OF PART ONE

Part Two   Revelations (Rewind)

(*THE REALITY of WEEK ONE*)

Perhaps the most renowned example of the development of a kidnapper – victim relationship, often referred to as Stockholm Syndrome, occurred in February 1974. College student, Patty Hearst, daughter of publishing tycoon, William Randolph Hearst, was kidnapped by a neo-revolutionary group in California.

Despite the demands of the group, the Symbionese Liberation Army (S.L.A.), being met, she was held prisoner, and eventually joined the radicals, assisting them in the robbery of a San Francisco bank. A photograph was published showing her holding a machine gun and she became a target for the F.B.I. Her explanation for her actions rested on her claim that she had been brainwashed into becoming a revolutionary and consequently was not responsible for supporting the cause of the S.L.A.

The victim needs desperately to be able to communicate at an early stage. Following the initial shock and trauma, fear sets in and each re-assurance is welcomed. Any hope of a positive outcome, however remote, is grasped and clung to as a life-line. Silence and the fear of the unknown breed inner sensations of absolute terror.

Both kidnapper and victim are players in the game, each attempting to manipulate the other's emotions to gain a perceived advantage. At an intellectual level this can create a bond whether it be in the form of admiration or abhorrence, trust or suspicion, dependant upon the tactics employed.

An understanding of each other's behavioural signals can lead not only to positive vibes between the two parties but a possible successful outcome. To the rescuers or negotiators, on the other hand, this merely presents a confusing representation of the situation and can be counter-productive towards the release of the victim. A wrong move can result in the destruction of the rapport with both kidnapper and victim reverting to their original roles.

Chapter 10

SATURDAY : Scott stood by the window and watched until the inspector drove away. He turned to his mother. "I think I'll go back up and take a shower. I feel rather unclean."

"What a nice man," she said clearing away the coffee cups. "I'm sure he'll find your briefcase. If I'm not here when you come down, dear, I'll have gone off to have my hair done. There's plenty to nibble in the `fridge if you get a little peckish whilst I'm out."

With that, she drifted into the kitchen and, after stacking the crockery in the dishwasher, began tidying the work surfaces. Scott scampered upstairs and sat on the end of his bed with mixed emotions. He was relieved to have had the opportunity to explain the actual course of events, but felt rather guilty towards the stranger who had approached him with the proposal, guilty that he had aborted the conspiracy in the first place and guilty that he had 'spilled the beans' to the police.

He wondered what might have been if he had gone through with it. Now he wondered what might ensue because of his spur of the moment actions. He selected a compact disk, inserted it into his music system, turned up the volume and headed for the shower to wash away all his negative thoughts.

*****

Having returned from Ashford, the black B.M.W. 6 series coupé crossed Blackfriars Bridge and continued along New Bridge Street, eventually pulling up outside a jewellers shop in Hatton Garden. The passenger door opened and Rebecca stepped out.

"Are you going back to yours or your fathers'?" she asked her cousin.

The Courier
James R. Vance

"Not made up my mind yet," replied David, "catch you later."

She slammed shut the door and entered the shop, still partly cross with him and his mood swings, still trying to figure his intentions following their sortie to Ashford. The car sped away and turned into Clerkenwell Road.

*****

Scott stepped from the shower somewhat refreshed, towelled himself dry and returned to his room to find some clean clothes. Dressed in a Tommy Hilfiger sweater, Levi's and Reebok trainers, he skipped downstairs and headed for the kitchen where he made himself a tuna sandwich. Apart from the music which was still pumping out from his bedroom, the house was quiet, indicating that his mother had already left for her trip to Canary Wharf.

Rather than stay at home lazing in front of the television, he decided to catch a bus to St. Katherine's Dock, meet up with his new friend Giulio and maybe later take the tube to Oxford Circus to do some shopping. At that point he was unaware of the black coupé with the smoked windows parked opposite.

Scott walked the short distance to the junction with Westferry Road and within a few minutes the bus arrived which would take him via Shadwell to Tower Gateway. As he walked down St. Katherine's Way towards the marina, he was still unaware of the vehicle which had tracked the bus and had now parked just below Tower Bridge. He wandered into the complex and found his friend cleaning the decking on the Guiseppe.

"It's going to rain," he shouted. "I reckon you're wasting your time."

Giulio looked up and waved Scott towards him. "Hi, thought you might call round. How about a trip up river later?"

"Maybe tomorrow. The weather's not very promising and I fancy a wander down Oxford Street. What about you?"

The Courier
James R. Vance

"Oh, no thanks. I'll finish off the cleaning before the rain kicks in. See what it's like in the morning. If it's a fine day we could motor up to Limehouse and try the Regents Canal."

"Sounds fine by me," said Scott and bidding his friend farewell, set off towards Tower Hill tube station.

The junction of East Smithfield and Tower Bridge approach road was extremely busy causing Scott to wait for several minutes before he could attempt to cross. Suddenly he heard a familiar voice accompanied by a tug on his arm.

"Remember me, sunshine?"

Scott spun around to face the stranger from Waterloo station and shuddered momentarily. *How did he find me here?*

"We need to talk," said the man, pulling Scott towards him.

"I haven't got it," protested Scott. "Honest I haven't got it. The police have it. Believe me, it's the truth."

He was ushered back along St. Katherine's Way as far as the black coupé, into which he was roughly bundled via the passenger side door. The stranger opened the driver's door, sat down, locked the car centrally and turned to face Scott.

"Now tell me what happened," he snarled.

Scott began to realize that this was no trivial escapade into which he had stumbled, but something more sinister and threatening. He wanted to throw up.

"I'm waiting," said the man.

The youngster related the events which had taken place at the station and described the visit of the detective inspector. The man listened intently without saying a word. He drummed his fingers against the hub of the steering wheel for several minutes while Scott became increasingly uncomfortable. He began to tremble, almost in unison with the man's staccato finger-play.

The silence was finally broken. "The woman who left your house earlier, your mother?" asked the man.

"Yes," replied Scott nervously. *My God, he knows where I live.*

"Where's she gone?"

128

The Courier
James R. Vance

"She's at the hairdressers, probably in Canary Wharf. That's where she normally goes."

"How long is she usually away?"

"Depends if she goes shopping….most times all day."

The man nodded as if pleased with what he had heard. "Who's the guy with the Searay?"

Scott was surprised that the man knew his boats. "A friend of mine, Giulio. He lives in one of the apartments," volunteered the youngster.

"Fasten your seat-belt, you are going to make amends."

Without further words, he started the engine, swung the vehicle around and headed back up to the lights at East Smithfield. Shortly they were sweeping into the Limehouse Link tunnel and turning onto Westferry Road. They passed Canary Wharf complex with Scott desperately craning his neck in the hope of seeing his mother. Suddenly they were outside Scott's house.

"I trust you have a key," said the man.

Scott nodded and reached into the pocket of his jeans.

"Get out."

The youngster was guided towards the front door which he opened and the man entered, relieving Scott of his small bunch of keys.

"Your bedroom," ordered the man.

Scott climbed the stairs, desperate to know what was going through the man's head. By the time he had stepped into the bedroom he was physically shaking. He backed away from him towards the window. The man cast his eyes around the room.

"Switch on your computer," he commanded.

With some relief, Scott flicked on the p.c.

"Now gather together some outdoor clothes and a toothbrush. Stuff them into a bag or something. We're going away for a few days."

Mystified, the youngster grabbed a holdall from the top of his wardrobe and, though shaking like a leaf, began to pack into it what he thought appropriate, considering the state of the weather. The man was typing something on the p.c.

The Courier
James R. Vance

"Is the printer connected?" he asked.

Scott nodded, wondering what he was up to. A sheet of A4 was disgorged from the printer and floated onto the floor. The man picked it up.

"Sellotape?" he asked.

"Try the drawer underneath," suggested Scott.

The man rummaged around a drawer full of oddments and withdrew a small roll of sticky tape. "Let's go," he snapped.

Scott grabbed his bag, still unzipped, and was forced downstairs. The man opened the living room door, looked around, walked to the television and taped the paper to the screen.

"Right, in the car," he said, pushing Scott towards the front door.

The man closed the door behind him, took stock of the street which was deserted, unlocked the car with his remote and told Scott to place his bag on the back seat. He opened the boot.

"Get in."

Scott looked at the man and started to shake again.

"I said, get in," he snapped again.

"But…but…"

The man pushed the youngster with such force that he tumbled into the well of the boot, bruising his forehead on the rim as he fell forward. The man grabbed the youth's legs, tucked them in with the rest of his bent torso and slammed down the boot lid.

Scott heard the engine start up and for the best part of an hour he was bounced around in the darkness as the car sped on its way. The vehicle eventually stopped and, apart from the drone of the six cylinder engine and the deep purr from the twin exhausts, an eerie silence pervaded the immediate exterior of his cramped space. Somewhere close by he heard a gentle whirring noise, followed by a dull thud.

The car moved slowly forwards, stopped and the engine died. The whirring sounded again, this time almost as an echo, followed once more by the thud. He felt the car tremble as a door opened and the driver stepped out. The boot was opened and he shaded his eyes partly from the glare of bright fluorescent lights

130

which shone above him and partly through terror of what might befall him.

"Get out."

The man stood over him whilst Scott eased his bruised and aching body from the confined recess of the car's boot. Unsteadily he stood up and realized that he was in a garage. The man opened a small door to his left and pushed him into a carpeted hallway. The man brushed past him and opened another door, revealing stone steps leading downwards. He switched on a light.

"Down there." The man pointed down the steps and Scott duly followed in the direction of the man's hand.

"Stay there."

The man closed the door, locking it with a key. Scott took stock of his surroundings. He was in a large tidy cellar, divided into two rooms. In the far right-hand corner there was an enamel sink with hot and cold taps, below which there was a large reel of hose and nearby some garden tools.

A large wooden door almost filled one wall, which, Scott presumed, led to the exterior, maybe to a garden. He tried the door but it was firmly locked. There were no windows. On another wall there were several shelves filled with an assortment of paint tins, plant pots and some packets of seeds. Against the rear wall stood an Atco cylinder motor mower and a Black and Decker strimmer.

Scott sat down on a long wooden bench next to the garden equipment and tried to figure what was in store for him. He was tentatively confident that he meant him no harm. What had he said at St. Katherine's? 'You are going to make amends'.

The sound of the door opening at the top of the stairs interrupted his thoughts. The man tossed down a pillow, a rolled-up sleeping bag, a nylon draw-string camping type of bag and the holdall of clothes from the car.

"Make yourself up a bed." He disappeared, locking the door behind him.

The draw-string bag contained a metal frame camp bed which Scott eventually assembled, placing the pillow and sleeping bag on it away from the cold concrete floor. A faint click and a whoosh from the smaller room adjacent to the steps attracted his attention. It contained the central heating boiler and the welcome feeling of warmth. Scott dragged the camp bed into the recess, reasoning that if he was here for some time, at least he would not freeze to death, though the fumes were of some concern.

Chapter 11

SATURDAY EVENING: Scott was experiencing a range of emotions. Initially he had been terrified, mostly by the thoughts of what might have been in store for him. Now his more recent feelings of anger at being in this situation had given way to the natural survival instinct of most human beings. He was contemplating possible ways of escaping from his predicament.

The door was locked, both at the top of the stairs and to the outside. There were no windows. His sole hope was to overpower the man, but that was a risk which had no guaranteed outcome. He decided to bide his time and look for opportunities. He desperately needed to discover the man's intentions. Again he returned to his remark about 'making amends'. What did the man mean by it?

As if to substantiate his suppositions, the door at the top of the stone stairs opened, revealing the man silhouetted against the harsh light of the carpeted hallway. He descended the steps carrying a tray.

"I've brought you a pizza and a flask of coffee," he announced and placed it on the wooden bench. He turned and went back upstairs, stopping momentarily. "If you need a toilet, bang on the door. You can use the cloakroom in the hallway." He disappeared locking the door behind him.

He needs me, thought Scott. Why else would he feed me? He munched a slice of pizza. It was hot and tasted good, as he had not eaten since the tuna sandwich earlier in the day. It suddenly dawned on him that he had been kidnapped. *Maybe I'm up for ransom, but that's pointless 'cos we're hardly rich.*

He poured some coffee. It was rather strong and too sweet. *It's the money in the briefcase, which he's after. Yes, that's it. He's holding me hostage for it. That's what he meant by ' making amends'. But what if they refuse to hand it over? Then what happens to me?*

Once more he became fearful for his own safety and his thoughts again turned to the chances of escaping. He drank some more coffee despite its unpleasant flavour, thinking it would keep him awake. He justified eating the remainder of the pizza if only it served to keep his strength up. He sat upright on the camp bed and contemplated his options, which, at that moment appeared extremely limited.

An hour must have passed when the door opened again. The man came part way down the steps. "It's time we talked," he announced. "You'd best come upstairs."

"Can I use the loo?" asked Scott.

"First on the left at the top," replied his captor.

Scott left the cold drab cellar and welcomed the warmth of a centrally heated house. The man indicated the cloakroom and waited close-by in the hallway. Scott reappeared and the man ushered him into a large tastefully furnished living room. He invited the youngster to sit at one end of an L-shaped sofa. The man sat on the longer end almost facing him.

The far end of the room was draped with gold and black heavy curtains which probably concealed either large windows or patio doors. An unlit glass chandelier hung from the centre of the ceiling, but the main lighting was provided by two bulbous, ornate table lamps with gold shades. Their black bases were decorated with gold Chinese lettering. The floor was highly polished parquet overlaid with several strategically placed Oriental rugs. Occasional tables and exotic ornaments gave the room an air of wealth and luxury.

Either he travels frequently to the far east or spends his free time shopping in Camden market, thought Scott.

The man interrupted his musings. "I've given the situation some thought and devised a game plan to recover what you stupidly lost, namely the briefcase. To recover it you will assist me and by so doing you will be also implicated if anything goes wrong. If you refuse, create problems, attempt to leave or contact anyone, your life and your mother's life will be in danger. Do you understand what I am saying?"

Scott nodded, fearing the worst.

"If it succeeds, you go free. You will be left in a position to volunteer whatever information you like, because my identity and whereabouts will be kept secret from you at all times. Do not ask questions. You will be told only what you need to know to help me rescue my investment."

The man rose from the sofa and stood by a Baroque style fireplace in Italian marble. "The boat, the one belonging to your friend. Is it in working order?"

"Yes. We've done some repairs and maintenance on it, but we've had it out on the river several times and last weekend I took it as far as Westminster."

"He allows you to take the controls?"

"He was working, so I took my mother out in it."

"You have access to it?"

"Oh, yes, sometimes I do work on it when he's not around."

"He gives you the keys?"

"No, I have my own set. Well I did until you nicked them from me at home."

The man turned away smiling. "Tomorrow, I have some purchases to make. You'll have to remain downstairs alone for some time. Now you must go to bed. If you need a pee in the night, use the sink. I'll wake you early with some food and a Sunday newspaper to keep you occupied. If you play ball with me, you'll be fine. Any nonsense and you know the consequences. Got it?"

Scott nodded, resigning himself to going along with him for the moment. The man escorted him to the door at the top of the cellar steps, watched him descend into his makeshift prison and once again locked the door.

Chapter 12

SUNDAY & MONDAY: During the next two days a tentative relationship developed between Scott and his captor. Though tense at times, it functioned based on the principle that they both needed each other, at least for the time being. There was an underlying comprehension of their shared commitment towards a successful outcome, the reward of which was freedom from the current situation. A mutual respect replaced the mistrust and wariness of the previous day.

A routine evolved with regard to the youngster's nourishment and personal needs. The man provided three light meals each day together with a flask of coffee (much improved) and a bottle of mineral water. He allowed Scott to watch some television with him in the darkened confines of the living room where the drapes remained closed and brought him a morning newspaper. Neither of them could understand why there were no snippets about the abduction, even in local news.

Domestic boundaries, however, were strictly imposed with specific areas in the house to which Scott was allowed access under supervision, the cellar, part of the hallway, the cloakroom and the living room during the evening. None of these areas provided any aspect to the exterior of the house.

Existing in this closed environment had heightened his sense of hearing to the degree that he knew that they were not too distant from a river, be it the Thames or otherwise. Several times he had heard the sounds of vessels using a nearby waterway whilst he lay quietly in the cellar and consequently he imagined that behind the large wooden door the garden probably led towards the banks of a river or canal.

The Courier
James R. Vance

He had also reflected on his hour long journey in the car boot, mostly a stop-start affair in traffic with few long stretches at speed. This disposed him to believe that, if the waterway in question was the River Thames they were either outside of the Greater London area in Kent or Essex, or alternatively somewhere west of London within the M25.

He was also aware of the noise of busy traffic, which seemed to emanate from the other side of the house, suggesting that a main road was fairly close. He suddenly wished that he had paid more attention to geography lessons, especially in relation to the topography of the south east of England.

The man occasionally disappeared, always locking him in the cellar and inevitably checking him out on his return. On Monday evening, after one such excursion from the house, he returned, spent some time outside in the garden area and eventually opened the top door to the cellar and asked Scott to join him in the living room. They sat in their usual places, but this time the man had drawn a low coffee table towards them on which were several sheets of paper containing drawings with notations added at various points.

The man spent the next hour or so explaining his plan of action and detailing Scott's involvement. Initially the youngster found it difficult to believe that the man was serious, especially when he produced a large blow-up doll for Scott to inflate and eventually dress with some of his own clothing from the cellar, but as each stage of the scheme unfolded he became more and more fascinated.

He found himself volunteering suggestions towards improvements and the fact that he was allowed to contribute gave him ownership of the proposals. It now materialized into the greatest adventure of his life. At that point in time neither of them knew the awesome consequences which would eventually transpire.

The Courier
James R. Vance

Chapter 13

TUESDAY: The man brought breakfast down to Scott in the cellar as usual but remained particularly quiet in contrast to the previous evening. Maybe nerves, thought Scott. A short time later he heard the man in the garden area again as though he was sawing timber. This continued on and off for a short period. Several hours of silence followed. It was mid-afternoon before the man returned, whereupon he brought Scott up from the cellar.

"Wear something warm. It's time," said the man. "I'm sorry, but to protect both of us and, particularly my anonimity, you will have to be blindfolded until we reach our target. I'll allow you to lie down on the rear seat instead of having to curl up in the boot, but stay low or the deal's off, if you get my drift."

He waited for his captive in the hallway. Scott put on a heavy sweater and donned his Helly Hansen anorak. The man blindfolded him, led him once more to the car, covered him with a tartan travelling rug and started the engine.

Scott heard the whirring noise and resultant thud again before the car sped off on its consequential journey. He was aware of the eventual destination from the briefing the previous evening, but, for the man's anonymity to continue, the location of his residence had to remain secret. The man had assured him that he would be able to recount his experience to the police and maybe later to the media, provided that he would have no knowledge of his whereabouts in a city of over seven million inhabitants.

As usual the traffic was heavy on the South Circular Road and as Battersea Park Road was no better, the man decided to cross the Thames at Chelsea Bridge, following the river to Westminster. He continued along Victoria Embankment to Upper and Lower Thames Street and finally turned into the public car park off East

Smithfield to access the marina at St. Katherine's Dock, whereupon he told Scott to remove his blindfold.

The plan to steal Giulio's cruiser had not initially made sense to Scott as the man had told him that he had already stolen another boat in which to carry out the drop. It appeared that the more complex the plan, the more difficult it would be to fathom. That seemed to be the logic.

They walked through the Boat Owners Only gate down to Giulio's berth where the Searay was moored and for the first time Scott saw the stolen cruiser alongside, looking very similar in appearance.

"Here, you'll need these," said the man as they approached the two cruisers. He tossed the set of keys which he had taken from the young man at his house the previous Saturday. Scott looked around nervously. Though he had taken Giulio's boat out several times previously, he felt guilty this time, aware that it was to be involved in an illicit act and that the man had failed to clarify if it was to be returned. The stolen cruiser had something bulky under a waterproof cover below the hood of the cockpit.

"I gather that's the inflatable dinghy," commented Scott, pointing at the bulky mass.

"And your doppelganger," replied the man. He glanced at his watch and looked upwards into the descending gloom. It was beginning to rain. "Perfect," he whispered.

They embarked onto their respective craft, which they both checked prior to starting the engines.

"What's your fuel situation?" shouted the man.

"Looks fine," replied Scott.

"Okay, follow me as far as Blackfriars, then continue to Embankment Pier as arranged. There's a floating restaurant just beyond Cleopatra's Needle. Tuck in behind it or next to the nearby pontoon. Keep your eyes open for me on the steps below the obelisk. I should be with you within the hour.

If I've not turned up by eight o'clock, something will have gone tits up, so take the boat back to its berth and go home. Remember, if you're stopped, you are Giulio and don't be

139

panicked by flashing blue lights, wailing sirens or river police. At least you'll know the party's in full swing!"

"What if I'm told to move on from the pier?"

"Do just that, but keep returning when it's safe to do so and always stay within view of the steps. Hopefully by the time I get there all the action will be concentrated downriver. Just act normally and you'll be fine. Don't forget, you are totally innocent and tomorrow you can tell the world about your adventure and have your fifteen minutes of fame. Can we go now?"

Scott nodded, still concerned about the complexity of the man's scheme, the two stolen boats, especially the other one and whether he would survive the ordeal intact. The two cruisers powered up, slipped their moorings and headed for the lock gates which would release them onto the River Thames.

Keeping to the right of the river they passed under the first span of Tower Bridge, observing the orange lights which glowed on the central arch. Both sides of the river danced with twinkling lights and the hustle of the oncoming rush hour. They passed by the floodlit ramparts of the Tower of London and headed upriver towards London Bridge.

H.M.S. Belfast loomed up on their port side as though it was waiting in the wings to receive its cue for action as the drama unfolded. Traffic on the river was somewhat quiet along this stretch possibly on account of the weather, but after passing under the central arch of London Bridge several trip boats were still plying their trade from the various piers upstream towards Westminster.

The two cruisers slowed after passing through the second arch of Blackfriars Bridge and pulled over towards the embankment between H.M.S. President and H.Q.S. Wellington. It was almost high tide which enabled them to keep close to the shadows of both the stone walls and the large vessels moored there. The man drew gently alongside the Giuseppe and checked his watch. He leaned across towards Scott.

"If it goes pear-shaped, I want you to know that I've had to treat you this way to protect you. Whatever happens tonight, you should remain blameless. I'll back you up, if we're both nicked. Don't forget, any funny business and there will be reprisals."

He turned up the throttle and sped across the river towards Stamford Wharf. It was dwarfed by the imposing edifice of the Oxo Tower which stood silhouetted against the faint glow of the almost defunct daylight. Pulling in towards the far bank, the man stopped the cruiser and launched the dinghy over the stern.

He checked the holding rope was secure and erected the effigy of Scott firmly in place between the plank seats of the R.I.B. Once again he looked at his watch and satisfied himself that it was now time to make his move. Stealthily he steered the cruiser with the dinghy in tow towards the right-hand pillar of the central arch of Blackfriars Bridge.

Fortunately, on account of the poor weather conditions, there were few people along Queens Walk to witness his manoeuvres. The commuters crossing the bridge itself were more concerned with conditions at street level than any episode taking place on the river. He held the boats in check amid the shadows of the bridge, consulted his watch, took out his mobile phone and called D.I. Massey's number.

Moments later the black bin liner thudded into the cockpit. With one movement the man slit open the plastic and shone a slim pencil torch inside. Wads of fifty pound notes still in their bank sleeves were illuminated by the beam. The man reached over the stern and, using the same sharp knife, cut loose the inflatable from the cruiser.

As it drifted away he reached out to the throttle and with a roar the boat reared up, disappearing further into the shadows below the bridge. Keeping tight to the south bank it passed the Tate Modern aiming for the central span of Southwark Bridge. Decreasing speed below the Millennium Bridge on his approach to Cannon Street Rail Bridge, the man headed for the two orange signal lights and held centre channel despite high water affording passage closer to the starboard bank. Running aground on one of the numerous shale banks would have courted disaster.

The Courier
James R. Vance

Poor visibility and reduced traffic on this narrow section of the waterway favoured an uneventful escape if he kept calm and did nothing to attract attention. His main concern was the possibility of a police launch in the immediate vicinity, but that was the only calculated risk which he had allowed for. Safely under London Bridge, he carefully steered the boat past the City Pier into the dark shadows behind H.M.S. Belfast and cut the engine. The cruiser swayed gently against its designated mooring, the galvanized metal ladder.

Stuffing the bin liner into a rucksack, the man ascended the ladder, vaulted over the railings at the top and casually walked past the Horniman at Hays into the Galleria. Passing Café Rouge, he stepped out alongside other commuters onto Tooley Street as three individuals rushed past him in the direction of the river.

Within minutes he was in London Bridge underground boarding a tube train to Waterloo where he would take the Bakerloo line to Embankment. It was raining heavily and Victoria Embankment was busy with traffic in both directions as the man with the rucksack emerged from the underground station exactly twenty six minutes after the bin liner had thudded down from Blackfriars Bridge.

He crossed to the river side of the road at a pedestrian crossing and walked down towards Cleopatra's Needle which rose up between the two black sphinxes on sentry duty. The Giuseppe was below the monument, gently bobbing in the water in tandem with the adjacent pontoon from the swell of a passing barge.

Scott spotted him as he approached the iron barrier at the top of the steps. He steered gently towards his accomplice and stood up in the cockpit, unzipping the protective hood which had been protecting him from the steady downpour.

"Everything okay with you?" enquired the man as he jumped aboard.

"Fine," replied Scott. "It's been really quiet, probably due to the rotten weather, apart from a police launch which has just shot past."

The Courier
James R. Vance

The man grinned. "They were a bit slow off the mark.
Right then, mission almost accomplished." The man removed the
rucksack and tossed it below. "I'm sorry, but you realize you'll
have to be blindfolded again 'til we reach base camp once more."

Scott nodded, resigned to the routine of the man's cloak
and dagger scenario. He made himself comfortable resting against
the rucksack in the gloom and diesel fumed well of the cockpit. He
listened as the man prepared the craft for the last stage of their
escapade. Suddenly he felt it lurch away from the pier and spin in a
circle several times before launching itself forwards.

Whilst passing time at Embankment Pier, the young man
had been analyzing the man's strategy and concluded that,
following their rendezvous, he would be heading upstream away
from the hub of activity which he had created east of Blackfriars. If
he had wanted to escape further eastwards, surely he would have
stationed Scott well beyond Tower Bridge, perhaps even as far as
the Isle of Dogs.

Despite the man's attempts to disguise the direction in
which the cruiser was now heading, Scott had convinced himself
that they were now cruising westwards. He sensed a sudden
change in the resonance of the engine and a slight change in the
density of the darkness. He assumed that they were passing
beneath Hungerford Bridge, the Charing Cross Rail Bridge.

Detecting this strange effect on his perceptions, he realized
that by concentrating and fine-tuning his senses to his situation,
hopefully he would be able to count the bridges to their
destination. Game on, he thought!

After Westminster Bridge he was unable to remember all
the names of individual bridges, but established that they had
probably passed beneath twelve more arches before the boat
eventually slowed down and turned to port. The man cut the engine
and Scott became aware of a musty dankness and calm.

The man helped him up and guided him onto some wooden
planking, which the young man assumed to be some kind of jetty
which the boat was now alongside. He ushered him through a
doorway and immediately Scott felt the rain on his face. He must

have moored the boat under cover, perhaps in a boathouse. The ground was now soft beneath his feet until he was asked to climb some steps which seemed to lead onto a smooth, hard surface. They stopped momentarily and he became aware of the jangle of keys. A door creaked open and closed behind them, again the keys came into play as it was securely locked.

"Welcome home," announced the man and removed Scott's blindfold. The youngster screwed up his eyes and blinked several times as he adjusted to the change in light. He was back in the cellar.

"You'd better dry off," said the man as he ascended the staircase. "I'll bring you something hot to drink and some food shortly." He disappeared into the hallway, locking the door behind him.

Scott heard the man outside beyond the large wooden door until it became quiet again apart from the sounds from the river and the noise of traffic passing the front of the house. He tried to picture the meandering course of the River Thames and remember the names of the thirteen bridges under which they had sailed since leaving Embankment Pier. Erroneously he concluded that they were possibly on the southern bank somewhere near Richmond, but that depended on how many bridges he had failed to recollect.

A short time later the man reappeared with a flask of coffee and a plateful of chicken sandwiches. He muttered a fairly discernible goodnight and left the cellar, again locking the door.

"And thank you for all your help," shouted Scott sarcastically as the door slammed shut. He reached for his snack and decided to get a good night's sleep since his release had been promised for the following day. However, he was suddenly startled by a loud crashing sound from above followed by a string of obscenities. A door banged followed by a deathly silence. He eventually fell asleep, still attempting to remember names of bridges and wondering what had upset the man upstairs.

Chapter 14

WEDNESDAY: Scott awoke to the sound of the door opening at the top of the cellar steps and, dragging himself into a sitting position on the camp bed, rubbed his eyes and looked upwards. The man seemed edgy and curtly told him to take a shower while he prepared some breakfast. With that he disappeared leaving the door open.

Scott slipped from his warm sleeping bag, grabbed a towel and his toiletries and headed upstairs. The man watched him from the kitchen. "You'd better come through here when you're dressed," he said.

A bowl of cereal, some hot coffee, fruit juice and toast were waiting for the young man when he finally entered the kitchen feeling clean and refreshed after the previous day's escapade. A window blind obscured the view outside and he was invited to sit at a round pine table set in an open brickwork alcove.

"You'll have to amuse yourself for the rest of the day. I've things to do," announced his captor. "I'll leave you some food and drink, but you'll be in the cellar again. Today's newspapers have arrived so you can wade through those. You'll be interested to know that we've got a mention. Apparently the police haven't made any statement to the media, so the general concensus is that we were terrorists escaping by the river! One tabloid even suggests a foiled plot to blow up the Houses of Parliament or MI6 headquarters near Vauxhall Bridge! Never mind, you can put them right tomorrow."

"Tomorrow?" queried Scott. "I thought you said you were letting me go today."

"Something cropped up last night," replied the man. "I'll fill you in later."

145

The Courier
James R. Vance

Following breakfast, Scott took himself off to the cellar with his newspapers and sustenance for the rest of the day. The door was locked leaving him with his thoughts and the various occasional sounds of the outside world which filtered into his subterranean room from the opposite sides of the house.

The man's strange behaviour last night and the change of plan announced this morning aroused suspicions which began to sound alarm bells. What had happened? What was the man up to today? Why was he being held prisoner for another twenty four hours? He decided to await his return and demand some answers. In the meantime there were the newspapers to catch up on.

It was late afternoon before Scott heard any movement in the house above. He anticipated some contact from the man but nothing was forthcoming. Instead silence reigned once again. He became aware of someone on the hard surface beyond the large wooden door and then the noise abated just as quickly.

He moved towards the door and pressed his ear against the damp timber panels. Suddenly he heard the distant roar of an engine. The man was in the boat. The sound of its motor seemed to increase in volume and gradually diminished giving the impression that it had sped away on the river. Scott concluded that he was returning the Giuseppe to its berth at St Katherine's Dock.

He returned to his half-completed crossword to await the man's return. Sprawled on the camp bed he dozed off and was eventually awakened by the noise of the door opening at the top of the stairs. The man stood there silhouetted against the light from the hallway.

"You'd better come up and eat, we have a journey to make later," he announced. The man had prepared a meal which they ate once again in the kitchen.

"After you've eaten, I'd like you to go back to the cellar, gather together your belongings and get some sleep."

"Am I finally going home?" enquired Scott, somewhat relieved by the man's announcement. "I thought you said it would be tomorrow."

"You ask too many questions," replied the man curtly.

The Courier
James R. Vance

"But you said…."

"I know what I said," he interrupted. "This is just the first stage of your…how shall I put it….your repatriation. It will be tomorrow, but we will be leaving before daybreak. I want you to be ready to go when I give the word."

"Why so early?"

"Timing, young man. You'll have noticed how smoothly it went yesterday. All down to timing. That was the secret of our success."

Scott took another mouthful of his meal and considered the possibility that the man had probably been in the armed services. He reflected that the events on the river had been planned like a military operation. He was strangely proud that he had been included in what had been referred to as a successful outcome. Justifiably, he had used the word 'our'. No longer was he a victim, but a partner. In some ways he was regretting that the adventure was drawing to a close.

"Will I really have to wear the blindfold again?" he asked, hoping that the man would restore to him normal status, especially as he was now his partner in crime.

"Only for a short while," replied the man. "Don't worry, it's nearly all over."

Sadly for both individuals, it was just beginning.

Chapter 15

THURSDAY: Scott only dozed intermittently since having been sent back down to the cellar, partly due to the knowledge that he would be wakened at some unearthly hour and also in anticipation of what outcome may be forthcoming. Finally he reached the point where he could stay awake no longer due to the weight of physical and mental exhaustion which had borne down on him. He sank into a deep sleep.

Within an instant, or so it seemed, he was aroused by a noise at the top of the stairs. The lights flickered on in the cellar, causing him to screw up his eyes as they adjusted to the sudden change. He glanced at the dial on his watch. Four thirty.

"Time to go," called out the man in a loud whisper, as though apologizing for the early interruption to the young man's slumber. "Get dressed, bring your holdall and meet me up here, and make it snappy. Remember what I said about timing. Oh, you'd also better bring the sleeping bag and pillow." The man disappeared from view.

Scott was too tired to consider the reason for the sleeping bag and five minutes later he was standing in the hallway, still sleepy but excited that the moment of release had arrived. He felt like one of the hostages which he had often seen on television expressing their relief and gratitude towards those who had negotiated on their behalf. The man approached with the blindfold.

"Sorry about that, but this time it's only temporary," he explained. He led him into what Scott had believed to be the garage and seated him in the passenger seat of the car, tossing his baggage into the boot. The car engine roared into life, yet to Scott it sounded different than on previous occasions. Despite the noise from the exhaust, he could still discern the usual whirring sound.

The Courier
James R. Vance

He had concluded that it was attributable to electrically operated garage doors.

There was little traffic at that time in the morning as they skirted Richmond Park to join the A3 dual carriageway passing between the park and Wimbledon Common. Thirty five minutes later the man turned and spoke for the first time since leaving the confines of the garage.

"Ok, you can slip off the blindfold now."

Scott removed the cloth cover from his face and stared out into a blackness only illuminated by the lights of other vehicles. After travelling some time in silence, he was about to ask where they were, when a road sign flashed by indicating that the next junction was the M23 to Gatwick. They were on the southern stretch of the M25.

Where is he taking me? thought Scott. He was still reticent to ask questions. They continued, each with their own thoughts, until the M25 veered away as the car sped onto the M26.

"Remember your Ashford house?" asked the man not waiting for a reply. "That will be your pick-up point," he added. "I'm leaving you there and will make arrangements for you to be collected by the police later in the day. I need a time gap to distance myself, so I'm afraid you'll have to hang about for a while. I've brought you some food and I'll get you a morning paper to read to keep you going."

"Why Ashford?" enquired Scott. "Why not Docklands?"

"Police presence there. This is a better option. It was this or dump you in a remote field somewhere and that's not my style, whatever you think of me."

"Thanks for the consideration," remarked Scott, beginning to wonder if the man was genuinely thoughtful or just plain stupid. *All this to merely hand me over?*

The miles slipped by until they turned off the motorway and stopped at a service station to pick up some newspapers. Scott thought about doing a runner but, being so close to freedom, it hardly seemed worth the risk and any possible adverse consequences. Soon they had turned into the road where Scott had lived with his father until his untimely death. At the top of the road the man drove the car into a small parking area adjacent to a parade of shops.

"We'll walk to the house," said the man. "Too much noise this early in the morning might wake up the curtain twitchers and alert the insomniacs."

The man opened the boot and passed the holdall and sleeping bag to Scott. He reached over and pulled out a plastic carrier. "Sustenance, whilst you await International Rescue," he whispered, pointing at the bag and smiling. The glow from a nearby streetlamp reflected from a black object which had now become exposed following the removal of the baggage. Scott's eyes were drawn towards a handle on the object, beneath which were some initials in gold letters.

The man followed his gaze and reached forward once more, lifting the black briefcase from the well of the car boot. "You can also take this. I've no further use for it," he remarked and, placing it at Scott's feet, quietly closed the boot lid and locked the vehicle.

Laden with their various bags, they walked down the road to the house and Scott followed the man to the rear kitchen door which he opened with a key.

"Luckily, I found it on your key ring," he explained, "or it could have meant breaking a window." He switched on a flashlight which he had intentionally left on the kitchen table and ushered Scott towards the staircase at the end of the hall.

"Up you go," he urged, pushing the young man towards the stairs. They reached the landing and the man switched on a small table lamp which was plugged into a socket close to the floor. Scott looked about him as he placed his luggage down and saw what appeared to be a well prepared confinement area, complete with handcuffs attached to a chain which was, in turn, fastened to the main balustrade at the junction of the staircase and the landing. House of horrors! thought Scott.

The doors leading off from the landing were closed (and probably locked as there were no keys showing) except for the bathroom door which remained open.

"It's just extra insurance for me until you are picked up," explained the man, somewhat apologetically. "The chain allows you access to the bathroom, but short of the window in there. The table lamp is your only light source, as I've removed the bulbs from the overhead lights. We don't want an empty house lit up like Blackpool illuminations, do we? You can bunk down on the floor in the sleeping bag if you need to and there's enough food and drink to keep you going. Are you right or left handed?"

"Right," volunteered Scott, still taken aback at the fact that the man had been here before to make these preparations. He convinced himself once again that he must have had some previous services experience as everything seemed planned like a military operation. Either that or he was an 'attention to detail fanatic'.

The man cuffed his left hand to the chain contraption. "Tell your rescuers that the key's downstairs on the kitchen table and I'll also leave your bunch there. The kitchen door will be left unlocked. I hope you don't get burgled!" he quipped. "Well, best be off, it'll be daylight soon. It's been nice knowing you."

"What was it all about?" asked Scott.

"A scam which went half right, but it's not over yet. I can't tell you any more than that. Thanks for your help. You did yourself proud." The man turned and disappeared downstairs.

Scott heard the kitchen door close gently and then silence. He imagined he heard someone call his name. I must be dreaming, he thought. The man also heard the voice as he walked away from the house. He carried on walking.

END OF PART TWO

Part Three   Dust to Dust

(*THE FALL-OUT*)

In one split second, every image, every thought, every memory, every sensation was erased, replaced by the blinding white flash heralding the cloak of terminal darkness. The accompanying noise was equal to the sound of Krakatoa splitting itself into that force of mass destruction which annihilated vast populations of Java and Sumatra.

Now there was only debris and dust, the floating evidence of man's devastating power, the suicide bomber's legacy of indiscriminate death.

Yet this was not Baghdad, nor Kabul nor even Tel Aviv. This was Leicester, the heart of England, where Moslems, Sikhs, Jews and Christians lived in harmony, where multi-racial cultures integrated into a viable society. What harbinger of evil had slipped un-noticed into this citadel of tolerance?

Chapter 16

FRIDAY MORNING: The heavy morning mist hung like a shroud over the river as Turner walked across to London Bridge City Pier. He reflected that, if the downstairs and upstairs lights had been switched off by two different people at the house in St. John's Wood, he was almost one hundred per cent certain that he had found the elusive young blonde. The old man's comment that he lived alone no longer stacked up.

Massey had suggested that he should leave the detective constable or his relief to continue the surveillance at Greville Road and, if a girl was to emerge the following morning, that he should follow her. Turner's time would be better employed checking out the main suspect with the boat.

P.C. Wilson was waiting for him on the pier. "Bloody freezing`, sir," commented the young constable.

"Any sign of him, yet?" asked Turner, too preoccupied to worry about the constable's state of health.

"No, sir." He glanced at his watch. "It's not quite eight thirty."

"What did you reckon to this guy when you met him last night?"

"He seemed okay, quite helpful really. He volunteered most of the information and had no qualms about showing the damage to his boathouse. Wicked pad he's got there. He must be earnin` a bob or two."

"Apparently forensics said there was a key left in the ignition when it was abandoned here. How do you explain that, if he maintains that it was stolen?"

"According to our man, there was a spare key hung inside the boathouse door, now no longer there."

"Seems far too convenient and coincidental to me," commented Turner, still not convinced. Feeling the chill of the damp morning air he pulled the collar of his coat up around his neck as a figure loomed out of the mist on the quayside above them.

"Good morning, constable. Can I join you?" It was David Joseph.

"Yes, by all means. Watch the gangway. It's rather slippery."

David gingerly made his way across and was introduced to D.S. Turner who was momentarily surprised by the stranger's smart appearance, contrasting vividly with the hooded figure in the video of the station concourse, if they were both one and the same. He motioned towards the cruiser swaying gently below them, which had been moored to some steps leading down from the pier.

"Can you identify it or would you like to take a closer look?"

153

The Courier
James R. Vance

David peered over the railing and cast his gaze over the object of their attention. "Fairly certain, same model, but can I go down?"

"Certainly. We need an absolutely positive I.D." replied Turner.

All three descended the steps and stood in the well of the boat. David looked inside the cockpit, returned, lifted a hinged seat top and inspected the contents stowed inside. He repeated the action with other seat tops before turning to the two police officers.

"Definitely my boat, the lockers are as they were, but it's been tampered with in several places. The craft number's been erased inside and …." He leaned over the side, "…the name and number have been obliterated."

"You reckon they used a spare key for the ignition?" challenged Turner.

"I keep one permanently on my key ring," replied David, "but have always kept a spare in the boathouse. It's there, you know, in case I need to start her up when I'm working on her."

"And that's the key which went missing?"

David glanced inside the cockpit. "Absolutely," he replied, "but it's been nicked. It's not in the ignition now."

"It was in the ignition, then?" probed Turner.

"Last time I saw the key it was hanging in the boathouse."

"When was that?"

"Probably sometime last week. I've been away on account of a car accident. I've already explained that to the officer here," snapped David, obviously rattled by Turner's manner.

"The key's with forensics. We just need to establish when the boat was stolen."

"Could have been anytime since Thursday of last week," added David.

"We'll need a full statement from you. Can you follow me to Blackfriars, so we can release the boat to you and return the spare key?"

"No problem," said David. "Can my cruiser stay here until I can get back to retrieve it? It may be later on today."

"Fine," answered Turner. "If you follow us, we'll get things moving."

The two men climbed back up to the pier and across the gangway to Queens Walk, leaving the young uniformed constable on guard duty at the entrance to the pier.

*****

Breakfast over, Massey set off with his colleagues along the N43 towards Ardres. The roads were damp from the early morning mist, but, unlike England, the skies were clear and the low autumn sun made driving difficult. They had been given directions to the school which entailed taking the D248 at le Pont d'Ardres towards Balinghem.

The school was situated down a single-track lane through a wooded area towards a lake. Initially they missed the turning but reversed back to see the sign which had been almost obliterated by the fronds of several large Leylandii firs.The track twisted and turned through the woodland, beyond which the surface of the lake glistened in the milky sunlight.

Rounding a tight bend in the narrow lane, they were confronted by two large stone pillars connected by slightly rusted double wrought iron gates. Set back at an angle from the lane, the whole structure interrupted a stone boundary wall which rose up about three metres in height as it snaked away below the canopy of chestnut and birch trees.

The car came to a halt on a gravel area in front of the gates. The words LE MANOIR were sculpted into each of the two stone pillars, though barely visible due to the effects of weathering. A wooden plaque, badly in need of a re-paint, was fixed to the angled wall. It displayed the name of the school (Blériot College) and beneath, in small lettering, advised the visitor to use the intercom for attention. D.C. French stepped out of the car and looked around the entrance for the device.

"It's here," he announced eventually, referring to the elusive intercom. He pointed towards the side of one of the pillars. "What should I say?" he asked the inspector.

The Courier
James R. Vance

"Ask if it's possible to enrol a student, as we've made a trip from England especially for that purpose," replied Massey. "Can you say all that in French?"

"Near as damn it, I expect," said French, adding hopefully, "anyway, they could be English." He walked towards the intercom and pressed the button. Nothing. He pressed it once more.

It crackled into life. "Bonjour," snapped the voice of Mme. Blanchard.

D.C. French attempted to explain the reason for their visit.

"Vous avez un rendezvous?" asked the cook.

"Non,.mais...." stammered French but he was abruptly interrupted.

"Attendez, s'il vous plaît," ordered Mme. Blanchard and the intercom went silent.

The young detective turned to the occupants of the car and shrugged his shoulders. "She's disappeared," he explained.

"Maybe she didn't understand you," suggested Massey. "Give it a couple of minutes and then try again."

French peered through the metal gates. His gaze followed a well-worn driveway which vanished round a bend behind the trees and dense shrubbery. He was able to discern the faint semblance of a large structure in the distance, but the foliage and reflections from the sun's rays made it difficult to distinguish any detail. His observations were interrupted by the voice of Mme. Blanchard.

"Entrez," commanded the voice.

French appeared perplexed until the gates started to swing open rather noisily and ponderously slowly. "Looks like we're in," he cried, returning to his seat in the car.

Massey started the engine and they followed the driveway through the trees until they reached an impressive building which sprawled before them. It stood grey and sombre but in places was brightly clad with reddened Boston ivy. Most of the windows were covered over by shutters desperate for a paint job.

The car halted in a courtyard surrounded on three sides by the stone frontage of Le Manoir. There was an eerie silence as the three occupants gazed up at the shuttered windows. It appeared cold, uninviting and deserted apart from the earlier disembodied voice of Mme. Blanchard.

Massey stepped from the vehicle. "I suppose we ought to knock," he suggested, nodding towards a rather imposing oak door atop a short flight of stone steps.

His companions joined him and all three suddenly became aware of a rhythmic creaking noise from beyond one corner of the building. They turned towards the sound to see a wooden wheelbarrow filled with logs appear round the corner followed by the less creaky frame of Marcel Dubois.

He stopped and greeted them. "Bonjour, Messieurs, Madame," he shouted, politely doffing his cap. Glancing at the car, he asked, "You are English?"

"Yes," replied Massey, relieved that someone here spoke his language, even though he only seemed to be the gardener. "You speak English, then?"

"I owe my life to you English. I feel it impolite that I not talk your language. It has its uses, sometimes." He pushed the squeaking barrow towards the main entrance. "You have the appointment?"

"I spoke to a lady on the intercom," interjected D.C. French, wondering why the old man was indebted to his countrymen.

"Ah, Mme. Blanchard. I go find her." Marcel parked his barrow and slowly mounted the steps as the heavy wooden door slowly opened to reveal Thierry Faudet.

"Tu as des clients," whispered Marcel, "les Anglais."

*****

D.S. Mullen had taken over from the night shift at St. Johns Wood and, with the car engine running to provide some heat against the early morning chill, he amused himself watching commuters setting off for work, inwardly guessing their occupations. Bored with this after about ten minutes, he picked up his copy of the Sun newspaper and turned to the Two-Speed Crossword, electing to use the Coffee Time clues first.

The Courier
James R. Vance

He completed several boxes and came to nine across: 'Paring Instrument'. What the hell's a paring instrument? he wondered. He glanced across at the Cryptic Clue: 'nineteenth century policeman will do spud bashing'. Feeling that he should know this one, he stayed with it, muttering copper, bobby, rozzer, plod.

Determined not to be defeated he lowered the newspaper and stared through the partly misted windscreen, tapping his ballpoint on the dashboard in the hope of inviting a modicum of inspiration.

A vague blurred sequence began to unfold before his eyes. Preoccupied by his endeavours to find a solution to nine across, he almost disregarded the distant wispy figure of a young blonde through the hazy condensation which had clouded the glass screen. Suddenly he became aware of reality once again.

"Bollocks," he mouthed, wiping away the globules of water from the window and casting the newspaper to one side..

The young lady stepped from the gateway of the Joseph residence and walked off at a brisk pace towards Maida Vale.

"Gotcha," cried D.S. Mullen and gently slipped the car into gear.

*****

"I don't care what you do with the car, just keep on her tail," replied Turner in response to Mullen's phone-call. "Look, I'm still at London Bridge Pier. Just keep me posted of any changes and I'll try to arrange some back-up for you. Where are you now?"

"Still following the number sixteen bus down Maida Vale," answered Mullen.

"Well if she makes any sudden changes and you have to dump the car, don't worry, I'll square it with the mayor if you get a parking ticket."

"You're so kind," said the detective sergeant and rang off.

He continued to follow the bus, staying in the bus lane. After passing close to the location of the Windsor Castle, the haunt of Frank Cannon and his associates, the young lady eventually alighted just short of the Westway.

Mullen turned the car into Bell Street, leaped out and, centrally locking it, raced back to see her disappear into the throng of other commuters heading for Edgeware Road tube station. Her journey took her via the Bakerloo line to Baker Street where she crossed to the Metropolitan line, finally leaving the underground at Faringdon station.

She walked a short way along Greville Street and, after turning into Hatton Garden, stopped at her uncle's jewellery shop where she began to unlock the metal shutters. Mullen stayed with her throughout and sent Turner a text message: *shes gon 2 work wat now?*

*****

Faudet invited the three police officers into the main entrance hall. "Bonjour. You 'ave a student, n'est-ce pas? "

"Oui," replied D.C. French.

"Ah, vous parlez français?"

"Un peu," volunteered the young detective.

"Très bien. Et vous cherchez des affaires avec l'école?"

"Er....pardon?" pleaded John French.

"You prefer I speak English?"

"It might speed things up a bit," added Massey, impatient with the useless banter.

"Suivez...follow," said Faudet walking across the hallway. "We go to le cabinet." He indicated a small office across the hallway.

Massey placed his arm on D.C. Croft's shoulder and turned to D.C. French. "As our man here speaks pretty good English, why don't you go and have a look at the school and see if it's to our liking. Maybe the old man over there could give you a guided tour. Ask him. Try out your best French accent." Winking knowingly, he nodded towards Marcel who was still loitering near the main doorway.

"Oh, yes, good idea," replied French, now grasping the underlying intent and glad to be relinquishing the responsibility of group translator. He approached Marcel. "Monsieur, any chance of a guided tour of the school?"

Dubois smiled and ushered him towards the open door. "Pas de problème. Come, young man. You must see le potager, my vegetable garden. It is the most, you say... abondant ...in the whole of the Pas de Calais. But you know at this time of year it is not at the best and so you must comprehend how it is in the spring and in the summer."

Massey and Croft sat in an office adjacent to the entrance hall assuming that Faudet was either the principal of the college or the administrator of the school's affairs. It threw them a little when he explained that he was merely the caretaker and that there were no persons in official capacity until the term re-commenced on the following Monday. Nevertheless Massey was determined to learn what he could from the visit.

He pushed Faudet enough to convince him that they were serious about enrolling their 'son' and, not wishing to have made the trip in vain, would appreciate an inspection of the facilities which would be on offer. Faudet's only concern appeared to be how they had learned of the schools existence.

This struck Massey as strange as it inferred that it was not in the public domain. D.C. Croft alleviated the situation by saying that it had been recommended to her by a social acquaintance whose nephew currently attended the college. This seemed to satisfy Faudet as he subsequently offered to show them round.

*****

Turner picked up Mullen's text message on the way back to Blackfriars. He called him. "Where are you now?"

"I'm enjoying a coffee across the street from Joseph's jewellers shop in Hatton Garden. It looks like she's there for the duration."

"Stay put. I'll divert someone to relieve you. Where's your car?"

The Courier
James R. Vance

"Still at Edgeware Road, I hope."

"You reckon she's running the shop?"

"Well, she's opened up and seems to be the only one there."

"Okay, forget the girl. We now know for certain that she exists. Get back to Edgeware, pick up the car and come over to Blackfriars. Stay in the car and call me when you're outside the nick. I'll be taking a statement from David Joseph and when I've finished I'll bring him down to the front entrance, shake his hand and thank him for his co-operation. Clock him and tail him. I'm hoping that he may lead us to Scott Morgan. Keep me posted on his whereabouts. I need to take a look in the boathouse at Barnes."

"What about the girl? What if she makes a move?"

"I'm playing a hunch. We've been staking everything on her but perhaps we're barking up the wrong tree. She appears to be acting normally, going about her business as usual, so maybe she's just an innocent pawn in the game. It's the bastard with the boat who's bugging me now. I'll still send someone down to eyeball the shop and also put surveillance back at St. John's Wood to keep an eye on the old man."

"You reckon that's where Scott is?"

"I'd put my money on the boat owner's pad at Barnes."

Turner rang off as he pulled up at Blackfriars. Glancing in his rear view mirror, he suddenly became aware that David Joseph was no longer behind him. He turned and leaned over the back of the front seats glaring through the rear screen. No sign of David's car which had been following him from Tooley Street.

"Shit," he muttered audibly, annoyed with allowing himself to be distracted by the phone-call to Mullen. He walked to the corner and looked back along Southwark Street. Again no sign of the car. He cursed out aloud.

*****

David's mobile shrilled as he followed Turner up Dukes Hill towards London Bridge. It was his father in an agitated state.

"What's the problem?"

161

The Courier
James R. Vance

"The Fixer's contacted me again. He wants the money today without fail. David, he threatened me. I'm frightened."

"Don't worry, I'm on my way. Yesterday I put the briefcase in your safe. Have it ready for me when I arrive."

"Yes, but what are you going to do?"

"Give him the money, like the man asks. See you shortly."

The traffic was heavy as he watched Turner join the queue heading along Southwark Street. David tucked in several vehicles behind as a white transit van waited to slip into the steady stream of cars. He beckoned him on and steered his car unobtrusively into the wake of the van out of Turner's vision. Unobserved, he turned onto Southwark Bridge, crossed the river towards the City and made for St. John's Wood via Finsbury and Regents Park. Traffic around St. Paul's cathedral was lighter than usual due to the cold autumn weather.

After a slight delay in the vicinity of King's Cross, he made good time around the outer circle of the park before exiting by the Central Mosque. Within thirty minutes from eluding D.S.Turner he turned into the driveway of his father's house and parked up.

Isaac Joseph welcomed his son by hugging him emotionally before he had even set foot inside the house. David was in a hurry, having conceived an alternative plan of action during the drive from London Bridge. He calmed his father with some comforting words.

Isaac made a note of The Fixer's contact number and passed it to David who, stuffing the piece of paper in his pocket, left almost immediately. He embraced his distressed father before tossing the briefcase onto the passenger seat of the car.

"Stay put and don't answer the door to anyone until I return later. Don't worry. Everything's going to be fine."

David left his father's house and, after first calling at a friend's house in Lambeth, headed for the M25 motorway.

*****

"It's been bloody clamped," exclaimed Mullen, pacing up and down angrily by Edgeware Road underground station.

The Courier
James R. Vance

"Well, take the tube down to Putney Bridge. There's a Firkin pub on the corner of Fulham High Street. I'll pick you up there on the way to Barnes. Sod the car for now, we can sort that later. We need to find David Joseph."

"What about St. John's Wood?"

"I've already sent McGovern across there to baby-sit the old man. I think you'll find it's a straight run through on the District Line. See you at Fulham."

Turner was still fuming at losing David Joseph. If he had lost his way or had a mishap, surely the guy would have called him. But why had he now become evasive when previously he had been so helpful and compliant towards the police? Why change now, unless he had finally bottled it? He thought about calling Massey, but determined to wait until he had something more substantial to report.

He decided to visit Anderson to see if there was any fresh evidence from the boat before setting out to meet Mullen at the pub near Putney Bridge. Anderson was alone in the laboratory peering intently through a microscope.

"I'm going to check out the boathouse at Barnes again. Is there anything in particular I should be looking for?"

The forensic expert passed him a clipboard. "Not much to go on I'm afraid. Has the owner identified it yet?"

"Yes, it's his boat, but he reckons it's been tampered with. Like you said, the registration markings have been erased."

"At least that saves running a trace to chase up ownership. We'll need his fingerprints to eliminate those we found on board."

"That might be a problem," said Turner and described the recent chain of events. He scanned the information on the clipboard sheets. "I see the rope fibres matched."

"If you're going to Barnes, it may be worth thoroughly checking the boathouse again. Remember the wood needed to keep the dummy upright?" Crossing the room, Anderson held up a large clear plastic bag containing the L-shaped frame which they had recovered from the RIB.

The Courier
James R. Vance

"The inflatable was definitely in tow with this boat so it's possible that the timber in the inflatable also came with the cruiser. If you look closely, the two pieces have been sawn from the same length of wood, which in turn has been sawn from a longer piece. The cuts on the sections here are fairly square, but the cut from the original is slightly angled. If you can find the missing piece at Barnes, it will connect the boathouse to the wooden frame, the frame to the inflatable and the inflatable to the cruiser."

"Maybe," replied Turner, "but if the boat was stolen from the boathouse, so might the wood be stolen."

"Bit of a coincidence, though," suggested Anderson.

"They're piling up thick and fast."

"What are?"

"Bloody coincidences. But, rest assured, I'll still check it out. The more evidence we have, maybe something might stick."

"Where's the cruiser now?"

"Still at City Pier. There's uniform keeping an eye on it. Have you still got the key?"

"Mm, do you want it?"

"I'll ask River Police to contact you. They can take custody of it, seeing as he's gone awol." Turner checked his watch and decided it was time to meet up with his colleague.

*****

David Joseph pulled off the M25 into Clackett Lane services, filled the tank up with fuel, parked the car, walked across to the shop, bought a coffee and a doughnut and made two telephone calls.

The first one put him through to Blackfriars Police Station, the second one to Detective Inspector Massey's mobile.

Satisfied with the results of the calls, he continued his journey to Ashford.

Chapter 17

FRIDAY AFTERNOON: The Firkin public house in Fulham is extremely cavernous inside and when Mullen entered there seemed to be more staff than customers. The flagstone floors and long wooden bench-type tables gave the impression that it was orientated towards students and connoisseurs of cask ale.

He chose to stand at the bar and ordered a pint of Dogsbollocks from the many varied and exotic sounding beers which were on offer. He fancied ordering some food but was unsure how long Turner would be, so he opted for a bag of chilli flavoured corn chips.

As if in tune with his thinking, his colleague arrived within several minutes. Turner was in no mood to delay and, hastily downing the last drop, Mullen followed him outside to the waiting car, still munching the corn chips.

"Debbie's just called me from the office. Apparently our friend Joseph phoned to say his father had been taken ill and he had to go over to St. John's Wood. That's his reason for suddenly shooting off. Again it seems far too convenient to me, but the flipside is that he's not at Barnes and we can have a snoop around."

Turner started the engine and the detectives turned onto Putney Bridge to cross the river and head towards Barnes.

"He's waiting for me to contact him to arrange another appointment for his statement, which we can do after we've checked out his boathouse. He's also been given a contact number for the River Police to get his boat back later, so hopefully we won't be disturbed. If it's all a load of bollocks, why did he agree to meet me at City Pier this morning? What do you reckon?"

The Courier
James R. Vance

"Why not check with McGovern to see if he's at his father's house, like he professes to be?"

"Good idea. Give him a bell."

Mullen took out his mobile phone. "Bloody hell," he cried. "That's it! It was peelers!".

"What?" quizzed Turner, totally bemused.

"You wouldn't understand," said Mullen smugly satisfied that he had solved nine across. He scrolled to his contact numbers and rang McGovern but only received the message 'number unobtainable'.

"Probably propping up some bar," he commented. "I'll send a text to call us asap. Where was he originally?"

"At Swiss Cottage, checking out the garage where Joseph alleged that he had his car repaired."

"It's hardly a spit from St. John's Wood. Surely he's there by now? Mind you, how many bars are there in between?"

Turner smiled. Andy McGovern was a bit of a scoundrel, but a bloody good copper, the type to have alongside when the going got tough. The car was now heading along Lower Richmond Road towards Barnes Common.

"By the way, what did you reckon to the girl?"

"Quite tasty, really."

Turner tutted and shook his head. "No, I meant compared to the photo of the one leaving the station."

"Difficult to say. To me, rear views of young ladies with long blonde hair all look the same. It's only when they turn round, you see the reality. They're either pretty fit or, sadly, some old wrinkly, desperately hanging on to her one remaining asset."

Their conversation was interrupted by a call on Mullen's mobile. "It's McGovern. He's at the house and there's still only the BMW and Audi in the driveway, no sign of young Joseph's Porche. What do you want him to do?"

"Tell him to sit tight. If our man turns up, he's to stay with him and to follow when he leaves."

Mullen relayed the message, laughed and said. "He wants to know how he's expected to keep up with a Porche in his clapped out 1.8 Vectra?"

"If he starts to lose him, tell him to stick his blue light on and book the bastard for speeding. Oh, and if he starts to head in our direction, he's to call us immediately."

"You really do not like this Joseph guy, do you?"

"It's him. I know it's him and I intend to nail him."

They continued the remainder of the journey in comparative silence and fifteen minutes later were outside the house at Barnes. There was no sign of the Porche.

*****

"Where the `ell's Loose?" snapped Frank Cannon.

Danny shrugged his shoulders. "Not a clue, boss. Said `e was off out. Didn't say where."

"Phone `im on `is mobile and tell `im to get back `ere smartish."

"Problem, boss?"

"Just `ad a call from The Fixer…said we can `ave our money back tonight. It's the usual swap at Waterloo."

"Same time?"

Cannon poured himself a drink. "Yeah, six o'clock. If `e's not back in time, yer'll `ave to do it."

"What we `andin` over?"

"They can `ave their bog roll back again and bloody-well like it."

"What they expectin`?"

"They can expect what they fuckin` like. They're gettin` bog roll and nuffin` else."

"In the briefcase, then?"

"Probably, `e just said same as usual, but no school-kids this time `cos of the `olidays. It's the newsstand nearest the burger bar. Said someone'll be sat on the bench nearest the stand with the briefcase on the deck next to `is legs. Suggest yer buy a newspaper, sit yerself down and let 'im walk away with our case. Soon as 'e's gone, scarper sharpish."

"I'd better try and track 'im down," said Danny, referring to Frank's son, Luke, not really fancying having to make the pick-up.

"If yer manage to find 'im, make sure 'e's back 'ere no later than four." Cannon sprawled in his armchair, smugly pleased that he could not only retrieve his cash, but also had the opportunity to pay back (in his mind) the original smart-arse who had put one over him in the first place. He decided to phone Mickey and Vince to announce the good news.

*****

Turner pulled the car over into a lay-by fifty metres short of David Joseph's house. A navy blue Vauxhall was already parked there.

"Who's on surveillance here?" asked Mullen.

"Seymour, I hope," replied Turner stepping from the car and approaching the parked vehicle. He tapped on the side window.

D.C. Kelly Seymour wound down the window. "I'd have preferred France to this," she remarked, smiling.

"Any visitors?"

"Not a soul."

"We're having a little snoop around the boathouse. If you see a Porche approaching, call me immediately. Is there a side entrance to the rear of the property?"

"There's a garden gate. I tried it when I first arrived to see if there was anyone about, but it's locked. You could try the path down to the river. You might be able to get access from there. At least you'll be out of sight from the road."

"Where's this path?"

"Right behind you. It runs from the lay-by down to an old towpath between the property and the river bank. I think there's a boundary wall along the length of his garden as far as the river, but I'm sure two strapping young men like you could climb over."

The Courier
James R. Vance

"O.k. we'll give it a try, despite Mullen's fat belly!" joked Turner. "Oh, and you never saw any of this, yes?"

"Any of what, sarge?"

"Good girl, see you shortly."

The pathway skirted a small copse on one side as far as the river. The perimeter wall of Joseph's residence rose up on the other side. The two detectives followed it down until they reached the old towpath which ran away along the banks of the Thames to their right. To their left, the wall stopped short of the river and extended at right angles parallel with the riverbank towards the boathouse which jutted out in the distance. Between that structure and the two officers a dense mass of hawthorn and prickly undergrowth barred their way.

Their only chances of reaching the boathouse were either by water or over the wall. They opted for the latter and backtracked until they found some crumbling brickwork where they could gain a foothold. Turner scaled the structure first and offered his hand to Mullen to assist him onto the sloping coping stones which capped off the top of the wall.

They dropped down into some dense shrubbery and emerged to skirt a broad lawned area across to the wooden boathouse. The broken rear door was slightly ajar and they entered, splitting their search on each side of the berthing bay between them. The wooden structure was badly in need of repair. Some of the timbers had rotted over a period of time and gaps in the roof allowed rainwater to trickle down the side walls leaving damp patches and, in some places, mould growth.

The mooring for the boat had been cut into the embankment and shored up with old railway sleepers, which were wet and slippery. The area around the bay had been concreted, but that was crumbling in various places. There was a dank, musty smell mingling with the strong reek of diesel fuel.

"Better watch your step," advised Turner. "Don't expect me to jump in after you."

"Ditto. What are we actually looking for?" enquired Mullen.

The Courier
James R. Vance

"Anything and everything, especially any lengths of marine timber," replied Turner, handing his colleague a pair of protective gloves. Methodically they searched both sides of the building, opening several lockers and rummaging through the contents of some well-worn tea chests. Turner found numerous lengths of timber but none to match the sections held in the forensic laboratory.

Mullen dragged a heavy package from one of the tea chests. At first glance it looked like a long bundle of oily rags wrapped around each other, but its weight suggested that something more rigid was concealed within.

One by one he removed each remnant of cloth to reveal two hand-painted boards inscribed with the words:

Jewel of the Thames

"What do you make of these, then?" he exclaimed holding them aloft for Turner to scrutinise.

"Where were those beauties?" cried Turner.

"Wrapped in rags at the bottom of this tea chest."

"I'll get Sarah to cross reference that with the Port of London Authority. If that's the current name of his boat, why would a thief go to the trouble of hiding them. Why not just chuck them in the river. Is there anything else in there?"

"Only some papers."

"Okay, put everything back as you found it. We're going to need a search warrant."

Mullen leaned across and reached down behind the tea chest. "Is this the timber you've been searching for?"

He held up a length of wood, one end of which was cut at a slight angle.

Turner grinned. "Got him. Now it's time to piece together all these bloody coincidences to create the reality."

At that moment his mobile rang. It was Debbie at Blackfriars. "Your Mr Joseph's phoned again. He says he's attending a couple of meetings this afternoon. Wants to know if he can call in on his way home at six o'clock tonight to make his statement?"

The Courier
James R. Vance

"Perfect," replied Turner, "and while you're confirming that, can you ask Sarah to check out the registration of his boat with Port of London. Find out if his current ownership matches the name, Jewel of the Thames. Oh, and tell Anderson in forensics that I've found his missing piece of wood."

"Piece of wood?"

"He'll know what I mean. By the way, did David Joseph say where he was calling from?"

"No, the number he gave me was a mobile number."

"Okay, thanks. We'll be heading back shortly."

They carefully replaced all they had disturbed, retraced their steps across the lawn and once more scaled the boundary wall. Back in the lay-by Turner asked Seymour to stay put until at least six o'clock in case Joseph returned in the meantime. He was still concerned that Scott Morgan had not been located, despite the mounting evidence against David Joseph.

*****

Massey was engaged in the guided tour of Le Manoir when his mobile rang. It flashed up 'number withheld' and, making his excuses, wandered onto an outside terrace to take the call, leaving Croft to continue the tour alone.

"Detective Massey?" enquired the muffled voice.

Massey suddenly became alert, the unmistakeable voice of his adversary immediately dragging him from the tedium of his visit to the school.

"You again. Where's Scott Morgan?" he demanded angrily.

"I am returning him to you today together with an opportunity to retrieve your toy money and to arrest a co-conspirator. Listen carefully. At six o'clock tonight Scott will be seated on a bench by the newsstand opposite the burger bar where you first found him. He will have a briefcase containing your toy money. If you watch and wait, someone will attempt to exchange his briefcase with their briefcase. The rest is up to you."

The phone went dead. Massey paced across the terrace and immediately contacted Turner to relay the substance of the anonymous call. Between them they decided on a strategy to act on the information which had just been communicated. Their main concern focussed on the need to provide sufficient protection for Scott Morgan, particularly if there was a chance of violence erupting at the scene.

Turner was now confused since the timing of the action at Waterloo coincided with David Joseph's appointment at Blackfriars. Maybe he wasn't involved. He had a decision to make. He brought Massey up to date with what had transpired in his absence.

"What do you think we should do with him?" he asked his superior.

"Arrest him when he comes in to make his statement," stated Massey emphatically.

"On what grounds?"

"Kidnapping and attempting to pervert the course of justice. Your evidence from the boathouse suggests that no theft took place, that he contrived the whole thing. If we can prove that he took the boat to Blackfriars and then to City Pier, that links him to the inflatable, which in turn links him to Scott via the dummy. Find out exactly what his movements were for the past week, get a search warrant for his house. You never know what else that may turn up and of course you will need the evidence from his boathouse. You also need a witness and, hopefully, he'll be waiting for you at the railway station at six tonight."

"If he is our man, I can't understand why he reported the boat as missing and is today releasing Scott to us. It doesn't make sense."

"You could interview the girl. Put pressure on her. Might not be a bad idea to do the same with his father. Look for any inconsistencies in their stories. Don't forget that you already have a witness to her involvement. According to Dawkins, Scott's next door neighbour in Ashford has spoken to a young blonde female, who, in turn was placed in that vicinity on the same day by the decorators at Scott's school."

The Courier
James R. Vance

"You're right of course. The links are so strong that it's got to be her. How are things going at your end?"

"Nothing so far. The school looks like any other privately run establishment. Unfortunately there's only a caretaker, a cook and some old guy who looks like the gardener. I've sent French off to quiz him. Croft and I are still performing the married couple scenario."

"How are you getting on with the language?"

"Fortunately, apart from the cook, the caretaker and the gardener seem to speak English fairly well, so we're communicating."

"When are you hoping to come back?"

"Originally tomorrow, but as circumstances are moving forward rapidly at your end, I'm now looking at tonight. When we've finished here, if we can't dig up details on the owners of the school, we'll need to visit the local town hall to see what we can discover. Best of luck at your end. Keep me posted on progress."

Massey once again visualised the tumbling brick walls. He sat on a small rustic bench at the end of the terrace and looked out across a vast expanse of lawn which sloped down towards the distant lake. Though excited by events in England, he nevertheless felt uneasy and not at all comfortable. Something was not quite right.

*****

There were a few local shoppers, mostly women with small children, wandering in and out of the shops on the parade. The black coupé purred almost noiselessly past them and parked at the far side of the parking area. David Joseph stepped out and walked briskly down the road towards Scott Morgan's previous residence.

There was no-one about as he slipped through the side gate into the garden beyond. The kitchen door was still closed despite being unlocked. He entered quietly and skipped upstairs to find Scott lying full length on the landing attempting a crossword in one of the newspapers which had been purchased the previous day.

The Courier
James R. Vance

"I thought I was supposed to be picked up yesterday. What happened?" snapped Scott, angrily.

"A slight change of plan. Just do as I say and you'll be reunited with your mother this evening."

"It's bloody uncomfortable here, you know... and it's cold. You're really freaking me out. First it was Wednesday, then Thursday and I'm still chained up. I trusted you."

"Calm down. It'll all be over in a few hours time. I just need you to do one more little job for me."

"No chance," exclaimed Scott. "I've had enough of your schemes and false promises. I resign!"

"Just listen. This time it'll help the police, not me. I want to sort of square things with them, but I need your help to achieve that. What d'you say?"

Scott stretched and stood up, rattling the chains. "You could start by removing this lot. You expect me to trust you. It's about time you trusted me."

David smiled and held out his hand. "Friends again?"

"Friends?" repeated Scott. "Some friend you are with locks, chains and blindfolds. I'd hate to be your enemy."

"Hey, sadly it was necessary. You're a good kid. Under different circumstances I'm sure we could have made a great team."

"I hardly know you, so I can't say. I don't understand. You have a beautiful house from what I've seen of it, flash cars, you're well dressed, you don't seem short of a few quid, so why, why all this? Or is your lifestyle the result of a life of crime?"

"Just the opposite, actually. This, as you put it, is pure excitement, simply adrenalin pumping and lots of fun."

"Mm, 'till you get caught."

"That could be up to you this time. We need to make a move. I'll get the key to release the handcuffs." David descended to the kitchen and promptly returned with the key to release Scott from his bonds.

"I'd offer you some coffee, but it's almost cold now," said Scott accusingly.

The Courier
James R. Vance

"How about sharing a pub lunch somewhere, before we complete our final assignment?" suggested David, ignoring the young man's pointed remark.

There he goes again, thought Scott, talking about 'our assignment'. *Yet further activity of a rather dubious nature is once again an exciting prospect. He has this knack of also getting my adrenalin pumping. How could I possibly let the guy down?*

"As long as you're paying," he replied.

They left together, locking the kitchen door behind them with Scott once again taking charge of his own keys and carrying his personal baggage.

As they strolled back towards the parade of shops, the lawn mower man watched from the shadows of his living room curtains as they disappeared up the road. Immediately, he scurried into his hallway where he rummaged amongst some papers on the telephone table to find Sergeant Dawkins' number.

*****

The three detectives completed their tour of the school and headed for the nearest bar where they could discuss their findings and any conclusions which they had reached. Following the same road away from the lake and Le Manoir, they turned towards Ardres and a short time later stopped at Le Café des Pêcheurs.

After ordering some drinks they shared their individual thoughts. "My first observation was the overall semblance of normality," said Massey. "According to the caretaker, it was set up by some consortium, the members of which currently carry out the role of school governors.

There's a headmaster and four teachers, all English with the exception of one French lady who teaches both French and English. The other staff comprises the three which we met today with additional cleaners and kitchen staff during term time plus a secretary who deals with all the admin."

"Whilst you were on the telephone I found out that student admissions only take place at the beginning of the school year in September," added D.C. Croft.

"How are they enrolled?" asked D.C. French

"Firstly by submitting an application before the first of March. I have the form here," she replied, handing the document across the table. "The applicant then has to sit an entrance examination in April and finally it has to be approved by the governors at their A.G.M. in July."

"It's not easy, then?" commented French.

"I'd like to know who are the governors," added Massey.

"The old guy was interesting," interjected French again. "He mentioned the governors…called it the organisation. Apparently five of them run the show, three are English, one is French and another is Dutch. He reckons they appear once a year, probably for that A.G.M. which you mentioned."

"Possibly," said Massey. "Maybe there's some reference to ownership at the council offices in Ardres."

"I'd be tempted to try the Mairie," suggested Croft. "In France most things have to have permission from Monsieur le Maire. Also the local Chamber of Commerce might be able to help and, of course, the taxation office."

"Okay." Massey glanced at his watch. "We've got all afternoon to make these enquiries, but we also need to bear in mind that it's vital to return to England asap." He went on to give an account of the anonymous phone call and to relate the conversation which he had held earlier with Turner. He leaned across towards D.C. French.

"You said the old man was interesting. In what way?"

"He took me down to his greenhouses and showed me round the gardens, he certainly knows a lot about plants and gardening."

"How the hell does he manage such a vast estate? He must be knocking on a bit." said Croft.

"He has a young guy from a local agricultural college who does all the heavy work. I think he's training him to take over when he eventually decides to hang his boots up."

"So what'sso interesting about his gardening expertise?" asked Massey, impatiently.

French continued. "He also gave me a potted history of his life story, from fighting in the war, captured by the Germans, escaping to England, coming over on D-day and ending up as a liaison officer for the Allies as Nazi Germany capitulated.

Apparently he was wounded during the push towards Paris and stayed on there with some desk-job until he transferred to the French zone, first in Austria, then at Strasburg. After the war he had another op on his dodgy leg, met a nurse, married her and ended up working for the Douane, the French customs authority at the Channel ports until he retired and took this part-time job here."

"Now that is interesting," stated Massey, "and I bet he still has contacts with French customs to this day."

"Possibly on the English side also," added Croft. "Might be worth checking with Revenue and Customs to see if anyone remembers him."

"Good point," said Massey. "We can also make enquiries with the local police and the customs at Calais on our way back to the tunnel. It's strange that an ex-customs official is working in an establishment which we suspect of some kind of smuggling activity. What would be the odds on that?"

"Just a small point," ventured French. "We don't know his name."

"You spent all that time with him and didn't ask his name?" demanded Massey.

"It's not the French way. It's considered impolite to probe into someone's private life, unless you're formally introduced or they offer the information."

"You're a bloody detective, for goodness sake."

Croft stepped between the two protagonists. "It's Dubois, Marcel Dubois," she announced.

"How the hell do you know that?" exclaimed French.

"There was a flyer on the notice board advertising weekly gardening classes each Monday and Thursday at six o'clock with the grounds-man, Monsieur Marcel Dubois, in the gardening storehouse for members only!"

"Well I never," remarked Massey. "How did you interpret all that?"

"It was in English, sir, you know for the English students."

"Did you observe anything else, which we may have missed?" asked Massey in a gently sarcastic manner.

"Yes, as a matter of fact," she replied. "There was a large carton in the main entrance hall. I took a look at the label." She took a small pad from her shoulder bag and read from it. "It had been delivered from Maroquinerie Desforges (SARL), Lyons."

"And what does all that mean?" asked Massey.

"Leather goods supplier called Desforges," interjected French. "The SARL bit's the equivalent of our private limited company. Don't ask me what it stands for."

Croft continued. "Anyway, as it had already been opened, I took a peek inside."

"And?" pressed Massey, curious as to where this was leading.

"Guess what?"

"I just can't wait," jibed French.

"It contained a consignment of large black briefcases."

"Well I never," quipped French. "Just what every student needs."

"Hang on a sec," declared Massey, suddenly serious. "A whole carton? Identical briefcases? All black?"

D.C. Croft nodded. "You thinking what I'm thinking, sir?"

"They're not student briefcases," exclaimed Massey. "They're courier briefcases!"

*****

The sleek, black coupé slipped effortlessly onto the M20 at junction five and headed north westwards towards the M25 and London. Scott was relieved to have no blindfold this time. Having just enjoyed a tasty meal in a country inn before joining the motorway, he was anticipating the events which lay ahead. Eventually they left the motorway system behind and continued along the A20 towards Lewisham. Traffic started to build as they approached the capital with its usual early Friday rush-hour exit from the city.

The conversation during the journey had ranged from football and sport in general to the various current events which Scott had read several times over in the newspapers during his confinement at the house. They chatted away like two close friends on a day out together, although David was conscious of steering in another direction any discussion which tended to drift towards his own personal life and circumstances.

Scott tried several times to discover if he had experienced time in the armed services, but David was clever enough to sidestep such issues. At Chislehurst, they pulled off the main road and stopped at a small, unpretentious public house in a side street.

"We'll have a drink here," said David, "and I'll fill you in on the game plan. We're okay for time, so there's no immediate rush."

They chose a corner table in the lounge bar away from the entrance door. The room was deserted apart from the girl at the bar who had served their drinks.

"We're heading back to Waterloo station, to where it all began."

"Is there some significance to that?" asked Scott, aware of the man's attention to detail.

"Not really, apart from the fact that certain events have forced the issue in that direction. It seemed appropriate to bring everything to a head in a situation where to some degree I had complete control, because, for obvious reasons I won't actually be there.

As I said to you earlier, it allows you to be safely handed over and, at the same time, it gives the police some kudos by arresting a possible suspect in the bigger picture. At least it'll give them something to chew on for a time."

"So, who's the person they're going to arrest?"

"I honestly don't know, but, rest assured, he'll certainly be of some interest to the police. I'll need your briefcase back again, but this time it'll be full of money. You will sit on the bench next to the newsstand opposite the burger bar, more or less close to where you stood originally. You'll have the briefcase at your feet. Someone will sit next to you to exchange briefcases. I suggest that you immediately pick up his case and walk away."

"Where do the police come in all of this?" asked Scott, envisaging possible feelings of vulnerability.

"The police are aware of the scenario and I am assuming that your safety will be their priority. That being the case, when you walk away, you will be instantly under their protection, which then gives them the opportunity to home in on the unsuspecting target, once he has grabbed hold of your briefcase."

"What happens then?"

"I would imagine that the suspect will be arrested and interrogated."

"What about me?"

"At some point you'll be de-briefed and you can then tell your amazing story."

Scott sipped his drink. "I'll sell it to the newspapers," he chuckled.

"Make sure it goes to the highest bidder," added David, smiling at the young man's enthusiasm and naively romantic view of the whole affair.

"It's a pity I can't involve you, though. You could have shared the fame."

"Yes, and a cell in Wormwood Scrubs," joked his companion.

"They'll ask me loads of questions about you. I'll have to answer some of them."

"Answer all of them. What do you know about me?"

"You're rich, you live in a smart house near a river or a canal, drive different cars, wear expensive clothes and know something about boats, although you don't have one yourself. You prefer to nick them!"

"Very good. How do you know that I drive different cars?"

"Well, I'm not very good on cars, better at boats really, but I know you first picked me up in a B.M.W., and sometimes at the house the engine noise sounded differently and today you're in another type altogether."

"And before you think about it, the car today doesn't belong to me. It's borrowed, so the registration number has no link to me. You also mentioned a river or canal?"

"Sounds again. I could hear river noises behind the house, you know boat sirens and boat engines."

"So, you could give them all that information and they wouldn't be any wiser as to my identity?"

"How could they? You could be one of several million people who live in and around London."

"What if they showed a photograph of me or took you to my house. What then?"

"How would they get a photo or find out where you lived?"

"Hypothetically, let's say it were to happen. How would you react then?"

"You mean, if I could actually identify you as the man who had set me up, kidnapped me, locked me up, blindfolded me and chained me to a staircase?"

"That's a damning indictment of my crimes."

"Fairly accurate, though."

They looked across the table at each other, neither of them very sure what thoughts were in the other one's head. Scott was enjoying the banter. He took another sip of his drink, dragging out the suspense. David leaned back in his chair, not too sure but displaying an air of complete nonchalance.

Scott grinned. "You're nothing like my kidnapper," he joked.

"What about the house?"

"He lived in a rat-infested smelly hovel."

"Well, I believe you, but will they?" David shook his head. His face was a picture of mock disbelief. "Not to worry, with a bit of luck, it won't come to that and even if it did…like you said…we have to trust each other."

David checked his watch. "Finish your drink then, it's time to go. I'll drop you at Lambeth North underground where you can take the tube to Waterloo. When you get there, go into the mainline station. Walk over towards the burger bar and sit yourself down opposite, next to the newsstand. If you see any police, ignore them. I expect there'll only be plain clothes about, that's if they've got any sense at all. Okay? Let's go."

They rejoined the A20 heading for central London, where each would perform their assigned roles in different places at the same time, unaware that the best laid plans.......!

*****

The incident room was already a cacophony of sound when Turner made his entrance accompanied by D.S. Mullen. The hubbub abated as they approached the desk.

"Finally got some action for you," declared Turner and the noise level increased again. He related the information from D.I. Massey and proceeded to outline the general game-plan which would be overseen by D.S. Mullen, as he himself would be at Blackfriars hopefully interviewing David Joseph.

"I've asked D.C. McGovern and D.C. Seymour to pick up the girl from Joseph's shop and bring her in for questioning. Ensure all the interview rooms are free, 'cos we'll have her, David Joseph, Scott Morgan and a.n.other from Waterloo to interview during the course of the evening and I want them kept separate."

He turned to the wipe-board where there was a sketch of the general layout of the station concourse, showing the newsstand, the burger bar and the main exit routes.

"D.S. Mullen will allot your various positions and movements. It's his call. I just want to emphasise that there's no room for cock-ups, either before, during or after the main action, but, and I mean a big but, keep it low key. There's no need to start a wave of panic. Don't forget it'll be awash with commuters and I don't want them causing chaos in the belief that it's some sort of terrorist attack."

On the board behind him Turner stuck a recent photo of Scott which had been handed to the police by Mrs. Morgan.

The Courier
James R. Vance

"This is the young man who is supposed to be waiting for us at the station. An exchange of briefcases is due to take place with someone unknown. Make the arrests quickly and quietly, including Scott. Cuff him normally and take them off once he's tucked away out of sight in the van. Explain it's for his own future safety. You know the drill. Any uniform plods about, just ignore them.

With regard to interviews back at the nick, I'll be already involved with young Joseph if it goes to plan. McGovern and Seymour can sort the girl and, possibly, D.I. Massey will have returned from his trip to unravel Scott Morgan's week-long saga."

The last remark was greeted by jeers, boos and innuendos with reference to the role of D.C. Croft on the trip to France. Turner left Mullen to restore order and go through the detail of the planned action for later in the day.

Back at his desk, he called McGovern to check that he and Seymour were organised to pick up the girl. A call also came through from Dawkins to report what the 'nosey neighbour' had witnessed that afternoon at Scott's old house.

"Where are you now?" asked Turner.

"Folkestone," replied Dawkins. "I can't really check it out until later this evening or tomorrow morning. The only other alternative is to get the local plod down there."

"No, don't do that. It could get messy. The way things are evolving, I don't think it really makes much difference anyway. Take a look in the morning. If you can gain access, have a snoop around and if you find anything interesting, we'll take it from there. You might also warn the next door neighbour that he could possibly be called to confirm the I.D. of the girl. It depends on how co-operative she is."

Turner outlined the current state of the investigation and thanked him for all his assistance so far. He decided to call Massey and update him. The frustrations of the previous week could now be brought to a successful conclusion, providing tonight's activity delivered the fruits of their collective endeavours.

183

Armed with renewed confidence, he spoke to Massey, who
was engaged in some Anglo-French diplomacy at the local Mairie
in Ardres as they attempted to acquire more information about the
school and its staff.

"I'll call you back when we've made some headway here,"
he told Turner. "Oh, just before you go, have you got a contact
number for Dawkins. I need him to make some enquiries with his
Revenue and Customs mates?"

Turner passed on the number. Though satisfied with the
state of play, he was still concerned about the role of David Joseph
in all this.He always seemed to be one step ahead.

*****

"About bloody time," ranted Frank Cannon as his son and
Danny entered the room. He looked at his watch. "Cuttin` it fine,
aren't yer?"

"I don't know what all the bleedin` fuss is about," retorted
Luke. "Danny `ere sez I've gotta be at the station for six. It's only
jus` gone four, so what's the panic?"

"I never know where to fuckin` find yer when I wan` yer
and you've gotta mobile that's never bleedin` switched on."

"I'm savin` the batteries."

"Bollocks, you've never saved a bleedin` thing in yer life.
Well, now's yer chance to save me some money, my money. The
Fixer's arranged a pick-up at six tonight, usual place. Some young
lad'll be on the seat next to the newsstand, briefcase at `is feet. It's
a straight swap. Go in, pick it up and fuck off. Danny can run yer
down there and wait outside for yer, so there's no `avin` to catch
the tube back. Five or ten minutes at the most."

"I take it that we're gettin` the money back."

"Too fuckin` true, so don't mess up this time."

"And `ow was I to know what was in the case the last
bloody time? Anyway, what's in my case this time?"

"Well, yer know `ow fair I am in all matters involvin`
money and as they're kindly returnin` what we `anded over last

184

time, you're 'andin' back what they gave us. It's only fair. What d'yer reckon Danny?"

"You couldn't be fairer, boss," replied his bodyguard, smiling smugly.

"Can I smack 'im one before I leave?" asked Loose, punching his fist into the palm of his other hand.

"Smack 'oo one?" snapped Cannon.

"The bastard who's finally bringin' our money back."

Frank Cannon leaped from his chair, exploding a stream of abuse into his son's face. "Fuckin' typical…'ow bloody stupid are yer? 'Ere we are, tryin' to make an unobtrusive bleedin' exchange and 'e wants to start fuckin' world war three in the middle of Waterloo station. I don't fuckin' believe it. I tell yer, if anyfin' goes wrong this time, I'll fuckin' swing for yer."

"They've abolished 'angin'," countered Loose.

"Any more smartarse remarks like that an' you'll be 'angin'….from the nearest bloody tree. Now go an' smarten yerself up, yer look like shit."

Cannon turned to Danny. "You'd better get that briefcase for 'im. Is it still full of that bog roll?"

"It's not been touched since we brought it back from the W.C that night. Boss, if yer not 'appy wiv 'im doin' the swap, I don't mind doin' it."

"Better if you stay in the car, then, if anyfin' does go wrong, you can both make a quick getaway. Just keep a fuckin' eye on 'im and tell 'im to keep it simple. 'E's done it loads of times before, so what could go wrong this bleedin' time?"

*****

Massey and his colleagues ascertained from a young lady at the Mairie that the school was registered to the Blériot Formation des Études Anglaises (SARL). To discover the number and names of the associates, they would have to consult the RCS (register du commerce et des sociétés), the relevant taxation centre or possibly the CFE (centre de formalités des enterprises) of the local chamber of commerce.

The Courier
James R. Vance

It was decided that this information could be gathered through official channels in England and the task was handed to D.C. French to pursue, following their return.

They also stopped off at the Gendarmerie across the square from the Mairie, where, reverting to their roles as police officers, enquiries were made regarding the backgrounds of not only Marcel Dubois but also Thiery Faudet. Unfortunately they were politely told to apply in writing as they were unable to provide any information without experiencing the process of French bureaucratic officialdom. Again, partly due to his moderate command of the language, this responsibility fell to D.C. French.

As their investigation proved somewhat fruitless, Massey decided that he'd had enough of France. He suggested that they head back to Eurotunnel at Coquelles and take the first available train to England in the hope that they would be in time to immerse themselves in the fallout from the planned activity at Waterloo station.

They left the police station and walked across the square to where they had parked their vehicle whilst debating whether to take some refreshment in a nearby bar. Before they could make a decision, a dark blue police car containing two gendarmes drew alongside. The driver wound down his window.

"I hear your demand at the Gendarmerie," he said. "You must ask also of Francis, the son of Dubois. I see him many time at Le Manoir. Something there is not good. You understand?"

"Thank you," said Massey. "This son, Francis, he lives with his father?"

"Non, he has un moulin...how you say...mill house? It is not in the town. It is near Guines, le Moulin d'Andres. I say no more. You must send letter of enquiry. Bon courage."

The gendarme tipped his cap and drove away. They all looked at each other and decided that some refreshment was definitely in order. The three detectives walked over to the Café de la Poste, where they ordered three grands cafés crèmes.

"Get the map out," said Massey. "Let's see where this Guines place is."

Discovering that the town was only a few kilometres distant and en route towards Coquelles, they opted to detour in that direction.

"The old guy never mentioned his son, then?" asked Massey, addressing D.C. French.

"He mostly talked about himself, really. There was no reference to a family, apart from his wife, who died just before he retired."

"It could be something quite innocent," suggested Croft. "Calling in to check on his father regularly seems pretty natural to me, especially as it's close to home."

"It's strange that the local gendarmerie think otherwise," countered Massey. "I'll wager that we've stumbled onto something rather shady here." They finished their coffees and took the D231 towards Guines.

Despite checking several by-ways and minor roads around the immediate area, including the small village of Andres, they were unable to find the elusive mill belonging to Francis Dubois. They questioned a few local inhabitants but were confronted each time by the Gallic shrug of the shoulders and the outspread arms.

They eventually gave up and decided to head for home, where their investigation could progress by data analysis in liaison with the appropriate authorities in France. Massey called Sergeant Dawkins before they arrived at Eurotunnel in the hope that he would be able to trace any links with Marcel Dubois through his contacts at the channel ports in England.

Deep down Massey was convinced that Blériot College was probably quite legitimate, but certain parties were possibly using it as a front for some kind of smuggling operation. The over-riding question, however, was to what extent?

Chapter 18

FRIDAY EVENING: Outwardly the station concourse appeared like any other Friday during the extended rush-hour period. Since some commuters headed homewards for the weekend to return late on Sunday or early on Monday morning, it started somewhat earlier than most other weekdays. Blending into the general scene, however, were members of Massey's team, strategically positioned for the forthcoming operation.

Turner had also contacted Sammy in security to ensure that all surveillance cameras were primed and in working order, especially those mounted on the wall above the burger bar. Unfortunately, the detective himself was at Blackfriars awaiting the arrival of his elusive interviewee.

David Joseph was at that moment parking the black Volvo S40, which he had earlier borrowed from his friend nearby, in a side street off Westminster Bridge Road adjacent to Lambeth North tube station.

The driver switched off the engine. "How are you feeling?" he asked Scott alongside him.

"Not sure really," he replied. "Excited, I suppose, in a scary sort of way, relieved that I'll soon be back at home and a little bit sad that we're going our separate ways."

"Are you still okay about going through with it?"

"Shitting myself, actually, wondering what might go wrong. It's strange that, when we were involved in all that business on the river, I was quite cool 'cos I knew somehow that I could rely on you. You always seemed to be in control with everything planned to the last detail. It's as though you're a specialist in this kind of thing. What were you, S.A.S., secret service, a spy, a mercenary soldier or all of those?"

"There you go again. Maybe one day I'll be able to enlighten you."

"Does that mean I'll see you again?"

"Who knows what the future holds….for both of us? At least you'll have plenty to tell your mates at school."

"I very much doubt they'll believe me."

"When the press get hold of this and you become a celebrity with all the media attention, they'll believe you." David looked at his watch. "Time to make a move."

"Will you be around when all this kicks off?"

"Fortunately, for me that is, I have to be somewhere else, so unfortunately the straight answer is no, I won't be around. Don't worry, I have every confidence in you." He winked at Scott. "And, of course, you've been trained by the best. Good luck and thanks. Maybe one day, under different circumstances…." His voice trailed away.

Scott reached over to the rear seat and grabbed his holdall and the briefcase which they had filled with the fake money. Without glancing back he walked nervously across to the tube station. As Scott descended towards the Bakerloo line, Massey and his two colleagues ascended the ramp from the Eurotunnel shuttle and drove to the exit road leading to the M20. Darkness was creeping in from the east as they sped onto the motorway, adding to the damp autumn gloom which had greeted their arrival in England. They journeyed in silence until Massey received a call on his mobile. It was Dawkins.

*****

The security video showed Scott walking away from the camera towards the newsstand, where he sat on the adjacent metal bench seat. Placing his holdall alongside him, as though reserving a place, he leaned forward and stood the briefcase upright next to his legs and partially under the bench. The timer in the bottom right hand corner of the screen showed five fifty four.

The assembled detectives watched intently as numerous commuters passed to and fro, some stopping to purchase an evening paper at the stand. At two minutes to six, a youth in jeans and leather jacket approached the newsstand. He idly leafed through the daily papers in the rack, while, at the same time, glancing several times towards the bench.

Eventually he walked over and sat close up against Scott's holdall, carefully placing a black briefcase next to the one below. Scott leaned forward, picked up the second case, swung his other baggage over his shoulder and walked off towards the main station exit. Immediately two plain clothes officers raced into view.

They apprehended the stunned youth whilst he was still on the bench, handcuffed him and frogmarched him off in the opposite direction to Scott, who was simultaneously surrounded by more officers and received similar treatment. The whole procedure took no more than two minutes, causing very little distraction to the commuters thronging the concourse.

"Well, that was neat and tidy," commented D.I. Massey as he watched the re-run. "Where's Scott now?"

"Interview room two, sir," replied a uniformed officer by the office door.

"I trust he's no longer cuffed."

"No," replied one of the detectives in Massey's team. "When we put them on we explained to him that it was to give the impression that it wasn't a fit-up. We also contacted his mother and he has since spoken to her following his arrival here."

"Has he given you much info yet?"

"Only that he was kidnapped by the guy who approached him and set him up at the station last week. He says he wants to talk to you."

"Okay. I'll be with him shortly. Look after him, he's our star witness. Is Turner still having no joy with David Joseph?"

"No, sir, he's denying everything. His brief's arrived now and demanding his release."

"Arrange a line-up. We'll get Scott to I.D. him. That'll sort him out."

"What about the girl. Did we bring her in?"

The Courier
James R. Vance

"D.S. Mullen and D.C. Seymour are with her now. Apparently she's Joseph's cousin. Reckon she just helps part-time at the jewellers shop in Hatton Garden. Said she last saw her cousin David yesterday morning as she left for the shop and that he's been staying at his father's house for the past week 'cos of some problem with his car. Gave her address as St. John's Wood, same as her uncle. Seemingly she has lived there since her parents died."

"So she's not admitting anything?"

"Not yet, sir."

"What about the other guy on the video tape?"

"Identified himself as Luke Cannon. Checked the database. There's no form, but his dad's Frank Cannon and he's got fingers in all sorts of pies."

"Any previous there?"

"Mostly receiving, but knocks about with some dodgy characters. The lad reckons he was set-up by some guy at the station who gave him the case to swap in return for a score!"

"Oh yes and where's that bloke now?"

"The lad's complaining that we scared him off!"

"I'm surrounded by bloody brick walls again," muttered the inspector.

"Pardon, sir?"

"Oh, nothing," replied Massey irritably. "Maybe Scott's testimony can help make sense of all this."

At that moment a uniformed officer appeared at the door.

"There's a Dave Finch on the phone for you, Inspector. He mentioned a Sergeant Dawkins."

"I'll take it in my office."

Massey left the video room and made his way to his office further along the corridor. He sat behind his desk and picked up the phone. "Massey here."

"Oh, hi, I'm Dave Finch, Revenue and Customs at Dover. Sergeant Dawkins asked me to call you about a French guy called Marcel Dubois."

"Oh, brilliant. That was quick," replied Massey. "Any joy?"

"Well, I'm too young to remember, but chatted to some of my more geriatric colleagues down here and the story goes that one of our guys, Freddie Wilson, and this Dubois guy were involved in some smuggling operation which came to light back in the eighties. It was when there was a lot of concern about tariffs and tax differentials in Europe vis-à-vis the U.K.

Apparently shipments of duty-free goods were passing through illegally with Dubois and his cronies on the French side and Wilson and his mates over here making the arrangements and receiving handsome pay-offs. When the shit hit the fan, they were instantly dismissed. No court action was taken against them to prevent adverse publicity for the service, but obviously their cards were well marked on both sides of the channel. That's it really."

"Well, thank you for taking time out," said Massey. "It supports something we're currently working on."

"No problem," replied Finch. "Oh, there was one other thing. Dubois apparently had a son who worked in shipping. Sorry, can't remember his name. It was thought at the time that he was also involved but, unfortunately, nothing could be proved."

"Francis," murmured Massey.

"Yes, that was it. You know of him too?"

"Not a lot, but I'm sure we will. Once again, thanks for all your help."

"Glad to be of some assistance, cheers!"

Massey replaced the handset and started to sketch on a blank piece of paper :-

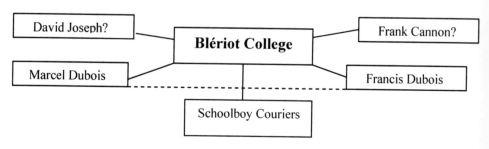

The school's got to be the link, he thought, need to find who owns it. Massey folded the paper, placed it in his pocket and walked down to interview room number two in the hope that Scott could knock down some of the brick walls which were confronting him.

*****

"What d'you mean…'e's been arrested?" Frank Cannon was again in one of his moods. He glowered at Danny. "I'm payin' yer to look after the prat."

"I did what you said. Dropped him off, waited outside and next thing the place is swarmin' wiv the fuzz and Loose is bein' dragged out to some police van wiv another lad."

"What other lad?"

"I dunno. Pobably the lad who was swappin' cases wiv 'im."

"I don't fuckin' believe this and I've still not got my bleedin' dosh. I should never 'ave sent the stupid little bastard. Serves 'im right if 'e gets banged up."

"D'yer think 'e'll say anyfin', boss?"

"I'll cut 'is fuckin' froat if 'e does."

Cannon marched up and down the room, muttering more obscenities. He wanted to call The Fixer, but was not really sure how he would take the bad news. He decided to call Mickey and Vince to meet him at the Windsor Castle and discuss the situation with them over a few drinks.

He convinced himself that this was the best course of action as they needed to be warned that their operations could also be compromised. Deep down he was concerned that Luke had never previously been in real trouble with the police and he was not too sure how his son would react.

Having overheard his phone calls, Danny asked, "What time we goin' to the W.C. then?"

Cannon checked his watch. "We'll go now before some bastard comes knockin' on the bleedin' door."

The Courier
James R. Vance

They left the house and, skirting Primrose Hill, drove down Prince Albert Road adjacent to the park in the direction of Lord's cricket ground, arriving in Maida Vale ten minutes later.

The public house was always busy on a Friday evening, so Frank negotiated the use of the back room with Cathy before ordering a drink for himself and Danny.

"Luke not with you tonight?" enquired the landlady.

"Nah, 'e's visitin' some mates souf of the river."

"Oh, that's nice," remarked Cathy, smiling. "It's time he got out more, rather than hang around with an old grouch like you, Frank."

"Less of the old, luv. Don't mind the grouchy bit. There's reasons for that. I'm surrounded by bloody idiots."

"Having a bad day, are we?" teased Cathy.

"It's been a bad week," added Danny.

Cannon scowled in Danny's direction.

"What?" pleaded his minder. "It's right innit?"

"There's no need to tell the fuckin' world about it!"

"Sorry I spoke," muttered Danny and retreated towards the back room.

"It's 'im," said Frank, trying to excuse the remark. "'E's not bin feelin' too good."

"You need to give him some time off," commented Cathy.

Cannon grunted, thinking that they all may get some time off if Luke spills the beans. He joined Danny in the quieter surroundings of the small meeting room and sat down to contemplate the options.

*****

"How are you feeling now?" asked Massey, leaning casually on the desk to put the young man at ease.

"Relieved to be on my way home, I suppose," replied Scott.

"Yes, it must have been a terrifying experience for you."

"Not terrifying. Exciting is how I would describe it."

"You weren't at all frightened?"

194

The Courier
James R. Vance

"At the beginning, I suppose, but once I realised that he needed me, I felt much safer."

"I'd like to get your version of events on tape, if you don't mind. Do you feel up to it now or would you prefer to get a good night's sleep and come back in the morning?"

"I don't mind, really. If you could do it now, I'd have the weekend to myself. It's up to you really."

"Okay. It's probably better now while everything's fresh in your mind. Having said that, you must come back to me if, maybe over the weekend, you think of anything you may have missed. I'll organise some tea and then set the wheels in motion."

Massey left the room and made his way to his office, sending Debbie to interview room one to interrupt D.S. Turner, who was still attempting to link David Joseph with the events of the past week. She beckoned the sergeant to temporarily terminate the interview and join her in the corridor.

"Problem?" asked Turner, closing the door to the interview room.

"Your boss wants you in his office."

"Did he say why?"

"I think he just wants an update."

"Do me a favour. Tell Joseph and his brief that I'll be back in two shakes of a you- know- what." Turner walked off to meet Massey in his office.

"What's the situation?"

"Not good," replied Turner. "He's spent some time with his brief and is still not budging from the stolen boat story. Everything we have is condemned as circumstantial by his brief and apparently, Mullen's having no joy with the girl."

"Did you get a search warrant for Barnes?"

"That's been knocked back for the same reason. Nothing substantial enough to justify one."

"Damn! I thought you had some evidence to prove he tampered with the boat."

"Inadmissable. That's what the warrant's for. We only found it when we broke in."

The Courier
James R. Vance

"Can't we say it was discovered when forensics investigated the alleged theft?"

"Not unless we tamper with the report."

"What about a line-up, while we've got Scott here?"

"That's being organised at this moment, but I bet the brief has something to say about that."

"Bollocks to the brief. Besides, he'll know that an objection will only raise doubts about his innocence. Emphasise that. Let me know when you're ready for me. I'm with Scott in room two. I also need to talk to you about France. I think we've stumbled onto something big."

They both returned to their respective interview rooms hoping for some shred of success. The inspector stopped off to ask D.C. Croft to join him, leaving D.C. French to pursue his French connection enquiries.

Massey introduced his detective constable and suggested that Scott recount the details of his kidnap and the ensuing events, while they videotaped his version, to which Scott had no objection. The inspector broke in occasionally to question and clarify certain points, but generally allowed the young man to tell the tale as he remembered it.

On several occasions, however, Massey sensed that Scott seemed to possess a selective memory in some key areas, particularly in relation to aspects which might have assisted in the identification of his captor. He probed on several occasions to ascertain details of the cars which the man had used, but Scott was always vague about the make, model, colour and style of vehicle.

Massey accepted that a blindfold was used to hide the location of the man's house, but found it inconceivable that the youngster had such sketchy recollection of the vehicles in which he was conveyed. Though a flimsy excuse, he accepted that fear and the threat of fear would have had some influence. He also fully understood his lack of desire to escape at several opportune moments on account of his regard for his mother's safety. As Scott quite rightly pointed out, he was unaware of how many others might have been involved.

Scott went on to describe his detention at the Ashford
house. Massey looked intently at his whole demeanour. Why was
he being evasive? Was he still scared? It didn't stack up. The
young man had earlier said that he felt safe with the man because
he was needed. How could a hostage feel safe with his kidnapper?
Oh, shit! Patty Hearst…Stockholm Syndrome! I need to put him
on the spot.

Debbie interupted the interview to inform Massey that
Turner was ready with the identification parade. D.C. Croft
stopped the recording.

"Can we conclude this shortly?" asked Massey. "I would
like to see if you can identify your kidnapper from a line-up."

Scott suddenly appeared nervous and extremely agitated.
The young man's reaction bothered him. He was reminded of their
first encounter on the Isle of Dogs when he had initially attempted
to hide the truth.

Aware of the youngster's sudden distress the inspector
leaned towards him, gently patting his arm. "Nothing to worry
about. They'll be behind a one-way glass screen and you won't be
visible at any time. D.S. Turner will be on hand to guide you
through the procedure and afterwards you can return here to
complete your intriguing story."

D.C. Croft escorted the hesitant youngster along the
corridor to a narrow room next to the area where the line-up was to
take place. Several similar looking individuals stood looking
directly at the screen. Scott could not believe his eyes. The man
who had kidnapped him and dropped him at Lambeth North tube
station two hours ago was nowhere to be seen. Massey was
unconvinced.

*****

After the police car had sped away from Blackfriars to re-
unite Scott with his mother, Massey sat in his office with Turner
and Mullen discussing the dilemma which now faced them. The
lack of physical evidence linking any of the evening's detainees

with Scott's abduction or the suspected criminal activity across the channel had created a seemingly insurmountable stumbling block.

He suggested that they renew their investigation from another direction, namely from France. He showed them the diagram which he had sketched earlier after receiving the call from Dave Finch.

"It depends on what D.C. French is able to conjure-up from his enquiries into the Dubois connection," commented the inspector. "Despite the negative results from the interviews, David and Rebecca Joseph are still suspected of involvement in the Scott Morgan escapade and I suggest that we should continue with their surveillance until such time as they slip up or we have something concrete with which to charge them."

"Do you reckon there's someone else involved?" asked Turner. "As Joseph wasn't identified by Scott, who really did kidnap him? Maybe an associate?"

"It's a possibility. I'm to blame for that cock-up. Scott was right. At his mother's house he described the guy to me as having light brownish hair in a ponytail, some kind of droopy moustache and shades. I should have checked out David Joseph before I suggested the line-up."

"Maybe I should have read your notes more closely," offered Turner, sharing the blame. "He couldn't have been more of a contrast…clean-shaven and bald as a coot. What about bringing in the neighbour from Scott's old house at Maidstone? He reckoned he spoke with the girl last Saturday. If he could identify her as being at the house, surely that puts her in the frame."

"According to Dawkins, he also said he saw Scott walking away from the house yesterday morning, yet Scott said that he was not released from the house until this afternoon. He's hardly reliable. If we put Miss Piggy in the line-up with a bunch of blondes, he'd probably pick her out!" exclaimed Massey.

The remark eased some of the tension. They laughed and nodded in agreement, though somewhat reluctantly.

"I've just had a thought," said Turner. "Where are the still photos that Sammy sent over?" Without waiting for an answer, he started sifting through the file of paperwork which they had accumulated during the week-long investigation. He brought back a folder containing photographs of images from the security videos at the station and began to spread them across the desk. "There you are," he cried triumphantly. "It's him!"

"Who?" asked Massey.

"The lad down the corridor. He's the one who disappeared towards the underground after the briefcases were exchanged." He turned to Massey. "You remember. We clocked him when we watched the replays in Sammy's office. He was the second lad in the school blazer with the strange badge. He also had his case switched, the one that Dawkins spotted. He's here in the interview room!"

"The one that we thought was the intended mark for the girl."

"Yes, that's the one."

"This is beginning to make some sense. Maybe today was a re-run to put things right amongst the villains of the piece. My anonymous phone-call could have been arranged for us to witness a sting in the tail or some form of payback. It's just possible."

"But where does Scott fit into all this?" asked Mullen, not quite up to speed with his boss's train of thought.

"Maybe using Scott was safer because he wouldn't be a suspect and only the other lad would be investigated for his part," replied Massey.

"Could it be that there's some feud going on between the Cannon family and Scott's kidnapper or even the Rebovkas," added Turner.

"I'm confused," admitted Mullen.

"Not surprising," remarked Massey. "Our mystery man has woven an intricate web all week. You've only got to listen to Scott's account of his experience to realise that the guy's playing a game of cat and mouse with, not just the law, but with his own fraternity."

"So what do we do about Cannon's lad?" asked Mullen

The Courier
James R. Vance

"Nothing," replied Massey. "Now that we've got some kind of overview of the situation, we keep an eye on him and particularly his dad. No point in continuing his interview as he's lying through his teeth and sticking to his fabrication. We know he's involved through the original drop at Waterloo. We can probably get more mileage by letting him think otherwise.

Let's continue the current surveillance on the Josephs. Somewhere along the line there's an organisation running a well-oiled smuggling operation. We just happened to stumble on one aspect of it through some possible malpractice of one of the participants. We need to find the head of the serpent, rather than chase its tail. In the meantime we should mainly concentrate on the French connection and monitor this band of brothers from a distance."

"At least you retrieved your case of dirty money," said Turner.

"And one of toilet tissue," added Mullen. "What the hell was that all about?"

"Just another of the oddities of the whole affair," sighed Massey. "We'll meet with the rest of the team first thing tomorrow and talk tactics. I don't know about you, but I'm knackered and badly in need of a shower, so I'm off home. You'd better release the girl and Cannon's lad before you go. I notice that David Joseph has already left the building."

"The solicitor wasn't happy," added Turner, "but his client walked off with a knowing smile, which said it all really."

Massey left for Streatham 'clutching a handful of straws in one hand and a sledgehammer in the other', quite prepared to use either one or both together to demolish the recurring brick wall.

*****

An intense gloom had descended upon the occupants of the back room at the Windsor Castle. The normally vociferous villains were in a strangely sombre mood. The shrill ring-tone of Frank Cannon's mobile broke the pervasive silence. It was his son, Luke.

The Courier
James R. Vance

"Where are yer now?" snarled Frank. "Well you'd better get yer arse up 'ere, smartish....yeah, the W.C." He switched off the mobile and turned to Vince and Mickey. "They've let 'im go, 'e's on 'is way 'ere."

"What's the score, then, 'ave they done 'im?" asked Vince.

"Dunno, 'e just said they'd let 'im go and 'e was on 'is way 'ome," replied Frank.

"So we're okay to carry on as normal," remarked Mickey, relieved that criminal activity was back on the agenda.

"I 'ardly bloody think so," snapped Frank. "Wevva 'e's bin charged or not, we've gotta soddin' problem. First we 'ave the case of bogroll 'anded over instead of the cash and now we 'ave my lad nicked by the pigs in broad bloody daylight."

"You said the drop was the normal time, six o' clock," commented Vince.

"What the fuck 'as that got to do wiv it?" asked Frank.

"Well it's dark at six," said Vince.

"Yu've fuckin' lost me," replied Frank, becoming more and more exasperated.

"Yer said it was in broad daylight..." Vince started to explain.

"I don't fuckin' believe this," exploded Frank Cannon. "Can someone get this bleedin' dipstick out of my face, before I twat 'im one. 'Ere's me tryin' to 'ave an intelligent conversation an' all 'e's bovvered about is what time the bloody sun sets!"

Danny rose from the table. "Shall I get another round of drinks?"

Three heads nodded in unison and the temperatures around the table dropped to a more congenial level. The topic of conversation drifted back to the consequential effects of the chinks which had recently appeared in the hitherto smooth-running system. They concurred that their previous decision to allow the lads at the school to monitor the situation during the following week should still stand. They also decided to reconvene at the end of next week to determine when and if to continue operations.

201

The Courier
James R. Vance

Once more Frank was appointed to contact The Fixer to ensure that he was made fully aware of recent events.

The discussion drifted into other common areas of interest, mostly centred on boxing and football until Luke finally arrived to brief them on the evening's events at Waterloo and Blackfriars. Though proud of his son's inventiveness to tell a pack of lies to the police, he kept his thoughts to himself since he could not accept that the police had actually taken it on board. If that were the case, in his mind, he questioned why they had been so lenient with Luke and queried their motives to readily release him.

Being the criminal that he was, suspicion always took precedence over trust, especially in matters connected with law enforcement. His other concern focussed on how the system had been breached. Was it someone within the organisation and, if so, why had they undermined an operation from which they had been benefiting? If someone from without was responsible, how had they infiltrated into an organisation which had been so secure for several years? These were niggling issues which had to be resolved before they could continue with any sustained confidence.

Keeping these considerations in mind, Frank Cannon swore to himself that whoever had caused this sudden breakdown would pay dearly. However, Frank was never that fortunate.

They finally left the public house at closing time, feeling content with their meeting even though little had been achieved. At that hour, satisfactory outcomes were more easily digested amid the haze of their excessive consumption of alcohol. Nevertheless, by the time they arrived back at Frank's house, his inner anger and fears had twisted his body tissues into a coiled spring of manic revenge.

*****

Massey poured himself a generous quantity of scotch to slurp with his takeaway Kentucky fried chicken, which he had purchased on his way home. He settled down to flick through the tv channels to find some entertaining programme to distract him from the pressures of the current investigation. The meal together with the alcohol and the soothing ambience of the central heating eventually took effect. Exhausted, he soon drifted into a deep sleep in spite of the cacophony of sound emanating from the 'Jonathon Ross Show'.

A clattering sound from the tumbling remnants of his left-over food as they slipped from his lap returned him briefly to the reality of his empty flat. The voluble Ross had already vacated the screen and had been replaced by a scheming Al Pacino in 'The Devil's Advocate'.

Somewhat refreshed by his enforced snooze, he rose and opted for a bottle of sixteen year old Tomintoul Malt to encourage the later continuance of a good night's sleep. Once again he settled back down in his easy chair and attempted to pick up the film's storyline. The telephone rang and languidly he reached over to answer the call.

"Hello, Raymond. It's me," announced a gentle female voice, a voice which Massey instantly recognised but had not heard since he had moved south. He sat upright and put down his glass, totally unaware of spilling some of the drink. Now he was wide awake.

"It's been a long time," he replied. "To what do I owe the honour?"

"I have some news," said his ex-wife, "and I thought that you should be the first to know, before one of our relatives or mutual friends spilled the beans. I'm getting married."

"Congratulations," declared Massey, wondering why she perceived it as of such importance to warrant a late phone-call. "What can I say? Anyone I know?"

"No, it's someone I met through work. You know how it goes."

"Have you known him long?"

"Long enough to know that this time it's for keeps."

"I thought that was the reason why we tied the knot," remarked Massey, having a slight dig.

"Ours was hardly a marriage," replied his ex. "You were never at home. I'd have seen more of you if I'd been one of your criminals. Let's face it, having to almost make an appointment to see your husband, hardly constitutes a relationship."

"So what does your latest victim do for a living? Obviously he's not a copper."

"Quite the opposite I would say. He's in the diplomatic service, hardly an apt description for your law enforcement cronies."

"Diplomacy is a pretty flimsy weapon when dealing with some of the villains who have crossed my path. So I presume he's based at the foreign office or does he jet-set around the world?"

"He's based in London at the French embassy, but he could be moved on to other parts of the globe if the French authorities decreed it. That's one of the reasons we're getting married as I'd be able to go with him and like you have just said, become a jet-setter."

"A French diplomat. Well, it's certainly a step up from being a copper's missus. When does this remarkable event take place, then?"

"Next week. Would you like an invite, just for old time's sake?"

"Love to be there to wish the happy couple bon voyage, but you know me, duty calls."

"Still chasing petty thieves and muggers, are we?"

"You'll be pleased to know that I've moved on a little since those days. Just this evening returned from following up an investigation in France, actually."

"What dizzy heights have you reached now, then? Have you joined Interpol?"

"No, just detective inspector with the met."

"My, my....we have gone up in the world."

"Yes, it's amazing how you can enrich your career prospects when there are no encumbrances dragging you back. It's good to offload some of the baggage occasionally."

"I take it there's no point in sending you an invite, then?"

"You never know. Pop one in the post. If I've wrapped up this current case, I may be ready for a little r and r. It could be quite amusing, knowing your penchant for foreign languages. How is your French accent, by the way?"

"Probably a damn sight better than yours. Anyway the service is in English and it's at Marylebone registry office. I'll pop an invite in tomorrow's post. You still at the same address in Streatham?"

"No point in my moving. As you said, I'm never at home."

"You'll never change. Well, hopefully see you on my big day."

"Second big day!"

"Oh yes, I forgot. The divorce was my first one."

"Well, you know what they say about the French. They're quite sincere when it comes to marriage, but they save their passion for their mistresses. At least when he doesn't come home, you'll know what he's up to!"

"Don't judge everyone by your own standards."

"Don't say that I didn't warn you."

"Goodbye, Raymond."

Massey replaced the handset and took a large slug of whisky. He finished the glass and decided to retire to bed. Perhaps tomorrow could be his big day.

Chapter 19

SATURDAY MORNING: Scott rose early, took an invigorating hot shower for the second time since his homecoming, put on some warm clothing and sped downstairs for some breakfast. His mother was already busying herself in the kitchen.

"Good morning, darling. How are you feeling now?" she enquired.

"Fine," replied Scott. "Is there any juice?"

"Certainly, dear. Would you like a nice cooked breakfast. I imagine you're ravenous after your ordeal?"

"No, thanks. Cereal and a yoghurt will be fine."

"I thought that we could spend a nice quiet day together. You must be exhausted after such a terrifying experience. I was absolutely distraught all week long, but so relieved now to have you safely home again. Maybe we could go shopping later. What do you think?"

"I'm going out," announced her son resolutely.

"But I've not seen you since last weekend and I thought we could spend some quality time together before you go back to school on Monday. That nice police lady said you would need some peace and quiet following the nightmare of your abduction."

Mrs. Morgan had steadfastly refused to use the term 'kidnap' in relation to her son's disappearance. In her mind it conjured up images of criminals or terrorists. She considered that 'abduction' was far softer and, in any case, she would have preferred her son to have been taken by aliens…they always came back from that experience, she reasoned! Scott was not so sure.

"It's not over yet," replied Scott. "I need to bring some closure to it all. Besides, I owe it to Giulio to explain about his boat, so I'm going down to the marina to see him."

The Courier
James R. Vance

"Surely that can wait until next weekend or perhaps you could phone him."

"I'll spend a quiet day with you tomorrow, mother. I promise."

Mrs. Morgan could see that her son was determined to spend time with his friend and resigned herself to her role of caring, but not always needed, motherhood.

"I'll cook us a nice meal for later. What time will you be home, dear?"

"Not sure. Probably about six. I'll phone you if it's any later."

"What about lunch? Would you like me to make you some sandwiches?"

"No, I'll be fine. I'll get something to eat at Giulio's."

"Now be careful dear, you know how I'll worry about you."

"Don't fuss, I'll be okay."

Scott finished his guzzle and go breakfast, grabbed his Helly Hansen jacket and walked out into the freshness of a cold but sunlit late October morning. He jogged and raced towards the main road, revelling in the abandon of his regained freedom. Deciding against taking a bus, he made his way across to Mudchute to catch the Docklands Light Railway which would take him via Canary Wharf to Tower Gateway, where he could walk down to St. Katherine's Dock.

A train pulled in shortly after he had walked onto the platform. He sat in his seat, intrigued by the fact that he was somehow special amongst the other passengers on account of his fascinating adventure. *I bet they've all had the same dull, unexciting, normal week living their boring routine lives. If only they knew what I'd been up to!*

He chuckled out loud involuntarily. Some passengers turned and gave him peculiar looks. He decided to look through the window and watch the landscape pass by, but the reflection of his face in the glass still bore the expression of a broad smile. Twenty five minutes later he strode into St. Katherine's Dock to be greeted by the usual sound of ropes and pulleys jangling against the masts of the various craft which were swaying and bobbing in the light breeze wafting across the marina.

Welcome back, he thought and headed for Giulio's apartment. He was about to ring the bell against his friend's nameplate when he heard a familiar voice call his name. Giulio was already in the marina working on his cruiser.

"You're back!" he exclaimed. "How are you? You okay now?"

"Fine," shouted Scott and made his way to the entrance gate for boat owners.

Giulio rushed up and grasped his hand. "Come on down and tell me all about it. There's a flask of coffee here and some croissants. I only got half the story from the police. Hey, and guess what! My boat was nicked and then suddenly she re-appeared, same as you... just like alien abductions! When did you come home?"

"Late last night," replied Scott. "You should talk with my mother."

"Your mother?"

"Don't worry. It'll keep." Scott shook his head in disbelief at his friend's comment about aliens. "I need a favour, hope you can help me out."

"Sure," said Giulio, stepping down into the boat. "What is it?"

"I need to tell you about what happened first, and then you'll know why I need your help."

They settled down in the well of the Searay where Giulio poured the coffee and handed out the croissants while Scott related the main episodes of his adventure. His friend listened intently, engrossed by Scott's incredulous account of the previous week's events.

The enforced theft and part played by the Giuseppe drew Giulio closer to the action, almost as though he himself had played a part in the escapade. Scott finished his Boys Own style dramatic tale of bravado and heroics by asking the favour which now had context.

Giulio leaped from his seat. "Let's do it!" he cried. "Let's sail into the unknown! No time like the present. How about now?"

"Absolutely!" yelled Scott and they danced around hugging each other so much that the cruiser was in danger of capsizing. They collapsed onto the padded seats to regain their breath.

"It could be dangerous," said Scott, gasping from the sudden burst of energy.

"After what you've been through? No way. Here's to the dynamic duo!" Giulio raised his plastic coffee cup. In his mind it could have been champagne. "Let battle commence!"

*****

The incident room was buzzing with chatter as D.I. Massey entered briskly, refreshed from a solid night's sleep. He crossed to the large table adjacent to the wall boards where D.S. Turner was in deep discussion with D.S. Mullen and D.C. French. The various conversations in the room slowly reduced in volume until there was complete silence apart from the intermittent ringing of telephones in the main office.

"Good morning," began the inspector. "First of all, thanks for your professionalism yesterday, especially at Waterloo which was carried out swiftly and discreetly. The fact that the operation received no media coverage bears that out. Today, however, we have other assignments, but first I want to go back to the beginning to help clarify the situation."

As he spoke, he moved amongst the team who were either seated or standing around the room in groups. The silence from his audience added an air of electric excitement to the room.

"Through a stroke of good fortune we have unearthed some kind of smuggling operation which, we believe, uses schoolboys as couriers between Calais and Dover. As yet, we have no evidence as to what they carry, how many of them are involved and their individual names, apart from Luke Cannon, interviewed last night.

The Courier
James R. Vance

All we know is that at least one of them uses Waterloo station as a drop for the contraband and a pick-up point for the payment. He was interviewed last night with regard to the operation which you expertly conducted, but with no reference to any smuggling activity. It is imperative that those involved are not alerted to the fact that we are aware of their operation. The couriers are only a small link in the chain.

We have identified the school in France which appears to be the centre or origin of these activities. D.C. French has been tasked to liaise with the appropriate authorities over there to establish ownership of the school and to investigate an ex French customs official who works there and also his son who may be involved. The investigation into the incident which alerted us to what is going on has, as most of you know, developed into something of a fiasco.

Fortunately Scott Morgan has been returned safely, apparently none the worse for his experience, but the original suspects, namely David Joseph and his cousin Rebecca Joseph, will become the focus of our investigation, commencing today. Whilst we can pursue enquiries into the French connection, I believe that, if we are able to charge the Josephs with the abduction and detention of Scott Morgan, together with perverting the course of justice, we will also have the opportunity to delve more deeply into their role vis-à-vis the smuggling racket."

Massey paused before returning to the table. The silence amongst the team had been broken by a crescendo of animated murmers.

The inspector continued his briefing. "We'll start by initiating telephone intercepts at the residences of Frank Cannon, father of the youth interviewed last night, David Joseph at Barnes, Rebecca Joseph at her uncle's house and their shop in Hatton Garden. I also want twenty four hour surveillance on each property and alongside all that we will apply this morning for a search warrant for the house at Barnes.

I also want to collect as much CCTV footage as we can from Hatton Garden and from the interior of Joseph's jewellery

210

shop which must have some security surveillance, plus Westferry Road in the vicinity of Canary Wharf where there must be numerous cameras and finally from St. Katherine's Way leading up to Tower Gateway including the Dock itself. All footage needs to cover last Saturday, especially the period after twelve noon."

The hubbub around the room indicated that the team were more than happy to finally make in-roads into what so far had been a frustrating investigation. Massey was also somewhat relieved and pressed on.

"Excluding D.C. French and D.C. Croft who can formally liaise with the French, team members will be assigned by D.S. Turner and D.S. Mullen who will be organising the various tasks following this meeting. Any questions or points to raise?"

Turner spoke first. "How will we get a warrant for Barnes? Nothing's changed since the last refusal."

"Forensics have come up with David Joseph's prints on some of the fake banknotes which we planted and dropped from Blackfriar's bridge," replied Massey.

"Scott Morgan said he was held captive for a day or so at his previous house in Ashford. Are we checking that out?" asked Croft, who had sat in on Scott's interview.

"I've asked Sergeant Dawkins to arrange a visit with SOCO from Ashford nick and following their investigation they will liaise with our forensics team here, depending on what they find."

"The kids go back to school on Monday," said Mullen. "Are we making any special arrangements to keep an eye on them?"

"If there's any activity, it won't take place until they return on Friday and, hopefully, by then we should have a list of students at the school and particularly those who are not full-time boarders, in other words those who commute each week. The other thing to bear in mind is that, if there are several operating as couriers, not all may be travelling into Waterloo. Conversely, not all commuting students could be couriers. Consequently there is considerable work ahead as soon as we have a definitive list."

The Courier
James R. Vance

"When do we raid the house at Barnes?" asked McGovern, looking forward to some action.

"As soon as we get our hands on a warrant. With luck, sometime today," replied Massey. He looked around the room for further questions. "Okay, let's sort out how we share this out and get the show on the road."

Turner motioned his boss to one side. "Can I have a word, boss?" They moved to a corner of the room. "These fingerprints on the banknotes. When was this discovered? Anderson never mentioned it."

"Anderson doesn't know yet. I need a quiet word in his shell-like. It's the only way we'll get access."

"Bloody hell," whispered Turner. "You're putting your head on the line. Will he play ball?"

"He knows that you found the missing wood and the name plaques from the boat. He knows, you know and I know the guy's involved and we need to nail him, not just for the business with Scott, but maybe we can put pressure on him to open up the remaining can of worms. Anderson will play."

"But Crime Prosecution won't go ahead without the evidence."

"Don't worry, we'll give C.P.S. the evidence. David Joseph's a clever sod, so we've got to be a damn sight smarter than we have been so far. We'll arrest his cousin at the same time, either at St. John's Wood or at the shop. I'll leave you to sort out the two teams for that as soon as I've procured the necessary search warrant."

Massey rubbed his hands together. "The sparring's over. The Josephs are on the ropes at last."

"I'm pleased that you're excited. Me, I've a bad feeling about this one," said Turner. He leaned against the wall, arms folded. Anxiety showed in his face. "Don't ask me why. It's just something in here." He placed a hand over his chest.

"That's not in your nature. I'm the worrier, not you," said Massey, reassuringly."You should be aware that I'm just putting on a brave face and hoping that we can get a result." He smiled.

"Hey, here's something to cheer you. I received a call from Helen last night. Did you know she's getting married?"

"Married?" asked Turner in disbelief. "Who the hell to?"

"Some foreign diplomat, apparently."

"Well, I've not had an invite. When is it?"

"Next week. Maybe it's lost in the post."

"I didn't even know that she was involved with anyone."

"Well, that's sisters for you. Always keeping secrets from baby brother!"

"I'll be damned," muttered Turner.

Massey left the incident room as the general chit-chat grew in volume, leaving Turner to assign the various roles to the team. Now he could attempt to re-gather his thoughts, scrambled as they were.

Why these mixed emotions? I should be more than excited. After a week of poor results, the investigation's finally gathering pace. Surely we're within touching distance. Deep within, Massey was not so sure. *Maybe it's this bloody wedding I have to contend with. Whatever the reason I must admit that I also have a bad feeling!*

*****

Giulio guided the cruiser gently out of the marina into the river Thames and opened the throttle as they headed upstream towards Tower Bridge. The morning air was cool, but they could feel the warmth of the sun's rays on the backs of their lifejackets as they ploughed through the wash of a passing barge.

En route Scott was keen to point out the various key locations which figured in the dramatic events earlier in the week. They continued at a steady eight knots until Embankment Pier came into view where they intended to commence their own adventure.

"How many bridges did you say you counted?" shouted Giulio above the roar of the engine as they approached Hungerford Bridge.

The Courier
James R. Vance

"Unlucky thirteen," replied Scott laughing. "Knowing me, I probably missed a few. I can't even remember if I counted this one."

"Not to worry. Let's start with it and see where your calculations take us."

He opened the throttle once more and gathered speed as they headed towards Westminster and the Houses of Parliament where they had to cross almost to mid-stream to avoid the security exclusion zone. The river was unusually busy for the time of year, possibly due to the sudden change in the weather, but the journey was uneventful apart from the interesting landmarks of the capital which frequently came into view.

For Scott it was a most enjoyable experience in complete contrast to his previous trip along this stretch of the river. In between drinking the remainder of the coffee flask, they chatted, sang songs and committed to memory the number of bridges under which they had passed. After a steady cruise upriver the Giuseppe passed from the shadows of Hammersmith Bridge into bright sunlight, following the elongated curve of the river Thames towards Chiswick Eyot.

"I think that was bridge number thirteen," professed Guilio. "How far do you reckon after that one?"

"I think it was some way, yet. He definitely turned to port at some point."

"So we keep a lookout for houses with a boathouse on the far bank, then?"

"I guess so," replied Scott, feeling somewhat confused. It had seemed so straightforward and logical at the time. The reality of the moment was so different. Normally it would have been difficult finding somewhere in the dark which had only been seen previously in daylight. This excursion was quite the opposite. How weird!

They passed the playing fields of St. Paul's School and headed towards Barnes. Scott was beginning to consider abandoning the escapade when Giulio suddenly pointed at a small wooden boathouse, badly in need of repair. "How about that?" he cried.

As they drew level with the structure, Scott became excited by the emergence of an impressive house set back from the river beyond sloping gardens. Giulio throttled back and they coasted several metres beyond the property.

"What say we give it a try?" he shouted.

"Worth a shot," agreed his companion.

Giulio swung the cruiser across the river and steered it towards the far bank. One door of the boathouse was open, swinging slightly with the breeze. They reached out and pulled open the other door, simultaneously dragging the boat into the berthing bay. Giulio switched off the engine.

"Now what?" he asked.

"Let's sneak up to the house and see if it's the one."

"How will you know?"

"It already smells the same," declared Scott, recalling the dank, musty stench of his original visit.

The house itself towered above the broad landscaped garden. It seemed so much smaller from the river. A raised terrace topped off by ornamental balustrades jutted out centrally, spreading along almost two thirds of the building. Steps from the main lawn connected the garden area to this flag-stoned patio area, which, in turn, was overlooked by large glazed doors.

They crossed the grassy slope and ascended the steps. To their right, some additional stone steps dropped down to a lower paved area leading to double timber doors set into the building below ground floor level. Scott convinced himself that he passed through those doors into the cellar on their flight from the Embankment Pier, as a broad path led up to that corner from the garden.

Giulio followed his gaze. "The curtains are drawn across the patio doors," he announced. "Can't see inside, but those doors down there aren't properly closed. Are we going in?"

"We've come this far," sighed Scott.

"What if he's at home?"

The Courier
James R. Vance

"That's the whole point. I need to see him again."

They warily descended to the lower patio and pulled back one of the wooden doors. Stealthily they crept inside.

"Well?" whispered Giulio. "Is this it?"

Scott stood in the middle of the cellar and took stock of his surroundings for the second time in a week. The Atco mower and the strimmer were near the far wall. The sink was to his left. The boiler room was beyond the stone steps to the hallway upstairs. It seemed so tidy and huge, nothing like the recollection of his 'prison' of the previous week. He crossed towards the opening into the small room.

"Is that where you slept?" asked Giulio, joining him and peering into the gloomy interior.

Before Scott could reply, the door at the top of the stone steps opened, lights were switched on and voices were heard. They were trapped.

"Quick," said Scott, grabbing Giulio by the arm. "In here."

They stumbled into the boiler room and pressed themselves up against the far wall. At that moment the thermostat on the gas burners cut in and startled them both. Giulio imagined that his heartbeat was echoing across the cellar. The voices became more audible as two men descended the stone steps.

"What's this place used for, then?" asked one of the voices.

"Mostly gardening equipment and the like," replied the second voice.

Scott recoiled further behind the boiler. "That's him," he whispered. "It's the man!"

"Who's the other guy?" asked Giulio.

"Don't know...ssh!"

The footsteps of the men resounded as they walked across the concrete floor.

"I'd better take a look around," said the first voice.

"Be my guest," came the reply.

A cone of light from a torch wafted across the far wall of the recess and the footsteps moved closer to their hiding place.

"What's in here?"

"Just the boiler room for the central heating."

Suddenly the figure of D.S. Mullen appeared in the open doorway and the beam swung round to shine on two astonished faces.

"Well I never," declared Mullen, recognising them from previous encounters. He half turned to face the open door at the top of the stairs. "Guv, down here," he shouted. "In the cellar. There's something you ought to see."

Within seconds several pairs of feet belonging to D.I. Massey, D.S. Turner and two other detectives cascaded down the steps. David Joseph stood rooted to the middle of the cellar, his mind racing, wondering what the detective had discovered. Only the previous night after returning from Blackfriars, he had cleared all vestiges of Scott's internment. *What on earth had the man found?*

"What is it sergeant?" asked Massey as he reached the last step.

Scott's heart almost stopped. Giulio's was still thumping loudly.

"In here, guv," said Mullen, stepping to one side to allow the inspector access..

Massey peered into the recess and looked at the white enamelled central heating unit, not quite sure of its significance. Mullen reached past him shining the torch into the shadows of the far corner.

Massey immediately saw bricks flying in every direction!

Chapter 20

SATURDAY AFTERNOON: Considering that a police investigation was underway, the atmosphere in David Joseph's lounge had been most convivial. The curtains were drawn back and there was a splendid view across the terrace towards the river Thames. Several white-suited individuals from forensics were still about, meticulously gathering evidence. Two of them were in view down by the boathouse. David Joseph had been read his rights and charged with the theft of Giulio's cruiser and Scott's abduction.

He readily confessed to both charges and offered no resistance to being arrested and taken to Blackfriars for a detailed interview. Indeed he promised to co-operate fully with the inspector before he was led away by D.S. Mullen and D.C. McGovern.

Due to their discovery in the cellar Scott and Giulio were already on their way with D.C. Croft to explain their unexpected involvement. D.I. Massey and D.S. Turner remained in the lounge still rather taken aback by the outcome of their visit.

"It's a mystery," remarked Massey. "Why get involved in all that when he has all this?" He waved his hand, gesturing towards the lavish interior.

"I knew it was him," conceded Turner, "but there are so many unanswered questions."

"I get the impression that there's a hidden motive to all this. Anyway, I'd best be off. Can you follow on? Just check that we have all the evidence we need for a watertight case."

Massey left the room, leaving Turner by the patio doors. The detective sergeant stayed for a moment watching several sculls rowing their way downriver from Duke's Meadow. It seemed so idyllic, hardly a portent for tragedy.

The Courier
James R. Vance

Wearing a white protective suit, Anderson appeared in the room. "Just thought I'd let you know that we're almost done here."

"Found everything from the boathouse?"

"All bagged up and labelled."

"What about photographs?"

"All done. A couple of the lads are finishing off upstairs."

"Fine, I'll see you later. Thanks."

D.S. Turner was a 'black and white' detective, a trait inherited from his time with Massey. Somehow this investigation appeared 'grey'. He concurred with Massey that an air of mystery still pervaded. Maybe the strange sensation within was his burning ambition to tie up all the loose ends to get a result.

The forensic team leader left. Turner took a final look around the room, still trying to find a motive for David Joseph's actions. The success of arresting their prime suspect was slightly tarnished by his immediate offer of co-operation. Was the man covering for someone else? Was there an accomplice? Scott failed to recognise him in the line-up, for example. Was Scott involved in some way? Turner was overcome by foreboding. Were they hiding something more sinister? He anticipated a long night ahead.

*****

David Joseph sat at the table sipping coffee from a plastic beaker. His solicitor sat alongside him. A tape deck was positioned at the far end of the table. In front of the machine were several new cassettes, still in their wrappers. Massey and Turner sat facing the self-confessed offender. A digital camcorder mounted on the wall also recorded the interview.

The relaxed atmosphere at Barnes had been replaced by a more formal approach in keeping with the location and the severity of the charges. Breaking the immediate silence, a clock ticked rhythmically but quietly on the far wall.

"I need to draw your attention to the background first," said David. "Several years ago my father was involved in some dishonest activities. You are probably already aware of that. He received a 'smack on the wrist' suspended sentence. He was doing okay until a friend of his in the business put him onto what you might call a nice little earner. As I was taking a more active role during this time, it was passed to me to follow up."

"I take it you're referring to the smuggling activity?" queried Massey.

"Absolutely. It was a very 'cloak and dagger' operation, but it worked," replied David. "It relies on total anonymity for its security. That was really the selling point for me. Over the years we've used it a few times without any problems."

"What were you using it for?" asked Turner

"Diamonds, precious stones," replied David, "and occasionally watches. Sometimes the real McCoy like Rolex, Gucci etc. Sometimes fakes. I suppose you'll also be charging me with VAT avoidance."

The solicitor leaned over and whispered something in David's ear.

Massey smiled, "Perhaps we'll leave that to Revenue and Customs. Anyway how does this foolproof system work?"

"I'll come to that later, if you don't mind," said David. "I want to explain to you why I've spent the last week drawing you in. For the past few months, I've been trying to negotiate a deal on a unit in Canary Wharf to expand the business.

One day, following a meeting which was principally about security, not just of the shop but of the whole Docklands area, London was hit by the terrorist attack on the underground. I immediately had recollections of the bombings by the I.R.A at St. Mary's Axe, Canary Wharf and Bishopsgate. I particularly remember the carnage at Bishopsgate as a friend almost lost her life there. Bizarrely, this same friend lost a colleague on July the seventh at Edgeware Road."

He took another sip of coffee. "Suddenly, I realised that this foolproof system as you called it, could allow more sinister items through, other than diamonds. It was then that I decided to end it, not just our involvement, but to actually stop these couriers from operating."

The Courier
James R. Vance

"So why didn't you just call Revenue and Customs, even anonymously?" asked Massey.

"I suppose it was arrogance and a little bit of greed," replied David. "I got it into my head that I would put a spanner in the works and keep on until they gave up. I worked out a scam where I could also make a final financial killing. Don't forget, I'd had some benefit from the system and in some way I was reluctant to shop them, as it were.

How does the saying go, 'honour amongst thieves'? Unfortunately, as you know, it all went pear-shaped, thanks to young Scott. I panicked slightly but then came up with a plan to recover the cash in the briefcase."

"Why did you make it so complicated?" asked Turner.

"I suppose to confuse you. As it unfolded it became a game and, strangely, I think Scott was beginning to enjoy it too. When I could see that the cash was gone, replaced by your interesting toy money, I came up with plan B. I needed to return Scott safely... you must understand that I could never have harmed him....and I still had to leave you with something to investigate further, namely the courier lad at the station."

"But why did you contact us about your missing boat?" asked Turner, still curious about his motive over that.

"Trying to be clever, again. I thought if I reported it stolen, it would deflect from me, just in case it was traced back. Initially I was just going to use one boat, the one from St. Katherine's Dock, but I thought that by using two, I could send you one way down the river, whilst I went in the other direction. In actual fact, it worked, until Scott and his pal appeared on the scene earlier today. I still don't know how he knew where I lived."

"Apparently, even though it was dark, by listening to the difference in the sound of the engine, he was able to count the bridges between Embankment Pier and your gaff," declared Turner smugly.

David smiled, "He's a clever sod, but the disguise fooled him. What you see is not always what you get."

"Why go to that much trouble?" queried Turner.

221

"Just part of the game and to protect Scott. Despite his involvement, the less he knew, the better it was for him. I anticipated an I.D. parade if you caught up with me. He may have lied, but I didn't want to subject him to have to make that choice. Consequently I shaved it all off."

"You've wasted a lot of valuable police time with this game of yours," said Massey sternly. "Let's get back to the real issue here. I want to know in detail how this smuggling operation works. First, though, we'll take a quick break."

He looked at the clock and his wristwatch. "Interview terminated at fifteen ten." The inspector switched off the tape recorder, removed and sealed the tape. The two detectives left the interview room.

"What do you think?" Massey stood by the front office with Turner.

"He's a total fruitcake," replied the sergeant, unapologetically.

"I'd say he was full of his own shit. Either that or he's an eccentric genius."

"Genius!" exclaimed Turner. "Could you imagine having him as a snout? It'd be like taking part in the Crystal Maze every time he fed you some info. I tell you he's nuts."

"It's a bit worrying, though."

"What is?"

"The possibility of someone smuggling in, say, components for a dirty bomb, apart from the chemical or biological agents themselves."

"I think he's just being alarmist. He sees himself as some caped crusader saving the world from the threat of terrorism. How are schoolkids going to get their hands on anything as deadly as that?"

"They're merely the couriers. I'm more concerned about who's supplying them and more importantly who could be on the receiving end."

"Well let's find out how it works and then we can snuff it out."

The Courier
James R. Vance

"Well he certainly seems prepared to talk about it, but I'm not totally convinced by his reasons for blowing it wide open."

The detectives returned to the interview room.

*****

Having explained their presence in the cellar at Barnes, Scott and Giulio were given a lift back to David Joseph's house by D.C. Croft to collect the Giuseppe. She had been asked by Massey to take down a short statement of how they had found the house and entered it so easily. His intention was to re-interview Scott later to corroborate any testimony elicited from David Joseph.

From the general conversation en route, she realised that Scott had been quite impressed by his captor. For the most part his comments on his adventure were quite complimentary, especially towards the treatment which he had received. She deemed it to be nothing more than hero worship from an impressionable youth.

A uniformed policeman was waiting near the main gateway. Behind him, blue and white police tapes with the repetitive message POLICE LINE DO NOT CROSS were blowing in the wind, blocking the entrance to the driveway.

"Is there anyone else still here?" asked the detective.

"I believe there are a couple of forensic guys inside the house," replied the officer.

"I'd better go with you," said Croft, turning to Scott and Giulio.

She escorted the two young men through the house onto the rear terrace. They crossed the garden to the boathouse where the Giuseppe was still moored and she waited until they had safely cast off to return downstream towards the capital.

Back in the house she chatted for a while with the two white-suited scene-of-crime officers as they packed up to leave. She wandered around the opulent rooms wondering how someone with this lifestyle could have risked everything for such a stupid scam. Opening the door to the cellar she found that the light had been left on.

The Courier
James R. Vance

She decided to snoop around what, until recently, had been Scott's temporary prison. It was extremely tidy, considering all the action that had taken place earlier. The door to the garden was still ajar and she closed it. Standing by the steps, it dawned on her that forensics had almost certainly missed this room, otherwise the door would have been closed. The commotion caused by finding the boys hiding in the recess had distracted everyone from their systematic search of the house.

There was not a lot to see apart from a mower, a strimmer, some gardening tools and a shelf full of paint pots and seed packets. He must be a keen gardener, she thought as she rummaged through the collection of packets. There were several varieties of flower seeds in addition to salad items such as tomato, lettuce, celery, spring onions and a mixture of vegetables.

He needs a greenhouse for this lot. It's amazing how all these tiny seeds grow into….. She suddenly held a packet with larger than usual seeds. Lettuce, was printed on the outside. She picked up another similarly labelled packet, yet the contents were barely palpable. Why the difference? Curious, she peeled open the packet with the larger lumps and looked inside. She gasped and poured the contents onto the bench. They glistened brightly, reflecting the light from above. "Wow!" she cried.

*****

"The initial contact with my old man was by phone," declared David Joseph as he began to explain the background to the smuggling operation. "He received a call requesting his mobile number and that was it. A few days later he received a text message giving him a contact number to call and a password.

However, he was instructed to use a public phone, not his mobile or land line. He made the call. A man using the alias, The Fixer, explained that the number he had dialled would be changed weekly or fortnightly for security reasons. Any new number would be communicated by text message.

He was also told that all orders for goods had to given to that number by public phone. It could also be used in an emergency. Confirmation of his order, its value and details of the drop would be transmitted by text to my father's mobile, identified by the original password. He was also informed that the newsstand at Waterloo would be his designated drop point, unless notified to the contrary. A few days later he was requested to collect an empty black briefcase which would be left by a schoolboy at the newsstand. Several weeks went by until my father decided to give it a go."

"I assume that it worked," commented Massey. "What I don't understand is how the various parties involved receive their cut."

"Not entirely sure," replied David. "I believe that the courier takes his slice of the cake from the cash which is handed over for the goods. Where the rest ends up, I haven't a clue."

"This courier," asked Turner, "is it always the same one?"

"I've not always seen them, but of those I have spotted I've never recognised them, so I presume there are several and they're interchangeable."

"You have no idea of their identities or who this so-called Fixer is?" inquired Massey.

"He doesn't have a French accent, does he?" interjected Turner, desperately seeking a lead.

David shrugged his shoulders. "I thought that's now your baby. I handed you a courier on a plate yesterday. Why don't you ask him?"

"That reminds me," said Massey seriously. "What happened to the contents of the original case which you casually lifted from our friend?"

"What original case?" asked David innocently.

"We have you on video switching cases shortly after Scott's outburst."

"Me? No, you must be mistaken," said David.

"What was in the briefcase, diamonds?"

"I don't know what you're talking about. I merely picked up a briefcase filled with schoolbooks."

The Courier
James R. Vance

Massey remained impassive, hoping that Tony Anderson and his team may have found some evidence at Barnes. "Okay, let's move on. You said earlier that you were concerned because something more sinister could be smuggled in. What did you mean by that?"

David's solicitor leaned across and said, "You don't have to answer that."

"I'm only after your opinion," remarked Massey. "You made the comment."

"I was thinking of drugs, I suppose."

"But it was in the context of the terrorism threat when you inferred the possibility."

"I'm no expert so I can't say," admitted David, "but you never know...."

David's solicitor leaned forward. "This interview seems to be going nowhere. Are you bringing any criminal charges against my client or not?"

Massey leaned back in his chair. "We'll take another short break. That will give us time to consider, not what felonies we're charging him with, but with how many. I'll send some coffee in for you. In the meantime, maybe you could advise your client as to the number of years he's likely to go down for."

The detectives checked the time again, switched off the tape recorder, removed and sealed the tape and left the room.

"I tend to agree with his brief," said Turner once they were outside in the corridor. "We've obtained his motives for his charade, flimsy though they are. The mechanics of the smuggling op seem fairly logical, but at the end of the day, we're no nearer to the organisation behind it all."

"I'm still unsure whether he's telling us everything," replied Massey. "If we could put more pressure on him, maybe we could delve a bit deeper."

"Like throwing the book at him," added Turner. "Not just kidnapping and theft, but extortion, perverting the course of justice, wasting police time, house-breaking at Ashford, smuggling. Is there more?"

The Courier
James R. Vance

"He doesn't seem too bothered about the charges. Perhaps he thinks we don't have sufficient evidence. No, I think he wants to cut a deal. He's given us so much already. Maybe he does have more but wants something in return. When we go back in, you lay all that lot on him. I'll see what I can get from him by offering to drop the debatable ones. Don't forget he still has direct access to this Fixer guy. Let's use him."

"Do you reckon he'll play ball?"

"Absolutely. He's already admitted to 'playing the game'. Now's his chance to play with the big boys!"

The detectives returned to the interview room and dangled the carrot. It was like a game of chess. Each opponent, having made a move, waited for the next move. They were playing David at his own game.

"How do you want to play it?" asked David finally.

A compromise was reached. An off-the-record discussion resulted in his promised co-operation in helping to expose the organisation behind the smuggling operation. In return, all charges would be dropped apart from abduction and theft plus an assurance that Rebecca would be exonerated due to her minimal participation and the fact that she had never been previously involved. She would merely receive a reprimand.

Turner was still mystified that he had agreed so readily. Massey explained that his involvement in the actual receipt of contraband goods would be taken up by Revenue and Customs. They released him on unconditional bail to report back on Monday morning.

*****

Later that afternoon the police officers on duty at Barnes were recalled and the house was handed back to David Joseph. He was driven home by his solicitor following his release from Blackfriars. The easterly wind had brought some heavy cloud which, in turn, had resulted in some intermittent drizzle. Feeling the drop in temperature now that the sun had disappeared, he opted for a hot shower and a change into warmer casual clothes.

The Courier
James R. Vance

Refreshed, he headed for the kitchen and sliced open a small baguette. He filled it with some crisp salad, two slices of left-over cooked beef and smeared it with course grain mustard. With a mug of hot coffee in his other hand he sat in the lounge with his snack watching the river through a sudden heavy downpour.

He decided to spend the night at his father's house. This would give him an opportunity to put him and Rebecca in the picture with regard to recent events.

Since the unexpected discovery of Scott in his cellar, he had been trying to make sense of the youngster's intrusion. He concluded that his companion of the previous week had wanted to make contact with him in a genuinely amicable kind of way.

With these thoughts on his mind during his improvised snack, he devised a plan to enlist Scott's help in thwarting the police in their eventual prosecution of him. He determined that it would be propitious to sow some seeds in that direction at the earliest opportunity, despite the prospect of a court appearance in the not too distant future.

He resolved, therefore, to drive to St. John's Wood via Docklands. En route he stopped to purchase a huge bouquet of flowers to placate Mrs. Morgan. It was dark when he arrived at Westferry Road and the rain had gradually turned to sleet. He parked the car and tentatively dashed across the paved walkway using the bouquet as an umbrella against the prevailing conditions. He confronted the same door where he had stood exactly one week previously. This time he had to ring the bell. The keys were back with Scott.

Mrs. Morgan presented herself in the doorway to be confronted by a smartly dressed young gentleman and a huge floral bouquet.

"Mrs. Morgan, I presume," said David. "Is Scott at home?"

She looked down at the bouquet, her expression vividly betraying her concerns. David immediately recognised the implication. "Oh, sorry," he apologised, "these are for you." He thrust the flowers towards her.

228

The Courier
James R. Vance

Scott's mother took them from him, totally bemused by the odd behaviour of this stranger at her door. At a loss for words, she was saved by the sound of Scott bounding down the stairs.

"Wow, it's you!" he cried.

"Who, dear?" asked his mother, even more confused.

"Tell you later," replied Scott and almost dragged the sleet-covered David into the lounge.

"Well, thank you for the flowers, whoever you are," said Mrs. Morgan, smiling graciously as she closed the door on the inclement weather beyond.

"My pleasure," said David. "Allow me to introduce myself, David Joseph, a close friend of your son."

"Oh, are you one of the boat people?" she asked, sniffing the bouquet.

"Yes, I also own a cruiser," he replied, hoping that she wasn't implying something else.

"I'll leave you to talk shop then, whilst I find a vase." She disappeared towards the kitchen, admiring the bouquet.

They sat alongside each other on the leather sofa near the window. Scott seemed delighted with the unforeseen visit which boded well for David's proposition.

"They let you go, then?" asked Scott, excited that his hero was liberated from police custody.

"Temporarily," replied David. "They've dropped the minor infringements of the law in exchange for my help in busting this smuggling ring."

"Great. So you're going to be working with the police?"

"Apparently, but they still intend to take me to court and prosecute me."

"For what?"

"Kidnapping you and nicking Giulio's cruiser."

"That's a bit much when you've offered to help them, especially as I told them you looked after me and had no intentions of harming me."

The Courier
James R. Vance

"Unfortunately that's not the way they see it. My solicitor says I could go down for between five and ten years, if the court finds me guilty."

Scott was devastated. He rose from the sofa and suddenly spun round animatedly to face his hero. "But they need me to prove that you did it," he cried.

"What are you getting at?" asked David, quietly confident that Scott was about to save him the effort of outlining his own preconceived scheme.

"I could say that you didn't kidnap me, that I went willingly."

"But what about the note, the threats and your imprisonment?"

"I could say it was all part of the plan."

"What plan?" asked David, realising that he might have to join in with some prompting.

"Not sure. Maybe we could think one up."

"I could say that I enlisted your help to alert the police about the smuggling operation and together we contrived a scheme to lead them in the right direction."

"Wicked! I'll have to change my statement, though." Deep in thought, Scott paced the room. "I know, I'll just say that you told me to give them that story to protect me. You said all along that the blindfolds, et cetera were for my own protection, and come to think of it, that's what I put in my statement."

"There's also the fact that we stole Giulio's boat."

"And the other one," lamented Scott.

David grinned. "The other one was my own boat, but that's another story."

"So we only nicked Giulio's," muttered Scott, somewhat relieved in the misguided belief that one stolen boat was not as bad as two. He sat down again and leaned towards David, smiling.

"No, we didn't."

"Didn't what?"

"We didn't nick Giulio's cruiser. We borrowed it. Don't forget, I have the keys and often take it out. You returned it. I just kept it longer than normal!" he declared.

"Would you two young gentlemen like some coffee?" chirped a maternal voice from the kitchen.

*****

Massey arranged to meet up with Turner, Mullen and McGovern on Sunday morning to discuss their options. Acute indigestion flooded his chest with a painful sensation as he left the office. He had not eaten a substantial meal since leaving France. His mind was focussed on food when he was interrupted by a breathless D.C. Croft as she entered the building.

"Can I have a word, sir?"

They withdrew into a side room, where she described her discovery in the cellar at Barnes.

"Where are the packets now?" asked Massey.

D.C. Croft dug deep into the side pocket of her waterproof and extracted a sealed plastic bag. "I think this is all of them. I searched the rest of the cellar and some of the other packets, but they were genuine. They all contained just seeds."

"You'd better book them in with forensics as part of the evidence recovered from the scene. They probably won't be needed for our case, but Revenue and Customs will certainly be interested. So he's still telling lies after all," mused the inspector.

"Beg your pardon, sir?" asked the detective constable.

"Oh, just reflecting on something that David Joseph said during his interview. We may have to use them if we find he's been telling porkies."

The inspector rose, thanked the D.C. for her initiative and headed home for food. Massey was tired. There was a conflict between mind and body. Despite his leather coat, the cold blustery chill of the night cut through him. The car heating system was a welcome antidote to the sick state of his aching physical well-being.

The Courier
James R. Vance

He reached Streatham feeling somewhat revived by the warmth afforded by the car's interior. Once inside his flat, he settled for a convenience meal of boil-in-the-bag fish with basmati rice before retiring to bed. He switched on a bedside lamp and started making some notes in preparation for the following day's meeting with his key team. Within minutes the telephone rang.

"Hello, Raymond, Dyson here. I think we need a little chat. How about tomorrow morning, say ten thirty. Let's make it fairly informal. Meet you at The Crusting Pipe in Covent Garden. Okay?"

"Fine," replied Massey, "Sorry I missed briefing you tonight. It was rather late when we finished and I think you had already left the building."

"Not to worry. You can bring me up to speed tomorrow. Good night."

Massey replaced the handset, pondering over his superior's unusual suggestion. It was totally out of character to want a Sunday meeting and in such a strange setting. What was his motive?

He decided to make more notes and contact his colleagues to keep the afternoon as opposed to the morning free for their individual team meeting. Maybe he would have something interesting to pass on from the Covent Garden rendezvous. His digestive system appeared to have eased following his meal, but his chest and arms ached irritatingly. He decided to call it a day and eventually fell asleep.

The Courier
James R. Vance

Chapter 21

SUNDAY MORNING: Massey decided to drive into central London as there was no congestion charge on a Sunday morning. He parked just off St. Martin's Lane and walked towards the West Piazza of Covent Garden. It was very busy, mostly tourists milling about the various café bars and restaurants. He crossed towards the Apple Market where the stall holders were selling their hand-crafted wares in a lively and colourful atmosphere. At the far end he could see a trio of performers entertaining the on-looking crowd with their antics.

Leaving the busy central area he descended the stairs into the lower courtyard where Detective Chief Inspector Dyson was seated at a table outside the Crusting Pipe Wine Bar.

"Good morning, Raymond," said the chief inspector, casually dressed in pressed Prada jeans, open-necked check shirt and powder blue lambs wool sweater.

Massey nodded in acknowledgement and joined his superior at the table.

"Coffee or would you prefer an early morning aperitif?" asked his boss.

"Coffee will be fine, thank you."

"Miss, over here please." He beckoned a young waitress. "What would you like, Raymond, expresso, latte, cappuccino?"

"Whatever. I don't really mind. You choose."

"Two large cappuccinos, my dear."

The waitress turned on her heels and walked away.

"I thought that you normally spent Sunday morning on the golf course," remarked Massey.

The Courier
James R. Vance

"Sometimes, Raymond, avoiding the rough is not just restricted to the fairways. This current case of yours. How is it progressing?"

"I believe we've tied up most of the loose ends with regard to our jeweller friend. We're now ready to move on the French connection which I outlined at our previous briefing."

"You have a game plan?"

"I've arranged a meeting this afternoon with some of the team to discuss how we move it forward." Massey was wondering where this was leading. He could have reported any outcome from his team discussion in the office. Why had he been invited here, and on a Sunday? He looked across at Dyson. "Is there a problem?"

"Ah, coffee," declared Dyson as the waitress reappeared with a tray..

The pause in the conversation made Massey uneasy. Should he repeat the question or wait? He decided to unwrap the complimentary biscuit served with the cappuccino. The chief inspector did likewise and also popped a sugar lump into the froth of his coffee. He looked out across the busy lower piazza.

"If you didn't know any better, you could be sitting at this table anywhere in Europe. Yet, here we are in the City of London, the cosmopolitan capital of democracy. This is special, Raymond. I'm sure you will agree that this is worth protecting. Despite the immense changes in our society, we still have our heritage and our traditions."

He leaned back on his chair and waved his arm in a semicircle taking in the panorama. "Over there we have St. Paul's Cathedral. Beyond that stands the Tower of London. To our right we find Buckingham Palace, Westminster Abbey, the Houses of Parliament and Big Ben, all symbols of our proud nation. Close by we find Bow Street, our ancestral home. Behind me stand the Royal Courts of Justice, which have presided over some of our most notorious trials. We must ensure that they epitomize our democratic way of life for future generations. It is our duty and as guardians of the law we must ensure that we perform that duty to the best of our abilities. Do you not agree?"

Massey nodded and sipped his coffee. To be invited to Covent Garden for a lecture on the merits of London's tourist attractions was not his ideal way of passing a Sunday morning.

"With regard to your current investigation, I believe it to be in the best interests for all concerned that the time has come to engage with other agencies," continued Dyson. "What do you think?"

"Such as?" asked Massey, not wishing to commit his true feelings. *The wily old bastard's up to something.*

"Are we dealing with smugglers or terrorists?" asked Dyson.

"The only evidence so far is of a rather sophisticated smuggling operation," replied Massey. "However, that doesn't rule out the possibility of it being used to bring in some pretty lethal merchandise."

"What do you think are the odds on that?"

"From the interview with David Joseph, I'm of the opinion that it was pure conjecture. There's obviously the possibility of drugs. He's admitted receiving diamonds amongst other valuable items and we now have hard evidence in support of that, but terrorism paraphernalia..." Massey shrugged his shoulders. "At this moment in time I can't see a connection to such a group."

"But it could not be ruled out?"

"We could test it."

"Test it? How do you mean, test it?"

"Joseph still has access to the system. He could simply ask for something of that nature and see what response he gets."

"Dangerous ground. Is he still in custody?"

Massey recounted the details of the previous evening's interview and his encounter with D.C. Croft as he left the station. The superior officer listened intently and referred back to the possibility of using other agencies.

"I was initially considering handing the case over to Revenue and Customs or, in the event of a more sinister threat, to the Terrorism Unit. If there was a possibility of, say, bio-terrorism involvement, there's a dedicated unit within Interpol based at Lyon in France.

At the end of the day, however, I do not wish to provoke a major security alert and be left with egg on my face, if we are only dealing with some petty V.A.T. dodgers. I need substantial evidence. Do you think you and your team can provide that without alerting the enemy, as it were, and treading on the wrong toes?"

"How far will your mandate allow us to go?"

"As far as the first sniff of a terrorist involvement. No further than that. How trustworthy is this Joseph chappie?"

"Until D.C. Croft's discovery, I was fairly confident. Now I'm not so sure."

"Is there any other way of sounding out this mystery so-called Fixer?"

"Not without sending up flares and blowing it wide open."

"I suggest you keep your contact on a very tight rein and supervise his every move. I want to be informed every step of the way. This meeting of yours this afternoon, who will be present?"

"Turner, Mullen and McGovern."

"Keep an eye on McGovern. I'm not too sure about his attitude. He can be a little gung-ho. Stay with just those three. The fewer who know what is going on, the better."

"I'll need to keep D.C. French involved as he's liaising with the gendarmerie across the water."

"Fine, but keep him abreast of things on a need to know basis. Can I leave you to push on with it?"

"No problem. I'll update you tomorrow."

"How about that aperitif now," suggested Dyson. "We can toast your forthcoming success." The chief inspector called a waitress over and ordered two dry Martinis.

One phone-call to D.I. Massey later that day would change everything.

*****

The Courier
James R. Vance

David Joseph had been unable to sleep. After rising early, he showered, dressed in some warm casual clothes and jumped in his car to take an early Sunday morning drive into Regents Park. On his return he found Rebecca still asleep so he opted for a leisurely walk into Kilburn. He returned later with a selection of Sunday newspapers. Rebecca was busy preparing vegetables in the kitchen.

"I thought that we were going out for Sunday lunch," he remarked, spreading open a copy of the Telegraph on the kitchen table.

"I decided to treat you," replied Rebecca. "There was some fresh salmon to use up and I thought it would be a nice change to enjoy a healthy meal at home. After the events of last week, we could do with some time together."

"Where's the old man?" asked her cousin, somewhat engrossed in his newspaper.

"Still pottering about in the garden, I believe. What he finds to do at this time of year I'll never know. At his age he should be relaxing and besides, the cold weather isn't good for him with his arthritis. Do you want to speak with him?"

"Not really," replied David. "I have no inclination to elaborate further on last night's explanation of my involvement with the police." His father had been far from impressed by his son's convoluted story following his late arrival at the house on the previous evening. The angry tirade had driven David to bed where he had spent most of the night mulling over his self-imposed disquiet and disaffection with the world in general.

"There's some fresh coffee in the filter if you fancy a hot drink to warm you," suggested Rebecca. David was still wearing his jacket and a scarf despite the warmth of the kitchen.

"I'm fine, thanks." Conscious of his outer clothing, he disappeared upstairs to change into something more appropriate for a centrally heated residence. A mobile phone on the nearby pine dresser signalled the receipt of a text. It was Isaac's mobile. Rebecca picked it up and opened the message.

The Courier
James R. Vance

'YOUR COVER HAS BEEN BROKEN. NOT ACCEPTABLE.
YOUR CONTRACT IS TERMINATED.'

It was from The Fixer. She called out to David, who
responded by bounding down the stairs whilst still easing himself
into an F.C.U.K. sweatshirt.

"What does it mean, terminated?" asked Rebecca.

"I presume that we can no longer import merchandise
through that channel," said David. "Shit. That's something else I'll
have to explain to the old man."

"No time like the present," quipped his cousin.

"I'll phone first to see if he'll change his decision," replied
David and explained to his cousin the terms of his commitment to
the police. He opened his wallet and withdrew a slip of paper
which, Rebecca assumed, contained the current contact number.
He reached over to pick up the mobile.

"I thought that you were supposed to use a public line,"
said Rebecca.

"Sod it," replied David. "If he can be awkward, so can I."
He dialled the number. It came up unobtainable.

"Damn him," muttered David. "He's already changed the
number so that we can't contact him."

"You had better talk to your father," suggested his cousin.

David slammed down the mobile and opened the door to
the garden. Rebecca followed him as far as the kitchen door and
watched him as he crossed the patio. He glanced around. No sign
of Isaac. He walked across to the garden shed and looked inside.
Again there was no trace.

A path led from the wooden shed through a rustic arch,
dense with Himalayan clematis. Beyond the arch and the adjoining
conifer hedge stretched a small vegetable plot which occupied
most of Isaac's time in the garden. His participation in the business
had decreased since David had assumed more control.
Consequently he had filled his expanding leisure hours with his
favourite pastime. The garden in itself had become quite a feature.

Some garden tools were strewn on the pathway in some
disorder. This was strange as his father was always tidy and

methodical. At the far side a short interwoven fence formed a screen which, in turn, hid an incinerator and compost container. He continued his search and reached the wooden fence.

The legs of his father's outstretched body jutted from the rear of the barrier. There appeared to be no movement from the crumpled figure lying amongst the scattered debris of decaying garden matter. David bent down towards the lifeless body of his father.

*****

"How about VX as an agent? That's what they used in the missiles in that film 'The Rock'," said McGovern.

"This is reality, not bloody Hollywood. It's too damn complicated," replied Mullen.

"Well, what about Sarin gas? That's what those Japanese nutters used in the Tokyo underground about ten years ago," continued McGovern.

"Why not keep it simple?" suggested Turner. "Ask for a small quantity of a virus like smallpox or that ebola one. That's reckoned to be lethal."

"I think we're missing the point here," interjected Massey. "We're talking about kids bringing in a biological warfare agent."

"I thought the plan was for Joseph to find out if it was available through his hot-line, not to actually have it delivered," remarked Turner.

"I'm just afraid that it could slip through the net. Think of the worst case scenario. We order it. They set the wheels in motion. We monitor the activity which it creates and catch them at it. But, let's say that we mess up or there's a misunderstanding with the French and it passes through the system. Some young lad could be carrying a deadly virus in his briefcase which he spills out over Waterloo station and we become public enemy number one!"

The four detectives had been sitting in the incident room for some time now. The agenda was focussed on their strategy to uncover the organisation behind the smuggling operation. Alongside of that they had to ascertain whether it could be infiltrated by a terrorist group. Returning to the original objective, Turner put forward a suggestion.

"How about if we made tentative enquiries about biological agents, but ordered something less destructive like a quantity of drugs? With that ploy we could monitor their activities at the other end and still discover if they had access to a more sinister market."

"How can you say that drugs are less destructive?" challenged Ricky Mullen.

"You know what I mean. A small quantity of coke or H isn't going to wipe out half the population of London."

"I can live with that," said Massey.

"So does half the population of London!" joked McGovern.

Alongside the repartee, they set about writing a script for David Joseph to use in his call to The Fixer. The atmosphere was buoyant in the belief that they were closing in on making a breakthrough. Massey brought them back down to earth when he recounted the content of his meeting with D.C.I. Dyson.

"I don't fuckin` believe it," exclaimed McGovern. "We do all the leg work then hand it over to bloody Special Ops and they get all the glory. Forget the drugs. Order that fuckin` ebola stuff. Let them sniff that up their bloody noses."

"I'm afraid it's out of our hands," said Massey quietly. "We have to be professional and ensure that we're squeaky clean on our part. If they then cock it up, that's their problem."

"I agree," said Turner. "Let's ensure we set them up with a perfect sting. If it goes wrong in its later stages, at least we'll come up smelling of roses."

"We should set the bastards up so that it does go wrong," declared McGovern.

"Knowing Special Ops, they'll manage that quite well without our help!" added Mullen.

That final remark eased their frustrations and they discussed the detail of their tactics. The words of D.C.I. Dyson were still ringing in Massey's ears about keeping David Joseph on a tight rein..How great a risk was there in trusting him? Could a strategy be devised where they had complete control all the time?

The Courier
James R. Vance

The complexities were immense. They were about to become involved in a scenario which could have fatal consequences, not just for those involved, but for the population of one of the world's major cities.

They were interrupted by a W.P.C. who entered the room and addressed D.I. Massey. "There's an urgent call for you, sir. Would you like me to put it through here?"

"Fine," replied the inspector, relieved by the break.

She left the room and a moment later the telephone rang.

"D.I. Massey, here."

"Good afternoon, Inspector. This is D.I. James at St John's Wood. I believe you have been investigating the Joseph family in our area. I suggest that you get yourself over to their house asap. Isaac Joseph is dead. A single bullet through the back of his head."

*****

There were road blocks on Kilburn High Road, Belsize Road, Abbey Road and Maida Vale. Traffic in the area was gridlocked. Fortunately it was not a weekday. Massey and Turner sped past the standing vehicles, flashing lights and siren clearing the way through. They parked up beyond the police cordon in Kilburn Priory and walked up the slight incline towards the square where the Josephs lived. It appeared to be isolated by armed police. A loudspeaker van toured the area asking residents to remain inside. Helicopters hovered above, adding menacing roars to the scene. The dramatic activity created the impression of a war zone. Massey saw only brick walls.

D.I. James met them at the entrance to the house and escorted the two detectives into a lounge where David and Rebecca were in conversation with a uniformed officer.

"I'll leave you to it," said the local detective inspector and beckoned the uniform to vacate the room.

It was the first time that Massey had seen Rebecca in the flesh. Despite smudges from her make-up…she had obviously been crying…she was far more beautiful than what he had observed on the video sequence at Waterloo. David introduced his

241

cousin and the two officers shook her hand. Massey recalled later her soft, delicate skin, comparing her to a china doll. They offered their condolences to both of them.

David was comparatively calm. "It was not meant to be him," he lamented. "It was my fault. The execution was for me."

Rebecca stroked his arm tenderly.

"Tell me what happened," said Massey calmly.

David and Rebecca described their morning at the house up to the moment when Isaac's body was discovered beyond the vegetable patch.

"Rest assured, we'll find the perpetrators," promised the inspector. "We are already working on a plan to flush them out."

"There's something else you ought to know," whispered David, "something that Becky and I decided not to tell the officers here." He explained about the text message, adding, "….with no contact number, your plan of action is probably a non-starter."

"What did you mean by the execution being for you?"

"It was my scam at the station which kick-started this chain of events. They must have known that I was responsible."

"Who are 'they'?"

"Your guess is as good as mine, Inspector," replied David Joseph.

Massey stood and looked directly at David and Rebecca. "We'll get the bastards even if we have to tear apart that school in France stone by stone."

"School?" asked Rebecca. "What school?"

"It was part of the set-up," explained David.

Massey turned his attention to Turner. "Let's have a word with forensics before we leave."

"What about tomorrow morning?" asked David.

"Spend the time with your cousin. I think she needs some t.l.c. and perhaps an explanation," replied Massey, unable to take his eyes off the young lady. "I'll be in touch. Call me if you come across anything which may help our enquiries."

The two detectives turned to leave. "Can you direct me to your garden?" asked Massey.

The Courier
James R. Vance

Turner's mobile rang as they stepped from the kitchen into a garden which was awash with white-suited forensic officers.

"I'll catch you up," he said to Massey and moved to a quiet part of the lawn. It was Mullen with further awesome news..

"You're not going to believe this. There's been a major explosion at Primrose Hill. They reckon it's a car bomb. At least two dead."

"Bloody hell," exclaimed Turner.

"Wait for the rest of it. The car was on Frank Cannon's driveway. We're already on our way."

"Shite Ricky! What have we got ourselves into? I'll tell the boss and doubtless see you there as soon as we've finished here."

Turner raced down the garden and broke the news.

"Well, we've certainly opened a can of worms," commented Massey. Maybe Detective Chief Inspector Dyson would get his own way after all.

Chapter 22

SUNDAY AFTERNOON: Massey's mind was racing as they approached Primrose Hill. From one war zone to another. He felt as though they were stepping into a live newsreel of a suicide bomb massacre in Al Fallujah or Mosul. Since the occupation, the Iraqi people confronted carnage like this, worse than this, every day of their terror-filled lives.

How did they cope? How did the security forces cope? Besides having to deal with such blood baths, their own lives were in constant jeopardy. And here it was once again on the mainland of the United Kingdom. God forbid that it would ever escalate to a similar level here. He shuddered at the thought.

As in St. John's Wood, the area around the Cannon residence was crammed with police vehicles and ambulances. There was also a fire crew at the main gateway to the house where the rescue team appeared to be generally stowing gear back on the tender. The still smouldering wreckage of a Cherokee Jeep was welded to the blackened crater of Frank Cannon's shattered driveway.

The two detectives stepped over the twisted frame of one of the vehicle's doors. It was spattered with dried blood and clinging remnants of burned flesh. A helicopter roared overhead as they passed the remains of two mangled torsos still strapped to the jagged metal outline of their seats in what remained of the four by four.

They were met at the entrance to the house by D.I. Jim Parker, heading the investigation from Camden Town.

"Not a pretty sight, eh?" he said and formally introduced himself.

The Courier
James R. Vance

"That must have been some explosion," commented
Turner. As he spoke, he glanced back at the widespread
destruction. The windows at the front of the building had
imploded, scattering fragments of glass, splintered wood and lethal
slivers of metal in all directions within the house. Several pieces
were embedded in furniture, the interior doors and even the walls.

"Any I.D. on the occupants?" asked Massey as they picked
their way through the debris of the hallway.

"Nothing positive as far as hard evidence until forensics
have done their stuff on what's left of the bodies," replied Parker.
"According to the son, it was his father and one of his employees."

"Where's the son now?" enquired Massey.

"He's making a statement to two of my team. They're
upstairs away from all this mayhem."

"I'd like a word with him before we leave," said Massey.
His tone indicated a demand rather than a request. "We
interviewed Luke Cannon a couple of days ago in relation to a
somewhat minor incident in which he had become involved."

"Connected to this havoc?" asked Parker.

"I shouldn't think so," said Massey with a rather matter-of-
fact response.

Turner coughed and quickly asked if the lad had thrown
any light on the incident.

"Apparently he was upstairs in his room when his father
and the other guy, Danny, I think he called him, left to meet some
friends for a lunch-time drink. Next thing he heard this almighty
explosion, the house shook and he raced downstairs. The heat from
the blazing vehicle held him back and he rushed inside to 'phone
the emergency services.

That's it really. I suppose that I ought to notify his friends
at the pub. The son seems to be all on his own, you know the story,
parents divorced. She's up north somewhere near Manchester."

"Which pub are his friends at?" asked Massey.

"One in Maida Vale. Er, something castle....the Windsor
Castle...that's the one."

The Courier
James R. Vance

"Well, we're going back to Kilburn afterwards. Perhaps we could call in and put them in the picture."

"Cheers," replied Parker. "Give us chance to get finished up here, though I think we'll be around for some time yet. Come upstairs and see if our guys have finished with him."

"Thank you," said Massey politely.

Turner grinned, impressed by the way his boss had calmly played the cards close to his chest. He was about to follow the two inspectors when Mullen and McGovern appeared in the hallway.

He waited until Massey and Parker were out of sight and quickly outlined the situation. He despatched them to the Windsor Castle to find and detain Cannon's mates until he and Massey could meet up with them. McGovern's eyes lit up at the mission. He could not think of anything better than spending Sunday lunchtime in a boozer, on official business! They quickly disappeared and Turner joined his boss upstairs.

Left alone with Luke Cannon, they commiserated with the tragedy which had befallen his family and suggested that he contact his mother, which he had not yet considered amid all the chaos. They reassured him that, because they were well aware of his father's involvement in the illicit smuggling operation, they were here to protect him from any repercussions.

Massey went on to explain that to achieve this, however, they needed his help to find those responsible for this terrible atrocity. During their discussion Luke told a similar story as David Joseph. They too had received the same text message which, in turn, had enraged his father. Uttering a steady stream of expletives… 'Swearin' like fuck!' as Luke described it… Frank and Danny had set off to meet up with some friends who were similarly involved with The Fixer. They got no further than the driveway.

"Who were they going to meet at the pub?" asked Massey.

"Not sure I should say," whispered Luke through his tears.

"Look, we're not after bringing any charges against them. We just need some help in tracking down those responsible for these atrocities." Massey put his arm around Luke's shoulder.

The Courier
James R. Vance

"Three people have died today, victims of two evil, cold-blooded executions. We must find these people before there are other killings. We need your help so that they can be brought to justice. Maybe your father's friends can help."

Luke wiped his hands across his bloodshot eyes and raised his head. He thought back to his let-off at Blackfriars. Brought up not to trust the police or any other aspect of the legal system, he eventually relented. These guys seemed pretty genuine and, besides, his father needed avenging.

"Mickey Driscoll and Vince Edwards. You'll find 'em at the Windsor Castle in Maida Vale. Can yer ask 'em to come and see me?"

"Do you have a contact number for your mother?" asked Turner.

Luke nodded and covered his face again with his hands. He had not seen his mother for several years. He wondered deep down if she could still be reached on that number. She had left home in Manchester during her teens and like so many young dreamers had found her way to the capital in search of fame and fortune. After several unrewarding jobs she found both aspirations in the arms of Frankie Cannon, together with an unplanned pregnancy.

Unfortunately his promises of the good life were financed by brown paper parcels with dodgy contents. She tolerated it when Luke was a youngster, but the constant fear of the knock on the door became too much to bear. She escaped back up the M1 and moved in with her sister in Urmston. The annual birthday and Christmas card with 'Luv Mum' was Luke's only contact.

"Maybe it might be a good idea if she could come and look after you," suggested Turner.

"I'll go round my girl's 'ouse when this lot's finished 'ere."

"You could be in for a long wait," advised Massey. "We'll ask your father's friends from the pub to come over and sort something out for you."

The two detectives left the room. On the way downstairs they spoke to D.I. Parker and suggested that a W.P.C. should perhaps take care of Luke Cannon until a responsible adult could

be found. Leaving the harrowing scene they set off towards Maida
Vale to link up with Mullen and McGovern.

*****

  The Windsor Castle was unusually quiet for a Sunday. The
detectives, sent on by Turner, were talking to two men at one end
of the bar. Massey and Turner walked across and introduced
themselves.

  "Is there somewhere more discreet where we can have a
chat?" he asked the older man.

  "Are you arrestin' us?"asked Mickey Driscoll.

  "I told you already. We need your help," said Mullen.

  Mickey leaned across the bar. "Caff, any chance of the
back room?"

  "Help yourself, luv. Frank not with you today?"

  "No, not today," he replied with a shake of his head. He led
the detectives to the meeting room, where they seated themselves
around the mahogany table.

  Massey outlined the current situation, omitting every detail
involving Scott Morgan or David Joseph and his family. He
focussed on their aim to apprehend whoever had been responsible
for the assassination of Frank Cannon and Danny. He explained
that they had evidence linking The Fixer to the atrocity at Primrose
Hill. To pursue their line of enquiry they needed to be able to make
contact using the same channel used for their smuggling operation.

  "What smugglin' operation?" asked Vince, attempting
misguidedly to bluff the detectives.

  "Look," said Massey. "We're aware of what's going on and
we know how the system works. We know about the school in
France and the students with the briefcases. We're not interested in
your criminal activities." Massey was content to gloss over that
fact. Revenue and Customs could follow that one up.

  "That particular scam is almost dead now anyway. This is a
murder investigation and you are the only guys who can help us to
apprehend the evil sod who killed your friend. Luke's counting on
you guys to help catch his dad's killers. Are you in or not?"

The Courier
James R. Vance

The two crooks looked at each other. Massey was praying that honour amongst thieves still existed at this level of criminality.

"What d'yer wanna know?" asked Mickey, after a thoughtful pause where he considered their current options to be few.

"We know that the lads have delivered goods in exchange for a briefcase containing payment. We have video tape of Luke's involvement. What happens to the cash?"

"'E takes 'is cut and passes it on to the supplier."

"How does he contact the supplier?"

"'E doesn't. Friday is delivery day. Monday is 'andover day. On 'is return trip to school, 'e exchanges 'is briefcase containin' the reddies for an empty one, which 'e then takes back to France."

"So who picks up the case with the cash?"

"Fucked if I know. Accordin' to the lads, it's usually a suit."

"You mean like a business man?"

"Yeah. That's what the lads said."

"Where does this exchange of the money take place?"

"Same place as Friday. If it's at Waterloo by the newsstand, it's same on the Monday. If it's bin switched at Paddington station under the 'angin' info block, it's delivered back there on Monday. Them's the rules."

"And that's the last you see of it?"

Mickey shrugged as if to say 'your guess is as good as mine'.

"You also have a contact number for this guy who calls himself The Fixer. We need that phone number and apparently it has just been changed."

"This mornin'", said Vince. "'Ow the 'ell did you know that?"

"It doesn't matter," continued Massey. "What's the new number?"

249

The Courier
James R. Vance

Mickey reached into his jacket pocket and pulled out a diary. He flicked through the pages to the day's date and slid it across the table to the detective.

"Thank you," said Massey and noted the number. "Now can I buy you guys a drink?"

"Is that it?" exclaimed Vince.

"What did you expect, a bloody three course meal?" retorted McGovern. He stood and walked towards the door. "I'll order so long as you're paying, boss."

"Use the fuckin' `atch. It's quicker," said Vince.

McGovern brought the drinks to the table. He was enjoying this. The conversation drifted towards the tragic events at Frank Cannon's house and Massey steered the conversation towards concern for Luke, managing to get a promise that either Mickey or Vince would look in on the lad on their way home.

As they were downing the last drops, Massey had one more request. "I'll need to borrow one of your mobiles for this Fixer character to be able to contact us. Oh, and your password as I understand that no names are used."

"Buy yer own fuckin` mobile," sneered Vince.

"Why one of ours?" asked Mickey.

"He may become suspicious if he can't recognise the number to which he sends the reply," said Massey. "We need to order something to set the wheels in motion across the water. That way we can monitor the operation and hopefully discover who is involved at that end."

"You'd better order yerself some mobile phones, then," interjected Vince.

Ignoring the remark, Mickey hesitated but passed his phone to the inspector. "Password's Silly Drockmice." He smiled. "They're normally ana...analogs? No, anagrams of the user's name. Make sure I get the phone back and you get Frank's killer."

"I promise," said Massey.

"`Ang about," said Vince. "What yer gonna phone the Fixer for?"

"That's our business," replied Massey.

The Courier
James R. Vance

"Well we don't phone 'im, except when it's urgent or we've got problems, unless we're oderin' sumfin and we're supposed to use public phones. The mobile's only for incomin' texts. So if yer usin' Mickey's phone, 'e'll fink it's 'im. So are yer orderin' or complainin'?"

"We were thinking of placing an order but we need Mickey's phone to receive the text message, don't we?"

"Look," said Mickey. "If yer use my password to order sumfin', the stuff'll just come back wiv my lad, Sean, 'cos they know that the courier and Silly Drockmice are the same outfit. But yer won't get a text to tell yer when and where. If yer wanna work the system, phone 'im up and say I've recommended yer and make sure yer use my password, not my name. All yer do is tell 'im yer want to order sumfin', give 'im yer name and mobile number. You'll get a text back with yer password, the drop site and a time."

"I fought coppers were supposed to be clever bastards," carped Vince. "In this outfit, there's couriers and there's traders and sometimes there's them like us, 'cos we're bofe!"

"So 'ow will orderin' sumfin' catch Frank's killer?" asked Mickey.

"I 'ope yer not stitchin' us up," chipped in Vince.

"As I said earlier, we need your help to gain more information about this Fixer guy. We believe there's a connection to what happened to Frank, but we've no hard evidence to work on. We've enough information to close down the operation. That's no problem and initially we were going after the major players, but now there's a murderer at large and that's a brand new ball game. By ordering some merchandise, we hope to track it and discover who's behind it all. You must realise that we already have enough evidence to charge all of you right now. We're offering to leave you alone in exchange for your co-operation."

"And 'ow do we know yer tellin' the trufe?" said Vince still full of misgivings. "All this could be just a load of shit."

"You just have to trust us," replied Mullen in support of his boss. Massey had answered most of the ripostes and the detective thought that it was time to show some solidarity against the constant flak, particularly from Vince.

The protagonists looked across at each other, digesting everything which had been discussed. Mickey finally punctured the awkward silence.

"We're only doin' this for Frank and 'is lad," he said. "So don't take any bleedin' liberties."

Massey smiled and handed the mobile back. "Nor mobiles, it seems."

*****

It was a subdued atmosphere in the incident room. The story-board still contained all the information which had been collated so far. There was some clutter on the various tables but no sign of the rest of the team. The four detectives sprawled in silence, three of them waiting for a cue from Massey. McGovern was the first to break the ice. He raised his right hand, pretended to scratch the top of his head, screwed up his eyes and pouted his bottom lip. "A fine mess you've got me into, Stanley," he quipped.

"I'm not so sure," replied Massey. "The murders were not on our manor, so the situation remains the same, apart from the business of making direct contact using David Joseph, which is no longer possible."

"What about Scott Morgan?" asked Turner. "Could he be a target?"

"I doubt there is any way of linking him," replied Massey. "I'd put my money on the motive for the murders being financial. There's a supplier waiting for payment, a middle man waiting for his cut and the fear that a lucrative money tree may have to be chopped because of the perceived cock-up between Frank Cannon and Isaac Joseph. Fortunately we're sitting here with both the cash and the diamonds."

"What's our next move, then?" asked Mullen.

"I'm going to suggest that we wait until tomorrow," replied his boss. "I'd like to know what progress French has made with the gendarmes and the school. Before we make contact I want to be one hundred per cent sure that we're in position to clock every resultant move on their part.

From the info given by David Joseph and Mickey Driscoll, after we link into the system and place an order, we'll eventually receive a text. It should give the time and location of the drop and obviously, the cost. Once we agree to take delivery of whatever we have ordered, the wheels will be turning."

"So what are we going to order then?" asked Mullen.

"I suggest that we stick with what we agreed and merely put some feelers out about the biochemical stuff as we only want to check on its availability. To set the delivery process in motion, we can just order something basic."

They all nodded in unison.

"How much help are we expected to give to the guys conducting the murder investigation?" asked Turner.

"It's a difficult one that," replied Massey. "Give them too much and they're likely to screw up our operation. On the other hand, if we don't co-operate, we'll be perceived as the glory seekers."

"Wouldn't it be easier if we just put them in the picture and asked them to tread softly, softly," suggested Mullen.

"Oh, yes," remarked McGovern. "Fat chance! One whiff of a suspect in France and that lot'll be organising a bloody booze cruise."

"The one thing in our favour," added Massey, "is that Dyson specifically asked me to keep it all between the four of us. Mind you, that was before this afternoon's bombshell. What do you reckon?"

"If that's what the big man ordered, you have no option other than to toe the line," said Turner, triumphantly. "End of discussion!"

"Let's call it a day, then," concluded the inspector. "We have a different agenda to pursue now. Let's meet first thing tomorrow, get an update from D.C. French and plan a constructive course of action. Agreed?"

"Just one point," added Mullen. "How are today's events being handled with regard to the media?"

"Already spoken to my counterparts in St. John's Wood and Camden. We've agreed to state that we have no evidence of a link between the two incidents and investigations are in hand. If we're absolutely forced into announcing some progress, we'll simply infer that it could possibly be related to gangland rivalries in a localised drugs war."

Having already spent some time at the pub earlier, they all decided to head for their respective homes.

Chapter 23

MONDAY MORNING: All the morning editions carried extensive reports of the events of Sunday. Most of the tabloids focussed on the carnage at Primrose Hill, it being the more visually dramatic of the two. Photographs of the burned out vehicle took centre space on the majority of front pages with some graphic headlines.

The Sun tabloid naturally displayed the most sensational and tasteless of them all with the word 'CANNONFODDER" and the remainder of the page was given over to a photo of the smouldering wreck on the driveway.

Thanks to the morbid curiosity of neighbours, two additional pages printed more pictures taken by mobile phone and digital cameras from nearby bedroom windows. One in particular showed a distraught Luke Cannon confronting the blazing wreck before he dashed back inside the house to contact the emergency services.

Massey decided to call all the team to the incident room. Copies of the morning newspapers were spread on the desk in front of him. When they were assembled he made an announcement stating that, due to the previous day's incidents, they would be handing over the ensuing murder enquiries to their counterparts at St. John's Wood and Camden, where a murder squad would be assembled to carry out that investigation. The David Joseph affair was partly concluded and the relative information gathered would be passed to Revenue and Customs.

Detective Sergeants Turner and Mullen and Detective Constable McGovern would continue to assist him (Massey) in probing the link between the school in France and the smuggling operation which they had uncovered. D.C. French would be co-opted as he had formed a relationship with the gendarmerie at Ardres and would continue his liaison until the investigation was completed. He thanked the team for their support during the previous week and suggested that they catch up on the more mundane activities which had been somewhat neglected.

He asked his three nominated detectives to remain in the room. D.C. French was also invited to join them. Massey asked him what progress he had made. The detective constable opened a file and passed several fax sheets across the table.

"These arrived this morning. They are lists in alphabetical order of students' names at the school together with their details. I've had a cursory glance through each one and it seems that the majority are English, with a few French and a smattering of Belgian and Dutch. There is a comment to check certain names. 'Regardez ces noms' has been scrawled at the top of the second page."

He looked directly at Massey. "Look at the D's in particular. What do you see?"

The inspector scanned the page, running down the list of names. The others stared at their copies, unsure of what they were expected to detect. Massey suddenly pointed at a name on the list.

"Dubois!" He exclaimed. "Julian Dubois, and the address, 'Le Moulin'. I remember. The mill we couldn't find. It must be the old man's grandson."

Mullen and McGovern looked at each other. "Can someone explain?" asked Mullen.

"The gardener at the school is called Marcel Dubois," replied French. "We've found out that apparently he has a dodgy background. He used to be in the Douane, French Customs, but was cashiered over some smuggling scam with an English guy employed by Customs at Dover. The French police also suspected the involvement of his son, Francis, but nothing was proven. However, they still think his son is involved in something similar now. He keeps turning up at the school which we believe is supplying the couriers. And now his son's name appears on the list of students and could also be involved."

"As yet there is no evidence to support this theory, consequently it is all conjecture," interrupted Massey. "If the guy's father works there and his son is a pupil there, surely it's only natural that he visits occasionally. Maybe we're putting two and two together and making five."

"On the other hand, we could be getting our sums right," suggested Turner. He addressed D.C. French. 'Why has each name got a 'T', 'S' or 'J' alongside it?"

"The 'T' stands for Trimestre, 'S' for Semaine and 'J for Jour which in English mean Term, Week and Day. I asked if they could be coded that way, so we could identify those who travelled in on a weekly basis. If we highlight the Brits who commute weekly...those with the letter 'S' alongside... maybe we could narrow it down to the possible couriers."

"Good thinking," added Massey. "Can I suggest that you take it one step further? Ask one of the girls to run the names and addresses of those commuting weekly through the database and cross-match them with any previous or any family criminal records."

At that moment the door opened and D.C. Croft appeared. "Excuse me sir, but D.C. French showed me his fax this morning."

"Just his fax?" joked McGovern.

"I've been thinking back to our visit," continued Croft, ignoring McGovern's trite remark.

"Go on," said Massey.

"Remember the poster on the notice board which advertised a 'members only' gardening club? It convenes every night on Mondays and Thursdays in some gardening storeroom. Monday's the day they all return and Thursday's the night before they go back to England. As it's organised by the gardener, a suspect gardener, could this be a sort of command centre for the smuggling operation?"

"It's an interesting thought," agreed Massey.

"A list of its members would be useful," added Turner.

"I'll get on it straightaway," said French. "I'm sure my friendly gendarme won't mind popping in. It could be interesting to see how many marry up to the other list."

"Good work," said Massey. "We'll follow that up. If you think of anything else, keep me posted and make yourself available on Friday, in case we have to intercept any couriers."

He turned to D.C. French. "Make sure that your gendarme continues his informal chats with the school principal. It's imperative that he doesn't alert the suspicions of that old gardener."

"Don't worry," said the detective constable. "He's making all his enquiries under the guise of keeping their records up-to-date. He's told him it's a new E.U. regulation concerning residency."

"That sounds credible. They bring in new legislation every five minutes. Whilst you're in touch, put out some feelers as to whether it would be possible for a phone tap at the school and the two Dubois residences. We also need a stand-by surveillance team to monitor activities at the school when we make our move. See what you can do."

The two detective constables left the room. Massey walked to the door ensuring that it was securely closed.

He turned to his detective sergeants. "We need to get down to the real nitty-gritty. If young Frenchie can get a result with his gendarme mates, we can place an order and speak with our principal target, The Fixer. Now what were the names of those bio-chemical agents?"

*****

Scott was on the 7.53am train from Waterloo, not relishing the idea of double sociology to kick-start the second part of the autumn term. Still immersed in his adventure of the previous week, he had day-dreamed his way from home to the station where his mother had kissed him on the cheek affectionately as she dropped him off. He had passed the newsstand from where the escapade

258

had originated, hardly noticing the dramatic headlines on the news placards.

As the South Eastern passenger train raced through the suburbs towards the Kent countryside he became aware of the front page of a fellow passenger's newspaper. In addition to the main story about a car bomb explosion, he spotted another featured story in the bottom right-hand corner. The headline leaped out at him. 'North London Jeweller Gunned Down'. He leaned forward and read the report, recoiling in horror as the story of the Josephs' tragedy unfolded.

David Joseph had given Scott his mobile number before he left Westferry Road on Saturday night, so that they could keep in touch in view of his potential court appearance. Scott immediately reached for his mobile and called him.

David answered and recounted what had happened. He seemed more concerned about Scott keeping a low profile and detached from the whole affair. It was difficult for the student to hold an open conversation surrounded as he was by commuters. They agreed to meet later in the week on some neutral ground. David thanked him for the call and said he would be in touch.

Scott looked at other students on the train, chatting, laughing and generally behaving like schoolchildren. He raised himself up in his seat and thought about the hunt for Isaac Joseph's killer. The briefcase on his lap was no ordinary briefcase. It had been cleverly prepared by 'M'. He patted the mobile in his inside pocket. It was a six round Walther PPK. He looked down at his watch...no ordinary watch...an Omega with a laser beam. The assassin will be hunted down and wasted. He looked at his reflection in the window. He was Bond, James Bond.

*****

"What about D.C.I.Dyson?" asked Turner. "We seem to be pressing on despite his directive to hand it over to Special Ops."

The four detectives were still mulling over the information which D.C. French had presented to them. Massey's mind was in overdrive.

The Courier
James R. Vance

"I'm seeing him later," replied Massey. "The events of yesterday should have distracted him sufficiently away from the French connection. He'll be too busy poking his nose into the other nicks' murder investigations. It should be sufficient to tell him that we're still pursuing our original lines of enquiry regarding the couriers."

"I take it that you're not going to tell him about ordering biochemical weapons, then?" remarked Ricky Mullen with a knowing wink.

"I think he's got enough on his plate at the moment," said Massey semi-seriously. "I'll inform him of our endeavours to identify and follow up potential suspects from the list of students. In any case there's little we can do until French confirms that everything's in place across the channel."

"We need to decide between a chemical and a biological agent in respect of our enquiry to this Fixer guy," said Turner.

"I thought we decided on Sarin," remarked McGovern.

"We didn't make a decision. At the end of the day, it doesn't really matter as we don't intend to order it, merely to ask about its availability," replied Turner.

"Let's go for the VX, the most deadly of them all," suggested McGovern.

"Surely it would be better to ask for the one that is easiest to get hold of," remarked Mullen.

"Using that line of reason, let's ask about the availability of several alternatives, rather than put our eggs in one basket and receive a negative," added Massey. "If we ask for only one, we may be missing the fact that others may be available. Give the guy a shopping list and see what he comes back with."

"The enquiry may not sound credible if we use that ploy," said Turner.

"Depends on how we couch it," said Massey. "If we explained that we have a genuine client who is looking at various options, including availability, speed of delivery, cost, et cetera, maybe he will bite. Don't forget this guy seems totally motivated

260

by money. Look at what happened yesterday because of his financial losses."

"Maybe we need to research biochemical agents more thoroughly before we make the final decision," suggested Turner.

"That's sensible," said Massey. "We're hardly experts in that field. Try the internet and come back with a proposal. Not much that we can do besides that so I suggest that you spend the rest of your day clearing desks of any outstanding business. We'll reconvene as soon as there's some positive news from France. I'm off to keep the D.C.I. sweet."

The meeting broke up. McGovern and Mullen returned to the main office and the coffee machine. Turner asked his boss if he had received the promised wedding invitation.

"To be honest, I'm so immersed in the twists and turns of this damn case that I haven't checked any mail today. In any case, I'm conditioned to the fact that the envelopes which drop through my letterbox are usually either bills or bloody circulars."

"Mine actually arrived this morning," announced Turner. "It must have been an afterthought. It's short notice, but the ceremony's at eleven on Wednesday morning at Marylbone Registry office. That's followed by a buffet luncheon reception at the Café Royal on Regent Street. Are you game?"

"Like you say, she's left it a bit late, but I reckon we could snatch an hour or two off. We deserve a break and a sip of Champers will go down nicely, thank you. Fancy meeting here first thing Wednesday morning? We could take a taxi to the registrar's, have a few drinks at the Café Royal and be back here shortly after lunchtime. Anyway, it'll give you the chance to meet your new brother-in-law."

"I hope he's better than the last one!" joked Turner. "Are you buying a present?"

"Not really thought about it." He stroked his chin. "How about a book on French cuisine? She was certainly no Delia Smith and, as she's marrying a French guy, she'll need some expertise. You know how highly they rate their culinary skills."

The Courier
James R. Vance

"She's marrying a bloody diplomat, for Christ's sake. She'll probably have her own chef."

"Okay, how about a book about the French Revolution in case she gets ideas above her station."

"I believe the guillotine suffered the same fate as the hangman's noose," replied Turner, still amused by the thought of his sister marrying into a pampered lifestyle.

Massey departed to meet up with Dyson. Turner returned to his desk, clicked onto the internet and typed 'dirty bombs' into Google.

Chapter 24

WEDNESDAY: For late October the weather had turned unusually mild after a bitterly cold weekend. The sun was breaking through the cloud cover as Massey and Turner jumped inside the taxi which they had ordered to take them to Marylbone registry office.

They crossed Blackfriars Bridge, cutting through Shoe Lane towards High Holborn. Avoiding the busy areas west of Kingsway, the taxi cut through Bloomsbury via Russell Square onto Euston Road. Taking the underpass they continued west into Marylbone Road, reaching the registrars as several other guests were climbing the steps to the ornate entrance.

Massey felt strange attending his ex-wife's wedding, but the split had never been acrimonious and, despite or possibly because of lack of contact, there was still a tentative bond between them. They had originally met years ago in Cheshire when he was a newly appointed detective sergeant and had inherited Chris Turner as a young detective constable in the team. The D.C.'s attractive sister had been introduced to him at a social function and, as the saying goes, the rest is history.

"What did you eventually buy as a wedding present?" asked Turner, drawing attention to the small package under his boss's arm.

"As I've never met him, her intended, I thought I should buy something personal for Helen, but something from which he would also benefit." Massey gently patted the parcel.

"And?" asked Turner impatiently.

"It's a Christian Dior perfume spray, French of course."

"You're suggesting that he wears perfume?"

The Courier
James R. Vance

"Hardly. No, it can sit there as a thing of beauty on her dresser where they can both admire it. Helen can adorn herself with the contents and he can breathe in the exotic scent."

"You've lost the plot!"

"It's the romantic in me. She always appreciated the finer things in life."

"So that's why she divorced you!"

They ascended the steps, enjoying the repartee, and entered the hollow sounding entrance foyer of the building which echoed with the clatter of footsteps on the tiled floor. On making enquiries they made their way up a further flight of stairs to a first floor waiting area where the bride and groom along with other guests were about to enter the marriage room.

Following the ceremony, an array of taxis and what appeared to be consulate limos ferried the wedding party the short distance to the Dauphin Suite of the Café Royal. There were the usual introductions. 'This is so-and-so…we've known each other for years…. you remember Aunt Geraldine…let me introduce you to Michel's best man….he's very close to President Chirac, did you know?......thank you so much for the lovely gift (what was it?)… I really didn't expect one….ah, champers!'

Massey felt like an outsider, as though he had gate-crashed some stranger's reception by mistake. Throughout his life, he had never been a party animal, preferring his own company to being part of the scene. Nevertheless, both he and Turner mingled, helping themselves to the lavish buffet and joining in the various toasts.

Before they departed, Massey was able to home in on his ex-wife during a lull in the celebrations. They sat together on a chaise longue in a quiet alcove.

"We met at the school's spring fair just before Easter, this year," recalled Helen as she brought her ex-husband up-to-date with her current beau.

"You're still teaching, then?" said Massey.

"More or less part-time now, but still at Hampstead, following my transfer down south. It's strange that we both ended up in the capital. I thought at first that you'd followed me here, but I eventually realised that you were too proud to consider that course of action.

Anyway, back to our first encounter. He was in the marquee looking quite lost and we started chatting. I discovered that his daughter, Amelie, was in one of my classes. It provided some common ground for both of us."

"So you've inherited a ready made family?"

"He also has a son, Christophe, slightly older than Amelie. However, the young man prefers to live with his mother somewhere near Paris. I've met him a couple of times when he's been over visiting his father.I found him to be extremely well mannered and very intelligent."

She took another sip of Champagne and looked directly into his eyes.

"So have you not found anyone?"

Massey smiled. "You know me, Helen...married to the job."

"Still saving the world, eh?"

"You could say that. What prompted you to marry the guy. You've not known him that long?"

"It just felt right. His divorce also came through in July, so we thought, why not?"

"Why did Michel get divorced?"

"It was a similar situation to ours, I imagine. He was never at home and they just drifted apart."

"So why fall into the same trap again?"

"It's different for him now. His kids are growing up and will shortly be carving out their own lives, giving him more freedom. I'll have the opportunity to accompany him on his travels and maybe see a bit more of the world."

"I can only wish you all the best." He raised his glass. "Here's to Monsieur et Madame...by the way what is your name now?"

The Courier
James R. Vance

Helen laughed. "I'm impressed with your command of the French language! Deneuve, Monsieur et Madame Deneuve, as in the great French film star, Catherine Deneuve."

Something in Massey's brain went click, some recollection, some recognition, and then it was gone. In that split second of the moment his mind registered one of those déjà vu scenarios which occurs at least once in almost everyone's lifetime. Was it déjà vu or did his brain stop for a nanosecond whilst real time marched on? Or did he really sense what was about to happen in that same cognitive flash? He thought so, but the memory or the premonition was just as instantly gone. Helen's voice snatched him back into the real world.

"You okay, Raymond?" she asked, disturbed by his frozen expression.

"Fine, yes fine," he replied automatically. "Congratulations to you both."

After the inevitable round of handshakes, several pecks on cheeks and the compulsory wave of the hand, the two detectives descended in a lift to the ground floor of the Café Royal. They strolled onto a busy Regent Street where the traffic seemed to be in a permanent jam. It was beginning to drizzle and they were fortunate to attract the attention of a cabbie, who was disgorging two elderly females from the interior of his taxi opposite. The cab made a u-turn and pulled up close by.

"Where to?" demanded the cabbie.

"The Ring on the corner of Blackfriars and The Cut, SE1," replied Massey. "You know it?"

"The boxing pub," replied the taxi driver.

"That's the one," said Massey.

"I thought we were going back to the office," said Turner.

"I don't know about you," said his boss, "but I need a couple of pints to draw a line under today."

Turner suddenly realised that his ex-brother-in-law had put on a brave face which had been masking his innermost emotions. Obviously he still had feelings for his sister. It was understandable that he was seeking some closure to the relationship. Maybe he could now get on with his own life once more.

Cutting through the side streets, the taxi eventually emerged onto Waterloo Bridge and crossed the river to the south bank. Twenty minutes after leaving Regent Street they were paying the fare and standing outside the Ring public house.

*****

Since the initial press coverage on Monday morning, the media had continued to follow the weekend's outrages, particularly the more noteworthy explosion at Primrose Hill. Each edition carried additional information as reporters delved more deeply into the affairs and the background of the Cannon family.

Organised crime became the main theme and speculation ran rife over possible suspect connections. The Sun, especially, was covering the story in ever increasing detail. Their Wednesday publication focussed on the plight of the son, Luke, and his relationship with his girlfriend.

She was obviously selling her story to provide the tabloid with a human interest factor. Unashamedly milking the opportunity for publicity she had allowed herself to be photographed in several tasteless poses and had even handed over photographs of Luke, who, despite all the attention, appeared to prefer to take a back-seat.

David and Rebecca Joseph had decamped to his house at Barnes, partly to avoid media intrusion and partly due to their discomfort of remaining at the murder scene. They were attempting to carry on with their lives despite the on-going police investigation. Rebecca was re-immersing herself in the Hatton Garden shop. David was continuing to pursue the potential development opportunities at Canary Wharf.

As he was spending most of his time on business at the Isle of Dogs, he had contacted Scott and arranged to meet him at Café Brera in the Jubilee Place Shopping Mall on Saturday morning. Following a meeting with the Canary Wharf Group P.L.C., he left One Canada Square on his way to the parking access when his attention was drawn to more headlines about Sunday's explosion on a placard at News on the Wharf.

Curious of the various tabloids and broadsheets covering the story from several differing angles, he saw a face which was instantly recognisable. It stared back at him beneath a headline 'THE LUKE OF LOVE'. *I know him. He's one of the couriers.* He purchased the newspaper.

*****

Their drinking session at the Ring was curtailed by Massey complaining of an acute bout of indigestion. Consequently one round of drinks was enough. Naturally he blamed a combination of the buffet and the Champagne at the reception. The rain had ceased and they walked back to the office, welcoming the opportunity to clear their heads. They were greeted by an excited D.C. French.

"The list has arrived," he cried, waving some sheets at the two detectives.

"What list?" asked Turner, his excitement quota having been exhausted for one day.

"The gardening club," continued French. "It's as we thought. There are only ten members, two are French and the other eight are English weekly boarders. One of the French lads is the gardener's grandson, Francis Dubois. The other one I don't recognise. I've made copies for each of you."

"O.k., bring it to my office and we'll take a look," said Massey.

They were joined by McGovern and Mullen. Massey spread the fax copies across his desk. Turner pointed at the eight English names.

"No surprise there," he said. "Luke Cannon, Sean Driscoll and Todd Edwards. If the devil could cast his net, eh? Don't recognise the other five."

Massey passed one of the copies to Mullen and McGovern. "There's a little job for the pair of you. Find out who the others are and do some background checks."

The Courier
James R. Vance

He glanced across at D.C. French. "You may as well follow up the other French lad." He looked at his watch. "Let's all re-convene first thing Friday and de-brief unless you unearth something vital."

"There's something else you should know," said D.C. French as he turned to leave. "They reckon that all the surveillance which you requested will be in place by the weekend."

"Well, that's a result," said Massey, knowing how slowly the wheels of French bureaucracy normally turn. "How did you manage that one?"

"It seems that they're just as keen to nail Dubois as we are."

"Let's hope that we're targeting the right guy, then. Keep the pressure on them. We need to make our move at this end. Tell them Friday at the latest."

The three detectives left the room. Turner picked up the remaining copy and browsed the list. "You reckon they're all couriers?"

"Apart from the French lads who don't commute, unless they have clients over there. If Dubois is our man, maybe his son is involved to support his granddad at the school. Who's the other lad?"

"According to this, he's a term boarder who lives in Erag....here, you've been to France. How do you pronounce all that?" Turner pushed the sheet across the desk.

Massey looked at the list. "Bloody hell," he exclaimed. "I knew it. As soon as she came out with it at the wedding reception, it struck a chord. Where's the original list?"

Turner looked at him quizzically. *What's somewhere in France got to do with the Café Royal? He's either flipped or still pissed.* "It's there on your desk," he replied.

Massey picked up the original fax copy. "That's where I'd seen it." He placed it back on the desk under his sergeant's nose. "We were asked to look at the D's. Remember? I immediately picked up on Dubois. Look at the name before it. Deneuve, Christophe Deneuve. That's Helen's new name, Deneuve. That's why it rang a bell." He was becoming more excited now. "Fetch the road map which we used in France. Let's see if the other bit fits."

Turner crossed to a cabinet with bookshelves and withdrew the AA Road Atlas. "What are we looking for?" he asked, still rather bemused.

"Turn to the list of place names at the back and find Eragny-sur-Oise."

Checking the spelling, he perused the myriad of French towns commencing with the letter E. He eventually announced its reference number on the map. "Page forty two, B two," stated Turner.

Massey flipped through to page forty two and placed his forefinger on the name, Eragny. "There it is!" he said triumphantly. "As I thought. It's just off the A15 from Paris." He smiled and looked directly at Turner. "The other French lad at the school appears to be your new nephew!"

Massey spent the next few minutes relating the conversation which he had held with Helen shortly before they had left the reception. They discussed the fact that there was still the possibility of others having the same name and even living in the same area of France close to Paris, but the coincidence was highly improbable. As they expanded on the implications, it also offered a solution to one of their unanswered questions. It was Turner who proposed it.

"What if Helen's new husband is the bag-man?"

"How do you mean?"

"When we asked Mickey Driscoll who picked up the briefcase holding the money, he said it was some guy in a suit. Could that be Michel Deneuve or one of his lackeys?"

"And legitimately taken back to France in the diplomatic bag. Bloody hell, it's so simple."

For the first time, they were lost for words. Their minds must have been racing with their own perceptions of the ensuing fall-out from the situation if it were to be true. Neither was prepared to suggest the possibility that Turner's sister, Massey's ex-wife could be party to it, could she? Massey's heart was pumping now. Could the brickwall be finally crumbling?

The two detectives left the office to go their separate ways home, both with a mountain of food for thought.Massey hesitated as he encountered the chill of the cold night air in contrast to the centrally heated offices.

Turner stopped and gripped his shoulder. "You okay, boss?" he asked.

Massey rubbed his chest and leaned against the entrance wall. "It's just this bloody indigestion I keep getting. I think I'm coming down with something. I ache all over and it feels like swollen glands in my neck."

"Probably starting with `flu," suggested Turner.

The inspector felt a pins and needles sensation in his arms, which felt like dead weights from his shoulders downwards.

The sensation spread to the rest of his body.

His bottom jaw ached immensely.

A vice-like grip seized his chest.

The pain was unbearable.

His skin felt cold and clammy, yet he was breaking into a sticky sweat.

The colour drained from him and his knees buckled.

Turner pushed open the door and shouted to the duty sergeant. "Call an ambulance immediately. He's having a heart attack."

Massey reached forwards and vomited. A uniformed constable appeared and they both supported Massey as he stumbled back inside the building. They seated him on a bench near the front desk.

"Ambulance on its way, sir," announced the sergeant.

Turner loosened the inspector's clothing and asked the constable to find some soluble aspirin. Massey was in considerable pain but holding on.

"I think I've just hit that bloody brickwall head-on, Chris," he whispered and closed his eyes.

The Courier
James R. Vance

*****

Debbie Collins still lived at home with her mum in Crouch End. Her dad was in Brixton jail for armed robbery. She had first met Luke Cannon outside the prison on visiting day. As the saying goes. 'Birds of a feather...'.   David Joseph traced her through information in the newspaper article and the local electoral list. He found the house just off Crouch End Hill.

The nineteen year old answered the knock at the door. Obviously expecting another interview or photo-shoot, her make-up was fresh, though slightly overdone. Her hair looked expertly layered, shattered by soft texture at the sides. She wore cream knee-length boots into which were tucked washed denim Donna Karen jeans. An aubergine lambs wool sweater, cut with a deep V which accentuated her ample cleavage completed the outfit.

"Hello," she said, affecting a 'Hollywood' smile.

"Debbie Collins?" asked David.

"Who would like to know?" she replied, broadening the smile.

"I'd like to speak with Luke, please," said David, ignoring her question.

Her demeanour changed immediately. "He's not available to nobody," she stated with a double negative.

"I think that he would wish to see me," continued David.

"And who are you?"

"I'm his original nightmare and, if he refuses to see me, it'll get worse."

"He doesn't want to know," she shouted. "Leave him alone." Stepping back, she attempted to close the door, but David held it firmly ajar.

"Who is it?" cried another female voice.

The stout figure of Mrs. Collins appeared in the background. She pushed past her daughter. "Who the hell are you...another bloody reporter?"

"I need to see Luke," said David. "I can help him. I know why his father was killed."

272

The Courier
James R. Vance

Mrs. Collins looked him up and down. "You don't look like a reporter or even a copper. You're too well dressed. You'd better come in."

He was led into a tidy but tastelessly furnished front room and asked to wait. The two women disappeared and after some distant muffled conversation, the door opened and a dishevelled Luke Cannon entered the room alone. David rose from the settee and offered his hand. Luke ignored him and slumped into an easy chair.

"My name's Joseph, David Joseph. We've met a couple of times, but you won't remember because you were too busy reading whilst we exchanged briefcases."

Luke raised his head.

"I've taken delivery of some of the merchandise which you have brought over from France, so I'm fully aware of the involvement of you, your father and others in this import business. Last weekend you lost your father in a terrible incident at your house. We have something in common. I lost my father in similar circumstances that very same day."

Luke was attentive but confused. He was insufficiently intelligent to comprehend the connection. Who was this stranger, bleating on about the death of their fathers? Perhaps he was some religious nutter who had come to sympathise. Why had he mentioned France? Maybe he was an undercover detective.

"What's all this gotta do wiv me?" asked Luke.

"Just over a week ago, through a chance mistake, I lost a briefcase full of money and you lost a briefcase containing diamonds at Waterloo station," said David, not wishing to expound further. "A hitherto foolproof operation went tits-up and the guy who runs it became rather more than a little bit mad. Because it wasn't resolved, retribution took place, the recipients being your father and my father."

Luke screwed his eyes and furrowed his brow, attempting to understand the gist of David's rhetoric.

"In other words, our two dads were assassinated because of a cock-up. Understand?"

Luke nodded. The simplicity of the last statement finally hit home.

"I need your help to nail the bastard responsible," continued David. "Don't you want the same?"

"Yeah, but 'ow can I 'elp?"

"You're just a courier. I'm just a receiver of contraband goods. Like your father our only contact was through a mobile number but I need to know who controls this operation over in France."

"They chopped us off."

"I know. It was the same with us, but you still have access to the mechanics of the operation at school over there. Surely you can finger some of the key players who supply the merchandise which you bring over."

"But I'm not going back."

"Why not?"

"There's no point, is there? They won't use me again. Dad's no longer 'ere to need the 'ooky stuff and apart from that, I'll probably get dun in like 'im."

"But you're the only one who has access to the system," argued David.

"Why not ask one of the other lads," suggested Luke.

"I don't know any other lads."

"I do," replied Luke.

*****

The ambulance with flashing lights and siren blaring hurtled down Union Street and within minutes would reach Guys Hospital. Turner sat alongside the prostrate inspector who was still conscious and breathing more easily through an oxygen mask. The paramedic was reassuring the two detectives that the patient would be fine as there had been little time lost between the onset of Massey's cardiac arrest and his imminent arrival at the coronary care unit. The vehicle came to a halt and the rear doors opened. The inspector entered the hospital on a trolley and was wheeled into a reception area.

274

The Courier
James R. Vance

A hive of activity swung into action as the medical team descended upon him. The routine questions were asked about allergies and medical history before catheters were inserted into his arms as the professional team worked to their strict systematic procedures. The morphine injection momentarily lifted the pain from his body as though he was off-loading a suit of armour.

Streptokinase, a thrombolitic clot-busting drug to prevent further damage to his heart was administered through the venflon which had been inserted into his arm. Ninety minutes later a printout from the electrocardiogram informed the staff that they had successfully stemmed the original onset. The next twenty four hours would be critical.

Massey drifted into a sound sleep. Turner spoke with the duty doctor to check on his friend's condition before leaving. He took a taxi back to his car at Blackfriars and set off home with deep concern for his long-term colleague. A day of so much promise was rapidly dissolving into a family nightmare in more ways than one.

.

Chapter 25

THURSDAY: Massey eased himself into an upright position and gratefully accepted the light breakfast that was offered. Despite the discomfort of a rather dull aching sensation throughout his whole body, he was surprised to feel fairly normal after the trauma of the previous evening. As in most hospitals, the first meal of the day was served rather early. Dawn had just arrived, heralded by the heavy pink glow of an overcast sunrise. He manoeuvred the various drip lines on his arms to one side as he attempted to carry the contents of the cereal bowl to his parched mouth.

A nurse explained that a regimen of blood tests, temperature readings, blood pressure checks and intermittent E.C.G.'s would become the daily routine over the next few days. His heart would also be tested and scrutinised for any apparent damage and all these results would determine the requisite treatment. He dozed fitfully as the C.C.U. gradually immersed itself into its normal pattern of activity.

Mid-way through the morning a consultant arrived to state the obvious, that he had sustained a minor cardiac arrest and his progress would be carefully monitored. He was visited by a student nurse, who asked politely if she could interview him about his experience whilst it was still fresh in his mind as she was researching symptoms of cardiovascular degeneration. Shortly afterwards the ward sister asked if he felt well enough to receive a visitor.

Though mentally alert, he was physically drained but acquiesced when told it was Chris Turner accompanied by a lady. When the newly-wed Madame Deneuve appeared alongside her brother, his exhaustion was temporarily thrust to one side. They seated themselves on each side of the bed.

"I thought you were off on your honeymoon," he whispered.

"We're flying to Paris tomorrow, having an overnight stay and on Saturday it's Air France to Guadeloupe. More to the point, how are you? I must admit you look in far better health than yesterday, despite what happened last night. I was devastated when Chris phoned."

"I think it must have been the shock of yesterday that caused it," teased Massey.

"Too much stress, darling. You should think about retirement."

"I'd be more stressed if all I had to look forward to was the History Channel and re-runs on UK Gold for the rest of my life."

"Well, if you, I mean when you get over this, I'm sure you'll be told to exercise more, so maybe you could join a fitness club or lead a more measured active lifestyle. Charging around after petty criminals and sitting in pubs with unhealthy specimens like my brother is not the solution. It's time to change. You're no longer the spring chicken that I remember."

"I hope you're not suggesting that I'm going to end up like this," said Turner. He faced his boss. "You scared the bloody life out of me last night. Promise you'll never do that again." He leaned over and gently ruffled Massey's hair. "How are you feeling now?"

"I must admit I'm knackered. It's amazing how it knocks the stuffing out of you."

"I thought you'd be in a private ward," said Helen.

"They're keeping me here for twenty four hours apparently. I'll be moved across tomorrow after some tests, provided that the results are o.k."

"Maybe we should go and let you get some rest," suggested Turner.

"Remember, you're in the best place," added Helen, rising from her seat. "It's amazing what they can do with heart problems

today. You'll probably come out of here a damn-sight fitter than
when you arrived."

"Anything you want bringing in?" asked his colleague.

"Just keep me updated," replied Massey.

"You should forget about work," added Helen. "Someone
else can carry on. Nobody's indispensable."

"If I get moved tomorrow, we can have a meeting in my
private ward," said Massey, ignoring her advice. "You need to
make that call, but first check with French. You'd better use your
name and mobile number as they won't allow me to use one here.
Mind you, I hope to be back on my feet by the weekend."

"Oh, there is one thing I should mention," said Turner.
"You're going to miss a funeral."

"I hope you're not referring to mine," quipped Massey.

Turner smiled. "Isaac Joseph, later today. The D.C.I.'s
offered to attend with me, to fly the flag, as it were."

"He's probably on the look out for suspects," remarked
Massey. "Where's it to be held?"

"Golders Green. A service in the synagogue followed by
internment in the Jewish Cemetery. Did you know that Jack
Rosenthal, the famous writer is buried there?"

"No, I didn't. Can we change the subject, please? You do
realise that I've just undergone a near-death experience?"

"So much for coming to cheer you up. I'm just wasting my
time," sighed Helen. "You'll never change, will you?" She leaned
over and kissed him on the cheek. "I'll phone Chris from Paris to
check on you."

"Where are you staying, the Hilton?" asked Massey.

"No, we're meeting up with Christophe, his son and staying
over. I'll be meeting his ex-wife. That should be interesting, n'est-
ce pas?"

"They live in Paris, then?"

"Just outside, I believe. Some place called Ragny or
something like that. Take care, my love. Enjoy the break." She
blew him a kiss and headed for the exit.

Massey and Turner stared at each other in silence.

The Courier
James R. Vance

*****

The synagogue off Finchley Road was crowded almost to capacity. Some mourners were family, some close friends, some business associates. Whatever their reasons for being there, most were Jewish, paying their respects to one of their own fraternity.

Amongst the congregation were those who had perceived Isaac Joseph's murder as yet another outrage against the Jewish community. To those people this atrocity could have taken place in Tel Aviv or Jerusalem. It was comparable to a suicide bomb attack by a Palestinian, an Iranian or any other extremist faction who condemned Israel as the enemy. Was this an extension of the turmoil in the Middle East? Was this an atrocity committed by Al Quaeda, Hamas or Hezbollah intent on spreading the net beyond the state of Israel itself? Was this a portent of the future?

These were questions in the minds of many who thronged this temple of worship. Iran had already threatened to wipe Israel off the face of the earth. By pointing the finger at Israel in such a way, were Jews world-wide about to be targeted? Amongst those present, only David Joseph and Detective Sergeant Chris Turner knew differently.

After the service and the internment itself, Detective Chief Inspector Dyson made a bee-line for D.I. James from St. John's Wood to discuss progress in the hunt for Joseph's assassin. Forensics had identified that he had been shot by a single bullet to the head with a Sig Sauer 9mm automatic pistol. It had been assumed that the gunshot had been masked by the noise from a Stihl 2-stroke motor strimmer which Isaac had been using at the time. The body had been left where it had dropped. The strimmer had continued running briefly until Isaac's grip had relaxed, causing a deep gash in the ground nearby. An empty shell case and several footprints were the only hard evidence from the crime scene.

D.S. Turner caught up with David and Rebecca Joseph before they left. They thanked him for attending the funeral and expressed their good wishes for D.I Massey's recovery. Nothing was mentioned about David's meeting with Luke Cannon and little was passed on from D.S. Turner about their proposed entrapment of The Fixer. Neither party seemed willing to be transparent, nor ready to pursue the matter further. It seemed that each was pursuing its own agenda, despite the prospect of an eventual collision course.

Chapter 26

FRIDAY: The atmosphere in the incident room was predictably subdued following the news of Massey's rush to hospital. Turner had phoned for an update on his condition before leaving home. The hospital had reported that there was no change and he was comfortable after a quiet night. The message was passed on to the other team members and a small group consisting of McGovern, Mullen, French and Croft joined him to discuss the on-going investigation.

"Last night I was assured that the French were making good progress with their surveillance set-up at the college. Consequently I made that first call to The Fixer to register our interest in using his services," explained Turner.

"What did he have to say?" asked McGovern.

"Not a lot," replied Turner. "Nothing of any significance. He asked for my name, address, mobile number and the password of who passed on his contact number. I was asking him when he would be in touch and the phone went dead. That was it. He just rang off as soon as he received the info he wanted."

"Was there any accent in his voice?" asked D.C. French.

"Nothing. It was almost like a recording. Just instant demands for each piece of info. All we can do now is wait."

"If we get a quick reply, at least we'll be in a position to move. I expect the French to be ready at their end by this evening at the latest," added French.

"How did you get on with checking out the other lads from over here?" asked Turner, addressing Mullen and McGovern.

"Quite interesting," replied Mullen. "As expected, they nearly all came from families with form. Two of the lads themselves had been done for shoplifting, but the rest were clean or at least they'd not been nicked."

"What sort of backgrounds did they share then, criminal-wise?"

Mullen picked up a small notebook where they had recorded the details. "The lad from Balham, his older brother was done for drug dealing, his dad for breaking and entering. There are two lads from the Peckham area. The father of one is doing time for armed robbery, the other comes from a family of petty thieves. He's one of the shoplifters."

"Well, that's three accounted for. What about the other two?"

"This is where it starts to get interesting," said Mullen. He turned to McGovern. "Here, you fill them in. You did the research on these two."

"There's a young lad from Barking with an interesting family. His dad has form stretching back years to when he was a West Ham supporter and was a member of the I.C.F., the infamous Inter City Firm. He was nicked several times for serious G.B.H. offences and later on, he did time for similar as a member of the National Front."

"Sounds like a nice bloke to meet in a dark alley," commented D.C. Croft.

"You may be nearer the truth than you think," continued McGovern. "He's now offering himself up as a candidate for the B.N.P."

"He's obviously got the credentials," remarked Mullen.

"What about the son?" asked Turner.

"Nothing on him," replied McGovern.

"Maybe he's straight," suggested Croft. "We have no evidence to suggest that any of these lads are involved. Just because they're members of some so-called gardening club doesn't necessarily identify them as couriers."

"What about the fifth one?" asked Turner.

McGovern smiled. "You're gonna love this one. His dad's a copper!"

The Courier
James R. Vance

"You're bloody joking," exclaimed Turner.

"London City mob, uniform."

"What rank?"

McGovern could hardly contain himself. "It gets better by the minute. He's a Chief Inspector!"

"Bloody hell. Do we know him?"

"Not come across him before. Jackson, Chief Inspector Jackson."

"It must be a co-incidence, surely?" added French.

"If that gardening club is a front for smuggling activities, he's got to be involved. Mind you, he could be doing it without the knowledge of his dad."

"What if he wasn't, though?" suggested Croft.

"Have we anything on this Chief Inspector?" asked Turner.

"Not checked him out yet. We thought that the boss should know first," said Mullen.

"He'll have another bloody heart attack with this," joked McGovern.

"By the way, where does Jackson live?" asked Turner.

"Hampstead."

"Bit posh, even for a Chief Inspector," commented French.

"I need to speak with the boss. Let's re-convene at five this afternoon," said Turner. He looked across at Mullen and McGovern. "It's Frank Cannon's funeral on Monday at Hoop Lane Crematorium in Golders Green. Can you two put in an appearance and check out the mourners?"

"It's hardly worth the bother. He's been cremated once already," quipped McGovern.

Mullen shook his head. "Your mouth will be the death of you one day." Addressing Turner, he said, "No problem with the funeral. We can renew some acquaintances. All the usual suspects should be there."

The two detectives stood up and made their way back to the main office.

"What about us. Do you want us back this afternoon?" asked Croft as she headed for the door.

"More than likely, but I'll let you know if it's otherwise after I've spoken with the boss," replied Turner.

The two detective constables left the room and Turner gathered up his papers with every intention of visiting the hospital. As he was about to leave, Debbie popped her head around the door.

"Before you leave, D.C.I. Dyson would like to see you in his office."

Bollocks, thought Turner. "Okay. Thanks Debbie."

He assumed that the chief inspector wanted an up-date on progress as Massey was temporarily out of action. Accordingly he prepared himself mentally before leaving the incident room.

*****

Massey was sitting upright in bed reading a newspaper when Turner entered the private ward to where he had been moved earlier.

"You look almost normal again," he said, handing him the obligatory bag of fresh fruit. He pulled up a chair and sat alongside the bed.

"I managed a shower this morning. It was the strangest sensation. I felt that everything had to be in slow motion. It's weird to be concerned about raising your arms too high and restricting the amount of effort you can put into such a mundane task. It's like learning to live all over again."

"You're progressing, though?"

"Still waiting for some results, but the blood tests and E.C.G.'s seem o.k. Enough of me, what's new?"

He'll never change, thought Turner. Here he is the day following a life-threatening heart attack and already he's back on the case. Little wonder my sister gave up on him. He related the substance of his meeting with the team while Massey listened intently. The inspector sipped some iced water before he commented.

"This is the strangest case we've ever been involved with. On the surface it appears to be a simple smuggling operation, yet we keep unearthing possible links which suggest that it's something far more sinister and that potentially some high-ranking people could be involved. Every corner we turn reveals the unexpected… an ex-customs official-cum-war hero, a foreign diplomat and now a bloody chief inspector, not to mention some guy known only as The Fixer. He'll probably turn out to be a top-ranking politician or a member of some royal family."

"We already have a politician. Don't forget the member of the British National Party."

"Hardly top-ranking."

"One never knows in this climate. These people are gaining ground with each terrorist atrocity." Turner lowered his voice. "Changing the subject slightly, I've got good news and bad news. Which first, considering your state of health?"

"The bad news is really that bad?"

"I reckon there should be a nurse on standby when I tell you."

"Give me the good news, then. Maybe it'll act as a counterbalance."

"I received two text messages on the way here. You're now addressing 'Trensh Curri', my new name!"

Massey looked at him quizzically and instantly the penny dropped. "The Fixer! You've had a reply. What else was in the message?"

"It confirmed the current number to contact for orders, specifically only from a public phone, my password and that delivery details would be sent by text. The second one identified my designated drop-point and that an empty briefcase is to be picked up there tonight."

"Bloody hell! That was quick. When did you call him?"

"Last night."

"What's the score on tracking him via the mobile number?"

"I made some enquiries with our techno boffins. They reckon that he's probably using several G.S.M. international cell phones and regularly switching sim cards."

"Clever guy. So where's our drop point?"

The Courier
James R. Vance

"Paddington Station. I need to be there at six thirty. I have to wait by the war memorial statue of a soldier. It's under the clock on platform one."

"Whoever this guy is, it springs to mind that he certainly knows London's main-line stations in some detail."

"Suggesting that he travels frequently?"

"Possibly or he's London based." Massey eased himself into a more comfortable position in his bed. "Anyway what was the bad news?"

"I was about to leave the office when I was summoned by D.C.I. Dyson."

"I should have guessed," moaned Massey. "That man is synonymous with bad news."

"He's decided that, as you could be out of action for some time, we will need a temporary replacement to, in his words, 'bring this investigation to a rapid and successful conclusion'. To effect this, a new Detective Inspector, who will report directly to him, will be joining the team on Monday morning. I think he intends to call in later today to bring you up to speed, as it were."

"The sly old bastard."

"He said that he would have taken control himself but for the pressure over the connection with the weekend assassinations where he is currently liaising with Camden and St. John's Wood."

"Do we know who's coming in?"

"Now for the really bad news. You'd better ring for the nurse! It's someone who's previously crossed his path from London City Police. I got the impression that there's also been some pressure from the Chief Constable. It's some female, who's supposed to be a rising star."

"A woman. From that lot! A rising star. You must be joking!" Massey slumped back on his pillows. "The sooner I'm out of here, the better."

"Don't push it. Get yourself healthy again. I'll still liaise with you and don't worry, I'll ensure McGovern stays close to her. He'll sort her out."

"Talk about kicking a man when he's down! It's this bloody investigation. You'll have to be extremely wary of what information she receives, especially that stuff concerning Helen. Let's keep that between the two of us for the time being. Feed my replacement with that chief inspector connection. If it comes to nothing, at least it will have occupied her time and if it unearths a can of worms, it'll be her career that's on the line. You said that he's with the same outfit. She must know him."

"It's good to see that there's still some fight left in you, but don't rush it."

"I'll beat this setback and this current case even if it kills me."

"A rather inappropriate threat under the current circumstances, wouldn't you say? I know what you mean, though. I'd feel exactly the same. Let's hope it doesn't come to that."

With those prophetic words still ringing in their ears, they bade farewell to each other.

*****

The black Porche slid to a gentle halt on Crouch End Hill. Several pairs of eyes stared from neighbouring houses expecting to see Debbie Collins emerge to be whisked away for another promo session. However they must have been disappointed when Luke Cannon appeared and opened the passenger door to join David Joseph. The car roared off and headed towards Central London.

*****

Turner quickly reported to the team about his meeting with D.C.I. Dyson and his subsequent visit to D.I. Massey. McGovern seemed pleased with his proposed role in shadowing a female inspector with a view to taking her eye off the ball. Since it was Friday, the day of the students' return from the college, coupled with Turner's assignment at another station, they decided to split into two groups.

D.S. Mullen, accompanied by D.C. Croft, was asked to cover Waterloo station to check out the students returning from

France. D.C. McGovern, together with D.C. French, was to stake out Paddington station as back-up for Turner's briefcase pick-up.

It was agreed to arm themselves with digital camera and video equipment for covertly recording any activity by potential couriers. The results could be matched against the lists which D.C. French had provided. Sammy in security at Waterloo and his counterpart, Frank, at Paddington were also contacted to ensure surveillance was functional at both locations.

*****

Scott was excited as he watched the countryside race by his window to be replaced by urban dwellings and eventually the congested sprawl of the capital. He was looking forward to his meeting with David Joseph in Canary Wharf the following morning. Apart from the news reports on the previous weekend's outrages, his week had been predictably boring. How he longed to leave school now that his appetite had been whetted by the irresponsible vicissitudes of adult life! The train pulled into Waterloo and he briskly made his way towards the kiosk where he would wait for his mother.

Two weeks had passed since the start of his memorable adventure. Deep down he was hoping for more action, convinced that David's story of helping the police would entail more involvement for him. Perhaps that was why he wanted the meeting.

Immersed in this daydream of further exploits as he stood by the newsstand to meet his mother, he became aware of two familiar faces. D.S. Mullen and D.C. Croft were seated in the Burger Bar looking like a normal couple having a snack. His reverie came to an abrupt halt as he re-lived the memory of his discovery in the cellar of David's house at Barnes. He was attempting to establish a reason for their presence when his mother arrived.

Glancing back at the detectives as Mrs. Morgan accompanied him towards the exit, he almost missed the next surprise sighting. Across the concourse was David Joseph in conversation with a casually dressed youth and two students attired in school uniform. What was going on?

He grabbed his mother's arm, stopping her abruptly. Should he approach David or ignore him? Maybe he was already working with the police officers sat in the Burger Bar. He recalled the set-up in which he had been involved when the police arrested that other youth. He looked more closely at the group. That is the other youth!

He was now convinced that another sting was in operation. He decided not to intervene in case he caused a foul-up. Naturally David would explain it all tomorrow. He quickly ushered his confused mother out of the station.

If Scott Morgan was surprised to see David Joseph and Luke Cannon with two students, it was no wonder that Mullen and Croft were equally taken aback. Having secretly taken photos and video shots of several students arriving onto the concourse, they were intrigued by this unexpected rendezvous.

The two detectives moved closer to get better shots. Mullen contacted Sammy on his mobile to ensure that he also had them in vision. How they wished that they had long distance microphones. Croft suggested that they should concentrate their video footage on their mouths. Maybe they could employ a lip reader to interpret the conversation between them. No sooner had they manoeuvred themselves into a good position than the four individuals split and left the concourse in different directions.

*****

D.C. French positioned himself on the stairs leading from platform one. D.C. McGovern loitered unobtrusively further down the platform towards the main concourse. Paddington station was busy. It was the tail-end of rush hour. D.S. Turner strolled up and down the platform in the vicinity of the clock, immersing himself in the waves of commuters who passed to and fro on their homeward journeys.

Six thirty came and went, but there was no sign of anyone delivering a black briefcase. Habit forced Turner to glance at his watch before checking with the clock jutting from the wall above him. At six forty he signalled to French to join him from the stairs. "Looks like no show," he said, disappointed. "See anything?"

"Apart from a couple of porters, one with a luggage trolley and a cleaner with one of those multi-purpose cleaning buggies, just commuters."

"Near the statue?"

"Well yes, but also on other parts of this platform."

"No school-kids?"

"None at all."

"Maybe we're at the wrong location," moaned Turner.

He wandered over closer to the statue which towered above him on a marble plinth in a small oval recess.

'IN HONOUR OF THOSE WHO SERVED IN THE WORLD WARS 1914 + 1918   1939 + 1945' was inscribed on the base.

'3312 MEN AND WOMEN OF THE GREAT WESTERN RAILWAY GAVE THEIR LIVES FOR KING AND COUNTRY' was engraved on the black slab below.

His eyes were drawn away from the stark words of commemoration towards the left of the statue. At first it looked like a continuation of the black marble section of wall which matched the base of the statue. It was also partially obscured by the sign advertising the entrance to the First Class Lounge. Suddenly he realised it jutted out slightly. It was a briefcase, a black briefcase.

"Bollocks! It was here all along."

"Perhaps the cleaner planted it," suggested French, "or maybe one of the porters."

Turner scanned the length of the platform. Not a cleaner nor a porter in sight. He picked up the briefcase after first wrapping a handkerchief around the handle.

"First stop, forensics for prints," he said.

The only person in the First Class Lounge continued reading the Financial Times, unaware of the activity on platform one. He was too busy checking his investments.

The Courier
James R. Vance

The two detectives strolled down to the main concourse to meet up with McGovern. Together they left Paddington station and headed towards Blackfriars and police headquarters, where Turner could hand over the briefcase to forensics. D.C. French was asked to check that the Gendarmerie in France were fully prepared. En route, Turner contacted Mullen and Croft to meet him and the others at The Ring.

By half past seven they had all arrived and were ordering their first pints apart from Croft who elected to have a bottle of Bud. After reporting back on the events at Paddington, the topic of conversation focussed on the diversion caused by David Joseph's meeting with Luke Cannon. They guessed that the other two students could have been Sean Driscoll and Todd Edwards, as their fathers were cronies of Frank Cannon. But the intriguing question revolved around the connection with Joseph.

"When we interviewed David Joseph, he said that he didn't recognise any of the couriers. He reckoned there were several of them and changed frequently. So, it's odds-on that he's made contact with them since, if he was telling the truth at his interview," pointed out Turner.

"But how would he know how to contact them?" asked Mullen.

"Maybe he waited at the station until he recognised them," suggested McGovern.

"Unlikely," replied Croft. "To find all three at the same time would have been impossible unless it had been pre-arranged."

"Luke Cannon's not returned to school, so he shouldn't really be there. He's been at his girlfriend's in Crouch End since last Sunday," added Turner. "Perhaps Joseph contacted him at her place."

"So how would he find him there?" asked McGovern.

"There's been loads of publicity about the Cannons all week," said Croft, "including the girlfriend. Anyone worth their salt could have tracked down those two. They were virtually demanding it, especially the girl."

The Courier
James R. Vance

"Well, there's a possible how," stated Turner. "We now need to discover why."

"And what they were discussing at the station," said McGovern.

"We may have the answer to that," replied Mullen. "We managed a few shots of them talking together before they split and Sammy in security has quite a bit on tape. Croft here suggested getting in a lip reader."

Their combined laughter was halted by Turner. "That's not a bad idea. If we learn what they were saying, it may give us a clue as to why they met in the first place."

"We could just pull them in and question them," suggested McGovern, preferring a more straightforward method.

"You mean torturing them until they spill the beans," joked Mullen.

"Well not quite that far."

"It certainly would be more effective, knowing how Andy operates," said Turner. "However, it could be more productive if we know and they don't know that we know, if you get my drift." He turned to Croft. "So, how many lip readers are you acquainted with?"

*****

Friday evening was always busy at the Windsor Castle. Early doors attracted commuters before they headed homewards. As the night wore on, they were replaced by locals and those professionals who stayed over the weekend in the capital. David Joseph arrived promptly at eight and thrust his way to the bar to order a glass of house red. He gingerly extricated himself from the mass at the bar and withdrew to a space near a corridor to await the arrival of Luke Cannon and his mates.

He vaguely remembered visiting the pub on a previous occasion following a test match at Lords between the M.C.C. and Australia. It had been during the summer and he had sat outside in the courtyard with some friends who were cricket fanatics. He was pleasantly surprised by the choice of venue for this meeting. The clientele was quality as were the general standards of the pub, the antithesis of what he had expected from the likes of Luke Cannon and his pals.

At that moment the teenager appeared in the main doorway accompanied by his young friends and two older men. David assumed that they were the fathers of Sean and Todd. They jostled through the crowd and led the way down the corridor to the back room, which Luke had booked with Cathy earlier. David duly followed and was invited to sit at the oval table. While Luke went to the hatch to order some drinks, Mickey Driscoll and Vince Edwards eyed David suspiciously.

"I believe yer want our lads to `elp you track down Frank's killer," said Mickey, assuming the senior role of the group following Frank's untimely demise. "I fought the cops were doin` that."

"It's personal," said David. "I lost my father also and I'm certain that both murders were arranged by the same person. As I explained to Luke, this Fixer guy seemed to hold my father and Frank responsible for some mix-up two weeks ago. I know that the stakes were high, yet the losses, though great, were still recoverable. To my mind their cold-blooded murders were completely iniquitous, perpetrated by some evil, power-hungry bastard. The whole business of last Sunday begs the question, where does it leave the rest of us and how safe are your lads in this venture?"

A silence ensued, punctuated only by some raucous laughter from the bar. The miscreants around the table attempted to digest what he had just stated and translate it into their level of understanding. Luke served the drinks, offering David another glass of red wine. He closed the hatch and joined them at the table.

"I agree wiv `im," said Luke. "I'm shittin` meself since me old man copped it."

"So what `ave you in mind?" asked Mickey, still trying to comprehend.

"I'm more or less aware of the system at this end, but I need to know how it operates over there. The more information

that I can gather should help me to track down this anonymous
Fixer guy. We can't rely on the police. Let's face it they're more
interested in nicking us for our illicit smuggling activities than
catching the killer of known felons. As far as they're concerned,
Frank's death and that of my father just means that there's two less
lawbreakers to keep an eye on."

David was attempting to influence them by playing on their
innate hatred of the police and their habit of closing ranks against a
common enemy. It seemed to be working.

"I fink `e's got a point," remarked Vince. "But it'll mean
the end of the lads bringin` stuff over, won't it?"

"Yes it will," replied David. "But it's a small price to pay
and don't forget there's more than one way to skin a rabbit. I'm
sure you'll find an alternative."

"What's rabbits got to do wiv it?" asked Vince.

As usual Mickey ignored him and turned to Sean and Todd.
"So, are you guys up for it?"

They nodded their heads. Luke said, "Count me out. I'm
not going back, but I'll `elp out at this end if you need me."

They all looked towards David. He fancied that he had won
them over. The rest would be easy. He leaned earnestly forwards.

"Tell me how the system works over there. Who gives you
the merchandise, where does it come from and how do you know
where to exchange it? The other query I've always wanted to know
is what happens to the money?"

Mickey answered first. "I can explain your last question.
The lads take their cut then leave the rest at the same drop point on
their way back on the Monday. In return they get an empty
briefcase which they `and over at school."

"So who makes the exchange with them?"

"Not a fuckin` clue. The lads reckon it's always some smart
bastard in a suit."

"Mmm, interesting," mused David. "What's the routine in
France, then?" He addressed the youths.

"There's a sort of gardenin` club, but it's not, if you see
what I mean," said Sean. "Near the main `ouse there's an old barn

and it's used for meetin's on Monday and Fursday nights. Monday we 'and over our empty cases and tell the old man if we've 'ad any problems. Fursday we get the cases back wiv the stuff in 'em and a card wiv all the info on."

"Who's the old man you referred to?" asked David.

"Dubois, the school gardener," said Luke. "It's like 'e's in charge of evryfin'. There's a big book 'e keeps on 'is desk in there where 'e writes evryfin' down. There's a computer there as well, but it's never switched on. 'E's probably too old to know 'ow to use it."

"So the school, the teachers and everyone knows what's going on?"

"Not fuckin' likely," replied Todd. "It's all a big secret. Only the lads doin' the runs are allowed in there."

"And the two French lads," added Sean.

"What two French lads?" asked David.

"One of 'em's the gardener's grandson. E's at the school and it's 'is dad who brings the stuff in evry Fursday mornin'. The other lad's from Paris. We don't really know why 'e's there but we fink 'is dad or someone must be sumfin' to do wiv it, 'cos 'e stays be'ind evry Fursday after the rest of us 'ave left the barn."

"If the school doesn't know what's going on, surely they must question these regular Thursday deliveries by this boy's father?"

"No, 'cos 'e comes in a wagon or a van and delivers stuff for the school as well, you know, cleanin' stuff, bog rolls and gardenin' fings. It's all stored in the barn, checked off and then taken across to the main school buildin'. Our stuff is kept separate and Dubois puts it in the briefcases ready for us on Fursday night."

"How easy is it to get access to this barn?"

"No fuckin' chance," replied Todd. "The door's always locked with a key and a padlock. The big window 'as solid wood shutters, which are fastened from the inside. It's like a bloody prison."

"Could either of you get copies of what he writes in this book on his desk?"

The Courier
James R. Vance

"Impossible," said Sean. "I've only bin near it once and it's wrote in French, so what's in it is anyone's guess. When `e's finished writin`, `e always locks it in `is desk."

"Sounds like a dead end," remarked Mickey.

The conversation ceased momentarily while everyone gathered their thoughts and wondered how else David Joseph could get hold of the information which he desperately needed. Luke finally broke the silence.

"There is anuvver way into the barn."

All heads turned in his direction.

"Through the tiny openin` in the end wall."

"It's too small," cried Todd, "and too bloody `igh up."

"Not if yer `ad a ladder and were a bit thin," retorted Luke.

"You'd `ave to be thinner than `im," replied Todd, pointing at Sean, "an` `e's that skinny `e ain't got no fuckin` shadow."

"It's better than bein` a fat slob like you," cried Sean.

"For fuck's sake, calm down," shouted Mickey. "Loose, `ow big d'you reckon this opening` is?"

"Probably about `alf a metre square."

"No way," argued Todd.

"Yer lookin` at it from the ground. It's a long way off. It's bound to look smaller," countered Luke.

"I was finkin` the same," said Sean.

"So how far from the ground is it?" asked David.

"About ten or twelve metres," replied Luke. "About as `igh as a gutter on a normal `ouse."

"To gain entry then, I'd need an extendable ladder," said David, "and someone slim enough to climb through the opening in the dark. It would have to be executed during the night."

"Then you've got a drop of ten metres or so inside the buildin`," added Mickey.

"A decent rope with a foothold loop could solve that," replied David.

"Whoever gets in that way could then open the shutters and let me in through the window and we could both make our escape the same way."

"I take it you `ave someone in mind," said Mickey.

Sean sat back in his chair. "Don't look at me. I shit meself when I'm `igh up on anyfin` and besides, gettin` out of the school's impossible at night, `cos it's all alarmed after ten firty."

"That's a point. Are there any security systems in place in the grounds of the school?"

"Only round the main buildin`," replied Luke. "The barn's some way off, so once yer over the wall, `cos the main gate'll be shut, yer okay."

"Can you draw me a sketch of the layout and directions to the school from Calais? I think a visit's in order sometime next week."

"What about yer skinny cat burglar?" asked Mickey.

"I think I know just the person," replied David, smiling confidently.

*****

Turner inserted his credit card and dialled the number. The call was answered with a question.

"Password?"

"Trensh Curri," he replied.

There was a brief silence.

"Place your order," said the voice.

"Can I order two kilos of cocaine?" he asked, tentatively.

"Quality?"

Not prepared for that, he instinctively said, "Pure, top notch."

"Anything further?"

"Yes, actually. Can you supply a quantity of the liquid chemical form of Sarin or VX?"

"VX could be difficult. I must make enquiries. Sarin is possible."

"How soon could Sarin be supplied?"

"The last time I supplied Sarin, it took two weeks."

"Is that two weeks from the initial order to when it will be delivered here?"

The Courier
James R. Vance

"Yes.......you wish to place an order?"

"I need to check first."

"Is that it?"

"For the time being, yes. Just the coke."

"You will receive a text to confirm delivery details and costs."

There was a click and the phone went dead.

Turner's head was spinning as he set off to visit Massey at the hospital. The words were still ringing in his ears. 'The last time I supplied Sarin, it took two weeks'. The short trip to Guys Hospital was a blur. He was now on automatic pilot.

A proven chemical biological agent had already been smuggled into the United Kingdom. Oh, shit! Who had ordered Sarin? he thought. How much had been delivered? Where was it now? And above all, why?

He parked the car near the private wing. He felt a shiver run down his neck. The cold night air was not the reason. The detective sergeant called D.C. French on his mobile before he entered the building. He asked him to advise the Gendarmerie that the wheels had been set in motion. He emphasised that they should only track any activities over there, not prevent the merchandise from passing through. Once the arrests had been made at the drop point, only then were the French to move in and round up any identified players at their end.

Massey was expecting him. He was sitting at the side of the bed, reading a magazine which he had selected from the stationery shop trolley. He looked up and realised by Turner's expression that something was amiss.

"Bad day at the office?" he enquired, sympathetically.

"You don't want to know," he replied and sat on a bedside chair. He sighed and began to recount the more recent events of the day.

"At least things are moving," commented Massey, deep in thought. "Do you fancy some tea or even a glass of wine? There's quite a reasonable bar menu here."

Turner smiled. "You always manage to take everything in your stride, whereas I tend to go off at a tangent."

"That's probably why I ended up in here. I keep my fears and anxieties too close. I should share them and relieve the tension more. Anyway, what is it to be? Tea, wine, coffee maybe or something even stronger?"

"After the remark from that bastard on the phone, I could do with a large brandy, but I'll settle for some tea."

Massey rang and ordered a pot of tea and biscuits.

"I'm not sure what to do about our friend, David Joseph. What do you reckon he's up to?" asked Turner.

"I would imagine that he's picked up on Frank Cannon's spectacular exit and maybe recognised his son from the media coverage. Don't forget they were both at the station for interviews at the same time. He is probably attempting to join forces. I can't see him achieving anything and it's doubtful that he could hinder our investigation any more than he has already. Let him carry on playing his little games for a while longer.

If he does cause problems we'll just bang him up. We've enough on him already, but at the moment we can do without the extra paperwork and hassle of charging him. At the end of the day, his arrest won't help us one iota in tracking down The Fixer."

"But I thought that he was supposed to be helping us."

"Quite, but if you think back, that fell apart when his contact was cut and his old man was gunned down. We no longer need him currently and it appears that young Scott is none the worse for his experience. In fact he seems to have relished it."

"Once we have flushed out the main players, we can pass his file, together with what we have on the others, over to Revenue and Customs. To be honest, I'm more interested in apprehending this Fixer chappie in the hope that it leads us to those responsible for the assassinations."

"I'll have to tell the D.C.I. about the Sarin when I report in tomorrow."

"He'll bring in MI5 and the anti-terrorism unit."

"They'll steamroller over everything we've worked towards."

"Not necessarily so. Don't forget political pressure is focussed on the prevention of terrorism. Their priority would be to direct their intelligence towards a potential bio-chemical bomb threat. If they received information that Sarin had entered the country, they would devote their limited resources towards discovering its destination rather than its source."

"So what should I tell Dyson?"

"Explain that the French are monitoring the supply chain and that a quantity of the chemical has been brought in by one of these couriers. We don't know who, how much and when, but that we are liaising with the French in the hope that their investigations will reveal more details. It keeps us on track and at the same time gives him more to think about in addition to the on-going murder enquiry."

"What are we going to do about Helen and her diplomat husband?"

"Absolutely nothing. It's only conjecture on our part and until some substantial evidence emerges we should just ignore it. If he is involved in some way, tough shit, he'll have to pay the price. I believe there's no way Helen could be involved."

At that moment tea arrived. The conversation turned to the state of the patient's health and his potential date of discharge from the hospital. He was due to undergo a cardiac catheter test at the weekend to measure pressures inside his heart, check the condition of his heart valves and to assess the state of his coronary arteries. Dependant upon the results, his release could be delayed by the need for cardiac surgery or treatment by angioplasty.

Massey had also learned that he would have to undergo several weeks of gradual rehabilitation before he would be allowed back to full-time work. This would include a programme of exercise and education about stress management, diet and relaxation.

Turner reckoned that the whole team could benefit from that. The discussion was having a noticeable effect on the inspector. Despite his determination and impetuosity to return to the investigation, he was far from ready. Turner suggested that he get some sleep. Just the mental strain of talking and interacting had tired him considerably. He said goodnight and promised to return the following day. The detectives parted company with the word 'Sarin' foremost in their minds.

Chapter 27

SATURDAY MORNING: Rebecca was having a breakfast of scrambled eggs on toast when David entered his kitchen and helped himself to coffee. He joined her at the round table in the alcove.

"How's your French?" he asked.

"My French what?" she snapped. She was not yet fully awake and certainly not in the mood for another one of his whims. Still annoyed with him about her recent arrest, she had listened at length to his explanation with total incredulity and was no longer prepared to give him any more leeway.

"You studied French at college, how good are you at speaking it?"

"Why?"

"I thought we could have a couple of days over there."

"I know you too well. What are you scheming now?"

"Okay. I'll level with you." David realised that no amount of charm or subtle patter would satisfy his cousin. For once he decided to be open with her. "I need some information which could help the police to trace dad's murderer. I told you that we wouldn't be charged in exchange for my helping them in their enquiries."

"I didn't think that included me."

"Quite. I just thought that it would look less suspicious if we visited that college which supplies the couriers as a couple."

"Visited the college as a couple," repeated Rebecca. "What are you up to?"

"We could be tourists or something."

"You're going all the way to France to call at some dodgy school as passing tourists? What are you going to say? 'Can we check the place out for an international smuggling ring?' You may consider the French to be gullible, but don't tar me with the same brush. Now tell me the truth."

He rose from the table. "Do you want more coffee?"

"David, stop prevaricating. What's going on?"

He poured himself another coffee and returned to the table where he outlined the gist of his meeting at the Windsor Castle. Rebecca listened patiently until he described how he intended to climb into the grounds of the college and break into a barn by lowering her through a small aperture where, attached to a rope, she would descend ten metres into the unknown in the darkness.

"Stop right there," cried Rebecca. "You're crazy." She left him to contemplate an empty coffee cup and the mental image of a small aperture in a barn wall.

*****

Before Turner had the opportunity to report to Detective Chief Inspector Dyson he was told, on arrival at Blackfriars, to attend a meeting in the incident room. The majority of the team had already assembled there along with several uniformed officers. The general concensus of opinion suggested that the temporary detective inspector, replacing D.I. Massey was about to be introduced. For some strange reason Monday had been brought forward to Saturday. Dyson eventually appeared in the doorway and ushered in a young, attractive brunette.

She carried with her a mountain of files, which initially hid the contours of her upper body. She stacked the paperwork on the table at the head of the room. Her long dark hair draped over her elegant shoulders and cascaded over her ample breasts which were accentuated by the lapels of her charcoal tailored jacket. She wore a matching knee length skirt and silver grey stilettos which complemented her long slim legs.

Dyson fussily offered her a chair which she declined, preferring to sit on the corner of the table with legs crossed. She threw her head back slightly, tossing her shiny locks over her shoulders, and placed both hands palm down slightly behind her. The pose was at the same time confident, defiant and sexy.

The Courier
James R. Vance

The room fell silent. The attention of everyone was captured by the seductive figure perched on the corner of an ordinary table. The vision before them resembled a decorative piece of sculptured beauty. D.C.I. Dyson coughed nervously and addressed the meeting despite the fact that not one pair of eyes was focussed on him.

"I'd like to introduce Detective Inspector Stephanie Harper. As you know D.I. Massey is recovering in hospital from a heart condition and D.I. Harper will be taking over his duties until such time as he is fit and well again to return to work. She was due to join the team on Monday but, after discussing progress so far, we both thought it essential to bring the appointment forward. I trust that you will afford her your full co-operation." He waved his hand in her direction and left the room.

"Her initials are spot on," whispered McGovern to Mullen. "She's certainly some D.I.S.H.!"

"Reckon you can manage her, then, 'sort her out', as the boss has suggested?"

"No problem, pal."

The buzz which had suddenly increased as the D.C.I. left the room dissipated just as quickly. The temporary inspector took centre stage. She remained seated on the table as she prepared to address the assembled team.

Unfortunately for the new inspector, her good looks were an immediate disadvantage. The majority of the team would see her progress to detective inspector to be bolstered by her appearance rather than earned by merit. The men would see her as a sexual challenge, male versus female. Alternatively the female team members would despise her for either having used her sexuality as a means to success or, conversely, been offered promotion because of it. However talented she may be, she would find it difficult to win them over. She was in a lose, lose situation.

"Good morning," she began. "I am here principally to take charge of the current investigation into the cross-channel smuggling operation. However I will also make myself available for advice to any officers who are engaged on other minor enquiries. Since learning of this appointment I have dedicated myself to scrutinising in minute detail all the files appertaining to this particular case."

She reached over and placed one hand on the stack of paperwork. Placing her free hand against her hip, she turned back to face her audience.

"Frankly, I am appalled that so little progress has been made during the past two weeks. It is almost as if there has been a reluctance to complete the task in hand. All that will change, commencing immediately. Though I am here on a temporary basis, I fully expect to put it to bed before I leave. I have an unsullied reputation with City Police and I expect it to remain intact."

"Is she saying she's a virgin?" whispered McGovern, causing numerous sniggers around him.

The inspector must have been aware of the suppressed sounds but continued without displaying any negative emotion.

"We will make a fresh start immediately after this meeting and I expect no relaxation of effort until we resolve this dereliction of duty. As some of you are presently more involved than others, I suggest that the following officers remain in the room: D.C. Croft, D.C. French, D.C. McGovern, D.S. Mullen and D.S. Turner. I will bring in other officers to join this small team as we progress. They will be selected on merit and specific expertise. The remainder can now return to work. Thank you."

She leaned over, opened several files spreading them across the table, sat down and waited until the room had emptied apart from her nominees, who were standing in a group, arms folded in a face-off type pose towards the far corner.

"Come closer," she said. "I don't bite."

"I'll bet she sucks okay, though," whispered McGovern.

Suffocating their laughter, they seated themselves in front of the table.

"You must be D.C. McGovern," she remarked. "I hear you always have a lot to say. That's fine but I must insist on total transparency of both opinions and actions within the team, no hidden agendas, open communication at all times. I expect complete commitment, positive responses and swift action. Before I outline my strategy, are there any questions?"

"Yes, I have a question," said McGovern.

"Oh, shit!" murmured Turner, softly.

"You're from London City Police, yes? Are you acquainted with a Chief Inspector Jackson?"

"Good old Andy," whispered Mullen. "Straight for the bloody jugular!"

*****

Café Brera was busy with weekend shoppers. Excited at the prospect of meeting up with his new hero, Scott had arrived in good time and had already consumed a large cup of coffee before David Joseph appeared on the scene. They greeted each other as long-lost friends might have done after years apart. Scott wasted no time.

"I spotted you at Waterloo yesterday. Are you working with the police already?"

Never slow to grasp an opportunity, David nodded in the affirmative. "I've been given an assignment and I need your help."

Scott leaned fervently across the table, hardly able to contain himself.

"Trouble is," said David, "I'm not sure whether you'll be able to manage to cover your involvement. I've been instructed to go to France. They need some vital information. Firstly, do you have a passport?"

"We're going to France?" asked Scott, excitedly. "When?"

"There's a problem. It'll mean an overnight stay and it needs to be kept absolutely secret. How will you explain that away to your mother?"

"When do we have to leave?"

"Monday evening at the latest, back on Tuesday."

"No problem. I can leave for school Monday morning, tell mum I'm staying at a mate's in Ashford and come home as normal on Tuesday night. What time on Monday?"

The Courier
James R. Vance

"I could pick you up when school finishes and we'll drive straight to Dover, pick up the ferry, carry out the mission and be back in England for breakfast on Tuesday morning. I'll drop you off at the school and no-one will be the wiser."

"You can pick me up earlier if you like. I've two free periods Monday afternoon, so I can be ready by a quarter to two."

"Fine. Be at the main gates by two o'clock."

"Where will we stay?"

"We won't. The job has to be carried out under cover of darkness, sometime during the dead of night. Do you reckon you'll have the stamina. It'll mean hardly any sleep for forty eight hours and also involve a bit of abseiling?"

"Great. I've done rock climbing at Brecon Beacons and at an activity centre at Eskdale in the Lake District on an outward bound course. I'll bring a change of clothes, something thick and warm for the night-time."

"Not too thick," warned David, reflecting on Luke's estimation of the size of the opening in the barn. "You do have a passport?"

"Absolutely. This is brill. Will it be dangerous?"

"Not really, probably hazardous would be a better description. I'll fill you in with all the details when I pick you up. Have we got a deal?"

"Too true," replied Scott. "When did you find out about this? Do the police know that I'm going with you?"

Unsure of when he had arranged this current meeting with Scott, David said that discussions had been taking place during the course of the week. He explained that the police would not be told of his involvement as it could be a security risk and he (Scott) had to promise not to tell anyone about it, not even his friend Giulio.

If the mission had a successful outcome, he assured Scott that his contribution would be recognised. David had achieved his objective, more easily than he could have imagined. Consequently he offered his apologies for having to leave for an urgent meeting, leaving the young man to mutate once again into his James Bond alter-ego.

*****

Detective Inspector Harper had obviously done her homework. Her immediate reaction to McGovern's question was to counter it by a rhetorical question which allowed her to retain control of the situation.

"Why have you singled out Chief Inspector Jackson? I assume that you consider his son could potentially be a courier. I find it strange that with the help of the police in France you have identified several youths who could be involved in this illicit smuggling ring, yet not one has been brought in for questioning. The exception is Luke Cannon, who was arrested in possession of a briefcase filled with banknotes and subsequently released without charge.

That brings me to another anomaly, David Joseph. No charges against him despite the fact that, in the course of leading you all a merry dance, he kidnapped some young student, held him hostage, made a ransom demand, stole a cruiser, lied about the theft of his own cruiser and admitted receiving hooky jewellery items to defraud Revenue and Customs. This man's an out-and-out criminal and still free, not even out on bail, still in possession of his passport. What on earth is going on or rather not going on?"

It was difficult to offer a legitimate excuse for what she had described without disclosing the sting which Massey had been organising. Somehow the suspicions of the inspector had to be deflected in a similar way that Dyson had been kept at bay. They had to give her something tangible to focus on otherwise she would destroy all the groundwork which had been prepared to trace The Fixer. Turner had an idea.

"May I bring you up to date, boss?" he asked.

"I would prefer to be addressed as ma'am," replied the inspector. "Carry on."

"It is planned to interview them, but we only received the list of students' names on Wednesday and as they were all in France until last night, it was somewhat impracticable to lift them. In the meantime we have checked them out and the intention was to question each and every one of them over the weekend. That apart, more serious incidents have overtaken those particular matters.

There have been, as you are well aware, three murders which are currently under investigation, albeit by St. John's Wood and Camden, but nonetheless possibly connected to our case. In addition, there is some far more serious news which, I am sure, you will wish to prioritise and act upon immediately."

The rest of the team looked across at Turner, wondering what bombshell he had kept in reserve. From what he had said so far, they realised that, not only was he trying to protect their current operation, but also that he was about to offer some juicy carrot to a rather ambitious inspector. But what had he withheld from them?

"Only this morning, guv, er ma'am," he continued, "we received a call from France with some terrifying news."

Once again the team were intrigued by Turner's words. What had he not told them or was he fabricating some nonsense to sidetrack her?

"One of the couriers has brought in a quantity of Sarin."

The team suddenly feared that he was about to spill the beans. How much was he going to divulge? They looked at the temporary inspector. How would she react?

"You're talking about a biochemical agent, sergeant?"

"Yes, ma'am, same as the one used in the Japanese underground."

"Have you told the D.C.I.?"

"I was on my way when I was summoned to attend your meeting. I fear that you may have to talk to MI5."

"That goes without saying. Have you any details?"

"According to the French police, it came via a telephone intercept. There's no info on how much, when or who was involved."

"Maybe one of these students which you identified as possible couriers can help."

"I doubt it ma'am. They bring in a briefcase without any knowledge of its contents. That's how the system works."

"I'll need to discuss the matter with the D.C.I. and take his advice. In the meantime maybe you could bring in these eight students for questioning."

"Does that include Luke Cannon, ma'am, 'cos he's already been interviewed?" asked McGovern.

"Of course it includes him. Apart from anything else, you'll be asking him about a completely different matter. After what D.S. Turner has just told us, you must give this utmost priority."

She once again addressed Turner. "By the way, what was the name of your French contact?"

"Not sure, ma'am," he said misleadingly. "To be honest he didn't leave his name. D.C. French has been liaising with them, but he wasn't around and I just took the message."

The inspector turned to D.C. French. "Who's your contact over there?"

French briefly looked across at Turner before he spoke. "To be honest, ma'am, there's several of them and they normally just say it's the Gendarmerie at Ardres and more often as not follow it up with a fax. You should have copies of them in your files. They've sometimes given me their names but I'm useless at French, so I can never remember them."

The others stifled their smiles.

"I suppose I should have expected nothing less," snapped the inspector, "appointing someone with no language skills to liaise with the police abroad."

D.I. Harper gathered up her files, stormed out of the room and marched off to see Dyson. Once she was out of earshot the team fell about laughing.

"Fuckin' fantastic," exclaimed McGovern. "What a story. I've got to hand it to you. That was quick thinking."

"Not me," replied Turner. "Thank French here. He backed me up brilliantly and to say that he was useless at the French language…well, that was the icing on the cake."

"But your story about the Sarin," began McGovern.

The Courier
James R. Vance

"It was no story, guys. One of the couriers has already brought in a quantity."

The smiles quickly faded.

Chapter 28

SATURDAY & SUNDAY: On a directive from D.I.Harper all eight youths on D.C. French's list were brought in for investigation during the weekend. They were questioned about their most recent activities in relation to consignments they had brought in from France. As the system prevented them from knowing the exact contents of each briefcase and the identity of the recipients, the information which was collated was of little value. Those couriers who had smuggled in merchandise for their own use or for their own families refrained from admitting to it.

Most of the youths offered little or no details, using excuses such as 'can't remember exactly' or 'not done any for months' and even 'business has been slack recently'. All of those questioned stated that they understood that the briefcases contained souvenirs from France. The only substantial data that was elicited, which the youths could hardly offer reasons to have forgotten, were the locations of the various drops. Most of those were specific sites at main-line stations, easily accessible by the underground system.

As far as the team were concerned it was a wasted exercise, but at least it satisfied the demands of D.I. Harper. As was to be expected, agents from MI5 descended on Blackfriars and interviewed the members of Massey's team individually. Prior to the visit they had all agreed to release a specially censored version of events, which naturally omitted their contact with The Fixer, the drugs order and the deals made with David Joseph, Mickey Driscoll and Vince Edwards.

D.C. French managed to get guarantees from the Gendarmerie to keep quiet about the sting operation, as it was to their advantage in their quest to nail Francis Dubois. They agreed to continue their surveillance activities until the following Friday.

The Courier
James R. Vance

Like their English counterparts they had no wish to see Special
Forces moving in, forcing their suspects underground.

It was almost eight fifteen when a weary Turner arrived at
Guys Hospital to visit his friend and colleague. The inspector was
in a buoyant mood considering that he had earlier in the day
undergone a minor angioplasty operation. He had spent about one
hour in the Catheter Suite where a stent had been inserted into his
right coronary artery to expand a restricted section, allowing the
blood to flow freely again. His main discomfort was caused by the
necessity to lie still until the catheter could be removed later in the
evening. He welcomed the appearance of Chris Turner to pass
away the interim period.

"You seem pleased with yourself," said Turner as he
flopped exhausted into the bedside chair. "Nice flowers," he
remarked, nodding towards a huge spray of red roses on a bedside
table.

"Helen," replied Massey. "She sent them from Paris before
setting off to Guadeloupe. Nice touch, I thought."

He went on to describe his experience in theatre. "Chris, it
was unbelievable. They only gave me a local anaesthetic in my
groin and I could actually see my heart pumping the blood around
my system on a monitor. It was like popping into the barber's for a
haircut!

To top it all, whilst they were poking around inside my
arteries, there was background music. I listened to The Moody
Blues with 'Knights in White Satin' as they were inserting the
stent. That was followed by Chris Rea with 'The Road from Hell'.
It was just a fantastic experience. You could describe it as a
musical operation in a theatre. An opera with me as the lead!" He
laughed and immediately grimaced with some discomfort.

He finally added that it was possible to be discharged
tomorrow or on Tuesday, provided that the final test results were
favourable. "I wondered if you could pick me up," said Massey.

"Call me on my mobile when you're ready. Who's going to
look after you at the flat?"

The Courier
James R. Vance

"They reckon I should be fine, so long as I don't overdo it. Could be back at work soon."

"Not before bloody time." Turner related the events of the weekend.

Though annoyed and somewhat frustrated at the actions of his replacement, Massey thanked his sergeant for how the team had responded.

"Heard any news about what David Joseph was up to with Luke Cannon and his pals?"

"Nothing. It's all very quiet on that front."

"How's the murder investigation going?"

"Don't ask. As you might expect it's going nowhere and Dyson's now steering them in our direction. I just hope we can keep them away from France until we can nab a courier with the evidence at our end. The gendarmes can then turn over the school and hopefully we'll have a case for C.P.S. I just need the breathing space of one week. I'm sure a text will arrive designating Friday as D-day."

"D-day?"

"Drop day. It just seemed appropriate. But you know what it's like with that lot at Camden. One whiff of a possible trip to France...it'll be like telling a child where the sweet jar is, but not to touch."

"A word of advice. If you or the gendarmes acquire any info which might help in tracing the Sarin, you must pass it on to MI5, whatever the consequences to our scenario. There could be lives at stake and none of us should have that on our conscience."

"It goes without saying. There's a team meeting tomorrow morning with Harper and Dyson. I don't know what their agenda will be next and we can't move with ours until I receive that text or the French guys report on any action at their end."

"If it's quiet, you could do some background checks on our French diplomat. Ask D.C. French to make some enquiries through his contacts over there, but don't mention the connection with us. You never know, we may be able to eliminate him which would ease our worries about Helen."

The Courier
James R. Vance

"I just hope that nothing transpires over the next few days to throw a spanner in the works."

"Well, as long as you keep a tight rein on the Camden mob and keep Dyson and Harper distracted, everything should go according to plan."

*****

An archway led from the opulent lounge into a minimalist dining area, the centrepiece of which was an oval glass table supported by perforated curves of highly polished stainless steel. Suspended above the table was a stainless steel lighting gondola. The matching dining chairs were curved like the table. Wide strips of cream leather formed the seat and back support of each chair. Art nouveau paintings in stainless steel frames decorated the walls and in the far corner a sculpture of assorted metal cubes cascaded from ceiling to floor. David had re-designed this part of the house shortly after moving in.

Rebecca appeared from the kitchen carrying a platter of chicken stir-fry and a dish of tomato and basil pasta which she had prepared. David opened a bottle of Anjou Cépage Cabernet 2003 and poured a glass for each of them. They sat facing each other and commenced the meal.

"You've been quiet all day," she remarked. "Are you still going ahead with it?"

"Everything is set for tomorrow night. I'll be leaving just after lunch."

"I've been thinking. I realise how you must feel about your father and I completely understand why you must at least try to avenge his death. You can't go on blaming yourself, so maybe this mission of yours is a way of not only absolving yourself, but possibly an opportunity to bring about some kind of closure. What I'm trying to say is that you have my full support and if you want me to dive through a window for you, just ask."

David took a sip of wine. "I already have a volunteer."

Rebecca frowned. "Not one of those villains you've been talking to?"

"What's the problem with those guys?"

"Well, they're from a criminal background. Your whole future could be ruined by them."

"We're hardly whiter than white, are we? If it makes you feel better, let's just say they're a lower class of criminal than we are."

"Which one is helping you, the one whose father died in the car bomb explosion?"

"None of them, actually. Scott's offered to help."

"Damn it, David, you can't take him. Why drag him into your devious plans once again. You're playing on his mis-guided hero worship of you. He's just a kid and besides, don't you think you've put him through enough already? If you are caught for breaking and entering, he'll also end up with a criminal record. You're hardly being fair with him."

"He enjoyed every minute of our escapade on the river. He can't wait for some more action. Anyway it's a done deal. He's coming with me."

Rebecca took a huge slug of wine. "That's it then. No arguments. I'm coming too, if only to look after the interests of that young man."

Chapter 29

MONDAY: D.I. Harper strode into the incident room without so much as a good morning and immediately launched into her demands.

"I want you to bring in the following suspects for detailed interrogation. Luke Cannon for possession of stolen money and V.A.T. avoidance, David Joseph for kidnapping, theft, extortion, perversion of the course of justice and V.A.T avoidance, his sister, Rebecca Joseph for aiding and abetting, Michael Driscoll and Vincent Edwards for V.A.T. avoidance. You have until the end of the day. Any questions?"

"I beg your pardon, ma'am," replied D.S. Turner. "Most of the evidence so far is purely circumstantial and, by the way, Rebecca is David Joseph's cousin, not his sister."

Ignoring his last remark, the inspector continued. "We have video footage, taped interviews together with, in some cases, an admission of guilt and witnesses who can testify to their misdemeanours. I don't see a problem."

"Luke Cannon was used by David Joseph to return our money back to us, fake money at that and he can hardly be charged with VAT avoidance as he's not a VAT registered trader, nor is there any evidence of his having purchased or sold on any merchandise, brought illegally into the country."

"But his father was trading and the son was supplying the goods to him."

"His father's dead, for Christ's sake and Luke will swear as did the rest of the youths that he believed he was just dropping off souvenirs."

"For which he was well recompensed."

The Courier
James R. Vance

"We've no evidential proof of that, only assumptions. His type do not possess bank accounts and he probably spends his cut as fast as he receives it. If we charge him, the defence will drive a ten ton truck through it. Also take the case of Rebecca Joseph. When she was interviewed she claimed no knowledge of her cousin's dealings and he stated in his interview that she was not party to his involvement. Again no evidence that she was involved."

"But we have her on video footage exchanging briefcases at the station."

"None of that footage can identify the blonde at the station as Rebecca Joseph."

"Fingerprints on the briefcase?"

"It was a cold day. She was wearing gloves."

Harper was ruffled. "We have the taxi driver's testimony and the neighbour at Ashford who spoke with her."

"The cabbie dropped the blonde on Maida Vale, not at her house and how many blondes do cabbies pick up each day? With regard to the guy at Ashford, you should speak to Sergeant Dawkins. If I remember rightly, his last description of the man was something like 'he's away with the fairies'. A good defence lawyer would tear them to shreds."

"I suppose that you also have good reasons for not arresting David Joseph," said the inspector, sarcastically.

"David Joseph is actually on our side. Admittedly he went about it in a totally bizarre fashion and sadly his father paid for his scam with his life. Until that moment he was in the process of assisting us in our enquiries and in return, we promised not to lean too heavily on him. He knows that he will be charged over the V.A.T. fraud and accepts that he will be found guilty. Bringing him in at this juncture will not provide us with any additional information and serve no purpose whatsoever.

Driscoll and Edwards are also guilty of fraud, but again we have no hard evidence. It will take an in-depth enquiry to discover the extent of their swindle and we believe that their cases should be handed to Revenue and Customs as they have the expertise in that field."

"You're virtually telling me then, that it is pointless bringing in any of these characters."

"We can bring them in, but I cannot honestly say what it will achieve."

D.I. Harper had been subdued. She sat facing the team, pensive in an effort to regain control. Seconds ticked by which seemed like minutes as she assessed her situation. There was no way out. The enquiry had reached an impasse as far as her comprehension of the situation. She turned to her other main strength, her charm.

"Well I must thank you for your expert analysis of the state of play," she said, smiling. "What do you reckon our next move should be?"

Turner looked across at his colleagues, who were inwardly sharing his victory, whilst he was stunned by her request. He needed to play for time. "I suggest that we wait for the French to make a move. I believe D.C. French would agree with that and update us with any progress?" he replied, glancing at his nominee.

"Certainly. The students are back today and there's some heavy surveillance now in place at the college. They've promised to contact us immediately they have anything to report."

Over the past week or so, the team had become extremely adept at imparting information of little value but with a hint of major importance.

"Fine," said Harper. "I suggest we meet again first thing in the morning. In the meantime I will speak with the D.C.I. and ask how we can be of further assistance to the murder enquiry teams and MI5. Thank you for a most illuminating discussion." She hesitated slightly. "I think I have the full picture now."

With those final words she left the room. Seconds before, the team had been preparing to congratulate themselves on another victory over 'she who must be obeyed' as McGovern had recently christened her. Her last remark, however, left them wondering whether she meant their depiction of events or the true state of play. D.I. Stephanie Harper had always survived by reason of her winning mentality.

*****

David parked the B.M.W. in the same place where he had stopped just over two weeks earlier, opposite the main entrance to the school. This time the road was much busier as the school was open for business. Rebecca sat beside him having insisted on making the trip. She had no intention of getting involved with the actual break-in at the barn, but argued that she could be useful not just on account of her reasonable command of French, but also as a look-out and driver if there were problems.

David had relented having experienced her tenacity and intransigence on several previous occasions. Even as a child she would remain obstinate until any protagonist relented.

Scott appeared earlier than arranged, such was his eagerness to be involved. He looked at Rebecca, not expecting David to be accompanied by anyone.

"You probably don't remember me," she said as he jumped into the rear of the car. "We exchanged briefcases quite recently." She smiled and offered her hand. "You can call me Becky."

"I thought it was just the two of us," remarked Scott, leaning over towards David. His tone suggested an air of disappointment.

"It was, but Becky's our insurance cover." David glanced in the rear view mirror and drove away towards Ashford and the M20.

Twenty minutes later they were passing the exit for the Channel Tunnel terminus at Folkestone before continuing on towards Dover. First stop before the ferry was Hertz Van Rental on Snargate Street. David had arranged to pick up a Mercedes Sprinter with a long wheel base as he needed the space to accommodate extension ladders. In addition, he was wary of using his own car too openly, especially for the planned escapade. He completed the paperwork and they transferred from the B.M.W. the paraphenalia they needed for the trip.

320

The Courier
James R. Vance

Shortly after three twenty they were boarding the Sea
France ferry bound for Calais. They sat in one of the bars and
discussed the game-plan for their mini adventure. The crossing
took an hour and fifteen minutes and following disembarkation
they by-passed Calais centre ville by joining the A16 and heading
west towards Boulogne.

Leaving the motorway at junction 13 they drove into
Coquelles to the Centre Commercial and parked outside Leroy
Merlin, a large D.I.Y. superstore. Here David purchased a set of
'échelle coulissante', the extension ladders needed to reach the
window in the barn. The load length of the van was 4.21 metres.
The ladders non-extended measured 3.95 metres.....a perfect fit!

Across the road from the store they spotted a Buffalo Grill,
where they elected to spend some time on an evening meal before
taking the N43 to Ardres. Following the meal they passed time by
drinking coffee in a town centre bar. Eventually they made their
way to Balinghem and followed the D228 in search of the lake.

In the darkness they became lost several times as they
attempted to find the road which led to Le Manoir. It was almost
twelve thirty when they spotted the sign for the college.

David guided the van through the twists and turns of the
track as it wove its way through the trees. Finally the main
gateway appeared in the headlights of the vehicle. They coasted
slowly for about a further two hundred metres before drawing to a
halt. Rebecca switched on an interior light and consulted David's
hand-drawn map which he had sketched in the Windsor Castle.
She looked across the road to a densely wooded area.

"There should be a narrow pathway through the trees
opposite to where you go over the wall," she remarked.

David leaned over his seat, unzipped one of the bags and
withdrew a torch. He directed the beam up and down the lane.

"It must be further along," he said and gently eased the van
forwards, still shining the torch at right angles.

"There it is," he cried as the light picked out a clearing in
the undergrowth. The vehicle stopped and he switched off the
engine. "Now comes the difficult bit."

The Courier
James R. Vance

They stepped out of the van into an eerie silence broken only by the distant hoot of an owl. Opening the rear doors, Scott and David gently withdrew the ladders whilst Rebecca shone the torch. Without extending them they propped the lightweight aluminium steps against the perimeter wall of the college.

David returned to the unzipped holdall in the van and lifted out two large bundles of 8 mm cord rope, a Black Diamond harness and several spare Screwgate karabiners clipped together.

"I presume that little lot's for me," whispered Scott.

David nodded and grinned as he helped Scott to don and adjust the harness. Satisfied, he passed him one of the bundles and a spare torch. Throwing the other bundle over his own shoulder, he gathered up the karabiners and whispered, "Let's go abseiling."

Rebecca settled herself in the driving seat and watched them disappear over the wall with their equipment and the ladders. The beams from their torches melted away into the black void beyond the wall, leaving her to contemplate a period of deathly silence and total darkness. She leaned over and as a precaution locked all the doors.

Scott and David picked their way stealthily through the shrubs and trees, each step seemingly cracking twigs and undergrowth with a resounding echo in the stillness of a cold, damp night. A large building appeared through the trees as they emerged from the wooded area onto an expanse of grass. David illuminated a stone wall which rose up to their left. He shone the beam upwards until it picked out a small aperture of blackness. It was the gable end of the barn.

Without speaking they withdrew the sections of ladder until it was fully extended and set it against the wall below the opening. David shone his torch up the ladder and was relieved to see that it reached to within a half metre beyond the entry point. He turned to Scott. "You still okay about this?"

The youngster gazed up at the hole. "If I can get through the opening, I'll be fine. It looks as though I'll have to go in head first. The ladder's not really long enough to go past it and drop in feet first."

The Courier
James R. Vance

"I was thinking the same. Mind you, if you can get a grip on the inside ledge, the rope will hold you there until you are able to turn upright again."

"I've abseiled before, so I'll be okay. As soon as I'm stable and in position, I'll play out the rope and drop down inside."

David wrapped the trailing rope securely around the nearest tree. Having connected and checked the tackle, Scott carefully ascended the ladder, whilst David guided him with the beam from his torch. They had adjusted the ladder so the final rung allowed the youngster to virtually access the opening head first.

As he mounted each rung his only concern was whether he would fit through the gap. His head eventually became level with the hole in the wall. He pushed his shoulders into the gap and shone his torch down into the interior of the barn.

It was cavernous. Massive oak beams stretched across the space between the side walls and narrower beams formed triangles above to support the tiled roof. The area below was partly obscured by several large packing cases and across one wall there appeared to be a large wooden structure. Opposite he could see the window which, he assumed he would open for David to enter. At the far end were large wooden doors.

Though much larger in size, it triggered recollections of David's cellar. He shuddered, partly from the cold night air, partly from fear but mostly from the memory.

Scott eased himself forwards, dislodging from the ledge some loose stones and rubble, which clattered down into the interior. It was impossible to grip anything and still drag his whole body through the gap. It was decision time, the moment of trust where the mind had to possess complete faith in the equipment.

He played out sufficient rope to exit the aperture and pushed away from the stone wall, launching himself into space amongst the rafters of the barn. He twisted violently and, in attempting to right himself, lost his grip on the torch. It tumbled, spinning into the darkness, its beam flashing in every direction like a deranged searchlight. It thudded onto the floor below and the light went out.

The Courier
James R. Vance

"Shit," muttered Scott under his breath and immediately set out to abseil down the barn wall in total darkness. On reaching the floor, he unbuckled himself from the rig and crawled on all fours to locate the torch. He was unable to find it as he crashed about into various solid objects, completely disorientated in the inky blackness. He looked upwards in an attempt to make out the position of the opening so that he might be able to pinpoint the wall. He strained his eyes through three hundred and sixty degrees. Nothing but blackness.

Outside, David had one eye on the shutters on the side wall of the building and the other on the aperture above him. There seemed to be no light from inside and no sound of any movement. Concerned that Scott may have fallen or worse, he decided to climb the ladders. His heart began to thump as he considered the possible consequences of Scott having incurred some kind of accident. At the top of the ladder he shone his torch through the gap.

"You're a saviour," whispered Scott loud enough for him to hear. The youngster explained his predicament and David leaned across the ledge shining the beam of light downwards.

"Found it," hissed Scott from below, as he retrieved the dropped torch. "I'll open the shutters for you."

Several minutes later David was clambering through the open widow. He closed the shutters behind him to conceal the light from their torches.

"I've already tried the desk over there," said Scott. "It's locked."

David shone his torch across the interior of the barn and swung it back to focus around the area of an old wooden desk. Two sets of three drawers which Scott had discovered to be locked supported each end. The beam came to rest on a computer monitor which sat on one end of the desk top.

"Let's try that. I've an idea that the p.c. holds the key to the info we're searching for."

"How do you know that?"

324

The Courier
James R. Vance

"Something the lads said. The old guy records everything
in some kind of ledger which is kept locked in the desk. Yet one of
the French students stays behind every Thursday after the others
have gone. I reckon he transfers all the info onto the p.c. Maybe he
e-mails it on to someone. Let's take a look."

Scott switched on the computer and whilst it booted, David
checked out the connections at the back.

"Perfect. There's a U.S.B. socket."

He reached inside his anorak and placed a U.S.B. key-fob
on the desk. "If there's any files worth copying we'll transfer them
onto this memory stick."

"What if there'd been no U.S.B. port?"

David patted his anorak pocket. "I've also brought some
blank disks. There was also the possible option of sending the files
to my own e-mail box, but that could have been a bit long-winded.
At the end of the day, we could always have nicked the computer!"

"You're always so organised," remarked Scott, still
mindful of their previous adventure. He had his hand on the mouse
as the desktop display came up with the programme icons. "That's
lucky, no password. What type of files are you looking for?"

"Excel or Word. Fortunately the French use Microsoft."
The desktop confirmed that. "You may find the keyboard slightly
different."

Scott clicked on the Excel logo and opened the list of files.
The computer was obviously not utilised to any great extent as
there were no more than a dozen or so listed. He opened the first
file in the list.

"It looks like a table of strange names, dates and various
other items," said Scott, trying to decipher the French words which
headed each column.

David leaned over as Scott scrolled down the list. David
grinned. "See that," he said pointing at the screen. "That's my
father."

Scott peered at the left hand column. David's finger picked
out 'Apache Jossi'.

"What on earth does that mean?" asked Scott.

The Courier
James R. Vance

"It's an anagram of Isaac Joseph, our password. I bet the rest of them are anagrams also. Brilliant! Close the file and we'll copy them all."

He inserted the key-fob into a U.S.B. port. Scott copied them across and followed up by copying all the Word files. David scanned around the various programmes for any other files which could have been of some use but found none.

"Click on that Wanadoo icon and see if we can check his e-mails."

Several seconds later they were looking at the Wanadoo home page.

"Where do you reckon we might find his e-mails?" asked David.

Scott studied the page and suggested 'messagerie'.

A box appeared listing two mail boxes. At the top was an instruction in French 'Choisissez un compte utilisateur.'

"What does that mean?" asked David.

"Choose your user account, I think."

"Which shall we choose, 'christophe.deneuve @ wanadoo.fr' or 'julian.dubois @ wanadoo.fr' ?"

"Take your pick," said Scott. "I really wouldn't know."

David clicked on the first one and it asked for 'mot de passe' , the password.

"Bollocks," said David. "We haven't time to play around with that. Shut it down and let's get out of here. Let me first write down those users' names. They may be useful later."

"What about the book in the desk?" asked Scott.

"Don't need it," replied David. "It's all on this, I hope! The beauty is that they'll never know we've taken a copy." He extracted the memory stick and zipped it into his jacket pocket.

They made their exit through the window, closed the shutters, gathered up the equipment and the extension ladders and headed for the trees. The temperature had dropped considerably and the light rain which was beginning to fall had turned to sleet by the time they reached the wall.

The Courier
James R. Vance

Rebecca had dozed intermittently during the long wait, but became aware of their return when flashes of light from the torches appeared in the trees beyond the college boundary wall. She jumped out of the van and opened the rear door.

With the ladders and equipment safely stowed inside, they turned the vehicle round in the narrow lane and headed back towards the main road. In the darkness and the swirling sleet neither the driver nor his passengers noticed the navy blue van parked in the trees opposite the main gate to the college. The word emblazoned in white letters on the door of the vehicle read quite simply, 'GENDARMERIE'.

Chapter 30

TUESDAY: A breathless D.C. French caught up with D.S. Turner as he entered the station at Blackfriars.

"Can I have a quiet word before you speak to anyone?" he asked.

They entered an empty interview room to avoid the early morning buzz of staff arriving in the office.

"There's been some activity over in France."

"What kind of activity?" asked Turner.

"The gendarmerie called me quite early on. I suppose it's that one hour difference in the time. Anyway, the surveillance team at the college reported that a white van was there during the early hours. A woman was with two guys who went over the wall with stepladders."

"So it wasn't a delivery then?"

"They were gone for about an hour, then returned with the steps and drove away."

"Just the steps?"

"They had some other gear as well."

"So they were nicking stuff?"

"No, apparently they came back with just the stuff they took in with them."

"How did the police see all this? It must have been dark?"

"The gendarmes said the two blokes were carrying torches and they were able to see everything quite clearly."

"Have they traced the van?"

French grinned. "You're not going to believe this. It had an English reg. I did a p.n.c. and found it was a rental van from Hertz at Dover."

"So?"

The Courier
James R. Vance

"I contacted Hertz and guess who hired the van?"

"You're not related to Sammy at Waterloo station are you?" asked Turner with a touch of déja vu.

"Sammy? Sammy who?"

"Forget it. So go on then, who rented it?"

French looked at Turner, still confused, but continued nonetheless. "At least we no longer need a lip-reader. It was a Mr. David Joseph."

"What the bloody hell is he doing over there?"

"It was only rented for twenty four hours. It's due back this afternoon."

"Thanks," said Turner, lost in thought. "I'll catch up with you later."

The detective sergeant headed for the main office. He stopped off at Debbie's desk and asked her to contact Dawkins at Ashford. Spotted by D.I. Harper, he was asked to join her in Massey's office which she had temporarily commandeered. Two middle aged men in suits were seated by her desk. Without introducing them she told Turner to sit down opposite. She deliberately closed the door and stood in a corner out of Turner's immediate vision.

"These gentlemen have some questions for you," she announced.

The younger looking of the two men spoke first. "I believe you and D.I. Massey first encountered this web of intrigue at Waterloo station."

"Excuse me," said Turner. "Who are you guys?"

"Agents Redwood and Mackenzie, MI5. This report of yours about a quantity of Sarin having been smuggled in by one of these school-kids. How accurate?"

"I only repeated what I heard in a phone-call."

"From the police at Ardres?"

"I reckon so," said Turner edgily. "I took a call which was meant for D.C. French who has been liaising with the gendarmerie over there."

"Yet they deny making the call. What was actually said?"

329

The Courier
James R. Vance

"Can't remember exactly. It took me by surprise."

"We know from your desktop that you have been researching chemical and biological weapons. Why?"

Turner was anxious now, wondering where this was leading. *The bastards have been bloody snooping on my computer.*

Having lied about the source of the information, he had either to continue with his fabrication or tell the truth, thereby dropping Massey and the rest of the team in it and possibly ruining the chances of the success of their current subterfuge. He decided to bluff it out.

"If you have read the transcript of the interview with David Joseph, you'll have seen that he referred to the possibility of such substances being brought in by these couriers."

"We have read the transcript, sergeant, and listened to the tapes," said the older man. "He only refers to, I quote, 'more sinister items'. He could have meant drugs. Why did you believe he meant dirty bomb components?"

Turner remembered David's Joseph's reference to July seventh.

"If you put it into its correct context within the interview, you'll understand why we interpreted his remark in that way."

The older man smiled. The detective was being tested.

"So why the research?"

"D.I. Massey thought we should be aware of the possibilities," replied Turner, growing in confidence.

"Do you personally believe that Sarin has entered the country illegally?"

Turner shrugged his shoulders. "It's not impossible. The students aren't aware of what they're carrying. They believe the briefcases contain souvenirs, don't they, inspector?" he replied, turning to D.I. Harper.

"Well, Inspector?" asked the younger agent.

"We interviewed several of them over the weekend," she explained. "They all stuck to the same story."

The older man stepped in and addressed Turner. "You seem to have a fair overview of their system, sergeant. If you wanted to trace a specific consignment, say for example a quantity of Sarin, how would you go about it?"

As far as Turner was concerned, they were already pursuing a course of action, which had to be protected. Whatever he suggested to these two agents could put their own plans in jeopardy. Maybe confusion would work.

"There are two conflicting investigations at the moment, even though they're both linked. A raid on the school might yield information about the courier activity, but could possibly obstruct the enquiry into the recent assassinations. It could drive the principal players in the smuggling operation underground and we might never identify The Fixer, who seems most likely to be responsible for the murders."

"But if we save lives, maybe thousands of lives by tracing the Sarin, surely, Sergeant, that justifies losing track of a suspected killer. Let's face it, the victims were themselves criminals."

"The French might have something to say if you go storming into their territory."

"Oh, I'm sure they'll be up for a joint venture. They have several suspects of their own whom they would be delighted to put away. It's time that suspects at our end were also brought in for questioning. I'm sure that Inspector Harper will make that her number one priority. Thank you for your time, sergeant. You can go now."

Turner rose from his chair, convinced that the secret service was about to trample over everything which they had been planning. He left the office with one thought in his mind. He needed to talk with Massey. He was expecting him to call any time, but maybe he wasn't being discharged today after all.

Debbie called him over. "Sergeant Dawkins isn't on duty 'till ten, sir. I've left a message for him to call you as soon as he starts his shift. Will you be in the office?"

"Thanks," said the detective. "You'd better tell him to contact me on my mobile. I'm not sure where I'll be today." Turner still had his mind on the guys from MI5. He immediately left the building.

The Courier
James R. Vance

*****

They had breakfast on the ferry before reaching the Port of Dover after a rather rough crossing. The wind had increased since they had left Ardres and it was raining heavily as David gently powered the Sprinter up the ramp and back onto the U.K. mainland.

They had arranged with Scott to drive him to his old house in Ashford where they could temporarily offload the extension ladders. Before returning to Dover with the hire van, they dropped him at the school where he could routinely fall back into a more normal day.

By nine forty five they had exchanged vehicles at the rental company and were once again in the B.M.W. heading towards London on the M20.

"I cannot believe how perfectly it went," remarked David.

Rebecca was also surprised by the lack of incident. "Like clockwork. A very pleasant trip, apart from the cold when I was sat waiting in that van. I trust that all the information on that memory-stick is what you are expecting."

"I couldn't get access to his e-mails unfortunately. I needed a password and there wasn't really time for trial and error. Mind you, I did get the computer users' names. I can't wait to plug this device into the p.c. back home."

"I assume you're taking a crash language course in French," said Rebecca with a touch of sarcasm.

"That's a point. I'll think of something. Maybe you can help."

Rebecca was loathe to be further implicated. "You know that you can't tackle this on your own. You might have accessed some vital information, but how do you intend to use it effectively?"

"I'm still not sure. Originally I promised the police that I would assist them in return for some leniency. Maybe now is the time to honour my commitment. What do you think?"

332

The Courier
James R. Vance

"These guys aren't petty criminals. Look what happened to Isaac. I would be more relaxed if you were no longer involved. I think it's sensible to let the proper authorities handle it from now on in."

"I'll contact Massey when we get home."

"I thought he was ill in hospital."

"Oh, yes. I'll try his sidekick, then. What was his name, Turner?"

They continued their journey unaware that at that very moment Sergeant Dawkins was about to contact D.S. Turner to inform him that, following a phone-call to Hertz, he had discovered that the Josephs had already left Dover.

*****

The grounds of the college were somewhat featureless, covered as they were with a dusting of overnight snow. The dazzle of a pale dawn sun reflected from the white expanse as Marcel Dubois parked his old Citroen in its usual spot adjacent to the barn. Stepping over the imprints of the tyres in the snow he unlocked the barn door, switched on the lights and filled up his Krups coffee machine.

He shuffled over to open the shutters and found that they and the windows were unlocked. He made fast the wooden doors in an open position and closed the windows to keep out the cold, still puzzling over his discovery. His initial thought was that someone had broken into the barn, but the desk was still secure, the computer was untouched and all the boxes and packages from the last delivery were as he had left them.

He noticed some rubble below the high loft opening, but that was not unusual as birds often disturbed the loose stone and dirt on the ledge. Marcel scratched his head, poured himself a hot coffee and lit his pipe. He leaned back in his well-worn armchair and contemplated the swirl of smoke rising from the smouldering Samson tobacco. He decided to phone Francis.

His son listened to his father's account of what he had found and suggested that he should contact Julian or Cristophe before they commenced their studies. They had the spare key to the barn and perhaps they had forgotten to lock up following their inputs to the computer the previous evening. Francis promised to stop by on his return from Oostende later during the day.

Marcel immediately phoned the two students on their mobiles. They affirmed that the barn was completely secure when they left, adding that it had been far too cold to have even contemplated opening the window or the shutters.

The old man finished his coffee and lolled back in the comfort of his chair. He stared at the window, puffing on his pipe and chewing on the mystery.

*****

Turner parked his car at Guys Hospital and walked to the entrance for the private wing. His mobile rang again. It was Massey.

"Hi, you'll be pleased to know that you can come and collect me. I've been paroled at last!"

"Where will I find you?"

"In the main reception lounge. How long will you be?"

"Two minutes," replied Turner and finished the call.

"You must be psychic," joked Massey when they met.

"Don't know about psychic, more like psychotic! I've lots to tell you, most of it bad."

He carried the inspector's travel-bag to the car and set off towards Streatham. Within ten minutes his mobile rang again. This time it was Mullen.

"Has bossy boots been in contact with you?"

"No, I'm in the car with Inspector Massey. I'm taking him home to Streatham."

"Great to know he's on the mend. Give him my regards and…"

Turner interrupted. "Here, talk to him yourself, I'll put it on speaker."

"Hi boss, hurry up back. We're missing you."

"What's she got you at now then?" asked the inspector.

"That's what I called about. I think she's had a rollicking from the D.C.I. who, in turn, has probably had one from those MI5 guys who were hovering about the office. Croft and I are on our way to pick up Mickey Driscoll and she's sent McGovern with French to lift Vince Edwards. She's been searching for Turner to go to Barnes to arrest David Joseph and his cousin."

"But I explained to her that all this was bloody pointless," said Turner.

"I know. I was there. What are we going to do?"

Massey interrupted them. "Since we left Guys, I've been hearing the full s.p. I suggest that you tell Driscoll to make himself scarce until at least the end of the week. Contact McGovern and tell him to do likewise with Edwards. You can then waste some considerable time trying to track them down. Of course you haven't spoken with me."

"Absolutely, sir. You're still laid up in hospital. What are you going to do about the Josephs?"

"Not a problem at the moment," added Turner. "They're definitely not at home and we have a vague idea where they might be, so we should be able to head that one off at the pass with a bit of luck."

"We'll work on that now," said Massey. "Thanks for the call, best of luck. Just make sure the others know the score."

The three-way conversation finished. "Where are we now?" asked the inspector.

"Just approaching Brixton."

"I've still got David Joseph's number logged into my mobile. Let's see if we can raise him." Massey dialled Joseph's mobile number and he answered immediately.

"This is Inspector Massey. Is it convenient to talk?"

"No problem. I thought you were laid up in hospital. How are you?"

"I'm fine. Listen, we have a slight problem. Where are you at this moment?"

David hesitated slightly. Why does he want to know? He decided to be straight with him.

The Courier
James R. Vance

"On the M20 near Maidstone. I was going to call you from home, well not you 'cos I thought you were still hospitalised. I was going to contact your sergeant, Turner, isn't it?"

"Yes, he's with me now. It's important that you don't go home. I'll explain later. There's a pub called The Bell at Godstone which is just off the M25 at junction six. Can you meet us there within the hour?"

"I don't see why not. What's it all about?"

"It'll keep," said Massey. "See you shortly."

"We're almost in Streatham," remarked Turner. "What's the score?"

"Oh, forget about Streatham. Carry on down the A23 to Purley and then take the A22 to the motorway. This way we can kill two birds with one stone. Let's just keep David Joseph away from your D.I. Harper and find out what he's been up to."

"Are you not overdoing it so quickly after your heart attack?"

"Who knows?" replied Massey. "Before the attack, I suppose that I pushed myself at one hundred per cent plus, quite unaware of my limitations. Afterwards you tend to perform at less than one hundred per cent because you are wary of the consequences and, if you push too hard, your body soon lets you know."

"That's referred to as death," said Turner cynically. "You should take it easy, one step at a time."

Massey smiled. "At least I know that there are limits now. I'm the lucky one. You'll keep pressing on until…bang, that's it… goodnight Vienna!"

"I'll take my chance. Everyone believes that they're invincible. I'm no different."

"I once thought that," reflected Massey. "I was fortunate to have been given a second chance. Not everyone is that fortunate… not even you."

"Whatever you say, boss."

After a few moments, Massey interrupted their thoughts. "Do you know she didn't even have the courtesy to visit me in hospital? Some replacement inspector!"

Turner smiled. Mister Cool was back.

That particular area of South London inside the M25 is normally busy with traffic. This day was no exception. Speed cameras, road works and the congestion itself made for a frustrating journey.

Turner also received a call from D.I. Harper asking him to meet her at Barnes. He stretched the truth by saying that he had only just left Guys Hospital with Massey and was on his way to Streatham. Despite arguing that the Josephs would be at work rather than at the house, he was still obliged to meet up with her. The traffic situation would have to be his excuse for arriving late.

Massey's comment was simply, 'Make the bitch wait'!

Turner dropped off Massey with his travel-bag in the car park of The Bell to enable him to continue the journey to fulfil the rendezvous with his temporary boss.

"How are you intending to get back to Streatham?" he asked before setting off.

"Contact me later. I'll fill you in with what I have in mind."

Massey entered through a rear door and found the Josephs waiting in a corner of the lounge bar. They seemed to be the only customers apart from two elderly gentlemen seated on bar stools opposite. David rose from his seat and greeted the inspector.

"Hi. How are you now?" he asked. "I thought you would be taking it easy after your ordeal."

"Still somewhat tired and wary of my limitations but hoping to be back to work soon," he replied.

"So this is just social, then? Something to drink?"

"Thanks. An orange juice will suffice."

Massey walked across to the corner table. "Miss Joseph, how nice to see you again, especially under rather different circumstances."

She smiled. "Please call me Becky. It's good to see you up and about."

The Courier
James R. Vance

Stunning as ever, thought Massey. He sat down as David arrived with his juice. "How was France, then?" he asked.

The cousins stole a glance at each other. "You know?" said David.

"You hardly covered your tracks. Who was the third person and how did you find the school? We experienced enough difficulty in broad daylight."

David recounted his meetings with Luke Cannon and the subsequent discussions with Mickey Driscoll and Vince Edwards. He explained Scott's involvement and described their escapade at the college. He finished by placing the U.S.B. key-fob on the table.

"We downloaded what we could."

Massey twirled it around in his hand, casting his mind back to the euro coin which Anderson had discovered in the original briefcase. Let's hope you reveal more than that, he thought. "So, what were you intending to do with it?" asked the inspector.

"If my original scam had gone as planned, we probably wouldn't be sat here now. As we know it went rather pear-shaped and I stupidly messed you about. You kindly offered to turn a partially blind eye in return for my help, but following my father's murder that opportunity was dashed. Hopefully this latest episode has given me the chance to discover who was behind the shooting and fulfil my promise to you."

David pushed the memory-stick towards Massey. "It's all yours. I trust that the information on there reveals the true identity of The Fixer and destroys the threats posed by his activities."

"You don't know what data is on there?"

"No. Time was of the essence, so we looked at one Excel file. It seemed rather interesting, so we just downloaded all the rest. I also made a note of the users' names on the computer. Our intention was to take a look at the data on the p.c. at home and pass on any information intrinsic to your enquiries. Your strange phone-call asking us to meet you here has changed all that."

Massey smiled and explained that there was a risk of being arrested by his over zealous temporary replacement. "Have you anywhere to lay low for a few days?" he asked.

"I suppose we could return to St. John's Wood," suggested Rebecca.

"I'm afraid they'll check that out when they find you're not at Barnes. I'd also stay away from the shop, if that's possible."

"How long are we talking about?" asked David.

"Friday at the earliest, but possibly Monday," said Massey, hoping that all their devious plans would have reached fruition by then.

He looked down at the key-fob. Maybe sooner, he thought. He looked across at David. "We need a computer."

"And probably an interpreter," he replied. "I should imagine that it's all in French."

"I know just the man for the job and a safe house for you guys. Care to give me a lift to Streatham?"

*****

Turner's new temporary boss was waiting at Barnes. D.C.I. Harper's frustration was evident by her hands-on-hip stance and the thunderous expression on her face. Turner pulled in behind her car expecting a tongue lashing. Summoning every ounce of composure, she merely announced that there was nobody at home.

He felt like saying, 'I told you so', but decided not to push his luck. She also informed him that Mullen and McGovern had also been unable to track down their quarries.

"We'll have to see what tomorrow brings," said Turner hoping that would be an end to it all.

"What's the name of that pub which they frequent?" she asked.

"Who frequent?"

"Driscoll and Edwards."

"Oh you mean the Windsor Castle in Maida Vale."

"Take me there," she said buoyantly. "That's where they'll be. You lead, I'll follow."

Shit, thought Turner, that's a possibility and more than likely McGovern will be propping up the bar with Mullen.

The Courier
James R. Vance

They set off, Turner leading the way and desperately trying to contact Mullen and McGovern. He was in luck. Mullen had returned to Blackfriars with Croft and McGovern had received a call from Massey to drop French off at his flat in Streatham.

He phoned Massey to put him in the picture and the inspector, in turn, related his conversation with the Josephs and outlined the arrangements he had made with regard to their temporary disappearance. Turner promised to join him at Streatham after he was able to offload D.C.I. Harper. All he hoped for now was to find no sign of Driscoll or Edwards at the Windsor Castle.

They parked the cars on Clifton Road and walked round the corner to the pub. A cold damp east wind gusting across from Maida Vale resulted in vacant tables outside the café bars which dominated this small backwater of Little Venice. The Windsor Castle was also unusually quiet for a lunch-time session.

Despite the search for the two wanted men appearing fruitless, D.I. Harper decided to stay for some refreshment. She ordered two coffees and they sat at one of the few tables opposite the bar. Turner's impatience showed as he checked his watch.

"How is Inspector Massey?" she asked.

"Looking remarkably well but still on the mend," replied the detective sergeant, "and desperate to be back on the job."

"I should imagine he'll have to spend some time on rehab before that. The D.C.I. expects us to put this business to bed in the next few days. I take it that I can count on your support."

"How does the D.C.I. come to that conclusion?"

"He believes that Special Ops together with their French counterparts will make a move shortly. We'll get the go-ahead to liaise with Revenue and Customs to nail all the protagonists at our end and with everyone legitimately banged up for questioning, he reckons MI5 will sort out any terrorism threat.

The whole operation has been given top priority from high up the chain of command. One whiff of a potential dirty bomb and the whole security network springs into action. We have to be alert

to any order that comes our way. I trust the team is prepared to
play their part."

"I suggest that you ask them."

"I'm asking you. As a newcomer I rely on you and D.S.
Mullen to give me feedback."

"How can I give you their reaction when only this minute,
you've told me what's going on?"

"You work alongside these guys. Will they be up for it?"

"They're loyal and committed. What more do you want me
to say?"

Turner sensed that Harper was feeling somewhat insecure,
that much was expected of her and maybe, maybe was slightly out
of her depth, especially knowing that Massey could be back on the
scene, albeit unofficially.

Under different circumstances, he could have adopted a
more positive attitude towards her. She was really quite
personable, attractive and at times extremely charming. Beneath
this allure, however she could be ruthlessly ambitious, stubborn
and demanding.

Because of these two extreme personas, she displayed
mood swings and inconsistency, making it difficult to form a
natural bond. She struck Turner as being a cross between the calm
reliance of Massey and the wild unpredictability of McGovern. He
decided that she could have been a good team player, but never
acceptable as team leader.

She must have been reading his thoughts. "Tell me,
sergeant, why is there an atmosphere of such apathy within this
team? From the moment I arrived I've had the impression that
none of you seem to care if this investigation progresses or not. Is
it always like that or," she hesitated for a split second, "is it me?"

"Not at all, ma'am. In my opinion it's the nature of the case
itself. Before you came on the scene, we were chasing shadows as
nothing of any consequence had actually happened, apart from that
business with David Joseph and Scott Morgan. Even then, we
weren't sure what we were actually investigating.

The Courier
James R. Vance

When the assassinations took place, we suddenly had a real crime to solve but it was immediately taken away from us as it wasn't on our patch. That decision de-motivated the team even further. Now we have an international smuggling ring and possible terrorist activity to investigate and that's being passed over to Special Operations. And you have the nerve to call us apathetic! How the hell do you think we should feel?"

Turner inwardly congratulated himself on his outburst, especially as it was a web of deceit woven with a mere thread of truth to disguise the reality of the current situation. How would she react?

Stephanie Harper was taken by surprise, but unreservedly accepted his explanation. "I'm sorry," she said. "Thank you for enlightening me. What can I do to help?"

It was a difficult question to which Turner could not give an honest response without referring to the team's parallel activity. He could hardly tell her to back off and keep her distance. She needed more involvement but with what? It had to be meaningful but of no threat to their subterfuge.

"Maybe in all this confusion, we've missed something. Perhaps it might be worth while if you reassessed the reports and interview statements so far. A fresh pair of eyes may spot something which we've not considered important." He was clutching at straws but hoping to buy some time.

"The D.C.I. gave me all the files before I took up the appointment, but perhaps you have a point. Now I have a more in-depth knowledge of the situation, a re-evaluation may put into context some key points which possibly didn't make sense at the time. It's Tuesday. Arrange a full team meeting for first thing Thursday morning."

Inwardly Turner sighed with relief but was still wondering what diversion could distract her for the remainder of the week. Hopefully she would unearth some fascinating detail from her perusal of the files. His thoughts were interrupted by her next pronouncement.

"By the way, you may be interested to know that according to forensics the cause of the explosion at Frank Cannon's house was a device triggered by the vehicle's ignition. House to house in the area has also revealed sightings of a dark saloon cruising in the area during the two days prior to the bomb going off. The same vehicle was spotted earlier that same morning in Primrose Hill, but unfortunately there has been no recall of its registration. It was reported to be an Audi, a B.M.W. or a Mercedes, so take your pick! Camden C.I.D. are thinking of going on Crimewatch with it."

"Any description of the saloon's occupants?"

"Blacked out windows apparently, not even the chance of a head-count."

"Obviously a professional hit. What about St. John's Wood?"

"Uniform's doing house to house there again tomorrow, checking vehicle activity this time."

"It's a pity those bloody cameras aren't yet operative. They could have saved us a lot of trouble when this thing first kicked off."

"I'll let you know if there's anything more when we meet up on Thursday. Tomorrow I shall be wading through this paperwork. What's on your agenda?"

"I'll check out the shop in Hatton Garden to see if I can track down either of the Josephs. Dependant upon the results of my visit I can join forces with Mullen and McGovern in tracking down Driscoll and Edwards. I also need to touch base with D.C. French with regard to any activity in France."

In fact he really wanted to see if French had uncovered any information on Michel Deneuve, but anything remotely connected to his sister was not for D.I. Harper's ears.

"That should keep the D.C.I. off my back. Thanks for the chat. See you Thursday." D.I. Harper finally made her exit to Turner's relief.

He could now head for Streatham and become a real detective again. He was tempted to stay for a beer, but time was of the essence and he desperately wanted to touch base with Massey. Maybe the boss could provide some liquid refreshment.

*****

"Make yourselves at home," said Massey, inviting the Josephs into his flat. "You can have my room, first on the left, Becky. David can share the spare room with me. Don't worry, there are twin beds. The bathroom's at the far end of the corridor." He walked towards the kitchen. "Not sure about food, not having been at home for a while. I'll send out for a takeaway. What do you fancy, Chinese, Indian, Pizza?"

On the way from Godstone he had offered to accommodate them overnight while suitable arrangements could be made to 'lose' them for a few days. It would also afford an opportunity to evaluate the contents of the key-fob, hence his summoning of D.C. French to assist in any necessary interpretation.

They agreed on a Chinese meal after consulting one of the inspector's collection of takeaway menus and ordered some extra portions knowing that they would be joined later by detectives McGovern, French and possibly Turner if he could escape the clutches of D.I. Harper.

"Whilst we're awaiting the others, how about a glass of wine?" suggested Massey. He turned to David Joseph. "The computer's over there if you want to switch it on and insert your magic stick."

David set it up and the inspector handed round the drinks. They watched the computer boot and David opened the new device starting with the Microsoft Word folder. There were several files, les Marchands, les Clients, les Livraisons, les Produits, les Mercures. Most appeared to be lists of names, some with addresses, telephone numbers, e-mail boxes and occasionally dates.

Between them they rationalised that they represented Dealers or Suppliers, Customers, Products and two others of which they were unsure. David returned to the file headed les Clients and explained that there was a similar one on the Excel folder with

more detailed information. He once again pointed out Apache Jossi
as an anagram of his father, Isaac Joseph.

"That's interesting," remarked Massey. "So all these
bizarre words are anagrams of customers' names. I reckon there's
a job for you, Becky. If you can print that file, David, your cousin
can make herself comfortable on the settee, deciphering that little
lot whilst we wait for the takeaway to arrive."

"How generous of you, Inspector," she said with a shy
smile, which he involuntarily returned.

David opened up the file on les Mercures. "It's a list of the
couriers," he announced. "Of course, les Mercures must be
Mercuries, messengers of the gods. Clever sod!"

Massey asked him to print off several hard copies of each
file. There appeared to be a long night of analysis ahead.

D.S. Turner arrived to find Massey's flat resembling a
cross between a Chinese takeaway and a press room. Strewn across
the floor were foil cartons of various oriental dishes, some partly
devoured, some still sealed and sheets of A4 paper which had been
disgorged from the printer. Massey's guests were squatting
amongst this chaotic scene attempting to interpret the data with the
help of D.C. French who had arrived earlier with D.C. McGovern.

"I thought you were supposed to be taking it easy," said
Turner, addressing the inspector.

"I am. I've got a houseful of Santa's helpers. Fancy some
Chinese?"

"I need a drink," replied Turner. "Any beer?"

"Only wine. Red or white?"

"What, no Scotch?"

"I think that was emptied when your sister called about her
wedding!"

Turner smiled. "No wonder you had a heart attack. A glass
of red will be fine, in fact anything alcoholic will suffice. Harper's
got them chasing up a dark saloon with blacked-out windows. I ask
you, in London! There must be bloody thousands. That woman's
dangerous."

Massey grinned. "I heard she was a bit of alright!"

"Sugar-coated cyanide!" Turner looked around the room. "Is this all the info from France?"

"Superb, isn't it? I think we've hit the jackpot."

They were interrupted by a shout from Rebccca. "Got another one!" she cried. "How about Silly Drockmice?"

"How the hell should we know?" retorted David. "It's taken you about ten minutes to work that one out."

"Mickey Driscoll," she announced triumphantly.

"There should also be a Vince Edwards amongst that lot somewhere," said McGovern.

"How about Cardew de Vins?" suggested Rebecca, consulting her list.

"What's all this about?" asked Turner.

"Anagrams of customers' names. In other words, all their passwords," replied Massey. "There appears to be a record of every activity and individual involved. We're attempting to decipher it all."

"Shit. What about my Trensh Curri?"

"Oh, it's there. She's already found that one. Don't forget, we had previously discussed that with David Joseph before his old man was knocked off. It's keeping Becky amused and she's doing okay. There are over twenty names on the list and she must have solved about half of them by now."

"It's Becky now, is it?" asked Turner with a knowing wink. "Where are you intending to hide them away?"

"They're staying here for the time being. I'm still on sick leave so it's their safe house."

Turner smiled and shook his head. "I've got to hand it to you. At death's door a few days ago and now, not only aiding and abetting, but also on the pull! You never cease to amaze me."

"Come off it, she's here with her cousin."

"Tell me it didn't cross your mind."

"Have some Chinese before it goes cold," said Massey and joined the rest of the group.

The Courier
James R. Vance

They all settled into a routine, each collating and cross-referencing the various pieces of data which they were able to extract from the information contained in the files.

D.C. French took on a roving role helping with translations. Massey asked Turner to filter the results into a format more specific to their investigation. Some of the data was historical and would be of greater value in a more broad-based prosecution.

Massey was especially interested in recent records which could identify key players in the operation and who might be implicated in the assassinations. More urgently, they needed to track the origin and destination of the Sarin transaction. By working together as the final filter mechanism, they were also afforded the opportunity to bury temporarily any data which might incriminate Turner's sister, Helen, who was still honeymooning in the Caribbean.

In the midst of this frenzied but organised activity, Turner received a call on his mobile. He took it in the kitchen. A few minutes later he re-joined Massey.

"I've got a date," he said.

"With whom?"

"Friday, six thirty under the clock at Paddington station."

"The Fixer?...Brilliant!"

"That means we can nab a courier with a briefcase full of drugs and hit the school by sending in the gendarmes."

"I've had another thought about that," said Massey. "What if we delayed the French move until we had set up our courier friend to hand over the briefcase, supposedly containing the cash, on the Monday morning. That way we could pick up the money handler."

"Or maybe tail him," suggested Turner.

"Need to think about that. We might have to go public, in other words bring in the D.C.I."

"I've got a feeling that we're going to have to do that anyhow. Going on what Stephanie Harper said earlier, our covert sting could get blown apart by MI5 going in mob-handed."

"Did The Fixer mention the biochemical agents?"

347

"Said he still needed more time on the VX, but again re-iterated that Sarin wasn't a problem. I said I'd wait until he had more info."

Massey looked across at the chaotic state of his living room. "Let's see what this lot reveals first, before we decide on whom to involve. They may believe that they're holding all the aces, but we could have the winning hand here. If that's the case, we can play the game on our terms."

The Courier
James R. Vance

Chapter 31

WEDNESDAY: The ad-hoc team had worked throughout the previous evening, sustained by provisions acquired by Rebecca from a local 'Twenty Four Seven' supermarket. They had been joined by D.C. Croft and D.S. Mullen during the course of the evening and Massey's flat had become so congested that he and Turner had retired to one of the bedrooms to analyse the data which was now flowing freely.

Shortly after midnight the inspector confessed to being exhausted and announced that maybe they should call it a day, get some sleep and re-assess what they had collated with fresh minds. They had been baffled by a staggering amount of coded information, despite their general understanding of most files. It was the fine detail which was lacking.

"If all these letters and numbers represent a word, whether it be in French or any other language, there are a lot of similar words or words with slight variations," said Turner. "For example MER4 and MAR4 crop up so many times as does LIV5, LIV6, LIV7 and so on.

Take the file on Silly Drockmice, which Becky identified as Mickey Driscoll, there's a list of dates all followed by a series of letters and numbers which are almost the same each time, apart from the odd number and letter change here and there. If we could work out just one line, the rest should be easy."

Massey nodded, more from tiredness than from any positive acknowledgement. He surveyed the reams of printed sheets which were scattered before them. Suddenly his face lit up. "Of course, we've the answer to one particular entry right here." He swung round to the open door of the bedroom and shouted along the corridor to David. "What was your father's password again?"

"Apache Jossi," came the reply.

"Can anyone put their hands on that file?"

"I think it's here amongst this lot," said Turner, shuffling printed sheets of A4 to find it."

David appeared at the door. "Got a problem?" he asked.

"More like a solution," said Massey. "On that Friday when Scott threw a spanner in your works, what were you expecting to take delivery of…diamonds?"

"Why ask, you've already nicked them from my cellar," remarked David ruefully.

"Here it is," said Turner, passing a sheet across.

Massey ran his finger down the list. "Assuming that it was your final transaction, it should be this one."

He read out the corresponding numbers and letters and said, "They're not dissimilar to any of the others which we've come across."

He paused and repeated the series of letters and numbers. "Of course," he announced, "they're not bloody words in some coded format, they're cross references to the various components of each transaction. MER is short for Mercury, the courier. Look up MER4, Mercury number 4, I'll bet it's Luke Cannon."

Turner found the Courier list and confirmed it.

"Similarly, MAR8, PRO12, LIV9 must also be cross references."

Rebecca had joined them in the doorway, holding another sheet. "I've found your MAR8, it's on le Fichier des Marchands…. numéro huit: Patrik van der Werff, Reestraat, Amsterdam. He's one of their contacts for diamonds and you'll probably find that PRO12 is short for Produit and will be information about the product."

"And no doubt LIV9 will be an abbreviation for Livraison neuf, delivery number nine," added French who had also joined them. "That will give details of the delivery, dates, times, costs, et cetera."

The Courier
James R. Vance

"It's finally making sense," said Massey. "We must have details here for every bloody transaction that's been made."

"Including Sarin," said Turner.

The room became silent for several seconds. Two words from the detective had created a poignant moment of reflection. The futility and indecision of the previous weeks had suddenly become frighteningly significant. At last it was game on.

Rebecca broke the silence. "What's Sarin?"

"Don't ask," said David. He turned to Massey. "You're saying that it's already happened?"

"We think so. Hopefully now, using this information we should be able to track it."

"I thought you were calling it a day," said Turner, still concerned that Massey was pushing himself too far, too early..

"And miss all the excitement? Where do we start?"

"What facts do we know?" asked French.

"Unfortunately only the name, Sarin."

"Try the Produit file first, then."

A scramble took place as all the data sheets were spread across one of the beds. D.C. French found it first listed against PRO19. With the help of his French dictionary, he translated the accompanying notes as best as he could.

"Sarin," stated French, "Sarin is one of the world's most dangerous chemical warfare agents, a substance toxic…the nervous system, attacks muscles and vital organs…breathed as gas or through the skin…suffocates…paralyzing muscles around…I think this word is the lungs. One hundred milligrams kills the average person in a few minutes if no antidote. Experts say sarin is more than 500 times more toxic than cyanide."

The room once more descended into silence, as they absorbed the horrendous implications of the description.

Massey broke the immediate silence. "What are the cross-references?" he asked.

"LIV1, MER8, C17 and MAR20," replied John. "Who's got the LIV sheet?"

"Never mind that one," said Massey. "Who was the courier?"

"That's MER8," added French.

Turner picked up the list of couriers. "MER8 is Frankie Smith."

"He's the lad from Barking. His dad's the BNP candidate," added McGovern. "He's the guy who used to be a member of the I.C.F. I think his dad's name is Trevor."

"Sounds like a tasty bloke," remarked David.

"And now for the main one," said John. "Who has the sheets on les Clients? We're looking for C17. That's who received the merchandise."

They all looked at each other as that list was not one of those spread out on the bed. Suddenly Rebecca realised that she had been working on that particular list of clients.

"Sorry, it's the one with the anagrams. I've left it in the living room." She disappeared for an instant, returned and handed the sheet to Massey. "C17 has not yet been converted. It's down here as Voters Mirth."

Once again the room fell silent as everyone attempted to break the code.

"Bloody hell," cried Turner. "That's an appropriate one. It's the courier's dad, the prospective B.N.P. candidate, Trevor Smith."

Massey once again stunned the room into silence. "What the fuck does a B.N.P. man want with a biochemical warfare agent?"

*****

They sat in Massey's living room drinking coffee and listening to McGovern's limited bio of Trevor Smith which had been compiled several days previously.

"I'm afraid you're going to have to pass this lot onto Dyson," said Massey. "It's taken precedent over our original objective of breaking the smuggling op. It's now a job for MI5 and the anti-terrorist unit. We can't sit on this any longer."

352

"What about the French lot?" asked Turner.

"I'm sure they'll become involved almost immediately. There are masses of intelligence to analyse on both sides of the channel. The sooner they have information on which to act, the better chance they have of not just recovering the Sarin, but preventing its deployment."

"Most of the relevant info from the French side seems to be already in our possession here," remarked Mullen.

"I agree," added Massey. "It appears that our old gardener, Marcel Dubois, has been cultivating more than prize vegetables in his potting shed." He turned to D.C. French. "It might be useful if your gendarmerie contacts could furnish us with as much detailed background info on the Dubois family as they can."

"Oh, that reminds me," interjected David Joseph. He reached into his pocket, extracted a slip of paper and passed it to D.C. French. "Besides Dubois, there's another name on there which may also be worth checking out."

The detective constable read out the two names written on the paper. "Julian Dubois and Cristophe Deneuve? Why those in particular?" he asked.

"They were the names of the computer users in the barn at the college."

"Shit!" muttered Massey under his breath and quickly glanced at Turner, who merely shrugged his shoulders in dismay.

"I wouldn't think any info on those two would yield much," said Massey, attempting to deflect the focus away from a possible connection to his ex-wife. "Their role seems limited to inputting data on the computer."

"I've already requested a trace on them, anyhow," remarked French. "If you remember, they were enrolled as members of the so-called gardening club. They were the only French names on that list. I expect to receive some info fairly soon."

"Let me have it as soon as you obtain it," said Massey, still hoping to be able to censor it before it went on file.

The Courier
James R. Vance

"Does this mean that tracking down my father's killer has been consigned to the waste bin?" asked David.

"Don't forget that inquiries are still on-going handled by C.I.D. at St. John's Wood."

"But if a major swoop is launched which involves this lot, it'll possibly drive the key players underground."

"Maybe," replied Massey, "maybe not. If a joint action leads to locating a potentially active terrorist cell which could threaten thousands of lives, it has to take priority."

David accepted the logic but Rebecca sensed that other issues were spinning around inside her cousin's head. He had that same expression on his face which she had witnessed after returning from her conversation with the mower man outside Scott's old house at Ashford. His reaction to negative news had been surprising then. His reaction to Massey's words was almost identical.

"In terms of passing all this info on to the D.C.I., I think that it would be less suspicious if I handled it," said the inspector. "If it's okay. by you David, I'll say that you phoned me about the data which you had acquired. I told you to bring it here so that it could be checked out before passing it on. The rest of you know nothing about this, just as I knew nothing about D.I. Harper's search for David and Becky."

He grinned and winked, confident that he still had the support of the team.

"I'll call Chris in the morning to come and pick up the key-fob and he can hand it over to that mob from MI5. If we all play our part, it provides a reason why David and Becky were not at home and it keeps the rest of you out of the picture. Let's see if the spooks have sufficient intelligence to decipher all the data."

"You mean you're only handing over the data, not the results we've produced here tonight?" asked Turner.

"They can earn their bloody inflated salaries and get something right for a change," replied Massey. "With their expertise, it shouldn't take long, but, at the same time, it may delay any action which could conflict with your plans for Friday evening or even Monday morning."

"You wily old sod," remarked Mullen, "with no disrespect, boss!"

Massey smiled and held up a hand in acknowledgement of his sergeant's back-handed compliment. "If we sent over the results of our efforts here, some low-life would lay claim to it as they climbed up some Director's arse. All I can do is thank you all for your endeavours, but I apologise that unfortunately, there are no commendations on offer."

"What shall we do with all the hard copy which we've produced?" asked French.

"Leave it here for the time being. I'm sure Becky can pass time away in the morning by filing it into some kind of order." He glanced in her direction. She smiled and nodded in agreement.

"What are we going to do about this Smith character who's possibly sitting on a lethal dose of Sarin?" asked Turner.

"As I said earlier, it's a job for MI5 and SO13. It's only going to delay any action against him until the end of the week. I suggest we call it a day and everyone can get some shut-eye. I'm knackered."

"Do you really want me to come over tomorrow or should I take the memory stick with me?" asked Chris.

"I'll call you some time during the morning. The call will be logged. With spooks everywhere, it covers your back. Also it gives us chance to ensure that we've extracted everything."

"You can just download it all straight onto your p.c. right now if you wish," suggested David.

"Some advice for you, young man. I'm no computer expert, but the less one has stored in that bloody machine over there, the less chance of ever being caught with your trousers down," said Massey.

Satisfied with the night's efforts, the working party finally went their separate ways. Massey checked his guests were au fait with the sleeping arrangements and headed for the kitchen to administer his first home dosage of the drugs prescribed by the hospital. Protected by twenty milligrams of Atorvastatin and ten milligrams of Ramipril he slipped exhausted under the duvet of one of the twin beds.

David wished goodnight to his cousin and stayed up for a short time planning his next steps. Twenty minutes later he had formulated a game plan and retired to bed, pleased with the outcomes of his sortie abroad.

*****

The Josephs left Massey's flat following a light breakfast, stating their intention of finding some hotel accommodation until the weekend or until they were given the 'all-clear'. They thanked the inspector for his hospitality and his concern for their well-being, wishing him success with the on-going investigation and a rapid return to work.

Once out of sight of the flat, David stopped the car and made a phone-call on his mobile. Rebecca was not yet party to his game-plan, but knew better than to ask questions. Over the years she had become familiar with his idiosyncratic behaviour when he was totally immersed in a project or strategy. She was aware that he would reveal all in his own good time.

The phone rang several times before it was answered. "Good morning," said David. "I would like to speak to Trevor, Trevor Smith."

Rebecca shot him a perfunctory glance and leaned back in her seat. *Now what's he up to?*

"I'm Trevor Smith. Who's that?" was the reply.

"We need to meet before mid-day. Your life and your son's life are in immediate danger. This is not a crank call. I am The Fixer and to prove that, I can tell you that your password is Voters Mirth. A car will pick you up at your house at precisely eleven thirty this morning. Be ready. Do I make myself clear?"

He hoped that the password would convince the man that it was a genuine call.

The Courier
James R. Vance

"You're The Fixer and you intend to pick me up at eleven thirty. I don't know what the fuck you're talking about, so you can piss off."

"If you want to gamble with your son's life, so be it. Dying through a lethal dose of Sarin is not a pretty sight and agonising torture for the victim."

The ensuing silence convinced David that he had the man's attention.

Trevor Smith was breathing heavily before replying. "I've meetings arranged.It's not convenient."

It appeared that he had quickly bought into David's scam. "Cancel them. It's vital that we meet. My colleague will pick you up at your address at Epping. You must come alone."

David ended the call and turned to Rebecca. "How convincing was that?" he demanded, switching on the ignition.

"I presume you know what you're doing, assuming the role of our mister Fixer," remarked his cousin as the car sped off towards Streatham High Road. "Are you going to explain my part in this latest scenario?"

"You just have to pick the guy up and deliver him to me."

"And where will you be?"

"In a pub restaurant, the Blacksmiths Arms at Thornwood Common."

"Where the hell is that?"

"Don't worry. We'll drive past his house which is in Epping according to last night's data and continue to the pub which I guess from my previous visit is about five minutes drive further on. You leave me there, double back for our man and deliver him to me."

"And what do I say to him when I pick him up?"

"Absolutely nothing. If he asks you any questions, all you need say is, 'I'm just the driver'. He'll accept that, if not out of concern for his son, certainly out of curiosity."

"Does Inspector Massey know about this?"

"All in good time," replied her cousin, as he headed towards Balham. Eventually they picked up the A3 and crossed the

Thames at London Bridge to join the A11 and the M11 towards
Epping. They reconnoitred the area before David dropped off at
the Blacksmiths Arms whilst Rebecca retraced the route back into
Epping to collect their 'guest'.

*****

Massey's select team of detectives descended upon him
later that morning to use up time they should have been spending
searching for Driscoll, Edwards and, of course, the Josephs. It was
also an opportunity to discuss the events of the previous evening
and the actions to be taken about the data from the computer. They
all agreed that they were sailing close to the wind in their handling
of the situation.

Consequently a decision was taken to justify their actions
by presenting a professional detailed dossier to D.I. Harper and
D.C.I. Dyson. The majority of the morning was taken in compiling
the appropriate information and drafting it into a suitable format.

Their main concern revolved around the question of how
they acquired the data in the first place. Massey had suggested
previously that he should name David Joseph as the provider.

"Why not state that the Gendarmerie sent it over?"
suggested French.

"We've tried that already, or rather I have with the spooks.
I managed to bluff it out with them, but it's too risky to use it
again," said Turner.

"How about an anonymous source?" offered McGovern.

"MI5 would want the full s.p. on that, using national
security as a lever," replied Massey

"Why not just tell the truth as you first suggested?" added
Croft.

The room went silent momentarily and all heads turned as
one in her direction.

"Excuse me," she said. "Am I flashing something I
shouldn't be flashing?"

"It's that word 'truth' that's the problem," said Turner,
smiling. "You know full well that honesty is not the best policy

with some superiors, present company excepted, of course. For one they won't believe you and two, if they couldn't discredit your story, they'd brand you as an out-and-out liar."

They laughed despite being no nearer to a solution.

"From what I have been told regarding your interim boss, the fact that David Joseph provided the info, especially by breaking and entering, won't do him any favours," stated Massey. "Also, if it was revealed that both he and Rebecca were here in my flat assisting in the de-coding process, it would not bode well for any of us."

"What if one of the couriers sent it to us?" asked Mullen. "Say, someone like Sean Driscoll or Todd Edwards? They would have had access to it, being members of that so-called gardening club."

"That's not a bad idea," agreed Massey, "provided that, whoever it is, will play ball with us."

"That's no problem," remarked McGovern. "We just lean on the bastards until they agree."

"Try the carrot instead of the stick for a change," said Massey. "They know we've enough on them already. The offer of a bit of leniency might appeal to their warped minds."

"Those bloody pills are sending you soft," joked Turner. "I vote we give it a try." He faced McGovern. "It was your idea, I suggest that you nail one of them on Friday when they're back. All in favour?"

Several heads nodded in unison.

"There's a meeting with D.I. Harper tomorrow morning," said Turner. "How about if I present it to her there?"

"Can I make a suggestion?" asked Massey and proceeded without waiting for approval. "Friday's your D-day with possible action across the water. Furthermore, she may have other news or info for you at the meeting which might provide some digression.

I believe it's important to present it in the first instance to D.C.I. Dyson, maybe in her presence. You may even wish to invite those two spooks who interrogated you, so that you can hand over the key-fob to them. Formalising it in such a way means that you would have to convene a meeting of all the parties concerned.

The point I'm trying to make is that, by instigating these avoidable delays, you'll be able to nab your courier at Paddington and set off the chain of events over in France before the heavy mob roll in. The added bonus is that your current assignments of hunting down D.I. Harper's petty criminals will be buried under the pile of shit which you're about to drop on the hierachy."

Having accepted Massey's advice, they decided that a beverage in the nearest pub would round off the morning's proceedings.

"Are you up to it?" Turner asked the boss.

"I'll buy the first round," he replied. "I think you all deserve it."

They cheered in the erroneous belief that progress was being made, despite the potential Sarin threat, the unknown identity of The Fixer and the lack of suspects for the assassinations. Deep in the recesses of his mind, Massey's brickwall was still standing. Nevertheless they headed for Streatham High Road and a convivial session in a pub.

*****

Rebecca returned to the Blacksmiths Arms accompanied by her 'guest'. David had positioned himself at a table near the window, where he was silhouetted against the bright sunlight of a late autumn morning. He was now wearing his heavily tinted Rayban shades and idly stirring the froth on his second cup of cappuccino. He rose to greet the potential BNP candidate from Barking, the former football hooligan, Trevor Smith.

"What's this all about then?" asked Voters Mirth.

David waved him to a chair opposite. Rebecca joined them by sitting to one side of the table.

"This is Trevor Smith," she announced to her cousin. Turning towards her 'guest', she said, "I'd like to introduce you to your contact, The Fixer."

The Courier
James R. Vance

Trevor stared at David. *So this is the guy who creams it by making 'disembodied' phone calls, whilst school-kids like my son take all the bloody risks. Little wonder that he can swan around in flash motors with a tasty bird at his side.*

He looked across at Rebecca and quickly reverted his gaze towards David. Where originally there had been resentment, now there was a deep sense of loathing, fuelled by his innate envy of middle and upper class wealth. Maybe this was his opportunity to redress the balance.

"Were you satisfied with it?" asked David.

"Satisfied with what?" he asked.

"The last consignment delivered by your son."

Trevor shifted uneasily in his chair, unsure whether this cool character opposite was for real. He wiped beads of foul-tempered sweat from his forehead with the back of his hand and subconsciously loosened another button on his less-than-white open-necked shirt. He was wearing a navy blue suit which cried out for a session with the local dry cleaning agency.

"I suppose so," he replied, not wishing at this point to commit himself to any loose talk.

"I would have thought that, for the amount of money involved, you would have expected a product of the highest quality." David was beginning to enjoy playing with the man's perceived discomfort. Rebecca likened the situation to watching two boxers sparring in the first round.

"Well, yeah, I think it was okay,"replied Trevor, still suspicious of where the conversation was leading.

"You've obviously not used the merchandise previously?"

Trevor quickly regained control of his original vexation and his persona reverted to type as his more natural hostility manifested itself. Seized by the reckless bravado more prevalent during his youth, he leaned across the table towards David. Instinctively Rebecca recoiled, anticipating some possible intention to assault her cousin. David did not even flinch.

"Look, what was all that crap about lives bein' in danger, especially my lad's?" he snarled.

The Courier
James R. Vance

"Exactly the point which I'm trying to establish," continued David, unfazed by the man's demeanour. "It was not up to standard, nor were the safety features built into the secure container. In fact the supplier is extremely distressed. He has demanded that it be recalled immediately as there is a danger of contamination to anyone who has handled it, including your son. Of course you will be fully reimbursed and compensated for any eventual consequences. If we can arrange a collection date we will instigate the necessary anti-contamination procedures to uplift it."

"I no longer have it. I acquired it for a friend of mine," announced Trevor, stalling for time.

Shit! thought David. He now leaned towards the man. "It is vital that he is contacted immediately. Where do we find him?"

"I'd better speak to him first," protested Trevor.

David slid his mobile phone across the table. "Do it. Do it now otherwise more lives could be at risk. I need to meet up with him at once."

Trevor was back in control. "He's in Barnet."

"That's not a problem. Call him and tell him that I can be there within the hour."

"He runs a boozer there. It's a kind of pub-cum-nightclub called Danders."

"What's his name?"

"He's a good mate. I don't want any nonsense."

"I'm concerned about his well-being, that's all."

"You'll need to ask for Taz Sharman."

"I take it with a name like that, he's not British."

"Born and bred here. We grew up together as kids in Bradford. His dad was Pakistani, but his mother was a Yorkshire lass. We went to school together and when his parents died, he came to live with us and moved south when my dad got a job at Ford Motors in Dagenham. He's a good mate, so if you screw with him, you'll have me to deal with."

David was confused. A candidate for the B.N.P. party being best friends with the son of a Pakistani did not really fit the profile. Was this guy feeding him crap?

The Courier
James R. Vance

"But you've nailed your colours to a B.N.P. mast. How does he cope with that?"

"He's one of us, mate. Like me, a big Hammers supporter. The lads think he's great even though he speaks with a broad Yorkshire accent and looks like Imran Khan."

"You'd better call him."

Trevor pushed the mobile back across the table and withdrew his own from his jacket pocket. "The number's programmed in," he explained. The call was made but only resulted in further complications for David. The Sarin had been forwarded on.

Trevor relayed a message. "He says if you go to Barnet, he'll explain how to find the guy who's currently in possession. He's in Leicester. He'll draw you a map, says it's too complex to describe over the phone."

In fact Taz wanted to check out this 'middle-man' who had unexpectedly burst onto the scene. To divulge sensitive information to a complete stranger over the phone was not a sensible course of action.

David looked over towards Rebecca. He had a feeling that he was being compromised. She in turn inclined her head in puzzlement and mouthed, 'What's going on?'

Her cousin stood up and offered his hand to Trevor. "You've done the right thing. By the way, why was the Sarin ordered in the first place?"

"Not a fuckin' clue," replied Trevor.

"You didn't query it?"

"I told you. He's a good mate. We trust each other. So is there any risk of contamination to me and my lad?"

"How long was it in your possession?"

"Only for a few days."

"I'll check it out with the supplier and get back to you."

Trevor Smith turned to face Rebecca. "I hope you're going to give me a lift back after all this?"

The Courier
James R. Vance

"We'll drop you on the way to Barnet," said David dourly, obviously dismayed at the inconclusive outcome from his visit. They left the Blacksmiths Arms and headed for Barnet via Epping.

*****

There was no car park at Danders, nor on the main street in Barnet. They eventually found some parking space behind Ye Olde Mitre Inn. Rebecca elected to stay with the vehicle whilst David met up with Trevor's friend. On the road to Barnet, David had outlined his intention to determine the location of the missing Sarin and to pass the information on to Massey's team. On the other hand, Rebecca, unclear as to his motives, had been convinced by David's performance that he planned to recover the chemical agent alone.

Her cousin had laughed it off, adamant that he was hardly brave enough to confront these people, but resolute enough to make sufficient inroads for the police to complete the mission. He hoped that this next meeting would provide the key to its whereabouts and bring about its recovery. All he wished for his efforts, he explained, was for the police to return the favour by bringing his father's killer to justice.

Taz Sharma was exactly as described. He greeted David with a warm smile and invited him into his private office, the walls of which were adorned with framed photographs of himself. Several were records of presentations and events with local dignitaries including the mayor. Others were family pictures or Taz involved in some sporting activity. The remainder were snapshots of promotions or celebration nights which had occurred within the nightclub.

In the majority of the photographs, he was immaculately dressed, whether he was in casual wear or more formally attired, as he was today, clothed in a light grey Armani suit, delicate pink Yves Saint Laurent shirt and burgundy tie. He was, as David aptly put it to Rebecca later, 'full of his own shit'.

The Courier
James R. Vance

He seated himself on a black leather swivel chair behind a polished mahogany desk inlaid with a rectangular work surface of rich red leather. He beckoned David to also take a seat.

"I'm sorry, but Trevor did not give me your name …something about a fixer?"

"You may call me Michael," replied David.

"So, we are in danger of contamination from a suspect package, I believe."

David explained the situation as he had earlier described it to Trevor Smith, emphasising the need to retrieve the faulty merchandise as quickly as possible.

"As Trevor explained to you, I'm also just a middle man here. To be honest with you, I never saw the stuff. I just arranged its delivery and subsequent despatch to the parties who made the original order. I can provide you with directions, but I'll need to contact you once I have arranged a convenient time."

"Why can't you do that now? It is urgent."

"The person I need to speak with is not available until Friday morning. He is out of the country until then. How well do you know Leicester?"

"Never been there."

"I'm afraid it has a rather complicated road system. The easiest way to reach your destination would be to enter via the A6 from Market Harborough. Here, I have prepared a sketch map for you." He pushed a sheet of paper across the desk.

"You will see from my diagram that you eventually pass through a place called Oadby. Stay on the dual carriageway until you reach the racecourse roundabout and then follow the signs to the city centre. About two kilometres further you will reach another roundabout at Victoria Park. Continue past the park, which is on your left, as far as the first set of traffic lights. Turn right there. That leads you into an area called Highfields which is a densely populated Moslem area of the city.

You'll see at the bottom of the sheet I have drawn a less complex street map of that specific area, showing the direction and the route to take. I will confirm the time and exact location to meet your contact after I have spoken with him. I will need a number to call."

"You'd better have my mobile number, as I am not sure where I will be on Friday."

Taz rose from his chair. "Would you like a drink before you leave?"

David declined and explained that his driver was waiting in the car. He thanked him for his assistance and left Danders still unconvinced about the strange relationship between two people who appeared to be ideologically at odds with each other. He returned towards London with Rebecca and with the impression that he had possibly been set up. But why and how? He decided that he would hand it all to Massey and his team. They were equipped to deal with the unforeseen.

"What was the outcome?" asked Rebecca.

"I have to wait. He needs to contact someone else."

"So, today's little escapade has been a waste of time?" Rebecca was still unable to see the point of her cousin's foray into 'enemy territory'.

"We'll see," replied David.

There it was again. Rebecca looked across at her cousin and noticed he was wearing that same smug expression that seemed to appear whenever he had reached an impasse. How could he remain so calm in the face of adversity?

The Courier
James R. Vance

Chapter 32

THURSDAY: One decisive moment in a lifetime can often determine that person's destiny. A chance meeting, a late connection, an unforeseen event, a misunderstanding, all pieces of the mosaic which forms the final picture of mortality. This fateful day was no exception. A missed phone call resulted in prophetic consequences.

It started badly with the pronouncement from D.I. Harper that Revenue and Customs were poised to intercept the couriers on Friday. As their destination stations could differ, it had been argued that no guarantees could be given to detain them all at their various points of disembarkation. Consequently it had been decided to pull them in at Dover before they embarked on their homeward journey to the capital.

Not only did this decision affect the drugs drop at Paddington, it also prevented Mullen from briefing one of the couriers to explain the hand-over of the USB key. In addition, it also thwarted their plans for surveillance of the cash drop on the following Monday. It had become evident that MI5 had already taken over and were hell-bent on making an impression. How this would enable them to trace the Sarin was a mystery to Turner and his colleagues, who had listened impassively to D.I. Harper's briefing.

"I take it that the spooks will now be investigating Driscoll, Edwards and the Josephs," he commented, hoping that they would now be absolved of this particular fruitless task.

"As this has become a major operation of significant importance to national security, I believe we must also play our part. The D.C.I. is particularly pleased that, without the intensity of your original investigation, all of this would have gone un-noticed and he is determined that you should still have some part to play in proceedings. To that end, the answer to your question is that we should still pursue these people in order to hand them over to MI5 for interview."

Turner was unsure whether to impart the news about the intelligence which they had in their possession from the USB key or to wait until he had spoken to Massey. Holding onto it seemed no longer appropriate as the hounds had been let loose and any delays would be of no consequence. Nevertheless he decided to wait.

The meeting concluded with D.I. Harper checking the accuracy of the files regarding the students and the relative information collated about Blériot College. This data had already been passed on to MI5. She had no further news about the assassinations, apart from the fact that little or no progress had been made.

As Turner left the incident room he received a call on his mobile. It was the pre-arranged contact from Massey about the USB key.

"We need to talk," said Turner. "I was about to drive over to your place." The detective sergeant briefly explained the new situation which faced them.

"Stay put," said Massey. "I'll contact Dyson direct and tell him the truth about how I received the key-fob. If you remember, when I met the D.C.I. at Covent Garden, he seemed okay about using David Joseph as a decoy, albeit in a slightly different way. I'll tell him that he sent it to me in good faith, that I have no knowledge of how he acquired it or of what it contains.

With all that's about to happen this weekend, I doubt that he'll challenge my story. Consequently, as far as he's concerned, our in-depth analysis of its contents never took place. I'll pass it on as arranged and it'll be up to the spooks to interpret the data. What do you reckon, two days for them to work it out?" Massey chuckled down the phone.

"How will you get it to him?"

The Courier
James R. Vance

"I need some fresh air. I'm coming in. I'll pop over to Blackfriars with it in the morning. My guess is that, if they manage to decipher any of it, they may even delay or postpone their activity planned for tomorrow. In that case, our sideshow may still be on the cards. You go off and have an easy day looking for Harper's criminals."

"I'm really pissed off with her now. She's so far up Dyson's arse that she'll agree to bloody anything. I just knew they'd bring in MI5 and ruin our plans. I need some action to get her out of my system."

"Well, if they get their finger out, I'm sure you'll all be co-opted once they've identified the B.N.P. guy as the Sarin recipient."

"Maybe we should tell them now."

"Let's just see how things pan out. I'll catch you later."

Massey rang off. Turner strolled into the main office and grabbed Mullen and McGovern. They headed for the Ring, the boxing pub.

*****

Whilst McGovern was ordering their first three pints of London Pride, David Joseph was reclining on his bed in the Millennium Knightsbridge Hotel in Sloane Street . He could have been at Barnes in the comfort of his own house considering the amount of effort that Turner and his colleagues were spending on tracking him down.

Rebecca had taken advantage of their situation and had headed off to explore the classic fashion houses and boutiques in the area before ending the day at Harrods. David, on the other hand, was restless for other reasons. He decided to walk up to Knightsbridge and crossed into the familiar territory of Hyde Park, where he had often met up with a business associate in the Dell restaurant.

He crossed onto South Carriage Drive via Albert Gate and walked over towards Serpentine Road. There were few people about probably due to the inclement weather. He stopped and looked across the peaceful expanse of Hyde Park. It was difficult to imagine how such serenity was devastated by the I.R.A. bombings in the summer of 1982. It had killed several soldiers of the Queen's Household Cavalry and seven horses whilst they were parading through the park. He was approaching the restaurant when he received a call on his mobile.

"Is that Michael?" asked a voice.

David was thrown momentarily until he realised who was calling and immediately he became attentive.

"My contact arrived back in England today," said Taz. "He will meet you tonight. I have a number which you must call when you arrive at the park in Leicester. He will direct you to a rendezvous where he will hand over the merchandise. You must come alone or he says the deal is off."

"I thought you said it would be Friday."

"He's arrived a day early. He says it must be tonight, as tomorrow he leaves for Pakistan."

"I will need to bring with me a specialist wearing protective clothing to handle the goods in question," argued David.

"Be that as it may, but only one of you will be allowed the final contact."

"What time are we talking about?"

"You must make the call at 7.00pm."

"Does this guy have a name?"

"You may call him Ahmed. I trust that we will be recompensed for the return of the faulty merchandise."

"It will be replaced. Arrangements will be made via your original contact."

Taz gave him the number to call and rang off.

David's adrenalin was pumping as he turned and retraced his path back to the hotel. It was beginning to drizzle and a biting wind blew across the open spaces from the direction of affluent Mayfair. He cancelled the restaurant visit. Other priorities occupied his thoughts. He decided to call D.I. Massey.

*****

370

The Courier
James R. Vance

Massey's phone rang. The caller was D.C. French.

"Thought I should tell you about some interesting information which I have received from France. It prompted me to carry out some research here and you'll be gobsmacked when I tell you what I've unearthed."

"Go on then," said Massey, smiling to himself over French's choice of words. "Gobsmack me!"

"I've found a connection between some of the suspects in this affair which are beyond belief. I've had to really go back in time. It's all part of an elaborate web of coincidence and conspiracy. I'm absolutely amazed by the story which I've unravelled. I'll fax you a copy of my notes later."

"How about skipping the warm-up and focussing on the main event," suggested Massey, more interested in facts rather than the detective constable's emotional enthusiasm.

"If you remember, I had a chat with the old gardener at Bleriot College during which time he spun me some tales of his war-time exploits. According to the gendarmerie version, Marcel Dubois spent some time in Freiburg towards the end of the war as a liaison officer between the 1st French Army and the U.S. Fifth and Seventh Armies. As more areas of the Western Front were liberated, he returned to Strasburg to deal with the repatriation of refugees in the French sector. Now this is where it starts to get interesting."

"I'm holding my breath," said Massey.

"Isaac Joseph and his brother fled Holland with their parents at the beginning of the war to stay with relatives in Luxembourg, but as the German occupation of Europe escalated, they were forced to take further flight. They bribed their way towards the south of France, using diamonds as currency. His father was a diamond cutter in Amsterdam.

To cut a long story short...this is the research which I carried out over here...along with some French resistance fighters, they were eventually picked up by German soldiers and shipped off to the Natzweiler – Struthof concentration camp in Alsace.

The Courier
James R. Vance

As the war drew to a close and the Allies marched through France, the camp was evacuated in September 1944 and in the confusion the Josephs hid their two young sons, leaving them behind. They were eventually found by local farmers who handed them to the American troops who stumbled on the camp in November of that year. They, in turn, passed the lads onto the French and guess who ended up trying to re-unite them with their family?"

"I'm intrigued, but from your story so far, I guess it was our friend Marcel Dubois."

"Spot on. Apparently their parents were taken to Dachau near Munich, but the trail went dead there and it was assumed that they were either exterminated or died on the death march to Tegernsee along with the other 7,000 Jews in April 1945. However, Dubois at some point traced an uncle who had been liberated from Bergen-Belsen and the boys were eventually brought by him to England to start a new life, where they eventually carried on the family tradition in diamonds."

"I assume that somehow they kept in touch with Dubois," added Massey.

"The uncle, who has since died, was forever grateful to Dubois and their friendship continued for long after the war. With him pursuing a career in Customs and his friend establishing a jewellery business in London, I suppose it was a match made in heaven."

"Well done," said Massey. "We now need to prove that Isaac Joseph and possibly his son, David, carried on where the uncle left off."

"Oh, there's more yet," continued John French. "Francis Dubois, Marcel's son went to the same Lycée as a guy called Michel Deneuve, where both attained the bac or baccalauréat. It's the university entrance examination. At this point they parted company, Francis ending up in a college universitaire, whilst Michel enrolled in a grande école and became a civil servant.

He entered the diplomatic service, interestingly in the French Embassy in Knightsbridge, whereas Francis became an entrepreneur with his own transport business. They kept in touch and their two sons, Cristophe and Julian both attend Blériot College. They're the two young guys who have the computer access. The building itself, Le Manoir was purchased by Dubois after he was dismissed from the Douane and it was his 'brain-child' to convert it into a college as a front for the continuance of their illicit smuggling operation."

"I see," said Massey, somewhat subdued by the detective's latest revelations.

"It's quite a cosy relationship when you think about it," added French. "Marcel Dubois as the master-mind, his son Francis as the supplier, Michel Deneuve, possibly as the money man …remember the reference to the men in suits who collect the cash-laden briefcases… and the two young lads as co-ordinators of the process. Old man Joseph was probably the original client and it spread from him."

"It's certainly feasible," replied Massey, "but who's The Fixer and why were Isaac Joseph and Frank Cannon bumped off? There's a missing link somewhere."

*****

David Joseph tried several times to contact D.I. Massey, but his phone seemed to be permanently engaged. He was running out of time and decided to contact D.S. Turner. By this time the detective had left the Ring and was back in his office. David stressed that he had some important and very urgent information for him.

Turner chose to meet up with him at the Millennium Hotel. Twenty minutes later he was in Joseph's room above the hustle and bustle of Sloan Street. The detective sergeant listened intently to his account of the meeting with Trevor Smith and his subsequent encounter with Taz Sharma.

"Why do you think you're being set up?" asked the detective.

"Not sure," replied David. "They seemed too acquiescent, almost as though their response was pre-planned."

The Courier
James R. Vance

"But that wouldn't have been possible, surely?
Furthermore, why would he offer to put you in touch with someone
who has the Sarin, if he didn't believe you?"

David went on to relate the instructions which he had
received from the recent phone call.

"Tonight?" said Turner. "He must be joking. How can you
arrange a pick-up at such short notice?"

"That's where you come in. I was hoping that you could
organise something."

Turner was in a dilemma. Here was a golden opportunity to
regain control of the substance which they had been trying to trace,
yet to arrange back-up and the possible involvement of CO19, the
firearms unit, SO13, the terrorist unit, locally based police in
Leicester and other emergency services, he would have to come
clean to justify his request, probably resulting in the end of
Massey's career and those of the team.

Was it worth taking the risk himself? If there was no Sarin
at the end of it all, it would be a case of nothing lost, nothing
gained, only a wasted trip up north. On the other hand, he was
desperate for some action and what a coup if he could hand over
the lethal substance before the security team became involved.

"This mini-drama of yours about the leakage. I assume it's
just a ruse?"

"Of course. I had to invent something to make them want to
give it up. If there was a leak, I'm sure it would have surfaced with
dreadful consequences by now."

"O.k. Here's what I propose." Turner glanced at his watch.
"It's almost three. I suggest we make a move, get out of London
before the rush hour and make Leicester before the deadline."

"What do you mean....we?" asked David, concerned about
what Turner had in mind.

"I'll need to grab Mullen and McGovern, just in case things
start to get heavy. In an unpredictable situation such as this, it's
important to have back-up."

"Oh, I thought you meant we...as in you and me," said
David relieved.

The Courier
James R. Vance

"No, it's too risky to involve you, even though they believe that you're The Fixer, that you're the main man. I can take your role as the contact. I'll need that number which you were given. If things go pear-shaped up there, I'll call in the heavy mob, in other words, McGovern. I'll be in touch later, wish me luck. It's time to get the show on the road."

*****

Massey's frustration was growing by the minute. D.C. French had left the inspector to assimilate and realise the implications of his latest report. On the one hand, it was obvious that the brickwall of the smuggling operation was about to come tumbling down, but there were other brickwalls still standing, namely the identity of The Fixer and the business surrounding the assassinations.

The link between the Joseph family and Dubois was undoubtedly strong but did it extend to David and Rebecca? The fact that there was a connection with Michel Deneuve had been gaining credence for some time and was hardly unexpected, but where did that leave Helen? Turner needed to be updated.

Massey's confinement for his recuperation period was stressing him out. In his mind he argued that he could reduce these harmful stress levels by becoming more closely involved. Had he not been absolutely fine the previous evening when the house was a hive of activity? He decided that it was time to return to the front line of duty.

He headed for the shower, smartened himself up, dressed in some warm clothing and set off for police headquarters at Blackfriars. He already had an excuse to be there as he had decided to hand over the key-fob to D.C.I. Dyson in person. It would also afford him the opportunity to discuss French's phone call with Turner and possibly meet the now infamous D.I. Harper.

*****

D.S. Turner was already approaching South Mimms services on the A1(M) when Massey arrived at Blackfriars.

375

Keeping pace behind Turner were Mullen and McGovern as the two cars sped their way towards Leicester. Fortunately they had escaped from the capital ahead of the evening rush hour and, despite the appalling weather conditions, were making good time. The rain was turning to sleet as they passed into more open countryside on their journey northwards.

None of the detectives had been in contact with French and, as Massey was anticipating meeting up with Turner at the office, they were all oblivious to the latest state of play. Foremost in Turner's mind was the recovery of the Sarin. The ensuing fallout regarding the involvement of Trevor Smith and Taz Sharma was, in his mind, another issue.

At least he had some action to anticipate instead of fulfilling the whims of a temporary inspector whose sole objective seemed to be the appeasement of the D.C.I. How he longed for the return of D.I. Massey. The working relationship with his superior was founded on mutual respect, something which could never be achieved with D.I. Harper.

*****

D.C.I. Dyson was pleasantly surprised to see Massey breeze into his office, perceiving his visit to be merely an expression of his return to health rather than his enthusiasm to return to work. He quickly realised that it was no courtesy visit, but something vital to the current investigation. He summoned D.I. Harper to join them and Massey passed over the USB, at the same time outlining the information which D.C. French had imparted, omitting any reference to Michel Deneuve.

D.I. Harper entered the room and Dyson formally introduced them to each other. Massey was impressed, not by her appearance but by Turner's accurate description of his temporary replacement.

"Have you had chance to check its content?" asked Dyson, holding the device which the inspector had handed to him.

The Courier
James R. Vance

"Unfortunately it's not only in French but in some kind of code. It appears to be a record of all the transactions and lists of the individuals involved in the smuggling operation."

"I feel that it should be passed over to MI5," suggested Harper.

"My thoughts entirely," remarked Massey.

"I'll contact them straightaway," said Dyson. "It appears that we've unearthed a real viper's nest. I must congratulate you both."

Why he was including D.I. Harper was completely beyond Massey as her contribution so far had been a hindrance according to his team. He offered his thanks, stating that he was eager to return to work as soon as possible. His remark was countered by an expression of disapproval by his opposite number. It must have registered with the D.C.I.

"That's really good news," he said. "If your doctor is happy to sign you off, the extra pair of hands will be most welcome. As the saying goes, 'two heads are better than one' and I'm sure that by working closely together, you'll be able to bring this prolonged investigation to a speedy conclusion."

The two inspectors looked at each other, forced a smile and inwardly seethed. Dyson was the epitome of compromise. They parted company and Massey went in search of Turner. Debbie caught sight of him across the office, prematurely welcomed him back and informed him that Turner, Mullen and McGovern had mysteriously left together without saying a word and certainly without speaking to D.I. Harper.

Massey thanked her and assumed that the three detectives had taken off on Harper's wild goose-chase to find her missing suspects. He left the building before contacting his sergeant on his mobile.

He listened to Turner's brief account of the day's events and the outline of his planned activity with a strange mixture of astonishment and trepidation. He asked him to make contact on arrival in Leicester to discuss the information from D.C. French in detail before he continued with the assignment. He sensed something untoward, but was unable to pin-point it. Something did not smell right.

Despite the latest revelations from D.C. French, there were so many questions swirling round in his head…..The Fixer, the assassinations, the French diplomat, the Sarin, the B.N.P. guy, the half-Pakistani friend…..and who was Ahmed? He returned to Streatham too stressed to worry about the state of his own stress.

*****

On June 14th 1645, almost three years after the start of the English Civil War, the decisive battle of Naseby took place. The Cromwellians pursued the defeated Royalists to Market Harborough before marching on to successfully attack Leicester. Three hundred and sixty years later Detective Sergeant Turner and his colleagues followed the same route into the same city with the sole intention of, this time, preventing a potential massacre.

They reached Victoria Park with time to spare and turned off the main London Road into an adjacent parking area. Turner took the opportunity to return the call to Massey before he stepped from the car to explain his plan to the others. The inspector expressed his concerns after recounting the gist of French's phone-call. Turner seemed more apprehensive about his sister's situation than his own current involvement.

He promised to call back after completing his bizarre mission, at the same time assuring Massey that he would be staying in open contact throughout with Mullen and McGovern who would be tailing him in close proximity.

At seven p.m. Turner took out his mobile and punched in the number which he had been given by David Joseph. It was answered by the man called Ahmed. He was instructed to cross the main road at the lights and to proceed down Melbourne Road, turning left into Needham Street. He was to continue over the railway bridge and to take the first road on the left, following it down under the railway arches to where he would find a white transit van which would be waiting with the merchandise. He was reminded to come alone or the deal was off.

The Courier
James R. Vance

Turner donned a white protective suit which he had acquired earlier from forensics to give the impression of authenticity and, for his own peace of mind, by erring on the side of caution. The three detectives had planned that he should make contact with whoever was in the van before Mullen and McGovern provided back-up to assist in making an arrest.

The convoy set off and followed the prescribed route. After crossing the railway, they swung left onto a badly-lit narrow lane which twisted away into the darkness and the incessant pouring rain. Mullen hung back slightly to conceal their vehicle until Turner reached the arches.

The speeding car hurtled downwards along the narrow winding road. In the darkness, he could barely discern the outline of old, grey factory buildings, the vestiges of a one-time industrial area. Away to his left he glimpsed the moon as it flitted between storm clouds, adding sporadic illumination to this dreary backdrop.

The green and gold minarets of a mosque rose up above this squalid landscape, glistening in the fitful glow. The road suddenly twisted sharply and descended steeply towards the railway bridge which spanned the narrow causeway.
As he approached and decelerated, he perceived a large vehicle which appeared to be stationary under the vaulted arch of the bridge.

The car screeched almost to a walking pace to squeeze through the narrow gap between the wall of the bridge and the petrol tanker, now more visible in the glare of the headlights. The detective momentarily glanced upwards at the driver, a young man with soulless eyes.

Turner suddenly realized something was amiss and his heart thumped out two heavy beats and then it stopped beating…. forever. The detonation destroyed the bridge and blew apart both the tanker and the car. Smoke and debris mushroomed upwards into the night sky. Fireballs from the petrol tanker scorched the road in both directions.

What had, seconds before, been a Victorian railway bridge had now become a huge smoking crater. Twisted iron sections of

The Courier
James R. Vance

rail-track snaked upwards, silhouetted against the greyish orange glow of carnage.

The suicide bomber had succeeded. The officer had no cause to feel any guilt about letting down his colleagues, nor could he accuse them of lack of support. Life's anxieties and concerns were now no more for him. Recriminations were matters for others to debate. He was now at peace with the world. Like the floating particles of dust which seconds before had been tangible evidence of life, one question hung over the desolate scene of devastation. Why had it come to this?

Chapter 33

THE NEXT WEEK: The doorbell to Massey's flat rang. He opened the door to reveal David and Rebecca Joseph. She was carrying a huge sheaf of flowers.

"We were devastated when we heard the news," she said, passing the flowers for David to hold. She leaned forward and hugged the inspector. "We know how close you were."

"You'd better come in," said Massey, stepping to one side.

"Thanks," said David, "but we've no wish to intrude. We would like to pay our respects and, if possible, attend the funeral, if you know what arrangements have been made."

"There's a cremation tomorrow morning at Camberwell New Cemetery in Newlands, followed by another ceremony the next day at Altrincham Crematorium in Cheshire. Apparently Chris had requested his ashes to be interred in the same plot there as his parents. If you contact Debbie at Blackfriars, she has all the details."

He took the flowers from David as the young man stepped back from the doorway.

"Thank you," said Rebecca. "Out of respect we assure you that we will attend at least one of them. Please accept our sincere condolences."

Massey watched them retreat down the path, reflecting on the strange relationship which had developed between poacher and gamekeeper. Many questions about David Joseph still revolved around inside his head. Was he involved in all this? What part did he play? Was Rebecca the innocent party he imagined her to be?

Always it came back to that one niggling question. Who was The Fixer? His thoughts went back to a remark passed by Scott Morgan when he described his first encounter with David

Joseph. His appearance was that of 'a normal businessman, he [David] was quite pleasant, not like a criminal'.

He placed the flowers in water in the kitchen sink and suddenly remembered David's description of himself during one of his interviews. 'What you see is not always what you get' and 'it was all part of a game'.

Massey retired to his living room to continue his reflections on the events of the weekend and the constant stream of evidence which was pouring forth, especially from the events in France. The raid on the college had still taken place on the Friday evening, irrespective of the events of the previous night.

Following the tragedy on Thursday, Mullen had stated that D.S. Turner had been extremely hyperactive and secretive when he had enlisted their assistance on that fateful afternoon. Information concerning the whereabouts of the Sarin had reached him from 'a reliable source'. That was all which they could elicit from him.

He had rattled on about D.I. Harper's handling of the case and seemed hell-bent on achieving a result in defiance of her approach. It was common knowledge that he had reacted strongly against her appointment, albeit as only temporary cover for D.I. Massey. Despite his demeanour, both he and McGovern trusted his judgement even though they received a relatively limited briefing about their roles in the planned activity in Leicester.

The only lead which had been followed had led to the arrests of Trevor Smith and Taz Sharma, who initially supported each other's attestation that the original approach for the Sarin was by two Asian guys, one of whom went by the name of Ahmed. The contact phone number given to D.S. Turner was no longer traceable and, as both corroborated visits by someone who called himself The Fixer, it was assumed that responsibility for the carnage was down to him.

A photo-fit was produced from their combined testimonies but even that could have been a million normal guys walking the streets of London. Strangely, Trevor Smith failed to mention the presence of the female driver who had accompanied the man called The Fixer and, at the end of the day there was nothing that directly linked The Fixer or even David with the tragedy which had befallen Chris Turner.

Over in France the gendarmerie had moved in on Le Manoir and Le Moulin at Andres, arresting both Marcel and his son, Francis, on suspicion of handling contraband goods, whilst at Dover all the students who were returning to England for the weekend were stopped and searched by Customs officials.

It emerged that Peter Jackson had been designated to carry the drugs earmarked for D.S. Turner for delivery at Paddington Station. This news was greeted with some amusement, as Chief Inspector Norman Jackson henceforth became known as 'Snortin` Norman'. It was one of the lighter moments in a weekend of tearful mourning for one of their own.

After flight AF621 from Pointe à Pitre at Guadeloupe touched down at Orly airport south of Paris, Interpol supported by members of the Fusion Task Force intercepted Michel Deneuve with a warrant for his arrest involving money laundering. Helen, his wife, was allowed to continue her journey to Heathrow, London where she was met by Massey, who had been informed of the situation.

She spent Saturday night at his flat before returning home to Hampstead on Sunday morning. Like her ex-husband she was astounded at the incredible allegations which had been levelled at her new husband, leading Massey to believe with some relief that she was totally innocent of any involvement. He openly discussed all the circumstantial evidence which they had unearthed and had presented to the French police, partly to justify the arrest which had taken place and also in the hope that Helen herself might shed some light on the diplomat's role.

She was unable to comprehend Michel's reasons for being involved, if any. As she pointed out, they each led a comfortable lifestyle, they were financially secure and both happy in their work. On her days off, she would often meet him at Knightsbridge, take a stroll in the park and stop off at the Dell restaurant which was a favourite haunt of his. Sometimes they would shop together in Harrods and have lunch together in one of the trendy restaurants nearby. They experienced an easy relationship together.

Why did he agree to co-operate with these people? She became even more distressed on learning of her stepson's minor involvement at the school. When she finally stepped into the taxi on Sunday morning, she was in a trance-like state, locked in her own nightmare world of false reality.

The inspector poured himself a glass of wine and sat in front of a blank television screen, attempting to come to terms with the loss of his friend and partner for so many years. Though still on the perimeter of events due to his obligatory convalescence, he was receiving regular reports from Blackfriars on progress as it happened.

Nevertheless, he continued to retrace in his mind every aspect of the case from the moment Sergeant Dawkins interceded in Scott Morgan's moment of panic. Between all the members of his team they had to have overlooked one shred, one piece of evidence, one link which would complete the collage of events and reveal the identity of The Fixer. He was unable to settle and decided to drive to the office. Parts of the brickwall had still to be demolished.

*****

The team seemed more concerned about D.S. Turners's untimely death than to worry about loose ends. There was nothing new to report, so after a wasted trip Massey decided to head back to the flat. Besides, an early start was called for tomorrow before driving to Cheshire for the internment service of his colleague's ashes. Deep in thought, he returned to his office to collect his briefcase, when he was interrupted by a W.P.C.

"There's a young gentleman to see you, sir. Says it's important, but wouldn't give his name. Reckons that he knows you from when you were up North. What should I tell him, sir?"

Massey was hardly in the mood for visitors, but was intrigued by her last remark. "You'd better show him in."

The Courier
James R. Vance

Moments later, the tanned features of Rob Smith appeared
in the doorway to his office. The undercover security agent who
had crossed his path during Massey's last case in Cheshire was
hardly a welcome sight.

"I'm here to offer my condolences with regard to the
untimely death of D.S. Turner. I believe that you were related."

Massey rose from his chair and nodded muted thanks.
"You've got a bloody nerve after your intervention in the Rebovka
case."

Smith ignored the remark. "If it's any consolation, your
sergeant's brave but foolhardy intervention identified the missing
links to a Midlands terrorist cell which we had under surveillance.
Their intended targets, however, had eluded us. Your guy opened
up a veritable can of worms. I commend his actions, but, at the
same time, I'm saddened that he paid such a horrendous price."

Massey walked around the desk and confronted the
Australian. "There's no bloody justice in this world when we lose a
good man like Chris Turner and you rescue a convicted killer like
Petra Rebovka from a life sentence. She should be rotting in jail,
not swanning around the West End adding glamour to your outfit."

Smith smiled. "May I sit down? I have an obligation to
explain."

Massey scowled. "Springing a bloody serial killer from
prison has no logical explanation."

"Inspector, she was not even tried, let alone convicted for
the serial killings."

"Come on, don't fuck with me. You know as well as I do
that she committed all those murders."

"She was tried and convicted of the murder of William
Day, no-one else. Her punishment for the crime was life
imprisonment, in other words to languish in jail at the taxpayers'
expense for at least the next twenty years. As this civilised country
has rejected the death penalty, that was the ultimate penance which
she could possibly pay. I'm not condoning what she did, but
surely, by using her in the fight against terrorism, that is a far
better way of repaying her debt to society? In a strange kinda way

she's atoning for her sins far more effectively than rotting in prison."

"Tell that to William Day."

"Point taken, but he was hardly a role model." Smith stood and moved towards the door. "You never know, Inspector, the recruitment of Petra Rebovka could become a blueprint for the future rehabilitation of some of society's more serious offenders. It's not unlike a higher level of community service, when you think about it."

"You're beginning to sound like a bloody liberal."

Rob Smith smiled. "Let's say that I'm a realist. Hopefully I'll be able to stand here one day with some evidence to prove my point. Don't forget that, at the end of the day, she could meet a similar fate to D.S. Turner whilst in the line of duty."

Massey sighed. "I'm still not convinced. My job is to arrest criminals and bring them to justice. Their bloody rehabilitation is not my concern." He paced across his office, becoming more than exasperated by this unexpected interruption.

He turned to face the man who appeared to enjoy operating in the murky backwaters of national security. "Despite your recognition of Chris Turner's role in exposing further terrorist links, we still haven't traced our principal suspect, The Fixer, who incidentally I still believe to be responsible for the murders at St. John's Wood and Primrose Hill. What are you guys going to do about that?"

"I'm a movie buff, Inspector. D'ya ever see The Great Escape?"

"Steve McQueen."

"That's the one. When the P.O.W.'s were planning their mass breakout, there was one guy who could lay his hands on the essentials, like a camera, a roll of film, passes, documents, etcetera."

"James Garner."

"Exactly. The fixer guy. That's who you're looking for. He's no terrorist, maybe not even a criminal. He's a player, an opportunist, an entrepreneur."

"But what about the two assassinations? Surely he must be the prime suspect?"

"From my understanding of your case, they were pro jobs, professional hit-man, hired assassin…whatever you want to call him. He, or she, probably leads quite a normal lifestyle. That type of individual does not wander about with 'assassin' stamped on his or her forehead."

"Is that your studied opinion?"

"I'm afraid so, mate. Anyway, that's your baby. I'm off to pastures new."

"Where next, then?"

"Sorry, that's classified info, Inspector."

"And the girl?"

"Petra?" Rob Smith smiled. "I'm afraid that's classified, too. See ya around, maybe."

The Australian swept out of the room. The inspector slumped back into his chair behind the desk. *Bloody brickwalls*!

*****

Massey reached the gateway of the crematorium at Dunham Massey in Cheshire and strolled into the parking area. He had just said a final farewell to Chris Turner, whose ashes were now at rest with those of his parents in the Garden of Remembrance.

A black B.M.W. coupe was quietly crunching the gravel beneath its squat run-flat radials as it headed for the exit. As it drew alongside the inspector, it stopped. The window of the driver's door slid gently into the body cavity below. The Josephs beckoned to him.

"Do you need a lift back to London?" asked David.

"I'm taking two more weeks leave, staying with some remnants of my far-flung family in the Lake District. Thanks all the same."

"That's nice for you," said Rebecca, leaning forward. "Enjoy the peace and tranquillity there. I believe it's a beautiful part of the country. Take care of yourself and don't forget to stay in touch."

"Thanks, Becky," said Massey, returning her smile. "I take it you're back to St. John's Wood now."

"Absolutely. The hotel in Knightsbridge where we hid ourselves away was okay but as you know, there's no place like home."

The black B.M.W. coupé gently moved off towards the exit. The faces of David and Rebecca disappeared behind the smoked window as it slowly and smoothly returned to its closed position.

Massey watched it roll out of view down the lane and momentarily shuddered as he experienced that déjà-vu sensation again. What was it this time? Something he had seen, something he had heard? He looked up to the heavens and the memory of Detective Sergeant Chris Turner forced teardrops from his eyes.

*****

The following day Scotland Yard announced that in conjunction with Specialist Operations it had again foiled a terrorist attack on London. Some tabloid newspapers reported a police raid on the Barking headquarters of the British National Front Party. Neither of these two events, commonplace at the time, gained any discernible media coverage.

As another New Labour scandal hit the headlines it seemed to be a good day to bury more significant news. Trevor Smith and Taz Sharma were arrested and taken to Paddington Green Police Station for questioning. Forensics eventually discovered that the type of remote device used to blow up the hijacked petrol tanker in Leicester was similar to the one used on Frank Cannon's Range Rover.

The young Moslem driver had also been strapped to his seat. D.N.A. tests eventually revealed his identity as that of a young British-born Moslem from Birmingham who had been missing for several days.

Later investigations found detailed drawings of connecting rail tunnels, escalators and passenger walkways at Euston and King's Cross underground stations on a laptop in the office at Danders in Barnet.

Comprehensive information on remote controlled magnetic exploding devices along with downloaded files on the building of the Channel Tunnel system were also discovered on the hard-drive of the main computer terminal at the offices of the B.N.P. in Barking. A plot to incriminate Moslem extremists in a mass Sarin attack on the London Tube system or possibly in the Channel Tunnel was averted. These news items were not reported and passed unnoticed.

The on-going investigation took a further bizarre twist several weeks later when the missing Sarin was finally discovered by an unsuspecting Maureen Cannon who had returned to the family home under the pretext of caring for her son, but was really more concerned about her inheritance. The hole in the cellar wall of the house in Primrose Hill had been the perfect hiding place for the sealed metal container holding the elusive tube.

It was still in full view in the cellar when the police raided the house once again following up their enquiries on the remote bomb connection. It was fortunate for the population of North London that she herself was unable to open the air-tight box.

The Fixer, whoever he was, vanished without a trace but Massey still had his suspicions.

*****

Detective Inspector Raymond Massey pushed his tired body several metres towards an outcrop of rock on the crest of Great Gable, which rose almost 900 metres above Wast Water at the heart of the Lake District's Western Fells. He stopped to take a breather. His heart was pounding. He was pushing out the boundaries. He removed his knitted woollen bob-hat and ran his hands through his thinning hair.

The view from almost three thousand feet was magnificent; the stillness was majestic in its silence. Nothing stirred. One could almost hear a pin drop. He glanced upwards at the jagged rocks ahead. The summit was out of sight, but only minutes beyond the ridge. His legs were heavy now, but one last effort would take him to where he wanted to be. Breathless from a morning which had started with some gentle fell-walking exercise, he finally reached the bronze memorial plaque dedicated to members of The Fell and Rock Climbing Club who had sacrificed their lives during World War I.

'Have regular exercise,' they had said at the hospital. He knew this was excessive and could have cost him dearly, but here it was tranquil and, in his mind, closer to heaven.

He sat on the loose stones with his back to the monument, which, in a few days time would be blessed with Remembrance Day poppy wreaths. The sky was clear, as was the air around him. To the south was Scafell Pike, the highest point in England, bathed in the golden glow of the western sun.

He smiled. For the first time in several weeks there was not a brickwall in sight. Here he could mourn for his friend in solitude and cast his mind back to the great times they had spent together.

He closed his eyes and soaked up the memories.

The Courier
THE END

James R. Vance
April 2009
e-mail: james.vance@orange.fr

Trilogy Series... book #1:

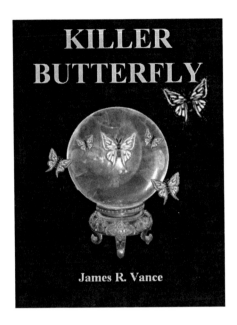

After visiting a fortune teller at a May fair, a teenage rebel sets out to fulfil her destiny of fame and fortune together with its associated materialistic lifestyle. The story centers around Petra, and the want to free herself from her perceived dysfunctional family into a world that opens her eyes to the power of her own femininity whilst striving towards her ultimate goal.

Just like this novel is part of a trilogy, the story can also be divided into 3 parts - each one symbolised by a stage in the life-cycle of a Butterfly...

Part 1. Chrysalis: Petra's future is influenced by the people who share her formative years.

Part 2. Metamorphosis: Traumatic events change Petra's life forever.

Part 3. Imago: Petra fulfils her destiny but not as she expects.

As she searches in vain for her prophesised fame she becomes the victim of the evil face of humanity.

Trilogy Series... book #3:

ANIMAL
INSTINCT

James R. Vance

The discovery of a naked body of a young female on a waste disposal site prompts an immediate police investigation, the responsibility of which is handed to Detective Inspector Massey. Working with a close-knit team in a town which appears to contain a number of renowned criminals, he is expected to bring about a speedy conclusion to the case.

The arrest of a murder suspect unexpectedly reveals the presence of a terrorist training camp in the heart of Cheshire. The motive for the murder becomes increasingly vague. Was the suspect, a local business man, also a terrorist? Did the young lady know too much? Was she involved in terrorist activities?

During the ensuing court case, the man's past life catches up with him, revealing that the murder was also a personal tragedy for the suspect. Who was the mysterious Jimmy Moran, who had arrived in the town? Had the police arrested the wrong man?

The Courier
James R. Vance

Printed in the United Kingdom by
Lightning Source UK Ltd., Milton Keynes
139276UK00001B/1/P